HOLD

MICHAEL DONKOR

HOLD

4th ESTATE • London

4th Estate
An imprint of HarperCollins*Publishers*
1 London Bridge Street
London SE1 9GF

www.4thEstate.co.uk

First published in Great Britain in 2018 by 4th Estate

1

A catalogue record for this book is
available from the British Library

ISBN 978-0-00-828034-5 (hardback)
ISBN 978-0-00-828035-2 (trade paperback)

Printed and bound in Great Britain by
CPI Group (UK) Ltd, Croydon CR0 4YY

MIX
Paper from
responsible sources
FSC® C007454

This book is produced from independently certified FSC paper
to ensure responsible forest management.

For more information visit: www.harpercollins.co.uk/green

For Patrick Netherton and Grace Opoku

Twi terms, phrases and expressions

Aane – Yes
Aba! – Exclamation of annoyance, disdain or disbelief
Aboa! – You beast!
Abrokyrie – Overseas
Abrokyriefoɔ – Foreigners
Abusuafoɔ – Extended family
Adɛn? – Why?
Adjei! – Exclamation of surprise or shock
Agoo? – May I come in?
Akwaaba – Welcome
Akwada bone! – Naughty child!
Amee – Please enter
Ampa – It's true
Ewurade – God
Ɛfɛ paaa – Very nice
Fri hɔ! – Go away!
Gyae – Stop
Gye nyame – Traditional symbol meaning 'only God'
Hwɛ – Look
Hwɛ w'anim! – Look at your face!
Kwadwo besia – An 'effeminate' man
Maame – Miss/Mistress
Me ba – I am coming
Me boa? – I lie?
Me da ase – I thank you

Me nua – My sibling

Me pa wo kyew/me sroe – Please (I beg you)

Me yare – I am sick

Nananom – Elders

Oburoni – White person

Oburoni wawu – Second-hand clothes ('the white man is dead')

Paaa – Sign of emphasis

Sa? – Really?

Wa bo dam! – You are mad!

Wa te? – Do you hear?

Wa ye adeε – Well done

Wo se sεn? – What did you say?

Wo wein? – Where are you?

Wo ye … – You are …

Won sere? – You won't laugh?

Yere – Wife

December 2002

The coffin was like a neat slice of wedding cake. Looping curls of silver and pink, fussy like best handwriting, wound around the box. It waited by the gashed earth that the men would rest it in. The mourners admired, clucking. Belinda made herself look at it. Her phone vibrated in her handbag but she let it rumble on. She brought her ankles together, fixed her head-tie and straightened her dress so that it was less bunched around her breasts. She passed her hand over her puffy face and then saw that eyeliner had rubbed onto her palm in streaks.

Belinda's inspection of her messy hands was interrupted by the shouting of the young pallbearers on the opposite side of the grave. They stripped off and swirled the cloths that had been draped over their torsos moments before, then called for hammers. Three little boys, perhaps six or seven years old, flitted back with tools heavier than their tiny limbs. The children hurried off with handfuls of sweet *chin chins*, nearly falling into the hole not meant for them and only laughing light squeals at how narrowly they had avoided an accident. Belinda wondered if she had ever laughed like that when she was their age.

The men started to thud away the casket's handles, eager for the shiniest decorations, the ones that would fetch the highest prices in the market. She knew it was what always happened at funerals, and that the bashing and breaking was no worse than anything else she had seen in the last few hours – but as the men's blows against the handles kept on coming, the sound became a hard hiccupping against Belinda's skull. Her chin jutted forward like it was being pulled and her whole body tightened. Belinda tapped the heel of her court shoe into the red earth, matching her galloping blood. Soon, wrenched free of its metal, the coffin's surfaces were all marked with deep black gouges.

Someone tried to move Belinda with a shove. She remained where she stood. The pallbearers strutted and touched their muscles. Some yelped for the crowd to cheer. There were whines from older mourners about sharing, relatives and fairness.

'Sister!' an excitable man said, pushing a brassy knob towards Belinda. She let it fall from his grasp and roll at her feet. It was not enough.

SPRING

1

Daban, Kumasi – March 2002

Belinda fidgeted in the dimness. She sat up, drawing her knees and the skimpy bedsheets close to her chest. Outside, the Imam's rising warble summoned the town's Muslims to prayer. The dawn began to take on peaches and golds and those colours spread through the blinds, across the whitewashed walls and over the child snuffling at Belinda's side.

All those months ago, on the morning that they had started working in Aunty and Uncle's house, Belinda and Mary had been shown the servants' quarters and were told that they would have to share a bed. To begin with, Belinda had found it uncomfortable: sleeping so close to a stranger, sleeping so close to someone who was not Mother. But, as with so many other things about the house, Belinda soon adapted to it and even came to like the whistling snore Mary often made. On that bed, each and every night, Mary slept in exactly the same position; with her small body coiled and her thumb stopping her mouth. Now Belinda watched Mary roll herself up even more tightly and chew on something invisible. She thought about shifting the loosened plait that swept across Mary's forehead.

Belinda turned from Mary and moved her palms in slow circles over her temples. The headache came from having to think doubly: once for Mary, once for herself; a daily chore more draining than the plumping of Aunty and Uncle's tasselly cushions, the washing of their smalls, the preparing of their complicated breakfasts.

Dangling her legs down and easing herself to the floor, Belinda quietly made her way to the bathroom. She stepped around the controller for the air con they never used and around the remains from the mosquito coil. She brushed by the rail on which their two tabards were hung. Belinda remembered the first time Aunty had said it – 'tabard' – and how confused Mary's expression had become because of the oddness of the word and the oddness of the flowery uniform Aunty insisted they wear when they cleaned. Belinda would miss that about Mary's face: how quickly and dramatically it could change.

Under the rusting showerhead, Belinda scrubbed with the medicinal bar of Neko. Steam rose and water splashed. In her mind Belinda heard again the sentences Aunty had promised would win Mary round. She yanked at a hair sprouting from her left, darker nipple, pulling it through bubbles. The root gathered into a frightened peak. She liked the sensation.

Returning to the bedroom, in the small mirror she was ridiculous: the heaped towel like a silly crown. For a moment, she forgot the day's requirements, and flicking her heels she pranced across the thin rug. Would Amma like that? Might jokes help heal that broken London girl? Or perhaps Belinda would be too embarrassed.

Mary shot up from beneath the covers and launched herself at Belinda's chest. Belinda pushed her off and Mary lost her balance, fell onto the bed.

'What is this? Are you a –? Are you a stupid –' Belinda lifted the towel higher. 'Grabbing for whatever you want, eh?'

'What you worried for?' Mary arched an eyebrow. 'I have seen all before. Nothing to be ashamed for. And we both knowing there is gap beneath shower door and I'm never pretending to be quiet about my watchings neither. You probably heard me while I was doing my staring. Even maybe you seen my tiny eye looking up,' Mary squinted hard, 'and you've never said nothing about nothing. So I think you must relax now. I only' – Mary tilted her head left, right, left – 'wanted to see how yours are different from mine.' She pulled up her vest and Belinda quickly rolled it down. A ringing quietened in Belinda's ears.

'And, and here is me ready to speak about treats for you,' Belinda began.

'You mean what? Miss Belinda?' Mary folded her arms. '*Adjei!* You standing there in a silence to be so unfair. *Adɛn?* I want to hear of this my special thing. Tell of it!'

'Less noise, Mary! You know Aunty and Uncle they have not yet woken.'

'Then tell the secret and I will use my nicest, sweet voice.'

Belinda headed towards the mirror and adjusted its angle slightly. 'Number one is that we have a day off.'

'*Wa bo dam!* Day off?!'

'*Aane.*'

'Day. Off. *Ewurade.* When, when have they ever given us one of those?' Mary rubbed her hands together. 'Today no getting them nasty stringy things from the drain in the dishwasher? No scrubbing the coffee stain on Uncle's best shirt again, even though everyone knows the mark is going to live there forever and ever amen!'

Mary laughed but soon stopped to count her stubby fingers. 'You said number one. And you said treats not treat. I know the thing called plurals. You speak as if we also having two and three and four and even more. So you have to complete please, Miss Belinda. What else?'

'Many great gifts from Aunty, Uncle and their guests Nana and Doctor Otuo. Many. But, but I will let them know they should change their minds and their plan. Because why should a naughty little girl get good things?'

'That question is too easy. Nasty people get nice all the time. Look at Uncle. He is farting in the night and afternoon, and then blaming it on Gardener or anyone else passing.' Mary threw up her arms. 'But he still got treasures from the UK and this massive palace he lives in with his own generator, own two housegirls in me and you and all kinds of rich visitors coming in.'

'Ah-ah! Your Uncle never, never farted! Take that one back.'

'What else is my treat?'

'Wait and see,' Belinda said.

2

Later that morning, under the fierce sun, for what felt to Belinda like hours they waited at the end of a long line outside Kumasi Zoo's gates. They stood behind three nurses who had powerful bottoms and who passed the time by repeatedly humming the old hymn about the force of God's constant love. Mary played with the green baubles Belinda had tied into her hair after she had promised to never again spy on Belinda showering. As they continued to queue, Mary crunched shards of dead banana leaves under her sandals and chattered away. Belinda tuned into and out of that overexcited flow of words: one of the larger clouds above, Mary was convinced, was shaped just like a fat man bending to touch his toes.

When they reached the stewardess in the crumbling admission booth, Belinda peeled and counted out cedis from the bundle of notes Nana and Aunty had given her. As Belinda paid, she became aware that Mary's talking had stopped. Belinda watched Mary stare at the stewardess. The cool seriousness of Mary's gaze made her seem much older than eleven. The little girl's grave eyes moved; to the young woman's hands that rested on a stack of brochures, to the polished things on the stewardess' shoulder pads, finally stopping on the stewardess' cap.

'Madam,' Mary said, suddenly beaming, 'I have to tell you, this your hat is very fine and well. So smart and proper. I like this golden edge it has a lot. Big congratulations on wearing it.'

'This is a most righteous praise.' The stewardess leaned forward, and with her face now poking out of the booth's shadows, her features were more visible to Belinda; the unusual fineness of the nose and cheekbones, the glossiness of her weave. 'What a polite and best-mannered young lady we have on our grounds this pleasant day. *Wa ye adeε.*'

Mary stood tall. 'The hat it looks like they made from a very beautiful and special material. Is it true? Can I please have one touch? I will not do any damages on it.'

'*Aba!*' Belinda tugged Mary's shirt. 'We not coming here to cause a nuisance or distraction for this officer. Let us go, please.'

'Is not a problem. I see no other visitors behind you at this time,' the stewardess offered.

'See, is not a problem.' Mary imitated the stewardess' casualness perfectly, shrugged and reached out. Belinda saw how much the hat's stiffness and texture seemed to please Mary. Mary began asking the stewardess how long she had had a job at the zoo, and what her favourite and worst things about working there were and which animals were the most annoying. Belinda jiggled her shoulders and pulled at the silly flouncy dress Nana and Aunty said she should wear because it was an important occasion. But even though she knew there were things to be done and things that she wanted done quickly, Belinda let Mary carry on. It seemed only fair.

The stewardess removed her fancy hat and placed it on Mary's head at an angle. The hat was far too big. The two of them found this very amusing. Now the stewardess whistled and called for one of her colleagues – a thin man with a square afro and sore patches around his mouth – to replace her in the booth, and she then offered to give the girls a tour. Mary did a wiggling dance of joy before marching forward. Belinda pulled at her dress again but stopped herself in case she ripped it.

Belinda wished having fun was more natural for her. When Nana and Aunty had called her out to the veranda earlier in the week to have the conversation that had started everything, the two women told her her face was too long. Nana and her husband Doctor Otuo had been staying at the house for a fortnight. Throughout their visit Belinda had been intrigued by the novelty of their preferences, how happy they were when tea was the exact 'right' temperature. But, as Belinda stood at the end of the veranda on that Tuesday evening, holding her hands behind her back, she was more confused than intrigued by Nana's advice that she 'be more lightened up'. Belinda saw no reason to relax: usually, once Belinda and Mary had taken the dinner plates away and cleaned down the kitchen's granite and marble, Aunty dismissed them. Then they had two uninterrupted hours of recreation time before lights out. Belinda had never been asked to return to the table after the evening meal was over. So she assumed she had made a mistake: perhaps the *egusi* stew had not been seasoned properly.

Waiting to hear her fate, a little dazzled by the stars decorating the sky and the candles she and Mary had placed everywhere at Aunty's request, Belinda had tried her best to be more at ease. She placed her arms at her sides loosely and tilted her head. In response, Aunty and Nana did sharp laughs at one another. Their chunky bracelets clattered and their wicker chairs creaked. They took sips of Gulder before falling silent. Every now and again, Belinda watched the oleanders in the garden as they trembled in the breeze, but then she worried that might seem rude so she focused on the two women as much as she could. Aunty complimented Belinda's hard work and effort, which made Belinda's tabard feel less restricting.

Nana nodded, her indigo headscarf wobbling a little as she did so. 'You doing really very well here, that's true. I have seen your greatness for myself during our holidaymaking here. Even before

I came to this place you should hear how your Aunty she praised you in every email she sent from her iBook PC, telling me of how she doesn't even have to lift one tiny finger ever, and of how you show a fine honour in all you do, how you making their retirement so beautiful and wonderful. I am so pleased for my dearest friend.'

'*Me da ase,*' Belinda said softly.

Aunty invited Belinda to sit, so Belinda did.

Nana went on, 'Especially the way you are with Mary. This sensible, calm way. I think that is really very good. You guiding her and caring for her. Is a blessed thing to watch.'

'Is so very nice to hear this. I thank God for all the blessings we receive in this house. Aunty and Uncle have shown a big kindness to me. And to Mary also. Is miracle my mother saw the small card for this job in Adum Post Office. Miracle *paaa*. I believe the Almighty helped them choose me.' When she finished speaking, Belinda felt breathless. Even the briefest reference to Mother could make her throat dry and strange.

For a time, no one spoke. Aunty flicked her Gulder's bottle-top. Belinda sucked in her lower lip. Eventually Nana tossed a napkin onto the table like it had offended her. 'Belinda. I will talk to you as a grown woman. Is that OK? No beating on bushes, *wa te*? I have to come direct to you because is the way of our people and will always be our way, *wa te*?'

'*Aane.*'

'Me I have a daughter in London. Amma. She is seventeen, very close to your own age. Maybe your Aunty has spoken of her. She is my one and only.' Nana unclasped her earrings and rattled them in her palm like dice. 'Let me tell you; she is very beautiful girl and the book-smartest you will ever find in the UK. *Ewurade!* Collecting only gold stars and speaking of all these clever ideas I haven't the foggiest. They even put her in *South London Gazette* once because of her brains!' Nana shook her head in disbelief. 'And when she has a break from doing her homeworks or doing paintings, we shop together in H&M and have nice chats. And she makes her father very proud so he doesn't even mind that he lacks a son and he never moans of how dear the private school fees are for his bank balance.'

Belinda took the napkin and folded it into quarters. 'Daznice,' she said. 'Sounds very nice for you.'

'It used to be nice.' Nana sighed, put down her Gulder. 'Past. We have to use past tense because is now lost and gone, you get me? As if in the blinking of a cloud of some smoke she has just become possessed. Not talking. Grumpy. Using just one word, two words for communication. As if she is carrying all of the world on her shoulders. Me, I am always trying to understand and asking her questions to work out what is happening to her, but I get nothing back. Only some rude cheekiness.'

'Madam. I am very sorry for this one.'

Nana hissed. 'And every stupid person in the world keeps talking to me about her hormones, hormones, hormones, but is more than this. I feel it. A mother knows. And her pain is paining me.' Aunty patted Nana's shoulder in the encouraging way that Belinda often did to Mary.

So Nana started to explain, drinking a little more and fussing whenever mosquitos came near her. When Nana spoke, she kept saying 'if' a lot, and saying it very slowly, as though Belinda had a choice to make. Nana talked and talked of her daughter's need for a good, wise, supportive friend like Belinda to help her. Smiling with excellent, gapless teeth, Nana listed the opportunities Belinda would enjoy if she came over to London to stay with them, said that Belinda could improve her education in a wonderful London school and get a future; said that, like Aunty and Uncle had, she and Doctor Otuo would send Mother a little money each month to help her because they knew Mother's shifts at the bar didn't pay enough. The talking about Mother's job at the chop bar, the thickness of Nana's perfume, the idea of moving again – all of it made

Belinda feel weightless and sick; like her chest was full of strange, drifting bubbles.

For a moment, Nana turned to Aunty. The two women held hands, their rings clicking against each other and their bracelets jangling again. 'Belinda,' Aunty exhaled, 'is a total heartbreak and pain for me to let you go. Feels too soon. Like you have been here some matter of days, and already –'

'Six months and some few weeks.'

'What?'

'Mary and I have been here six months and maybe two weeks in addition.'

'Yes,' Aunty said, now touching the papery skin at her throat. 'And that is a heartbreak. But this is what my great friend says she needs and what Amma needs. So, out of a loyalty and from a care, I let you go.'

Belinda traced the silver pattern marking the napkin's edge. The cicadas played their long, dull tune. She had so many questions but found that her mouth only asked one: 'You mentioning just me. What of Mary? She stays here?'

'Yes,' Nana said without eye contact, 'she stays here.'

'Oh. Oh.' Belinda concentrated on the napkin again but its busy design became too much for her.

Nana and Aunty behaved like everything would be easy. Belinda worried it would not be. Even so, she nodded along then got down on her knees to thank them because she knew her role and place, understood how things should be. And, at their feet, she bowed her head and gave praise in quiet phrases because getting further away from what she had left in the village was more of a blessing than either Nana or Aunty could understand.

It was decided that Belinda should take Mary out for a day trip to tell her the news. Let her have a bit of sugar to help swallow the pill. It was decided that a visit to the zoo would be just right. It was decided that they had struck on a great plan. And so, in a voice faraway and unlike her own, Belinda told them Mary would like the zoo, especially seeing the monkeys, because Mary loved the cleverness of their tails.

But now, as Belinda and Mary stopped at a water fountain near the snakes' enclosure to wait for the stewardess to take a gulp, Mary seemed much more interested in ostriches than monkeys.

'So, where are they hiding?' Mary demanded, pointing at a grainy picture of the birds in the brochure.

The stewardess wiped her mouth and admired the lushness in front of them, a wooden stick clutched under her arm. Belinda studied the view too. Sighing, Mary snapped away with the tiny camera borrowed from Aunty. The zoo was beautiful, rich with orchids shooting from dark bushes like eager hands, thickening the air with sweetness. Cashew trees were everywhere, loaded with leathery fruit. Even the lizards here seemed different, striped with hotter colour. Small streams cut across the land, flickering with unknown fish. Every now and again, the tops of trees rang with cries.

'The ostriches?' Mary asked firmly.

'If you revise your memory of the noticeboard encountered on your entry, you will recall that we have sadly to inform you of this suspension of this ostriches. They have been removed from our care due to budget cut. Me, I'm not supposed to be revealing to you such. I'm to declare this ostriches has been loan to a Washington Zoo, in United States of America, so it gives us a prestige and you feel proud your nation's zoo-oh, giving its animals to the West.' The stewardess pushed the sweaty licks of hair from her eyes. 'Sorry. Is lie. We have sold our ostriches. Sold. Because how can you be keeping grand big birds in country like this when too many here still have no simple reading, writing and such things?'

'Cro-co-diles here!' Mary pointed to the words on a sun-bleached arrow. Belinda's arm swung as Mary released her grip and skipped up a dirt track.

'Careful, oh! He come from the Northern region – and we have left him unfed for some four days – budget cuts!' The stewardess headed in Mary's direction.

Following, walking through foliage, Belinda bit her nails, spitting out the red varnish that broke onto her tongue. Belinda wanted the right sort of place: somewhere hidden; theirs for that moment. But visitors busy with their own intimacies occupied all places the path led. An Indian couple wearing matching baseball caps, necks looped with binoculars, sat on a bench. A father near the porcupines opened his briefcase in front of three waiting children. The three nurses from the entry queue unlinked their hooked arms; one stopped to rub her hip. And if that wasn't bad enough, there were no pockets on Belinda's dress, and so after Mary got a generous share of the cash Belinda had been given to pay for the day, Belinda squeezed the remaining cedis into her bra, giving herself an uncomfortable, monstrous breast. The high-heels Aunty and Nana said made her feet 'feminine' pinched her toes and were more painful than stomach cramps.

'I face the most severe of high recriminations if the girl comes lost. *Akwada bone! Wo wein?*' The stewardess hopped, checked the air around her, shouted in the direction in which Mary had sped off. 'This crocodile will be bearing the most emptiest of stomachs, small child. He will come, snapping for even your no-meat ankles. You must exact caution!'

Mary jumped up from behind a tree. Belinda leapt with shock.

'Why does budget cut have to mean bad signs?' Mary asked the stewardess. 'I mean how long we have been walking for and have I seen one cro-co-dile? No, Mrs. No even one of them to snap at my size-five feet.'

'This one has so much lip!' The stewardess became suddenly playful, extending her hand to Mary.

'You will take me?'

'I will take you.'

Mary asked the stewardess her name, then asked if she was married and about being married. Behind, wrestling with the layers of her long gold dress, Belinda remembered what women claimed about fat-cheeked babies who did not cry when they were passed between relatives. 'Oh, he is such a good boy – he goes to anyone!' Though she would have hated being compared like that, Mary had that same ease. Belinda wiped away something sticky from her neck, fallen from the canopy above. She considered beginning with reassurances about the smallness of the loss. There would be a new Belinda soon, surely. Another plain girl from some bush-place, come to clean Aunty and Uncle's fine-fine retirement villa nicely. All Mary needed to do was introduce herself politely, show this housegirl where the towels and things were, and then they could start. It would be easy to go to this new Belinda. Good for Mary, even. Yes. But Belinda knew Mary would ask if she herself was so replaceable; if a new Mary would be found so easily. Belinda could not mention Amma.

Ahead, through the heat's shimmers, the stewardess 'Priscilla' lifted her staff, pushed a curtain of leaves aside and ushered Mary beneath. Belinda stumbled forward. Tired fencing and browning grasses ringed the swamp. Dragonflies and midges rose and fell in the steam. Broken wood and lengths of something like soiled rope drifted across the surface and Belinda understood their slowness. Peaks of mud forced up through the water. A dripping sound worried the silent air and the sickly light.

'Ladies and no gentleman, I am presenting … Reginald!'

Mary applauded, but soon Belinda saw her face squash when it became obvious that the clapping fell deafly. Cross-legged on the wet soil where Priscilla joined her, Mary said, 'I don't like Reginald for a crocodile's name. Tell me his local one. On, on which day was he born?'

'He arrived here some three years. Big men brought him in a truck all far from Bolgatanga.'

'Which. Day. Please?'

'I believe the delivery came on a Tuesday, so –'

'So we will say that. Let us call for Kwabena. Come.' Belinda made her way to them, cursed the shoes, squatted as the other two did, and clapped towards the water. 'Kwabena?! *Aba!* Eh? You want to be shy? *Adɛn?*'

Nothing. Nothing but stillness.

'There are, erm, tarantulas also for us to show you? Erm.'

'I hate spiders. And anyway, I have spiders at my house, at my Aunty and Uncle house where I do clean, we do cleaning, *Ino be so*, Belinda? They, they come into bathroom. They don't mind the cockroaches. Neither do we.' Mary shifted her attention between Belinda and Priscilla dizzily and then became strict. 'They not our real Uncle or Aunty, by the way. But you know how we have to use these words for our elders out of a tradition and respect and I am a 100 per cent respectful child.'

Belinda wondered what sort of companion she would have chosen for herself, if a choice had been offered. Half a year ago, when the driver took Belinda from Adurubaa and from Mother, then made his unexpected stop near Baniekrom, what if some other girl had stepped into the car and gently introduced herself?

The water tore apart. The three of them staggered backwards. Diamonds jumped and splashed as Kwabena dashed forward. He snapped at the fence and Belinda gulped. His roaming eyes were massive, dark planets. His fat, knobbed tail whipped, sending up water again as Mary screamed. His long jaw flipped and crashed shut with a sound like falling bricks or breaking glass. He scuttled back.

'I didn't even get to be taking one single picture,' Mary moaned, pointing the camera at the ripples Kwabena had left. Belinda did not breathe. He was enormous. He had not yet shot out of the water but she knew he could leap and reach high enough to brush the trees and drop onto her, onto all of them. They would be crushed. Mangled beneath his rough belly.

'You see that bucket over there? Listen, do you see that bucket over there?' Belinda heard Priscilla softening. Mary, giving in to her tears now, sobbed. 'Listen: in that bucket are bits of meat – collect it. I didn't want to waste, but …'

Belinda said nothing as Mary ran to a nearby hut and returned with a dripping chunk.

'Good girl! See your friend? Not so courageous and bold like you. She seeming like she has come across a ghost, or is in preparation for the vomiting.' Belinda tried to find it funny. 'When he comes up again, you throw this meat at him, OK? OK then. Here we go. Kwabena, Kwabena –'

Priscilla paused, tapped Belinda on the shoulder. 'Help me, madam? Madam?'

Belinda added her calls, irritated by a wavering in her voice that wouldn't shift. Within seconds a blur of grey, brown, pink and green rose again, thrashing even more this time.

'Throw, throw!'

With a bark, Mary launched the meat. It hit Kwabena's snout and he began tearing at flesh before he and the red block disappeared into bubbles. Belinda gasped.

'That. That. That. The most brilliant thing!'

Belinda looked over at Mary's cheeks. They were streaked with tears, mucus, sweat, water, blood.

The zoo's canteen was a long, narrow room painted in sludgy tones, filled with rows of wooden tables. Each bore a matching island of condiments, bent cutlery and a miniature Ghanaian flag. Rusted ceiling fans dropped dust on the customers below. No one complained. A plump attendant wearing a splattered apron manned the till beneath a calendar, which, for the month of April, showed Jesus bursting through light. A chewing stick drooped from one corner of the woman's mouth. A thin cat lay at her feet. Somewhere in the back a radio crackled silly jingles into the oiliness.

Beneath their table, Belinda crossed her ankles, hoping to control her quaking thigh. Her plan seemed to work until she started fidgeting with the ketchup's lid instead. She rattled the can of Coke and watched Mary push Red-Red around her plate.

'Finish all, Mary, to grow up big and strong, eh?'

'You know Red-Red it always take me a long time to eat because –'

'Mary – eat not talk, *wa te*?'

Mary wriggled off her seat. She began bouncing the ball Priscilla had convinced them to buy from the gift shop, along with mugs, rubbers, T-shirts, posters, bracelets, catalogues and sun hats that were all stored in heavy bags that spilled at their feet.

Boing. Catch. Boing. Catch. Boing. Catch.

Belinda considered taking the ball away, though the waitress who delivered more serviettes appeared undisturbed by Mary's playing. And now Mary bounced it on the vacant table opposite. The ball knocked over a pot of salt. Mary ran to tidy up, then continued to bounce it on an empty seat.

Boing. Catch. Boing. Catch. Boing. Catch. Pleasure shone across Mary's face.

'You are not hungry, Mary?'

Boing. Catch. Boing. Catch.

'Mary?'

Two old men sat to the right of Belinda, one much larger than the other, both engrossed in *Oware*. They lifted and dropped the grey counters delicately. Each of the bigger man's moves began with a chuckle. Arching forward, his competitor hummed. Belinda noticed the piled pesewas between them. A group of white tourists pointed at the game. There were five of them, possibly students, nibbling boiled groundnuts off a large map. She heard them talking about how friendly the 'locals' were. Mary's rhythm slowed as she threw the ball at the ceiling, zigzagging around the fans.

Boing. Catch. Boing. Catch.

Belinda shovelled steaming rice into her mouth and saw the slimmer player getting up from his seat and pacing around the table, checking his lot from different angles.

Boing. Catch. Boing.

Mary, at the counter now, made the cat screech. The waitress hummed. Belinda cracked two knuckles. Mary got one of the white tourists to his feet. His blond hair flew up as Mary threw the ball and he followed it.

Ta. Ta. Tap. Boing. Catch. Boing. Catch.

'When you came from your mother's vagina,' Belinda heard, 'it is pressing hard on your own head and making your brain stupid – too easy for me to win this!'

The slimmer man bobbed around, his fat challenger flaring his nostrils.

Boing. Catch. Boing. Ca–

The student leapt forward now, his loose, tie-dyed shirt inflating as he picked up Mary and chucked her into the air. The ball rolled outside. The mad cat pursued it.

'MARY!'

Mary landed. Everyone stopped. The white man stood still. The old men forgot their game.

Heat ran across Belinda's chest. 'Come. And. Eat.'

Mary apologised to the student, who blushed and shook Mary's hand.

'Where's the ball gone?' Mary asked as she sat.

'We can get another one, eh? For now, you just eat.'

'OK, OK. I don't know why you talking all rude and quick to me.'

'Sorry. I don't mean to. I don't mean to at all.'

'Hmm.'

'And that, my friend, is a win!' the fat man roared.

'Is *Oware* in a way same like our Connect 4 only different? Do we have an *Oware* at Aunty and Uncle's that they may let us borrow? My father use to –'

'Mary, you are nearly a grown-up now, aren't you? Almost twelve years?' Belinda began, with false brightness.

'I can stand up to anyone who is even trying to come close to fighting me. I will even beat seventeen-year-old you if you try. If that's what you talking about?'

'Part of it. Part.'

'What else are you meaning then?'

Belinda flattened rice on the plate. 'Being a grown-up is about needing less then less. As you get older, things get taken away. But you are OK with it. With losing the things, because you can sort of – you can make up for the lost thing yourself. You can be looking after yourself. The teddy bear goes. The mum and dad go. And is not problem.'

'I don't know if I really understand it, Belinda. And – from your face – I don't think you do either.' Mary wiped orange grease from the corner of her mouth. 'Can't we go back for one more ball?'

'No we cannot. We cannot.'

'But, Belinda –'

'You won't always get your own way. As adult, you won't always get your own way. *Wa te?*'

'The opposite. Adults have –'

'You get strong by being disappointed sometimes. I know that is a truth.'

'What?'

'It is for best.' Every part of Belinda's body readied to run out of the canteen. She denied each one. 'This Nana who has stayed in the house for some weeks now?'

'What of her? I told you: out of ten, I think I would give her about five and a half. She's OK and I really like all the nice dresses she wear and her nice lighter face, but she also a bit weird? I know she is a Ghanaian truly, but is as if all those years over in the Great Britain for working like Uncle and Aunty did something crazy-crazy to her mind. She keeps looking at me with a funny eye when I'm only offering her more Supermalt or something. Or maybe is even only because she is getting old and that is the reason she cannot hang on to all of her marbles.'

'She and the husband have said for me to travel from the house. They will take me to their London, eh? You, you have it? Aunty and Uncle, they say yes. They know is a great thing. I will not come back. You. You will not see me. It is for the best.' It was right that the words came out slowly.

'Tomorrow? You leave tomorrow, eh?'

'No. We wait for papers – they have to pay someone at the Embassy. Something like this.'

'I. I knew that we would not be forever. I knew one day it will happen, but.'

'*Aane.*'

Mary stopped to fish ice cubes out of her Coke, then looked up. 'You? You, you're RUBBISH, hearing me?' Mary stood and pointed. 'You so … RUBBISH! And you right, I don't need you. Not only because I'm adult. But because I'm better than you.'

'Mary –'

'So go take your stupid self to London. You go do it, I don't care. I'm not even crying one tear.'

The white man came over. 'Is everything cool here?' He fingered wooden beads at his neck.

'Perfect and fine. Please, good day.'

'I was only …' He shuffled back to his muttering friends.

'I am not clever enough for London, or something, eh? My letters and number not so excellent like yours. Eh? Not pretty enough? My hair is too rough for London?' Mary grabbed the baubles on her head, tossed them, loosened the two bunches. 'I am sorry Aunty and Uncle did not pay for me to go to hairdresser to get nice plaits like you to show off at Nana and the husband. I am sorry no one is giving me shiny dress to wear!'

Belinda reached towards her.

'You don't come near.'

'We –'

'I said YOU DON'T EVER COME NEAR ME.'

The white people were gathering their backpacks. The radio had stopped.

'You been lying, isn't it? All of this, when we together, like we doing this all together, that's how I thought. Only now I see you just a smelling liar. You been thinking I am most rubbish girl, *ino be so*? Been laughing with Nana. Been counting days until something like this is happening, yes?'

Mary's nodding frightened Belinda; it was as if the electricity that sometimes pulsed through her own body had been passed on.

'You don't care what is happening to me at all, do you? You have nice flight to London, they get you husband and a palace. And me? They will send me back.' Mary paced. 'You bloody –'

'Swearing! Who is teaching you swearing?'

'FUCKING. FUCKING. No one is FUCKING ever coming to see me from my home village. No Papa. No Grandma. And now, you telling me Uncle and Aunty will drive me back there, push me out of the door and leave me? That is what going to be happening, Belinda. Because they don't want only me. We came as two. Two.' She flopped to the floor like a cheap doll.

Belinda crouched down.

'I –'

'FUCKING. And also, SHIT. You. Your dress is ugly and I hate your idiot shoes!' Mary lashed out, pushed an unsteady Belinda and ran through the coloured strips of plastic in the doorway.

Splayed on the linoleum, Belinda wanted to shout after her friend. But nothing came out.

Encumbered by the bags, Belinda found Mary sitting on one of the security guard's stools at the zoo's exit.

'If you misbehave, they may beat you,' Belinda panted. Gravel crackled under her feet. 'For your own benefit and peace, I say this to you.'

Belinda stopped, caught her breath and squared herself for Mary's next insult. But Mary only hopped down from the stool, ran up to the bars of the main gate and stroked them. She tried to fit her head through one of the loops in its rusting pattern. Belinda knew she would be unsuccessful but thought it best to let her try.

'Mary, you don't –'

Mary returned to the stool, pulled herself up, kicked her legs backwards and forwards. Neither of them were skilled at fights like this. Mary started well but continuing was difficult. It was true what she had suggested: Mary wasn't clever enough. She was incapable of creating some plan to keep everything safe and the same.

'You don't have to carry my things. They are mine. I will carry.' Belinda watched Mary hop off the stool again and come forward to struggle with the shopping herself. 'We should go.'

Mary walked on, leaning down towards the fuller bag, limping with the weight. 'When we are late and Aunty wants to coming finding a person to be blaming, don't push me up. I am doing hurry hurry and you want to be waiting and playing. Not time for one of your daydreaming now.'

Led by a tall woman with a clipboard, a snaking line of loud schoolchildren marched past, two by two, pristine in their blue and white and straw sun hats – not the usual brown and yellow most wore to school, and that Belinda had been so proud to wear in Adurubaa. Blue and white meant somewhere expensive. Their scrubbed faces and clean feet in matching blue sandals, agreed with her guess. Belinda watched Mary hobble to one side to make way for them. Then a hunched Mary turned her thinking face to the sky, to the showy swallows dipping and dipping there.

3

That evening, back at Aunty and Uncle's, Belinda twisted the kitchen tap firmly and was amazed again by the water's purity, so different from the gritty coughings of the communal pump back in the village. She picked up her terracotta *asanka*, its complicated decoration of interlocking diamonds matching the design of the kitchen's smart grey tiles, and placed the bowl beneath the tap's steady flow, tilting it so shallow waves skimmed its grooved inside.

In the *tro tro* on the way home from the zoo, Belinda had done her best to enjoy Mary's sulking silence. Mary's quietness as they went through Bekwai and Melcom should have given them both a moment to calm; time for Belinda to realise the threat had passed. She had told Mary that she was leaving and so the worst was over. But Mary's silence had not been calming at all. Mary's eyes were narrowed, her jaw set, her mouth mean.

Mary seemed slightly less distant when they arrived back in Daban and they returned to the familiarity of their routine. In their room Mary unpacked the bags, arranging everything they had bought in rows in the small cabinet by her side of the bed. Belinda listed the tasks that needed doing in preparation for the evening meal and Mary listened to and acknowledged each clear order. They both slipped out of their clothes and then put on their matching uniforms at the same time.

Belinda's swilling of water round the *asanka*, the rhythm of Mary scouring saucepans at the kitchen's island and the drain's glugging were disrupted by a shout. Another shout came and Belinda glanced through the window's louvres. Near the pool, lit up by the sunset, Uncle was thrusting tilapia at Aunty. Aunty was screaming and clutching her breast. Shaking and stroking his bald head, Uncle threw the fish onto the barbecue, then waved towards Aunty until she fiddled with something in her hands. Belinda recognised the voice that soon came from speakers as Sarah Vaughan's because Aunty and Uncle played this CD so often. The woman's voice spread and slid and spread.

'*Aba!* They always causing a complete racket when we try and concentrate,' Mary pounded her fist. 'Don't they know that we like to have a peace when we make them *eto*?'

Since Belinda arrived in Daban, Uncle often told Belinda he planned to make the most of his retirement, laughing his roundest laugh as he said it. 'Making the most' seemed to mean eating, listening to the trumpet man Miles Davis or the lady Sarah Vaughan, sleeping in the day, drinking, and playing pranks like that one with the fish. Mary kept on scouring, Uncle bullied a reluctant Aunty into dancing with him and yet again Belinda found it difficult to imagine that man handling all the big monies they said he dealt with in London. He must have changed himself a lot between there and here. Pulling the tough green skin from four plantains, she wondered if she could change so much in her own lifetime. Tossing the peelings in the rubbish, something made her flip the louvres down. She laid the pale plantains side by side on the chopping board, like tired infants ready for sleep, then sliced them fast.

'And so please start the boiling, *me pa wo kyew*.'

'I shall do that one, Belinda.'

Belinda turned her attention to the Scotch bonnets, using the knife to scrape out some but not all of the peppers' seeds, allowing the meal to keep its fire as Aunty and Uncle liked. Belinda heard pleasing grunts of effort as Mary carried the heavy pan to the stove; heard the click of the kettle, the clattering as the little girl rested the pan on the hob, the crackle as she lit the match, the whispering of poured hot water and salt, the plop as she let the eggs go.

'Now, Belinda, pass me plantain, please.'

With a nod, Belinda did as she was told, watching Mary drop the plantain pieces into the water too.

'You know the story of this one?' Belinda asked, pulling the roots off two onions.

'*Wo se sɛn?*'

'What *eto* is for.'

'You tell me.'

'Is the egg, really. That's the important part of it all.'

'How is that?' Mary stood on the tips of her toes to reach the shelf with the seasoning and tall bottles on. She grabbed the deep red palm oil and set it on the side.

'So on the wedding day they will give the *eto* to the bride. In the morning, perhaps; I don't know. And they will give it to her as we will to Uncle and Aunty. I mean that after it has been prepared – we've mixed together the mashed plantain, fried onion, nuts and things – they will place a boiled egg on the dish. Then all the elders and everyone will watch the bride. Because she has to eat the whole egg in one go. Without biting or chewing anything at all. Swallow in one.'

'*Adɛn?*'

'The elders' rule is that if you consume it all in one then you will have many, many children. But if you bite even one small bite into the thing then is like you are eating into your unborn child and you will never have any children ever and after. Is their word.'

'*Sa?*'

'*Aane.* Is what they have always said. Now collect the roasting groundnuts, I beg.'

Mary bent down to the oven, waved away heat and pulled out the tray, nuts crackling against the foil. Belinda busied herself with chopping the onions, the heels of her hands wiping back hot tears.

'Miss Belinda, I have some feelings about this one you have told.'

'Of course you do. I will be pleased to hear them.'

'Thank you kindly. So I don't believe the story is a truth. Boiled egg to tell of later babies? No, I don't agree with this one. And, also, sound to me like a horrible thing to do to a lady on her wedding day when you are already full of nerves and fears. *Adjei!* Why ask a girl to stand in front of the publics to watch her choke and become ashame? And, also, what if she choke so much on the egg it comes up from her mouth onto her princess dress? Can you imagine? Where have I placed the salt?'

'Your mind is a sieve. Is over there. There, by the pan.'

'You are correct. There it is. Is always the same: Belinda always right; Belinda never fail.'

The sharpness of Mary's comment hung in the air. Belinda worked the pestle in the *asanka*, using her weight against the ingredients, grinding together the slippery onion and pepper. She stopped.

'Yes, it sounds funny to me also. I don't think I would ever be able to do it myself. My mouth is too small and not well equipped for such a thing. Look.'

Belinda turned round and opened her mouth as wide as she could, her lips and neck strained and stinging, embarrassment fierce across her cheeks. Mary laughed. Belinda liked that and began to cool.

'You're a nonsense, Belinda.'

'Only sometimes.'

'Yes. Only sometimes.'

Mary interrupted Belinda's grinding to add a pinch of salt to the spicy paste forming. Dusting off her fingers, the little girl coughed

like Uncle did before giving an instruction and let her shoulders
fall. 'I have to do an apology. I suppose.'

'No.'

'Yes.'

'For what? I don't mind. Truly.' Belinda moved to the teak
cupboards to find the frying pan. She placed it on the hob next to
the boiling water.

'You do, Belinda. You do. I think you hate things like a big
shouting like I was doing in the zoo. You not use to it. So I have to
say sorry. Because I know you hate that one.'

'I don't hate anything, Mary. Hating is very, very evil. That's why
it hurt me so badly when you used that word about me. Saying
how you hate me. *Adɛn?*'

'But it was my true feelings in that minute. Now: not so. Then:
it was my God's honest. You, you prefer me to lie as Pinocchio?
Pretend I was really the happiest?'

'No, but –'

'You will want me, like me better if I didn't speak anything at
all? But I find that a difficult one.'

Belinda smiled to herself, placing a flat palm just above the
frying pan to check its readiness. She tipped in the palm oil then
tested the texture of the boiling plantain and the eggs, to find they
both needed longer. 'You seem to do a very good job of not speaking on the *tro tro, me boa?*'

'Not really.'

'*Wo se sɛn?*'

'In my head I had very long talk with you. Very long.'

'*Sa?*' Belinda scooped the contents of the *asanka* into the frying
pan and took a big step back while the oil hissed.

'The conversation did not go good at all. You, you kept on
trying as if to make me feel better. So annoying to me. So I got
bored and I took some ice water from off your bag and spill it all
over the top of your head. Sorry about that one, also.'

Mary did a small bow and Belinda went at her with a tea towel. The little girl pretended to have been wounded by one of the swipes. She pouted, winked, then returned to the high shelves to find plates, water glasses, place mats.

Belinda took the frying pan from the flames and poured the freshly fried ingredients into the *asanka* where they would wait for the plantain. Before seeking out her pestle again, Belinda checked on Mary, who was inspecting the crockery like Aunty had showed them to do on the first morning they had arrived.

There had been so many things to take in during that morning when Aunty, queen-like, had patted her headwrap as she showed them the house and its grounds, walking through echoing white corridors and grand arches and perfect gardens; past chaise longues and chandeliers and flashing glass-topped tables. So many rooms that Mother would have been jealous of but that left Belinda's stomach feeling like it would fall through her feet. Throughout the tour, Belinda remembered, Mary had stared at the faint marks her flip-flops left on the squeaky floor, and Belinda had nodded while memorising Aunty's endless notes about brands of bleach and meal times so she could recite them to Mary later, in the comfort of their new bedroom, when she hoped the girl might be less frightened. Now, as Mary polished silverware, Belinda wanted to offer her praise and kindness. She could work well. That was important and deserved to be recognised. So, smiling, Belinda opened her mouth, but then Mary dropped a fork. Mary did not flinch. Instead, staring ahead at the cupboards with their spotless, bronzed handles, Mary began to speak.

'Once, in my hometown, a boy called Akwesi from a compound nearby to ours he won some test at Sunday School. Test or competition. Something like this. So he had been handed a reward. That day, I learn the foolish word for the prize he was getting. They call it a hula hoop. So much hu hu hu. Funny to me. Anyway, the boy was a selfish. He never said yes if any neighbour children we did ask to play with the thing. He only knew to refuse us.' Mary picked up the fork, started wiping it. 'It was pretty, Belinda. They made the hula with all rainbow colours and they even tied ribbon to some parts. But I didn't mind too much that I couldn't play on the thing because I got to watch Akwesi using it. He use to stand, in the middle of the yard, with all us children clapping and clapping. And he will spin so quick with all the colours flying up and all over. And when he was spinning like that my heart it went running and running and my smile was really smiling. Because how beautiful. *Wa te?* And I thought I could never feel anything nicer or happier than watching Akwesi in that way. Then. Then I met you. So.'

Mary took out a slotted spoon, dipped it into the water and transferred the two eggs into her hands. She yelped at the heat of the things bouncing in her palms. She blew on them and hopped. Struggling, her fingers tried picking off the eggs' shells by jabbing. Defeated, she rolled the eggs onto the black worktop and whimpered. Outside, Sarah Vaughan held a low note for a long time then melted into nothing.

Belinda straightened her spine, hunched her back then straightened it again. In a scrunch of kitchen towel, she gathered up the two eggs carefully and pressed them against the worktop until cracks appeared across them. She picked at the first one with patient fingernails until she could uncurl the whole shell with a few swift pulls. Then she repeated it on the next.

Hoping it would be enough because it was all she had and all she could do, Belinda stepped forward and held Mary's wrists gently, feeling the slight bones there, as well as the little girl's latest insect bites. Turning the hands over, it was good to see no scalding, only one or two pinker patches in places.

'You brave to grab those eggs so fast, Mary.'

'No, stupid.'

Still clutching her wrists, the boiling pot rumbling away, Belinda walked Mary to the tap and ran her fingers under the cold, just to be safe. At the sink, their four eyes fixed on the shut louvres behind which the evening sky now glowed. Droplets dripped down the tiled splashback, and Mary's obedient palms cupped water. The two girls remained like that for much longer than they needed to.

SUMMER

4

London – August 2002

A gentle voice came down in a different language. Then another. And then another.

A loud child was silenced with a sweet that crackled out of its wrapper.

Strip lighting overhead, black arrows on yellow, corridors with moving floors.

A scared man reached into his pocket for an L-shaped plastic tube, sucked hard and brought colour into his cheeks.

Queuing.

Strip lighting overhead, black arrows on yellow, corridors with moving floors.

A demanding woman – probably a Nigerian with all that around her neck, in her ears, in her nose – had lost the passport, oh! Lost the passport, oh! Yey, has lost dis here the paaaaassport, oh-ho!

Being watched by a white lady with a man's tie, then watched by a black eye on a stick.

Holding back blinks. Stamp.

Strip lighting overhead, queuing, corridors with moving floors.

The beeping.

The thing to do next: reach the gathering at the tracks that went in a big loop. Stooped older women stood beside concerned men.

Bored toddlers harassed teddies' limbs. Lots of tutting at watches, followed by sighing when suitcases came through the lazy mouth. Belinda pulled her luggage to a trolley. Directed by the movement of crowds, she found an exit. Squeezing the trolley's handle was settling.

Busy shops and families waited on the other side of a long silver rail. Where was Nana, wearing one of those bright, swirling dresses Belinda so loved, so unlike anything Aunty might wear; dresses that, over Nana and Doctor Otuo's fortnight in Daban, had shown Belinda parrots, peacocks and toucans?

Tight smiles, wet eyes and wrung hands sprang open. Embraces were long. How would she greet Nana? Perhaps she could kiss her on the cheeks – one on each, neatly timed – like she had seen the women do on Aunty's *The Bold and The Beautiful*. It would show how grown-up she planned to be. Belinda's eyes stung.

'Over here! Liam, over here! Ohmygodohmygod.'

Belinda checked again, trying not to be distracted by the shouting, by WHSmith, The Body Shop. Moving to the side of the wiggling queue of passengers behind her, she dug out the emergency numbers scribbled in Aunty's parting gift, a leather notebook. Belinda scanned for somewhere to make that first call. Then her eyes stopped on the sign.

She'd never seen her name written like that. The seven letters were cut from a special kind of paper, bordered with something glittery, like the hems of expensive christening gowns. Pretty and sugary, the sign hid a face. Its holder had a tatty mound of plaits tied with ribbon. Cubes drawn in scratchy purple and black lines covered the girl's top; colours to match the plaits. How satisfying to wash a pattern like that. Mary would have marvelled at it. Belinda moved closer and saw that the fingernails spilling onto the 'B' and 'A' were painted purple and black too. There were dark scribbles – letters? – on the wrists.

'It is … me? You are Amma?'

Her name disappeared. The girl's skin was as rich as Supermalt, darker even than Doctor Otuo's. Though the girl's eyes were puffy, their quickness was obvious. Her breath, Belinda noticed, was stale and bitter like Uncle's if he returned home late from the city. Amma pointed in the direction for Belinda to move and soon they stood opposite each other like old enemies ready to resolve a grudge. Belinda considered leaning forward. Even though she had never learnt how to do them from Mother, Belinda had started to be better at 'hugs'. She had recently begun to drop her shoulders during them, and to almost enjoy the sensation of someone else's warmth coming through into her own chest. Belinda coughed, tilted her body and Amma returned the embrace just as mechanically. Then, in one clean motion, the girl took Belinda's bag.

'Here we are then. And – to get this done ASAP: Yes, my hair is messy. I know that. And it might be inconceivable, but I do quite like it like this. So.' Belinda stared. 'Let's head, yes?'

Scrambling behind as Amma marched off, Belinda wanted to praise the girl's beauty – her good height, cheeks, bottom, all better than Belinda's. But now the girl frowned, grabbed her stomach and stopped outside Boots. After a pause she started to walk again, trying for a smile, muttering: 'Sorry. Sorry.' Belinda wanted to reassure her that there was no need for apology, but then sliding doors parted, they were outside and Amma's hailing hand swept the air.

In the taxi, Amma didn't bother to soothe Belinda's fear that London was one big black road with cars. The motorway gradually thinned out into smaller roads, where there were stores selling rows of plastic bodies – some naked, some clothed – frozen in the middle of dances. People pushed prams and pressed buttons on their cell phones. Some children had hoods on their heads, and some men sat begging for money underneath boxes in the wall where others queued. Why so much queuing if things were supposed to be modern and working here? The cars drove more slowly in this non-motorway part of London and spent too long at traffic lights. Amma slept and sometimes lolled onto Belinda's shoulder, only to bob up seconds later, refusing to meet Belinda's eyes, preferring instead to stroke her seatbelt or hunt the dirt beneath her nails.

Belinda concentrated on the meter and its blinking from 33 to 34. Then they zipped across a bridge over slack water, and then to somewhere the signs called Clapham Junction. Clapham, she was pleased with herself for recalling, was where the Otuos had recently bought an extra house which they weren't intending to live in, which made little sense to her, but had seemed to make Nana very happy. A plain of green opened up to the right. On it, a man with sunglasses pointed to a pink diamond of cloth floating in the sky. Others were lobbing balls around. Others slept on blankets like the matted tramps at Adum. Some ate lazily from baskets. Many of the girls appeared to have come out dressed incompletely, in colourful knickers and bras, so Belinda folded her arms over her chest. Was it the Brockwell Park Nana had told her about?

'We are almost near, not so?'

'Yeah.' Amma stopped, the seatbelt fascinating her again. 'Yeah, nearly.'

'That place it looks … it looks very nice. For playing. Relaxing. And you lucky, to have such things. We don't have such like this in the middle of Kumasi.'

The driver turned a corner and they lurched into each other. Belinda felt Amma stiffen.

5

A strange white flower bloomed on the ceiling of the front room in which she waited. Beneath her feet, wooden floors – wide strips, scarred with pale patches. To her left, through a folded back partition, was the dining room, a dark, bloody cave with a long table set as though guests were expected soon.

Belinda had had such grand visions of her new home. She was unsurprised that the reality matched none of them. Aunty and Uncle's house was so much *wider*; in Daban the houses of all those other *bogahs*, consultants, accountants, lawyers, returned from overseas had been, too, with rooms coming out from everywhere, rooms that had no purpose, bathrooms for guests, for no one; annexes and servants' quarters to the back and sides. Didn't Nana and Doctor Otuo feel boxed in or too small here? Why did the cars pass right in front of the house – where was the perimeter wall? The swimming pool?

Unlike Belinda, whose fingers now pinched each other until she pushed her hands away, Mother had been calm when the biggest change came. On the last day of the Easter vacation, Mother should have returned from the Comm Centre in the middle of Adurubaa with the yellow Western Union receipt to put with the others in the battered tin. She didn't. Her return to their room that afternoon was ghostly. Belinda was distracted from the Jollof on the stove by the tinkle of keys. Mother waited in the doorway for a moment, very still, very stiff. Mother's sweep of hair, turning brownish from sitting in the sun, perhaps seemed more wild than usual. Mother dropped onto the bed and kept her stare on the blistered wall.

'It concerns you, also,' Mother had said, evenly.

Belinda turned the temperature down and flipped the dishcloth over her shoulder. The paper in Mother's weak grasp was blue and the first example of her father's handwriting Belinda had been allowed to see. Her first real evidence of his existence. On his Aerogramme, his words came in writing more girlish than her own. The careful characters made the letter's news bite even harder. Though short, it needed to be read again and again: the noise of the Akuapem children next door, playing their stupid clapping game, always as loud as though in the room with them. Mother had sighed, and sighed, and sighed, and then rose to scrape the bottom of the pan, Belinda assumed, to check that it had caught slightly, for added smokiness. The note ended without even an attempt at apology for no longer being able to pay the school fees. Mother turned the dial down lower so the flame sputtered. Her eyebrows were raised, and her whole face tightened when she had turned around to conclude, 'That's that then. We find something else for you to do.'

Now, under the huge white rose, Belinda snapped her knees together to stop herself from thinking. She picked up the remote control, then put it down. Nana was taking far too long in the bathroom. Belinda's attention fell on a sticky brown ring on the coffee table. The sun seemed to show a grey film on all of the surfaces.

'Nana? Amma?'

Belinda approached the mantelpiece, extended a finger and dragged it along a shelf, drawing a deep and perfectly straight line. A ball of fuzz gathered. Certainly, it would be an intrusion and a rudeness, but returning to the sofa? That would be a laziness. Walking out, she found herself in a corridor, the end of which was lit up from below. The steps moaned at her heels and took her into

an airy kitchen, everything here a hospital-white impossible to
achieve in dusty Kumasi. So much white: cups, plates, floor. One
unplastered, crumbling wall shouted difference. But, perhaps not
a hospital at all, instead more like a factory: the polished metal of
the cupboards, the cooker, the upside-down chimney above the
hob, the fridge, the bins, the clock on that messier wall reminded
her of cruel machines. The kitchen lacked wood, pottery –
anything homely. Beneath the sink, sprays that smelled safe and
familiar were carefully arranged. The man on Mr Muscle was
good. Belinda lunged for it.

Back upstairs, she wanted to clap as the foam's bubbles crackled
over the splodges on the table and the coiling in the small of her
back stopped. She heard a muffled shouting somewhere and then
the slamming of a door. Belinda shoved away the cloth and can.
Tell-tale Mr Muscle rolled out from beneath the table, grinning at
her.

'Sorry! I'm only –'

'No, it's me. I caught her upstairs and … we talked.' Nana
flopped onto the sofa. Belinda copied.

'OK.'

'What will it take to have her sit? You, you see how she leapt off
from the cab as if please, as if thank you and hello they gone out
of fashion?' Nana froze with the tiny folds around her eyes
stretched and her hands begging. 'She apologises to you and must
have a lie down because of this late returning last night. What kind
of introduction?'

'I don't mind. She has been so very kind and helpful to me in
the taxi, on the way. So.'

'It was this AS results yesterday and so she has to celebrate with
the friends or whatever. All A grades. That's all I hear her shouting
when she ran from this house, to leave me reading about her
success from some small paper on the side. All A grades.' Belinda
liked Nana's soft chuckle. 'I want to even sit her down to announce

how joyful we are, and, and we give a great thanks – but will she come and talk as we do now?' Nana pulled her red cardigan tighter over her white shirt.

'She –'

'Maybe your first of the mission is to find out her last twenty-four hours for me, eh? I am, I am certain she has done nothing … untoward? But, I need to … be informed of such things.'

'Mission sounds too big for a, a small one as me.'

'*Sa?* For me, mission is exact and right.'

'I –'

'Praise God your Aunty she released you for this – even as she wanted to keep you and your fine work to herself. But that, my dear, is what loyalty truly mean. You sacrifice for one another when is like that, you get me? You have to.'

'*Aane.*'

Nana shifted the tiny tail of her lizard brooch so it sat more proudly on the swell of her left breast. 'Always sticking together. From day one, our Confirmation ceremony.' Nana's earrings danced. 'We were something so beautiful. Special.'

'I am sure of it.'

Belinda chewed the inside of her cheek. Nana moved the lizard's tail back again.

'And. And you can be Amma's good friend too. Eh? Show her your goodness. Tear her out from whatever making her behaving in these ways. Tantrum. Silence. Crying.'

Belinda stared at her palms as if checking the lines there would not somehow reveal something. She sat on her hands.

Goodness? So good that her mother, creator of such goodness, sent her away without doubt or hesitation. So good that her father didn't wait around to see what the goodness he bred looked like. Had she ever seen goodness back home when she was growing up? For her and for Mother the village had offered little in the way of anything like that. The village was a place of turned backs and rolled eyes, suspicion, spit. *Goodness*. Belinda knew she would always have to struggle hard to get anywhere near it. But she would never let Nana know that. Nana did not want to know about that. Belinda forced her weight down onto her hands more firmly.

'*Adjei!* I'm doing it, aren't I? Don't o-ver-whelm. They put it like that, your Aunty, my Otuo, both of them. O-ver-whelm was their term, and I was all like, no, I'll be playin' it cool, cool. This is not cool, is it? I must be making you hot, eh?'

A rolling Mr Muscle encouraged her near her feet, but everything was too much and too fast for Belinda to work out how to respond.

'Listen to me! I'm so jumbled up and excited!' Nana tapped her knuckles against her forehead and raised perfect eyebrows. 'I meant to start with it, my great plan. Sorry sorry, eh? Bad Nana. Call me that one. Rap my wrist. There, there is this excellent occasion to introduce you to our community here, to present you nicely, in some weeks. Amma she complains I shouldn't demand so much of her time but perhaps you might ask her to – or tell her you will like to observe the *Ghanafoɔ*. *Ghanafoɔ* is our –'

Belinda was grateful for the door's click, the rush of cars and wind, the footsteps bringing in Doctor Otuo. He muttered about being stuck up a tube, said underground was terrible. Belinda breathed and her chest felt like it might expand endlessly.

'My succour and splendour,' Doctor Otuo bowed to his wife and she replied with a curtsy. 'Our new daughter? *Akwaaba*. You are more than welcome.'

He seemed thinner than he had done during their visit to Daban, more tired. He slapped Belinda's back and the weight of his man's hands was a whip to her. She shot up, took his briefcase and the jacket slung over his arm.

'Madam, we have prepared something for him to –?'

'I have leftover okra and fish –'

'We cannot let him be hungry, eh, Ma?'

Belinda zipped off, put the Doctor's things on hooks and clattered into the kitchen. The busy washing machine tickled the whole room.

'Belinda!' Nana yelled.

Belinda bobbed beneath the swinging saucepans, flipped open the fridge and dismissed tins with lids curled back, wilting greens and brown sauces in Tupperware. Then, yes, a glossy orange stew. Without even tasting it, she knew it would need Maggi and the rest.

'Belinda?'

Doctor and Nana's approaching footsteps stirred a feeling within. She searched for cayenne, nutmeg and a little ginger. Pinch, pinch, pinch from each. The feeling flung itself between her kidneys, liver, unable to escape through the belly button even though its head butted and tried to pierce.

Doctor shook his head. 'Calm, child. Calm yourself down.'

She scraped the pan, careful to get the delicious bits from the bottom, scooped a man-sized portion onto a plate and brought the rice closer. Not enough pilchards in this stew, not enough at all. Slam, bang: the dish thrust into the microwave, her fingers skipped over the numbers and the bowl spun, and now Mary would have done the same, spinning in circles until she collapsed, giggling.

'Belinda? You, lady, are quite the dervish. I was expecting to come down to a pigsty, the amount of noise.'

'You are a hardworking, sir. That is one that Uncle told me of you back home. He had me learn it; that I am never to see you in your house because there will always be a big money crisis for you to repair, or you are with some book until late in the study reading even more of this tax laws. He tells me on top of this I am to treat you as well as I treated him. And I will honour, for this is the greatest kindness you have shown me. In having me here. Isn't that right?'

The feeling bounced high and landed on its back, its legs tickling Belinda's diaphragm as Doctor Otuo hummed and slid a cell phone and then a booklet across the table in her direction. The booklet's cover showed a young woman with unusually large glasses. The glasses had no frames. The woman focused on a cylinder; a metal candle. Upside down, Belinda read *Abacus Educational Centre*. Beside that, in similar but smaller letters, *Committed to your boldest future*.

'We want you here for learning, Belinda. No cooking-cleaning-ironing-cooking. You must learn, eh? Eh hehhn.'

6

It probably would be a 'good idea' for Amma to do as Nana had suggested the day before and 'think about her room' and the slippery leggings and exhausted knickers on the floor. But as Golden Belinda stuttered the Lord's Prayer or whatever downstairs, Amma sat at her desk, rested her head on peaked knuckles and promised she wouldn't open the little trinket box to her side. She pulled her baggy black sleeves down as far as they could go and pushed her thumbs through the holes torn for them. Her insides sloshed again. She groaned.

Yesterday had been AS Results Day: Amma and all the other prefects had been garlanded with As. Clutching certificates they did a show of being surprised, relieved. Going home after the results was not an option. Party! Max from Alleyn's! With his fat house near Dulwich Village? Off they went. Max's dad laid boxes of wine and buckets of beers on the long dining table before high-fiving his son on his way out.

As soon as the door shut, before anyone could protest, Amma swiped the Beaujolais. She ran to the basement, slipped off her Converse and stationed herself in the corner of their library to hide. Until the Addie Lees and faggy final kisses at 5 or 6 a.m., Max's front room would sweatily ripple with skaters in children's jewellery, students from Camberwell doing Art Foundations, adjusting dungarees and wearing tiny hats, and the chavvier girls in jeans revealing a tasty inch of arse crack; the Stella-ed up young Tories, thick of lip, expansive of forehead and primed for showy debate. On the edges of the dancing and grinding, over fuzzy Drum'n'Bass, conversation would offer nothing of importance or comfort. It never did. So if you ever came across someone whose words stopped the passage of time – that someone needed keeping. There hadn't been anything, or any conversation like that since Brunswick. The icy February half-term on which everything rested seemed far away. Amma ran her finger back and forth inside her collar to soothe herself.

Last night, in Max's parents' bookish hollow, Amma dodged the enquiries of wide-eyed heads-round-the-door. Music rumbled above her and she ploughed through the wine with gusto, liking its poetic blackening of her tongue, reaching up for Lorca, Yates, Bowen, whoever. She read random pages to herself. She scribbled the names of writers new to her on the inside of her wrist. Of course, she knew she was being a dick; it seemed impossible to stop that.

Ignoring the trinket box's fussily carved lid, Amma rubbed at the smudged names now. She picked up a hair grip from her desk and sucked its ends until the little black buds came off, then spat them at the glass: tiny bullets. Perhaps last night was equally about Belinda, about her coming. For Amma the idea of a visitor itched at her. No privacy. Someone watching, asking questions. Someone else to think about. She shifted on the cushion. She could have tried harder with Belinda in the taxi. Amma had sometimes even wondered what it might be like to have a black friend. But, as they'd travelled from the airport, in her peripheral vision Amma had seen Belinda's face – the generous eyes, the ample mouth, in fact almost everything slightly too big – flicker and flicker and twist, fighting to stay controlled.

The interruption of Mum's voice was no shock. 'Amma? Amma Otuo? *Adɛn!* Your own father comes and you leave it for a guest to do greetings. *Maame;* you need to reconsider that one.'

Amma got to her feet. She would have to leave the safety of her desk for three people downstairs who hadn't the tools to understand her. And perhaps they couldn't really be blamed for that. We're born where we're born, led to believe what we're led to believe. The second part of that construction was particularly problematic. She pulled on her black and purple plaits to yank herself out of the mood.

'Coming, Mummy dearest,' Amma said, sarcasm the most immediate and pathetic of refuges.

7

Belinda broke the conversation, taking a long breath to ease the kinks as she spoke into the receiver. Using a casual, easy-going tone with Mary proved difficult. She tried again.

'And, and, how is our Aunty?'

'Our Aunty is very fine. But I think you have spoken to her before me, isn't it?' Mary said.

'Yes.'

'Then you could hear she is fine for yourself. I am looking after her well well. Uncle also. You are not for to worry.'

'I do not ... Worry.'

'Dazgood, for you. Lucky and nice. To not have worrying. In your English castle.'

'And you? You are fine, also?'

'Yes, Belinda, me I am doing absolute OK.'

She imagined Mary by the veranda, cradling the phone. Mary sounded different, even though it had only been three days.

'I cannot hear very clear, Belinda. Belinda? You gots to be speaking it loud or else I will not be getting you.'

'I did not say anything.'

'Oh.'

'I –'

'I –'

They giggled. 'You before me, Belinda.'

'I can't believe that I'm here. And seeing it without you. So much.'

'Tell me all now.'

Pleased to hear something like enthusiasm from the other end, Belinda straightened the phone's coil.

'Is, I don't know. So … the exact place in London where they stay is called Herne Hill. Even though I have seen no hill yet. And I have asked several times. And … And … every road has tar. And there are many poor, poor people sitting in the street. And I have seen churches like castles, bigger than even Central Post Office. And post? Mary, the letters come to your door. Each day. No catching *tro tro* or taxi to collect it from town and queuing.'

'*Sa?*'

'The cats? They sleep in the bed with the white people. *Adjei!* Like a small child. And, Mary, this one would be disgusting you-oh: on the television they kiss the animal as if it hasn't roamed the town eating sewage.'

'It cannot be!'

Mary cackled and Belinda leant on the landing wall, drinking in the scratchy sound.

'I. I feel a big guilt and a sickness. When I think about you.'

'That's not polite if I give you a sickness.'

'I thought you might still have rage. Sometimes. Anger is hard to die.'

'My sister, I'm too busy for such things.'

'Eh-hehhn.'

'Only reason I might be coming angry is that you missing it out.'

'You mean what?'

'I mean you talk all long as this and can't even mention the girl, not even one time? Cats and Post Office? What of your new princess friend?'

'Oh. Amma.'

'"Oh. Amma." Yes, Amma. When you said to me you were going there to meet this Amma princess friend I thought: wow wow wow! That will bring you a great fun *paaa*.'

'I remember.' When Belinda had finally told Mary that the Otuos had a teenage daughter, Mary was, to Belinda's initial relief, interested rather than envious as she had feared. Mary had bounced up and down on their sunken bed, shouting Amma's name repeatedly until Belinda made her stop.

'Tell me,' Mary continued now, 'tell me about her face, the face of this Amma – what is it like? Very black? Black like me? Black like you? Or a fair one?'

'She is black.'

'Ah-ah! Come: Does she have different smell from you and I? How is it? How is her smell? Is coming like flowers, I bet that.'

'I haven't. I haven't been up so close I am putting my nose against –'

'OK, OK. But, maybe if not that one, what about her voice? Her white voice? Do her white voice as an impression so I can learn it to show Gardener tomorrow. He will like it very much.'

'I can't.'

'Why? You holding all back.' Mary tutted. Then she began to whisper loudly, 'Oh! She standing too near so you have become shy and have to do it as secret. OK, OK …'

'Is not that. I. I haven't even heard her speaking many times.'

'*Sa?*'

Belinda thought her statement sounded unbelievable too, but in the days since arriving mostly Amma had been 'out'. The longest she had spent with Amma was in the taxi: a memory that brought a tackiness to the roof of Belinda's mouth.

'The girl, she. She seem to be very quiet. Which is no problem, of course. If that is how she like to be. I don't have a right to force her. Is only … Well, nothing. Is too early to –'

'Spit out, Belinda. We haven't the whole of the day for it. The phone card will beep soon.'

'I only feel sometimes as if is when I speak – to do thank you at a dinner time, or, or asking about weather because Aunty told me they will like this type of conversation – when I do this, is almost like Amma does a noise similar to laughing. Laughing at me. At my expense. Is not a big laugh. Not louder than, maybe, a cough showing you fever comes. But I hear it. And yet I have offered no funny words. And then I think about the sound again, in my own time, and I wonder if it is a rudeness. Why rudeness at me? She hasn't had a cause. I give her none. I. I feel scared enough to do any speaking here. In case I get it wrong. Or say a thing they won't like. And this Amma's weird noise it isn't helping me. *Wa te?*'

'If I was there, I would like to take one of those Science Magnification glasses and put it up on her.'

'Still so silly, eh?'

'If we check it again, you are the silly thing: What? You going to sit there and not even ask the girl one question about why, and why she behave as this?'

'Will she even answer me? She doesn't have to.'

'My sister, if one is a quiet, you have to find clever tricks for to stop them being as that. Sneak into her to make her chat properly.' Mary kissed her teeth. 'Everyone always tell me you are the clever one, with your old schooling. Now seem as though it fell from your head on the plane.'

'And what do you know of planes? Oh, I forgot, you are in aeroplanes all of the time, isn't it? Like a smaller Naomi Campbell.'

'*Aboa!*' Mary laughed. *Aboa* was Mother's insult of choice too; it was what Belinda had expected to hear the evening when Mother lurched towards their room after work and found charred fabric on the pillow. How stupid of Belinda to wait for that mean sound. Of course Mother had only quietly brushed off the pile of ash, then padded over to the sink to clean the black stuff off her hands. Belinda remembered listening to the water and the scratching of the sponge, thinking that no amount of washing could help Mother now.

'Never. Do. Swearing, Mary. Is bad.'

'You think of that as a swear? I have a lot better swears than that one.'

'Promise me to never. It show you to be a wicked person, and is not true of you. You are better. Promise it. Never.'

'Stop being all this weird and drama, and go for to talk with the girl. I want to find out about her. If you can't even do that then I should never have allowed you and said is all right for you to go in the first place. Is waste of everyone's time if you not collecting good information.'

'*Maame?* You allowed me?!'

'*Agoo! Me pa wo kyew, agoo!*'

The local carpenter's daughter's braying in the background behind Mary's chuckling, deepened Belinda's smile. 'Greet Afua for me, w–'

'So I'm going now because my little friend is here for a break. She beat up some small boys down in Sokoban who call her ugly or some like this, and she took their football as a revenge. So now we have a ball for fun. Is a bit busted and old, maybe why come they let a girl take it without proper fighting. I don't care. We never have a ball before, did we, Belinda? I cannot be more excited than I am.'

'Well done.'

'Eh eh? Listen to this heavy heavy speaking voice now. Well done: you sound as a big old dog would or a big old man. You don't have to be as miserable. Even though you have no football as me, you still have a chance to play games with your Amma.'

'Yes.'

'Yes. I know it. Trust your Mary. I never lie.'

8

The following afternoon Belinda asked Nana for the kitchen scales. She wasn't frightened when informed they were 'electronic' while Nana tied her into an apron. The small glass shelf presented to her was mean-faced, like the calculator from SS2. Belinda squared her shoulders at it.

'*Me pa wo kyew*, leave me please to shape and fry the *bofruit*, and you please ask your Amma to join us for a taste of these in perhaps half an hour. In that upstairs living room, or whatever you have call it before. For a change? And I will prepare the coffee in the special pushing-in thing I've seen she uses.'

Belinda wondered if their hopeful smiles matched. Perhaps that possibility kept the smile there long after Nana had gone, and Belinda was alone, tapping eggs against the bowl, licking swipes through leftover batter, dropping sweet dough into blipping oil. With the cooking done, the grin remained as she arranged the grainy globes and fanned napkins. Her hands slipped into the breakfast tray's rounded slots, a feeling that reminded her of teaching Mary to carry properly and not to balance food on the head any longer. The grin stayed as she transported the doughnuts and coffee, each step an effort against the jangling of porcelain. Her cheeks contracted as she saw Amma.

Amma's head faced the ceiling, ignoring the crouching mother in front of her who struggled up to full height. Amma's skyward expression was of concentration, set on the plaster vines weaving the whiteness above.

Belinda pressed her lips together, then slowly relaxed them out and breathed. 'Shouldn't, shouldn't be surprise to you? You got them in all the rooms. But me, I never saw anything like these patterns and designs and things on the ceilings before. Is very pretty, but I'm almost thinking how did someone come up with the idea to put them up there? Who was the first one to do it and why?'

'You won't help your sister, eh? She has prepared for you this special, and so –'

'Belinda, totally. Yeah. Thank you.' Amma took the tray from Belinda's strict grip, lowering it to the coffee table. Belinda thought the girl smelled so clean and flowery, despite all the dirty shades of black and mud and grey she wore. 'This is very kind – thanks – and there's no need to be so utterly patronising, Mum.'

'I'm only trying to get you to –'

'We don't need to have a discussion about everything.'

'OK, Amma. That's OK. No one is trying to be difficult here.'

'I'm not trying to be anything. It appears that I just am.'

'No. No. Belinda has prepared something for you to enjoy. That is the thing for now. To enjoy. Do that, eh?'

The stretched final note made Belinda play with her earlobes, as if touches to their softness would help. Amma rolled on the armchair towards the food. She rested her elbows limply on legs splayed like a man's, then pulled herself forward to press the cafetière's plunger.

'I don't suppose you want some, Be?'

'No. I mean, no thank you. Is very strong for me, even if I know you like it as such.' Amma's forehead moved, dipped slightly. 'I hope you like it well.'

'Sure I will.' Amma splashed in milk, eased back and seemed to wait for the next move, next sentence. In its absence, Amma shook her head and sucked shiny wetness off her little finger. She reached out and bit a *bofruit*. Belinda almost felt sorry for the doughnut collapsing under the assault. Although, of course, she felt sorrier for herself.

The decoration of this upstairs room, Belinda thought, might have been the reason why the conversation between the two standing and one sitting snagged. The second living room seemed silly, not for living in at all. Belinda had only been allowed to a museum once: a compulsory Cultural History trip Mother saved hard for. This was another museum. Kente scarves meant for celebrations were flattened behind glass, rainbowing walls. Alongside them, huge paintings of bloody sunsets and kola trees, women loaded with pots, curved elders relying on long sticks for support. But the black figures in the pictures were wiry and stretched, and the backgrounds painted in something smoky; these were images of a place so much dreamier than Belinda's recollection of that world.

Rather than books, the bookcases were for ornaments and framed papers. One set of shelves presented several documents, bordered with complicated black swirls. Each was marked with shiny holographic stamps, like sweet wrappers. Most had Amma's details written in important letters, the middle name Danquah misspelt in different ways. On remaining shelves, jutting their arms, rows of *akuaba* stood to attention. The fertility dolls' inflamed heads and pinched features always seemed odd to Belinda; ugliness for objects meant to bring a pretty, fat baby into the world seemed wrong.

'You see how Belinda is fascinated by our traditional things? You enjoy my collection? The dolls?'

'Is a very big one … very unusual to have.'

'They're, er, very – very surly, aren't they, Ma? You almost want to pick up the little darlings and ask them what their bloody beef is,' Amma said, mouth full.

'Bloody beef? What is a bloody beef to do with these, Amma?'

But Nana interjected, 'I suppose how the whites they sometime collect these stamps, buttons and whatnot, this is my version. I told myself every time I went back to our homeland I will collect one or two to bring back, trying to find something nice that will complement the ones I already have, you know? First it was a bit for juju as well, I cannot deny that.' Nana flexed her golden fingers and rearranged some of her loose, greying curls. 'Even after all these years of collecting and hoping and praying, when my little girl actually came, I still kept getting more, because I … they give me a sense of protection. Or something along lines like that. You get me?'

'Hanging on to the past, Mater. Get rid, *non*? I'm sure Oxfam would be delighted to receive a job lot of these lovelies – and what a beautiful symmetry there'd be: African gems saving African lives. Et cetera.'

'A big-time joker. That's good for you. Congrats to the comedienne. If your father wasn't in his work, I'm sure he will be here with you, also laughing it up and having a great fun. But when I talk of that time before you? Me, I can't find any funny at all. A hard, hard time to wait for you, Amma – my very, very hardest time.'

Her hand waved Amma's reply aside. Nana bent down for a napkin and nestled it and a doughnut in her palm. Belinda wondered if she should have added a dash of lemon juice, to sharpen the taste.

Nana seemed amused by something. 'Maybe the third or fourth time when I'm starting to gather all the dolls, I go home for a visit; my mother was unwell deep inside her back. Complaining and coming up with such horrible ideas: how the spine is rotten off and will soon fall out. *Adjei!* Can you imagine this nastiness? Anyway, when I was staying in the compound that time, everyone was joking of this *kwadwo besia* who had passed through the village – eh, Belinda, how can we explain *kwadwo besia* for her?'

Belinda blinked several times, tugged the striped strap of her apron and then shrugged.

'Is like one of those … sissies. Those, erm, Lily Savage, Edna Everage. Amma; I used to ask you if Margarita Pracatan is one? Anyway, anyway: they told me he carried his own *akuaba* on his back as though he is a real woman, wanting a child like I. And I thought; no, they are lying about this one, it cannot be like that, you can't take the mimicking so far. But on one afternoon, I saw him! Is like when you see a Father Christmas for the first time in the shopping centre. He was knocking on someone's door to beg for change. *Adjei*, I never knew anything such as this, Belinda. More than six feet and with a dress for a nightclub with sparkles, only covering his buttocks and let you see all of the big legs – and his hair? A wig like he has fetched it from the roadside. Trampled. And a massive one of these dolls strapped to his back in our normal way as if he is a normal. We laughed! We. Laughed. My mum had been bedridden for weeks and moaning moaning, suddenly she is laughing so much we fear that she would urinate! All the little ones came with sticks and bad pawpaws to throw at the him–her, and as he is running away, the *kwadwo besia* cannot even get out quickly enough because he can't walk in the women's shoes!'

Nana stopped to chomp and wipe away a pretend tear of laughter. Belinda wished that Amma hadn't turned to the ceiling again, with her jaw even more fixed. Belinda wished Amma wasn't closing her eyes, making her face so peaceful and breathing so steady when Belinda sensed that those were not the girl's actual feelings.

'I only thought *kwadwo besia* was on the television. For comedy. Not in real life. It must be very great to encounter one in the flesh,' Belinda tried.

'And why you so serious, Miss Otuo? I think that's one of my favourite tales. Not even gonna do a little smile for me? Tough crowd here, innit?!'

'*Kwadwo be-sia. Kwad-wo be-sia,*' Amma whispered, before adding with force, 'I've got memories of Ghana all of my own.'

'Yes! Good! Share with your sister Belinda also. Excellent.' Nana settled into one of the armchairs and invited Belinda to take the other. 'Seem like you not interested in back home matters. You giving all your excuses not to come at Easter when you could have met Belinda at your Aunty's fine place – some parts of Kumasi now are so beautiful you even feel as though you are in Los –'

'I bet you don't remember this one, Mum.'

'We are all ears.'

'I was in Year 2, or something. It might have been your home-town or Dad's we were going to. And I insisted you gave me the plastic bag with all the money in for the relatives; there was tons of it. So we were, like, walking, and I was being all bossy with the bag and probably trying to show off with the, like, two words of Twi I'd picked up, because showing off was totally my thing back then.'

'Back then?!'

'We were getting closer to the actual village and I saw all these orange clay or mud or whatever houses next to each other. They had these slits for doors that I thought were really small, and I said to you something, like, about how Ghana was only for skinny people or something equally insensitive, I'm sure …'

Belinda watched Amma stretch the ripped thumb-holes in her jumper.

'We kept walking, and then this massive queue, like, appeared? Everyone in it was all, like, jostley and impatient. And facing the queue – sort of like everyone had come to see him – there was this little boy and he was crying. I think he was probably about four or five because I wondered if we could be friends. That's when I noticed his hands and feet. They were tied up. And the dude at the front of the queue, like, whipped off his, his, flip-flop, his – *challewate.*'

'We pronounce as cha-la-watt –'

'And went completely psycho all over the little boy. Laying into him with it. Even when he screamed and shit –'

'Amma –'

'And then, like, yeah, I got that everyone else in the line was getting ready to do the same: they were all bending down to take off the one shoe. And we walked past and made small talk when all the uncles arrived, and they said nice things until you handed them cash.'

'Amma.'

'So that's probably the thing I remember most about Ghana. Yeah.'

'I don't think that's a very good story.'

'No?'

'Is it necessary, Amma? Eh?'

'For, for the *bofruit*, I used a recipe I have known since I was a small girl. My trick is adding the vanilla. Is expensive, that's why people they don't like to add, but if you have only one pod, and you use only a few of the small small beans in it, is sufficient. It will give plenty of flavour. In your cupboards I noticed you have many vanillas. So. No problem.'

Outside, the still, white sky seemed to be the sigh Amma released. 'It doesn't matter. Really. It doesn't. None of it does.'

The words travelled lightly from her, along with other, more muttered phrases. Amma stood, walked out, and Belinda's hands flapped, forgetting how to hide in pockets. Nana's head was bowed, and she let herself hang like that for a while, as if dragged by the small pendant at her neck, and Belinda reassured herself by looking at the exposed, biscuit-coloured nape, knowing how soft it must be to touch. Belinda wondered if Nana had ever found somewhere quiet and hidden to cry, like she had done in the early days at Aunty and Uncle's. Crouching in the tool shed, with an oily rag in her mouth and the tears unable to come out was the worst one, on an airless Wednesday. She had ironed and stored Uncle's

handkerchiefs for three hours without stopping. The instructions
were that they needed to be folded identically. After attending to
at least fifty, it came on her: a falling, falling feeling that had her
scuttling around until she found safety, away, breathing fast
amongst spanners and wrenches and nails.

It was difficult for Belinda to remember exactly what had
brought on that sensation. If it was just the grinding nature of the
work. Or a fear that she always had in those early days in Daban,
that her dirty, village hands might leave a grimy trace or mark on
the fine fabrics she was being asked to handle. Or fear that Aunty
would ask her a question about Mother's life and that Aunty's
clipped voice might make Belinda say too much. Or if the horrible
feeling was prompted by the loneliness of being somewhere new,
despite the small girl who shadowed her for most of the day. What
Belinda could remember clearly was the pressure of the cloth in
her mouth; the silencing, muffling force of the fabric on the back
of her throat. Painful but comforting at the same time.

Belinda wanted to ask Nana what she should do next but was
interrupted by Amma's return to the room – a swish of loosened
plaits, sweep of sleeves, stomp of boots.

'These are fucking delicious, Be.'

Amma collected three more *bofruit* and swept away. Belinda's
stirring hands stilled.

9

Even though Amma found the idea of a 'black Eve' trite, and even though she didn't want to be looked at, Amma had agreed to pose that Wednesday afternoon because it was Helena who had asked. Same old, same old: when they were at Prep School and Helena didn't want to stand next to that girl in assembly or be the nurse again at playtime, there was a lilt in the enunciation of her requests or elegance in the fiddling of her fine, yellow hair that invariably won. So in Helena's Dulwich conservatory, amongst arrayed yuccas, a coerced Amma found herself holding a Granny Smith at eye level, all for the sake of Helena's Art coursework. Amma had never 'sat' for a portrait before, and the hot awkwardness as she suppressed fidgety itches was something she had no desire to experience ever again. Opposite, as if in response to Amma's internalised disdain, Helena squinted. Amma watched her baroquely flourish the brush and dab the painting with finality.

'And now for that promised hashy hash,' Helena stopped to change the CD from De La Soul to Bob Dylan, wiped her hands on her faded T-shirt with Babar on it, then reached for the wooden pipe to her left and tapped ash from its bowl. She wrestled with her pockets. 'The dark cloud hasn't, like, lifted then, *ma petite sœur*?' Helena said, peering into the retrieved baggie.

'What?'

'Obviously I'm talking about how you've been Lily Long-Face all afternoon.'

'You told me I should "do pensive", so I'm doing –'

'– And what about how dry you were at Max's? Mmm? I needed you there, man.'

'I *was* there.'

'Come on, Am. Support was required. Lavender needed controlling. She's becoming a real joke. It's like she's forgotten that she's actually, er, supposed to be a feminist?'

Amma rotated her neck until it clicked, then popped the apple on the nearest bookcase.

'Yeah. You're probably right. Definitely. Yeah.'

'What?'

'Nothing. Let's not talk about Max's. Please.'

'Fine. That's totally fine.' Helena flicked her lighter, took a gulp and let out a luxuriant horn of white. 'I don't want you to do or say anything you'd be … uncomfortable with.'

Amma rolled her eyes.

'Am, I'm trying to be nice. You're acting like you need someone to be nice to you. Like you want that? So I'm doing my best. OK?'

Helena wiped her tiny mouth with a splattered sleeve and passed the pipe over. Amma inhaled a deeper lungful, then replied through strained exhalation.

'Really. Let's chat about something else. As uncharacteristic as it seems, the urge for the ordinary is pressing on me hard, dearest.'

'That sounds really odd, and … disgusting.'

'But I didn't mean it like that.'

The two girls sat in silence, the milky sunlight playing with the air's bluish haze. Amma rested the pipe by the apple. She wanted to leave, but that would be terrible. She closed her eyes and told herself she could start again. When she opened them, Helena was back at the easel, frowning.

'What? What's wrong?' Amma asked.

'You've really fucked the mood of this painting.'

'How short-lived kindness and concern are with –'

'Seriously. You've … like, infected it with some sort of weird Daria gloom and shit.'

'What's the one about a workman and his tools?' Amma hopped up, lighter in the head, and walked over to Helena, muttering, 'Workwoman. Her tools.'

Amma saw wildness on the canvas. Dragged, dripping bars of dirty brown and licks of red. Darker waves near the top. Scratched bits, etched with the pointed end of the brush perhaps. Mum would stand right up close to the thing and complain she couldn't see what was supposed to be the fruit, what was supposed to be a leg, what was supposed to be an eye. To Amma, the swirl of wet colour in front of her, its indistinctness, the frightening sense that it might morph or become something more, was entirely familiar. She chuckled.

'What's funny?'

'I was thinking to myself. Sorry. Nothing.'

'Why don't you *think* to me as well? It's only right and proper.'

Helena's eyebrows and forehead were working so much that the glittery bindi she had decided to wear slipped off. Amma picked it up, passed it over. She watched Helena press the dot back onto herself primly. Helena checked herself in one of the conservatory's windows and Amma saw how pleased she seemed; how easily that pleasure arose.

'When have you been most scared?' Amma asked her.

'Funny question.'

'Try. Go on.'

'What do you need to know for?'

'Why so reluctant, *ma chérie*?'

Helena's pinking eyes flashed. 'When I thought I might drown. But you know about that. So you're probably after something –'

'Doesn't matter. Keep going.'

'So, OK, I was about eight or something. Mum was going out with that creepy cellist then.'

'Eugh, yeah. With the teeth and the fingernails.'

'The three of us were in Cornwall. He'd never been and Mum was, like, too happs about showing him everything and blah blah. Some afternoon we were on the beach and I swam in the sea. And I hadn't swum out like crazily far or anything because I'm a good girl and know the rules –'

'Indeed, indeed.'

'And I, I had a cramp, like, winding round my leg, like squeezing it? I had no clue what was happening. Fucking terrible, man. Swallowing water. Yelling. It felt like I was doing that for hours, but that's what happens in those, like, crisis moments, isn't it? Time stretches? I bet it was probably only fifteen seconds or something before the cellist came and got me. So I suppose he was good for something.' Helena laughed lightly, reached for a different brush.

Amma didn't like what she was doing: forcing her friend to perform to prove a point to herself, a point she already understood and whose recognition would bring about no change. But the truth was unavoidable, as Amma watched the excitement with which Helena spoke as she recalled details. Fear was easy for Helena, maybe because it could be talked out, later. Amma could not breezily say what she wanted to; could not play it for laughs.

Amma coughed and shook her head when Helena offered the pipe. She returned to the raffia armchair and picked up the apple. 'OK, let's keep going then. Was it like this?' Amma tried to replicate how her body had been. 'Or this?'

'What, now? We're back on? I can't keep up.'

'More like this? H? More like this?'

Gravely, Helena cleaned her brush in murky water, sniffed and sighed, but Amma only half-heard, because she was looking at the apple's buffed skin, wondering how Helena would react if she pressed in the three soft brown bruises on its surface: three tiny dips of disgusting tenderness.

10

Earlier that day, in Belinda's new bedroom, Nana picked through Belinda's belongings. Belinda looked on, tightly wrapping her fingers around her thumbs. Nana inspected each item, making disappointed noises in response to every T-shirt or pair of shorts. Nana started moaning about how she never got to have a girly, girly shopping time any more. Nana talked about Belinda exploring her new ends; she thought they should do it quickly, before the sticky weather broke. Nana promised they would have too much fun together.

So they headed out for Marks and Spencer. Belinda walked just behind Nana as they made their way along noisy Brixton High Road. Flat, late summer heat hung from Belinda's shoulders. The sky was bored, the traffic was angry. Everything around them beeped or screamed. People on bikes turned around to swear at people in cars. Three striped white vans with swirling blue lights moaned. Buses bent round corners looking like sick caterpillars. Both Nana and Belinda were careful to avoid stubby black bins that choked on packets and bottles, and that made Nana hiss 'Lambeth Council' like those words were bad *kenkey* on her tongue. A tall man with wheels on his shoes sailed through it all peacefully. He overtook them until he became a thin, upright line between all the bodies in the distance. There was no space; the road was too full, the pavement too narrow to hold all the people pushing along it. Nana marched on, pointing forward with two certain fingers, swinging her yellow handbag with the little LVs on it. Belinda tried to match the pace but she kept nearly bumping into everyone because the surroundings pulled at her attention so much.

On her left, outside a huge shop – Iceland – a group of children played silver drums that were like the buckets she had used when fetching water from the stream when the village pump wasn't working. The children's music was a wobbling sound that shimmered on the air. Two women with flopping hats stopped to dance in front of the band, wiggling their bottoms and holding their breasts. Near an even bigger store – Morleys – muscled men wearing small vests had arranged themselves in a circle. They casually held big guns made from coloured plastic. A joke of an army. They pressed their pretend weapons into the ground as though steadying themselves. A larger circle of girls formed around the men. The girls picked at the small jewels growing out of their belly buttons, touched the drawings on their arms, talked to the little dogs at their heels that bit at nothing. Every few seconds one of the men pulled a trigger and water sprayed. The girls shouted like they were surprised, the dogs became furious and the men all shook hands. Nana muttered. Belinda wished she could make out the words but Nana seemed to be trying hard to speak very quietly.

Opposite Superdrug, Belinda tripped and landed on her knees. A girl in a red cap with a wad of leaflets in her hands helped Belinda back up. Through a giggle, the girl asked Belinda if she was OK. It took Belinda time to get to her feet and to understand what had been said because she was distracted by the picture on the leaflet: a black baby with squeezed eyes and tears moistening dusty cheeks. The girl asked Nana to do something about saving children for only £5 a month. Nana was not interested.

Belinda knew what crowds were like. She had battled through New Tafo. She had been in packs of brave pedestrians who ran across the crazy junction near Kwadwo Kannin Street. But it was different when so many of the rushing faces of the crowd were white.

Obviously she had seen *oburoni* before: Leonardo DiCaprio and Julia Roberts in the magazines Aunty left on the bathroom floor, the big men on the news, the silly young man in the zoo, the families at Heathrow. Belinda was familiar with the idea that their hair was weird, their voices weirder, like the sound ignored the mouth and came out through the nose. But here they were even stranger. They seemed so determined. Or focused. Yes, their pale stares were very focused on something important. And they themselves were important too, with their heads up and shoulders square and faces on the edge of anger. They were certainly too important to notice her. But if, for a second, they did let their gazes drop on her, would they dislike what they saw? Would the sight of her bring more red to their faces? Stepping aside for a child who was held back by a stretchy leash surely meant for one of the yapping dogs, Belinda wondered if Nana had ever felt the same foolish fear of whites. She wondered how Nana had quieted it. Because how could you live here with that prickling fear? How could you breathe, think, do anything?

Finally, they got to Marks and Spencer. As they passed through sliding doors, Belinda tried to find the source of the whining background music. Nana moved them on, drawn by various red signs. Belinda squinted in the hard light. Rails of dresses divided the space, blocks of shifting pattern. Alongside those were tables of blouses: some folded, others slumping messily towards the floor. Women grabbed things from hangers, checked tags trailing from cuffs before tossing the things back. Younger girls – the daughters of these women? – found everything funny and so kept laughing and showing tiny teeth held together by metal wires. Nana swung round and pressed a green top with only one sleeve against Belinda's chest, smoothing it down with firm strokes. Belinda held her breath as Nana screwed up her nose, dropped the top then tried out a blue version. Nana didn't like that one either.

They went on like that for a while; with Nana thrusting spotty, frilly, velvety things at Belinda. After what felt like ten minutes, with dampness collecting at the back of Belinda's knees, Belinda's eyes found the Childrenswear section ahead. It was marked out by a poster that hung down from the ceiling. In the poster, a mixed-race girl wore the stupidest of smiles. Many of the adverts here had mixed-race girls in them, Belinda realised. After Nana ushered Belinda into a changing room, Belinda snorted because she knew exactly what Mary would want to do. Mary would want to tear the picture down, stamp on it and tell 'someone in charge' that they should replace it with something much, much better: a nice photo of her. Belinda snorted again. The white cubicle around her was neat and tight, her reflection in the mirror was still. The shoppers' chatter had reduced to just a swishing in the background. There was nothing but that silly thought of Mary and coolness around her ankles. But then a hand poked through the curtain. It clutched three denim shirts.

11

Gossiping like the dried women Belinda had seen outside Costcutter on Norwood Road, Mary talked about how Aunty and Uncle planned to build their children, Antoinette and Stephen, little 'holiday cabins' near the house. Belinda could have joined in, telling Mary about the Otuos' flats, houses they didn't even need to live in, houses built for strangers. Pim-lic-o. Vaux-hall. The newest one in Clap-ham, but she didn't.

The landing that surrounded her – painted in a polite shade she now knew to call 'Duck Egg' – was dull, so she played with the corsage Nana had bought her from Monsoon, an unexpected prize. Pretty, flopping and delicate. The sort of thing Belinda would have thought hard about before showing to Mother. Like if she had collected pebbles coming home from school, all miraculously equal in size, shape, and colour. Because, though difficult to imagine precisely how Mother might take the moment's specialness, the ending of it was certain. It felt so very wrong to be frightened of your own mother.

Belinda stopped touching the flower. She noticed a change in Mary's speed at the end of the line.

'And of yourself?'

'Myself what?'

'Don't be a parrot parrot, Belinda.'

'Am, am well. I suppose I am making tiny small moves to make it better.'

'What better?'

'With Amma. That's the main thing, anyway.'

'*Aane!* I said to you, not so? You are a winner.' Mary's noise implied a deep wisdom. 'Tell me then.'

'There's not so much new, if I'm totally true. The most is that she, she decided to shorten my name. Give me nickname. Be. Not the whole Belinda as usual. Only "Be". Good, eh?'

'Be? As in … Be?'

'Yes. Exactly right.'

'Baby name – as though she trying to small you to littler than you are. A less scary one. What did my Belinda do to scare the queen white girl?! Ah ah, it must be big to have her cutting your name so you lose your power!'

'I think she did it because is nice. Friendly.'

'Maybe. Maybe I misunderstand. That happens sometimes.' Mary paused. 'You have a way of naming her also? Your new thick as thieves, or however they call it?'

'No. Not really. Same as last time, we don't really talk to one another so there is no need for that. Only a few days she has used this Be so far. That's the time she has said the most. So I'm hoping and hopeful.'

'Her tongue still not opening? And you been there these two weeks? *Kai!* Not only me with a problems then.'

'Problems? Like what?'

'Only usual. Normal. Same.'

'How you mean? Spit it out, Mary. Or "Mare". Mare has good feel about it?'

Mary breathed a serious whoosh down the receiver.

'For the whole life I have to have only small small conversations with you and then I scrape up the bird poos on the veranda, and then a hundred years will be done and I will have Uncle's grey hair on my head. Is it? I'm to only spend my days pushing that annoying glass cloth on all the glasses for so many hours to be sure when Aunty comes to check everything is correct. And you remember how the cloth itches my hands. And how long it take to get them white watermarks out. It make me even hate water, knowing how much time I spend on all those glasses, even though I have to drink it or else you would die.' Mary kissed her teeth. 'Is like I'm only waiting for Aunty to smile on me and tell me I can stop that one now to then do another job on the list. How can I do that forever? Is like a robot without dreams.'

Belinda twisted the anglepoise lamp on the side table away, its glare unwanted. 'Don't forget, Mary: we are lucky to have found ourselves in that house.'

'Lucky? I don't feel that at all. Opposite.'

'Yes, it can be a tough task sometimes –'

'Sometimes? Is all times. Every day I'm sitting here in the kitchen with my crossed legs on the floor, trying –'

'You have to imagine. That's how I told myself.'

'Imagine what?'

'Imagine that you are the kind of girl that can cope with it, even if you are not. Even, imagine you are the type that enjoys it all. If you cannot do it as Mary, be someone else when you work, eh? *Wa te?*' Mary hummed. 'You tell me, eh, tell me now, let's play – what is the girl who doesn't mind fishing in the plugholes for the hairs? Let us give –'

'She a mad girl; you can have that for free.'

'Let us give her name and age and story. Come on, Mary. At least try. Close your eyes.'

'OK. Only so you are happy.'

'Hey, mini-madam! I can see they are still open.'

'A witch! My sister is an oversea witch.'

'Close them!'

'I am.'

'Good girl.'

'Now, can she have any name I like to choose?'

'Go ahead.'

'Errrrrrm. I like for her to be Cynthia. Obviously is far too white for me, but I always think that it sounds how an angel would breathe.'

'That's very grand and for a princess. OK. OK, Cynthia. And how old is Cynthia?'

'Thirteen. The beginning of grown-ups.'

'Excellent ... you doing well.'

'I thank you.'

'And ... tell me, what is Cynthia's favourite task to do around the house? What is the one when she wake up, she's most looking forward to?'

'Is a hard one, but ... maybe she really enjoys to grind the pepper for *Kontomire*. She mash it in the mortar very well to give it the most delicious taste.'

'Good.'

'And also, the onion part also. She thinks is amazing and magic that from only slicing them, it waters your eyes as much as that, as though you really have something to cry about even if you're feeling in a normal or even a fine fine mood.'

'And here I put something else about Cynthia – if, if you don't mind me adding also?'

'I suppose I will let you.'

'She has no fears. So when she has to climb on the step ladder to get to the dirty ceiling corners or to wipe the fans, even though inside she is trembling a little, she can still do it. And another one of her favourites is cleaning the glasses.'

'Why would any human being on earth choose that one?'

'She, she loves how the glasses all look when they lined up on the shelves. She calls it perfect: with the light ... She sees them and she thinks of heaven, like her angel name. And, yes, the cloth can hurt her fingers a bit sometimes. But the tingle tingle is good. It means that she's not a lazy person, like all the old men from her village who are drinking on the road and then crying for their wife to get their food for the evening when the bottle is empty. She's a doing person –'

'*Adjei!* We have left Cynthia homeless and without a home-town! That's very bad of us. We call her Fante, for that nice yellow-yellowy skin. Maybe she is from some small place by Takoradi.'

'Main point is Cynthia likes the hard work. It gives her a pride, to, to feel as though she is doing something not nothing.'

'Is she pretty?'

'Very. Miss World 2002.'

'She has very nice white teeth, all neat, and a nice dress with all patterns on the arms that was very expensive to sew.'

'OK.'

'And she stands very tall and straight. And when she walk anywhere is with her head up, and she is very proper, never drag-ging her feet in the floor like when I normally walk.'

'Exactly. So, when next time you doing the latest chore or Aunty is asking you for a help with something else – remember that you are Cynthia, and, and Cynthia will leap up for it with a big smile and that head up.'

'I suppose I will do it the first time. Even if it sound a bit weird. You clear that it sound weird, isn't it?'

'Is like I heard on one of Aunty's *Oprah*. You remember her? The black billionaire with the jewels on her throat?'

'Your Aunty is still a fan for it: GTV, 3 p.m. every day. I'm still watching it round the door. All those ladies moaning and moan-ing around the place.'

'On one I watched, Oprah she told one of the crying ladies, "Fake it 'til ya make it."'

'*Wo se sɛn?*'

'Is like … you pretend to be as Cynthia for long enough and then one day you will see that you have … have become her.'

'*Sa?*'

'I think so.'

'I like the idea. Of changing, magically. Remind me of how you became different when you used to read to me. One minute you are like a monster, and then you are like you are a dog, and then like you are dead. And I nearly believed it all. Very entertaining. You were top marks at it, is true-oh.'

'*Me da ase.*'

'Maybe is right for you again, Belinda.'

'*Wo se sɛn?*'

'You can do anything now you are over in that different place. All different sorts of things from how you behaved here. But all you are doing is sweet pastry and getting all happy because she gives you name as for a puppy dog.'

'That's rude. Aren't you ashamed to speak like that to someone who spent the money and time to call you?' The space between Belinda's shoulder blades seemed to contract and throb.

'Sorry. I. No, you're right.' There was a shy shuffle. 'Shall we talk about some other? I don't want my sister to leave thinking only badly of me when she put down the phone.'

Belinda could see Mary's thinking face, deeply lined, as if it were in front of her, glowing dark against the pale walls. 'Go on, discuss again about Christina Aguilera and the half trousers she wears. They sound really impossible and nasty!'

12

The third surprise – after the ease with which Belinda knocked, and the calmness of Amma at the bedroom door – was the poster. Belinda shivered at it. It wasn't nearly as big as the grand Sunlight Soap billboard in Daban. But, as a darkly smocked Amma invited her in and Belinda positioned herself on the edge of the bed, the image punched her. The black woman in it was possibly singing, more likely screaming. She had wide, bush baby eyes, pricked ears and bared teeth. Her licked lips wanted to swallow the microphone, a microphone with a foam head as perfectly round as the woman's bald one. A costume of glossy black feathers like those on vultures sprouted from her shoulders and beneath this, chains dripped. In the corner, written in razored letters, was the word 'Skin'. Belinda turned her whole body away from the juju picture. She wanted to get started. She placed her hand on the top of her thigh, her new jeans absorbing some of her palm's wetness. She wished the sweat would stop, wished that her heartbeat could be a little less persistent, demanding. She tried to focus. She would begin with the music; the odd, shaking whine in the background that Amma twitched and swayed to.

Belinda did a smile and tried twitching too.

'Yeah. Not everyone likes it,' Amma said.

'It's new for me. Usually I only know some of the Highlife artists and a few Americans. But this isn't one of those. So, what, what is the song, and who is the person singing, anyway?'

'It's Thom Yorke, it's Radiohead, from *Romeo and Juliet*, the film? I'll turn it down. Sorry.'

Amma crawled across the duvet and pressed buttons. 'I dunno, I suppose, like, I like the haunting quality his voice has? And the guitars: how they plod through. I've never been the best at describing music.'

'What is the quality you mean?'

'It's … searching, and … I don't know. Nothing. Nothing.'

Belinda reached past Amma, and turned the same buttons in the opposite direction. The song came back louder; now the voice spat out hard questions and rude words, over and over again.

'I hope you never feeling as angry like this man. Would be dreadful.'

'Is he angry?'

'Of course. Listen to the abuse.'

'Is anger the only reason for sentiments, words, like that? Really?'

Belinda shrugged, trying her best to be light, cheerful. Her spit tasted bitter like bad *kenkey*.

'That's all you've got? A little humph? A little blah humph.'

'Amma?'

'Blah humph.'

'Amma?'

'Goodbye.'

Amma rolled over and buried herself under pillows. The girl would not speak or move, but Belinda could be patient; she had learnt patience in Daban. She nodded to herself and looked around the room for help.

The room was a big hexagon, sliced horizontally across its middle. Two walls slanting towards long windows were plastered with messy sketched drawings that spread out around the Skin woman. If Amma was responsible for these, she was very clever for sketching them so realistically. But as well as being almost as sharp as photos, they were also very horrible. Most seemed to be of small animals – curled storybook mice or things like grasscutters – only with their faces twisted in on themselves. Painted in the thin greys and nearly greens Belinda knew from dishwater, they seemed injured, some oozing a blackness that could only be old blood. In between these were scratchy pencil scribblings, bits from newspapers and wise phrases written in red; there were woolly receipts, letters with grand letterheads, more newspaper cuttings; drawings of women with melon heads, saucer eyes and balloon breasts; black and white shots of people marching with banners. And the books? Piled in tall stacks between the small tables and the armchair. Open, closed, upturned.

Though the desk and the fancy box that sat on it amongst torn pages interested Belinda, it would be very inappropriate to rifle through someone's papers. So she bounced over to the busiest wall, where photos wept blue glue – or gum. In the photos, Amma became a dark, smudged stillness in the middle of gleaming white girls, all of them with pink on their cheeks and clutching one hip like they were scolding. Twinkly and smooth-skinned, in each moment they were having a better time than in the last. Sometimes, they were in small photos like the one in Belinda's passport. In those they clung to each other and Belinda noted how easily Amma seemed to let these people push up close to her, and how much she seemed to be enjoying it. Amma's prettiness – proud cheeks and fine lips – was obvious.

A soft patting noise encouraged Belinda to turn.

'Actually you should sit. If you like. Or whatever. You look ridiculously awkward.'

Belinda moved back to the bed where Amma had now stopped talking, and instead was crouching forward, pursuing a splinter in her toe. The black Skin woman caught Belinda's attention again. The expression was frightening but full of strength. Belinda shifted and sat up taller.

'You never even ask me. Not even your ma, now I come to think of it. None of you.'

'What?'

'When we talk of our homeland. No chance for Belinda to add anything at all. So, so don't I even have an opinion worth counting? And I'm the one who was there basically some minutes ago. I'm the one who has it fresh in the mind as though it's here to hold in front of me. I'm the one who sees it in their sleep.'

'Oh God –'

'Don't use His name like that.'

'I'm actually an atheist.'

'Of course a girl like you is atheist.'

'What's a girl like me?'

'Is an expression. Isn't it? Have, have I got the wording wrong?' Belinda flicked her glance towards, then away from, the pointed teeth in the poster. 'Listen, I … I only want us to hear each other. Eh?'

In Belinda's pause, Amma grabbed a teddy bear as big as a well-fed toddler and pressed it against herself.

'Even if I only have some seventeen years in my life, I have had a great, great pain. And even sometimes I closed my eyes hard to hope that when my eyes come open, if I have squeezed enough, the pain will have disappear into thin air. It never did. I don't need that kind of sadness again. No one does. *Wa te?*'

'And people tell me *I'm* fucking melodramatic.'

Blood swelled Belinda's temples. 'Name it as you want.'

'I'm only saying you're coming on quite strong. Chill.'

'Was strong. The feeling was strong. And that's the best I can describe. Maybe you cannot understand and cannot even care to give an attempt to understand.'

Belinda watched Amma pull the toy's ears until neat and symmetrical, then bring his paws up, as if to protect him from

difficult sights. Belinda needed to move before the softness of the
moment passed.

'I think you are going to come with me and your mother.'

'What?'

'How you're acting and behaving – is achieved nothing. So now
do another.' Belinda let the rising inside keep on and on. 'It's a
cultural event your ma wants for us to attend.'

'No.'

'I only say is something cultural. Your ma promises there will
be Nollywoods and people talking of our politics and serving
Chichinga and *Kelewele*. And is something you will do for me.
Because I hope, under it all, you are a human being with a soul. I
have hope.'

'But – but not fucking that *Ghanafoɔ* group thing! No fucking
way.'

'*Aba?! Adɛn? Ghanafoɔ* sound very nice to me. Is good for
people from our community to come together and to discuss our
traditions and so on. Is –'

Belinda dodged the flying bear. Perhaps it was a joke, a joke the
whites liked to play, but Amma's burnt expression didn't seem like
that. Belinda wanted to run down the stairs and reorganise the
strange ordering of tins in Nana's cupboards. She wanted to de-ice
the chest freezer she had seen was thick with white fuzz and
smelly. Anything. Anything was better than having things hurled
at her by the girl turning the music back up.

13

The Otuos' Spenser Road was smart, marked by pointy black lampposts like those outside the Huxtables' on *The Cosby Show* repeats Aunty loved. Each morning from her new window, Belinda saw men swinging briefcases and women flicking scarves called pashminas. But late the following Saturday afternoon, as Nana, Belinda and Amma walked from the house in matching wrappers, a few minutes away on Railton Road, they were somewhere unrecognisable. Clusters of tired buildings were interrupted by a betting shop, an 'off licence', the Jamaican Take Away, 'Chick 'n' Grillz'. And none of them sold what they promised. Fronts were smashed or boarded up. Even the earlier rain seemed to have collected more dangerously here, lapping at Nana's peep-toes. A gust came at Belinda with a rumour of nearby bins, beer, and spoiled fruit. She couldn't understand why anyone would want to hold a meeting – or was it a party? – around here.

Before she was able to ask where exactly they were headed, the shock of a dusty man with matted braids stopped her as he passed by. A sort of hat – thick threads in red and black, crisscrossing – covered the top of his head, and he was singing softly, softly to himself and down at the empty plastic bag he circled through the air. Belinda hurried closer to Nana and Amma, but the man was nonplussed and nodded, perhaps in response to the extravagance of their glittering, green outfits. Amma wolf-whistled back. The unexpected noise set Belinda's teeth on edge. Nana stopped walking, her heels gently scraping as they came to rest.

'I think he would be a fantastic Caliban. *Non?*' Amma offered. Nana's shoulders fell.

'Part of me wonders if there is any point in asking, but. If in any small way you possibly can do it, please try to hold this, your … humour in check? We haven't come to spoil anything for anyone. Such a nice family, the Yeboahs, eh? With those good twin boys – doing something clever like Mathematics … Engineering?'

'Oh, please tell me they won't be there? Fuck sake. They're such drippy drip drips. Especially the taller one. I told you he texts me sometimes, right? What's he called: Kweku? Kwadwo? Eugh. Like, I'm always like, why are you bothering? As if I'd reply. So weird and lame.'

'Mrs Yeboah,' Nana continued loudly, 'and her husband have worked very hard on this. Is a big thing to have so many guests and you know we will all have to stay until at least midnight, and they have to keep watering and feeding and watering. They not having much. So is down to you to respect the hospitality. Hold. Your. Beak.'

'What was that man? The one who went beside us?' Belinda tried, keen not to lose the day's excitement to another of their arguments. 'Since I'm arriving in these three weeks I have sometimes seen some others like that around, having that hairstyle. They do it for what?'

'Is Ras-ta-far-ian. Is for those West Indians, isn't it? Is probably against the PC law to say, but the hair comes, this dreadlocks, as these West Indians can get hooked on narcotics drugs, eh? And they, they lose all respect for themselves. I-ma-gine. The hair, Belinda, the hair is unwashed for months. I know! How can you carry on as that if you are decent? You will see many, many, many more as we getting closer by the station. Try not to stare, eh?'

At the far end of a large compound bordered by little rounded cylinders, Nana led them towards a monstrous tower. Somewhere near, the laughter of playing children looped, round and round again, and Belinda wanted to stay with the sound and its soothing: the closest she had been to Mary in days. Amma, however, kept checking the air, chasing something that slipped and hid. Nana was all preparation: pressing the buzzer, unbunching the messy ruches in Amma's top, straightening Amma's rucksack, pressing the wrinkles from Amma's brow.

'A frown like when you were little girl,' Nana said, saddened by a realisation Belinda could not quite interpret.

Nana dotted perfume behind their ears, a cleaned toilet smell which tickled Belinda's throat all the way up three shadowy flights of stairs, with chewed handrails and stained walls.

'Come on, my little darlin' slow coaches.'

Now, another door – No. 33 – and Nana was anything but slow. As soon as a mean metal grille flew back, Nana disappeared into a packed flat full of showy headdresses, thick crucifixes on necks and polished brogues. She nodded to a Hiplife beat and Belinda enjoyed Nana's sketch of a dance through the small corridor. Between the bodies, Belinda made out dowdy brown wallpaper lining the passageway. Much brighter than this, Nana shimmied, her hips and voice clearing a path amongst so many black faces. Nana pushed her red lips into cheeks and slapped broad male backs. They chuckled after she struck; they found her strength funny, it seemed.

'Parts the sea more impressively than that Moses of yours.'

Amma began their entry, picking past a suited uncle brushing his forehead with an old handkerchief, and a concerned grandmother who ushered them in. '*Akwaaba, abusuafoɔ, akwaaba,*' someone else mumbled. Amma and Belinda bleated gratitude like goats. They carried on through the busy hallway and found space was so scarce that the crowd spilled into the frenetic kitchen to chat, to admire each other's hooped earrings. Careful not to nudge the Kente framed painting of Christ, Belinda saw steaminess ahead: hot racks of roasted *brobe* and plantain were hoisted high to avoid complicated hairdos.

Amma struggled in the *tro tro* tightness; Belinda heard her phrasebook Twi fail. Amma stuttered through limp apologies that amused listeners and, as they inched forward, Amma was mocked in her mother tongue. An aunty with a huge birthmark near her hairline tugged Belinda's ear. She asked if 'this child has the disability? Is the girl your sister afflicted by cruel Down's Syndrome? Is the explanation for the water in her mouth?'

The girls wriggled into the living room, through red, yellow and green bunting. Belinda and Amma nodded 'hellos' to the congregation of mewing infants and to flashy men in high-waisted trousers. Rather than replying, the guests directed their energies towards *chin chins*, monkey nuts, popcorn, cashews.

Belinda found the room's attempt to impress touching, if not a little silly – the bunting was too much, for example. The smell of dust and mechanical heat from recent Hoovering was strong, and the carpet's renewed red blazed up as best as it could in the weak English sunlight. In the corner opposite, two aloe veras guarded the noisy television, the left one almost covering a lick of damp. A dark, too-large cabinet held perhaps fifteen brass carriage clocks, and amongst these a troupe of glass animals in acrobatic positions: chimpanzees in headlocks, elephants balancing on one hoof.

Another aunty bustled through, speaking to everyone and no one at the same time: 'Dripping Cokes coming, innit, excuse! And fetch them seat. We not living in caves here. Politeness for ladies.'

'Well, this is quite the turn-up,' Amma said, suggestively.

'In what way and why turn up?'

'Usually, I don't get this far. On the rare occasions that I'm dragged along it's totally a case of "not heard, so let's not see her". I'm relegated to the children's area. In this sort of, er, venue, it'll be one of the rooms out there. Like, me and a handful of eight to twelves, shoved in a box room, with the coats and handbags. Some so-and-so throws in a pirate DVD and a Walkers multipack and I'm left to entertain for the duration. And, like, one of the more attentive parents might check every now and then that I haven't massacred the darlings, if they can be bothered. It usually ends up with me letting the girls plait my hair, or I get the girls to gang up on the naughty idiot boys.'

An uncle placed two pouffes in front of the television and switched it off, seconds before the starting pistol popped. Unable to contain their disappointment, men clapped their knees. Amma and Belinda sat. Belinda watched as Amma spoke faster and faster.

'When I was really, really little and I came to these things I was the most enormous show-off. Dad was around a bit more then because he was, like, less senior, and he'd sort of parade me about, and he'd make me do these little performances for everyone: whatever I'd learnt in ballet that week, or conjugating shit in Latin for everyone. And I'd stand in the middle of the room, literally,' she pointed ahead of her, 'then he'd get everyone to clap and sometimes they'd slip me a fiver or whatever.'

Amma pressed neat her ankles together, just visible below the wrapper's shiny green hem. For some reason Belinda remembered Mary's little white church socks, topped with the frothy lace torn by too many loving touches.

'I can't imagine you performing anything. Sorry. I hope that doesn't cause offence.'

'No. No. Sort of seems like another person.' Amma placed her hands in her lap, formally.

Belinda observed her scanning the room and its large *Gye Nyame* poster, the scratched glass panels that led to a tiny balcony for mad pigeons, the unpredictable gestures of an Albino uncle. Like a fly hopping between surfaces, everything seemed to quietly disturb Amma's eyes. She wrestled with some annoyance at the small of her back, then smiled a thin smile. In Belinda's chest, a wave rose and died. She bent towards Amma, whispering.

'You see that one over there?'

'Where?'

'The woman. The one holding the sunglasses?'

'Yeah,' Amma spotted her, nearer the fatter aloe: the short, cinnamon woman with long, sharp fingernails painted to match her copper wig. 'Yeah. Yeah?'

'In our language, she has been talking talking about you since we're arriving. I have heard all. The conversation is strange. First, I am thinking that the woman is perhaps … incorrect, erm, in the head? To begin with, she is saying to the man behind that you remind of her grandmother. You are the grandmother, returned.'

'Is that so?'

'It's true that is those are the words coming from her. But no, is not true about that you are anyone's grandmother, the second coming of. No, this woman is clearly wanting the attention of that man, you see him also?'

Again, Belinda watched Amma follow subtle direction, towards the short gentleman with scarification and an eager manner.

'Yikes. Not a looker. Flares? Who wears flares?'

'No, no. Again, that is true, he seems to me ridiculous also. But for some reason, this lady is finding his company very pleasant for her. And so she keeps telling him more big big stories to keep him there.'

'Like what?'

'Oh, oh. So, first you are the dead and departed coming back to earth to frighten all of us. Then, the second she is telling that no, she is mistaken, in actual correct fact you are exact same like the cruel first wife of her former husband.'

'Who knew I had such a generic face? And what's his response? He seems really, like, into it? Like, with all that patting and his silly doe-eyed staring at her boobs and that.'

'First, pass me some groundnut, eh?'

As Amma obliged, the cinnamon woman clung to her man, nails sinking into his generous shoulder padding. She muttered something to him. Belinda caught the gist and tutted.

'The woman believes now that the two of us are jealous of her. Apparently, we have been staring at the man too much and we are jealous that he has not come to greet one of us or even perhaps asked us if we will be dancing with him later in the evening. The one best word I have learnt since I come here is the word farcical.'

Belinda and Amma laughed and the room's attention shifted towards them. Perhaps that caused Belinda to slide off the pouffe with a tiny yell. She reached out for balance. Amma signalled for her to stand and wait while she pulled Belinda's pouffe back into shape. For a moment, they smiled at each other, and even if Belinda knew such a reaction to be silly, she could not deny that for the seconds their shared expression lasted, she felt more solid: she touched her own elbows and wrists, and liked their correct heaviness.

'What's wrong? Have you got sore –'

The bitty background noises gathered into longer rabbling: Nana entered, waving a clipboard, conducting patchy clapping.

'*Agoo?*' Nana asked.

'*Amee!*' The crowd responded.

'Oh God, here she comes. Keep your subtitley magic going.'

Trying to be discreet, Nana mimed a zipping motion towards the two girls. Nana's sweeping glare rested on Belinda too long to be shrugged off. Belinda squeezed the edges of the pouffe, switched her new phone to silent and sucked in her lips as Nana turned to the room, shy in the face of their praise, bowing her head at appropriate times. Belinda looked up at her as Nana pointed her clipboard heavenward, rejoicing in God's name, calling the occasion and their togetherness a blessing. They all knew that was right, so Belinda and the others let out firm Amens. Only Belinda noticed and itched at Amma's silence. Rustling in the wrapper that Belinda saw was inspiring bursts of envious whispering, Nana cleared space for the libation.

Amma tapped Belinda's shoulder pertly. 'I –'

'The elder will come to give his offering to the ancestors. This is how our people we have always done it.'

Belinda swivelled away to face two identical and identically suited young men with long, shiny jheri curls entering the room. Their hairstyle looked so wet and licked that Belinda almost winced, but that would have been a wrong to the hobbling old man they supported, guiding him through until he called for them to stop. The elder pulled himself, with grimaces, to his tallest height, the work stretching the skin of his neck. He smiled, then groped the air, wanting someone to pass him the customary glass of Schnapps. Nana obliged with a curtsy.

'I kept my word. Did it. Did it all. Came, saw. Not quite the third, but still …' Amma whispered.

'What?'

'It's my turn now.'

Amma swivelled and wriggled. 'Watch this,' she mouthed, and then that mouth released a series of retches. Her eyes started to dribble.

'Water!' Nana fanned her with the clipboard. Clear liquid ran down Amma's chin.

'Mum, I'm gonna throw –' Another, louder retching loosed. Two tired uncles sitting on opposite sides of the room screwed up their noses, shook their heads and clucked. Using low, certain voices they said 'no' over and over again. In Adurubaa, Belinda had become so familiar with that tone – with that word said in exactly that tone. She wanted the men to shut up.

'Take her, Belinda! Take her to fetch water! She can't, she can't here!'

'I need … eugh, it's the heat, Mum, so claustroph–'

The cinnamon woman's moan of disgust louder than all the rest.

'Go – and quick! *Ewurade!*'

Belinda saw the two suited boys stand. She dragged Amma back the way they had come, accidentally elbowing soft bellies, stepping on toes, thickening the gossip. On the other side of the grille, in the breeze near the stairwell, Belinda panted. Amma panted. Then Amma straightened herself out.

'A stunning show, no? All that bulimic dabbling in Year 9 is finally proving useful. Win.'

'Amma –'

'Relax.' She rolled up her wrapper to form a scandalous kind of skirt. 'It was only like half a term and everyone was doing it, and I'm not dead, so … oh, fix your little guilty, grumpy face.'

Outside, fat and nasty houses squatted close to the ground, their windows decorated with knickerish nets. On these streets, children thinner than Mary wobbled around on bikes with huge wheels. In some places, dog mess crisped. Grey, bobbled buildings, like the one they'd left minutes before, shot up hundreds of feet. Amma suddenly ran.

'Wait!'

Off they went: up black-and-white roads, so horns beeped; up through the old women in drifting bubbles-on-wheels and the walls of slow-moving boys with hoods that descended as they flitted by. They zipped past the disinfected freshness and shrieks of the Leisure Centre, and the security guard at Tesco who Belinda was convinced was shouting in Fante, past the red mouth of the butcher's. They continued, without explanation, Amma's rucksack thud, thud, thudding past a bus stop, and Belinda wanted to know if they shouldn't wait too, like the others who formed a sensible line under the shelter's clear hat. Her chest began to sting with the fear of what Nana would do if Belinda couldn't turn them round. The pinch lessened the more Belinda concentrated on the changing pitch of Amma's laugh as they flew. They ran by another bus stop, and a swearing man who pushed a trolley bulging with enve-lopes. Then past a knot of big men by the McDonald's, and over the crossing at KFC, even though the traffic lights said no, Belinda apologising into swerved prams.

They came to an avenue that sharply curled from the main road. Belinda really wanted to stop rather than just slow down, as Amma's pace instructed. Here was a little corner of Kejetia – Kejetia transformed. Electric Avenue. Though jowlier versions of the heroes in Aunty's Bollywoods were everywhere here, Belinda knew this place was not truly for them. It was not the pale sun making her warm, but the sight of salons filled with rows of black women. While Amma scrabbled in her bag for water, Belinda saw behind oily glass and fluorescent signs, women dramatically caped, their hair shining with relaxers, chattering easily as Mother never could have done. Hands draped over counters, half a set done out in golds and blacks, their remaining nails waiting to dazzle too. Out on the pavement, Belinda inhaled deep and ignored the phone's vibration in her pocket, instead taking in the sweetness of the loud gospel that came from somewhere. No one else seemed lightened by the salvation offered; workers were too busy hauling boxes of bananas and spinach stamped with flags. Balancing loads on heads, the men edged around stalls selling string vests, leggings, towers of aluminium cooking pots, large enough for half of Adurubaa. The burdened men were particularly careful to avoid the scrunched, older shoppers and their *Ghana Must Go* bags, and that made Belinda smile.

Belinda was yanked off again, Amma feeling renewed. And they were back on Railton and Amma was whooping. White passers-by clapped. Belinda wanted to know what was good about this black girl showing her uncreamed legs to the world and surely only running herself and Belinda even further into Nana's bad books. And as they turned closer towards Spenser, if they were only headed home, what was so joyful?

Belinda doubled over. 'We will stop now I think.' Her breath came harder than after Calisthenics. 'I think that is a better idea. Stop.'

'Oh, come on – we're, we're nearly there.'

'Can we walk then? My insides –'

'I like running, don't you? It helps me feel … freer?'

The sign told Belinda they were entering Brockwell Park by the 'Lido Entrance'. They searched for space away from businessmen loosening their ties and couples giggling at each other. Bits of leaves blew at Belinda as they walked across thirsty grass, and she flapped the itchy debris in the air, looking like she was warding off the sunset beyond the trees.

'A lido is what, exactly?' she asked, after wiping irritated eyes.

'It's a swimming pool, but, like, outside. It's really cool, that one.'

'Oh, my Aunty and Uncle have their own of these. Not for everyone else, though: only for them solely. They liked to sit around it and stare at it and sleep by it in the daytime. I never used, obviously, because first it belonged to them and also because I cannot swim. No one ever teaches you that in the village. No one ever teaches you many things.' She sensed her unintentional seriousness and jerked her body. Words came, tumbling. 'I have dreamed of what it would be like in water like that – surrounded on all the sides and only floating. I think it would be peaceful. I, I bet you and your white friends come here all the time, to enjoy it?'

'White friends?'

'Those in your photos? I suppose you must be … excited to see them in school after this long vacation?'

'Let's head up there? I want to change.' Amma wriggled, skipped ahead. 'Keep an eye out for pervs.' She skipped into bushes and through branches. Belinda glimpsed flashes of Amma's dark arms before she soon emerged, back in her all-black; a loose top that fell off the shoulder, a long skirt, her hair held in place by vicious pencils.

'Much more me.' Amma posed. Belinda frowned.

'I think I preferred it when we were wearing the same thing. Customary dress. Was nice. Two peas in the pod for once.'

'Hmm.' Amma released the balled green wrapper she clutched and spread it out.

'It will get damp and be ruined. Don't you know the expense?! Is real Dutch wax we are wearing!'

'Worry less, Be.'

What a silly thing for the girl to demand. Especially as, after patting the cloth for Belinda to sit, Amma then produced a small bottle and white packet from her rucksack.

'What. Are. What?'

Crossed arms crushing her chest, Belinda watched Amma take a considered sip of whisky. Amma winced, then tore foil and put a cigarette to her lips. She lit and inhaled, behaving as if she had tasted the most delicious thing. The games Amma played with the soft, disappearing smoke sickened Belinda.

'Don't worry, there's lining for our stomachs too.'

'Eh?'

Amma offered two sad sandwiches bundled in clingfilm that Belinda snatched up for inspection. Creaminess poured from their sides.

'This – we left our home-food for this?'

'I thought I was on fairly safe ground with a BLT?'

'No. Not safe.'

Belinda thrust it back, and sat with arms still crossed, sulking like Mary. She thought again.

'Sorry. I have been impolite. I want to apologise for my actions. I only wish I didn't feel as though these things that you are doing are not right. But that is how I feel in my heart. And now you have involved me in them. All this – cigarettes, alcohol – it will be smelling on me. Me.'

Nearby, three slim and cylindrical dogs bounced up, barked accusations at each other and strained their leads.

'They're gross, aren't they? Really creepy.' Amma inhaled again.

'I was thinking the same thing.'

'Yeah.'

Belinda watched Amma swing the bottle out towards her. Belinda's eyebrows arched. 'When did you buy this one even?'

'It's Dad's. He never drinks it. So I took it.' Amma drank more. It seemed like it burned down her. 'I don't even really like spirits. I don't think he does either.'

'No.'

'What's your dad like?' Amma paused. Belinda tried to freeze but something inside her ear ticked like termites. 'Your face has changed again. Sorry. I'm sorry. That's personal. I'm holding my beak now. Pinky promise.'

Belinda coughed and passed her fingers over Amma's wrapper that was flattened on the grass and soaking up moisture in tiny patches.

With Mary, Belinda had become expert at avoiding proper discussion of Adurubaa. Belinda had surprised herself at the quickness of her own thinking; if ever Mary came close to asking about the details of Belinda's life before Daban, Belinda invented distractions that satisfied her young friend's need to win at something, anything – how fast can you shuck these corns? How many singlets can you hang on the washing line in these two minutes? Or Belinda pointed out a problem Mary needed to solve – the unswept backyard, marks on the bathroom louvres – and needed to solve before Aunty or Uncle noticed.

If Mary's curiosity and questions persisted, and they often did, Belinda pushed harder to get the silence she wanted: she emphasised the authority of her age and threatened the removal of rewards like Fan Ices or watching *telenovelas* in recreation time. And that usually worked because rewards were a new and special and favourite thing for Mary. For both of them. Whenever Belinda used these tactics Mary called her behaviour weird or confusionist, judgements that somehow made Belinda's heart work to a mad rhythm, but that wasn't important. As Amma sighed into the distance, Belinda wondered if, to get to know this girl, to understand and help her in any real way as Nana wished, Belinda would have to offer more of herself than she had given to Mary, something more truthful. She played with the fabric again, experimented with pressing its delicate pattern of cut-out circles and triangles.

It was hard to begin in a way that would allow her to keep control. And what words wouldn't say too much but would give just enough? Phrases took shape in her mind but they disappeared when she started to grasp their meaning. Belinda breathed out and her lungs felt taut. She lifted her hands from the cloth.

'My father I've never known. I do know that he is abroad someplace. But that is all. He could be anywhere or anything. I. I don't have a great sadness about it, really. Or I don't think I do. Because I can't miss it, can I? I never had it.' The wrapper's kaleidoscoping greens blurred. She started again, even more carefully this time. 'Sometimes I do try to imagine what his face might have been like as he was leaving the house, for the last time, and the expression on it. Why I think of that, I can't tell. But I do. When I'm thinking of it, his face is coming to my mind as so angry, like the blood will even explode from his cheeks and he is slamming the doors and whatnot. Other times, I think: no, his face will have to have been quieter. Closer to tears. I don't know.'

Amma's head flopped back and then returned to its normal position. 'You probably think I'm totally, like, over-lucky with two of them around. Well, sort of around.'

'Is that why you have the problem? Because your pa is not at home often? And he used to be more?'

'Who says there's a problem, Be?' Amma slapped the earth then drove her cigarette into it. 'Why am I always a fucking problem to you lot and nothing else?'

'That is never what I meant.'

'I bet this would be going a lot more smoothly if you had a fucking drink – here!'

'Then – no – please – we will have to put up with it going more bumpy bumpy.'

The girls laughed at Belinda's silliness, but more at the messy sloshing Belinda's rejection of the whisky brought about. Belinda was frightened to touch the spill on the wrapper, so Amma blotted it out and licked the excess off her fingers. Amma stopped and looked blankly at her rucksack's complicated zips then gulped.

'You flare up and you burst and you flare. You, you have to see that as a problem? That you can't … what is the best way for describing this? You can't still yourself and be happy as a still person?'

'I have stilled myself.'

'How? Your way of being is, is so … hot.'

'Do you ever feel like you've betrayed yourself?'

'How does that follow?'

'I mean, like, you've betrayed who you think you are. Have you ever had a moment when you're suddenly, like: Fuck, I thought I was like *that* – in my head, I'm always like *that* – but I can't be because I'm not being like *that* at all?' Amma swigged, tore at grass again. 'I could be roaring. Absolutely, like, roaring away. Like it's a fucking opera. I've got every right. But I'm trying to survive it and ride it out quietly. I've got my grades, I've done the fucking Summer Homework. I know what needs doing –'

'Then why –'

'And maybe sometimes maybe, maybe I'm not so great at it and the mask slips. Shock fucking horror.'

Amma reached for another cigarette and struggled with the lighter. Shaking it, tapping it, swearing more. Directed by something, Belinda reached forward. Her thumb withdrew across the spark wheel. A polite flame rose. Amma lit. Belinda knew she was good with lighters.

'Thanks.'

Belinda's laugh was dark. 'A nice "thanks" in the middle of all this rudeness and bad manners?'

'It's not my intention to be rude to you, Be.' Amma inhaled. 'See? I can't do or say anything. That is precisely why I'm fucked.'

'What?'

'I'm fucked.'

'What?'

Amma removed the cigarette from her mouth, spoke to its glowing end. 'Nothing. Nothing at all.'

Spaces grew and stretched in Belinda's head. Her hand reached up, fiddled with the knifing end of a cornrow. Another conversation she had held lightly now slipped from her entirely. Unable to stop the picking, picking, picking at the crisp hairs, Belinda turned away from the smoking figure to the view of the park – a world freshly washed and scrubbed even though the rain had fallen hours ago. That was better. The leaves of sturdy trees twinkled and winked to show off their best green, a green not quite as rich or filling or shiny as the green she knew from home. She could not bring herself to deal with the phone shaking in her pocket again.

'I only want to put it simply. That if you have any sadness in you, I am sorry for it. Nobody should hurt.'

'It doesn't matter. I suppose, like, this is the sort of stuff that makes us human?'

And, at that, Belinda felt the whole cornrow unravel.

*

Later, Belinda followed Amma into the house, sniffing herself once more, in spite of reassurances and spritzes with Impulse. But no toe-tapping Nana waited in the corridor in a nightdress as frilled as Aunty's. Soundless. Only the buzz of fridges and marching of clocks; none of the fired questions she had imagined.

'Bit shit to turn in at nine, but I don't want to be around when Mum gets back later.'

'Oh yes. She will come later. I remember. Small hours *Ghanafoɔ* goes on until.'

'You've towels, et cetera?'

'Of course I do, by now. You can go off. Please. I'll take care of myself.'

'I'll be in my room.'

Belinda watched Amma sway up to the top of the stairs until she disappeared. Then Belinda pinched her arms again and again and again. A price needed paying. Brushing past the umbrella stand, she pecked towards the front room. She sucked in and became dizzy, but started piling old newspapers and letters on the coffee table in the way she had seen that Doctor Otuo liked. She recycled the crossword pages that he could only half complete. All cups and glasses were taken to the dishwasher. The dishwasher was unloaded, reloaded. She wanted more, to clean more: sprayed 'sorry' on all the surfaces, then swept the word away with fast movements of the cloth. Even if she had been instructed otherwise, this was better. Her fingertips flaked. Until she thought she might undo their stitches, she picked the lint and fluff from the throws that brightened the sofas, and then spotted one of Amma's butts hidden beneath a cushion. Belinda paused.

In the village, before Mother left for shifts at Misty's Chop Bar each evening, she smoked beside the window. Did Mother stand there because her daughter hated the smell? Or because she wanted to stare across into the next house? Next door, the family had a television all the other locals were invited to watch. Belinda liked to think that it was the first reason. When Mother took the last, long puff, she would flap at Belinda, mutter something about returning and flick the butt out onto the stoop. Without fail, Belinda would pick it up later. They looked so pretty: hunched little white things wrapped with the ribbon of red that was Mother's lipstick. Belinda kept the butts, hundreds of them, in a twist of newspaper beneath the bed. Sometimes she would take them out and pet them, or line them up, or arrange them into letters spelling out her name and Mother's name, next to each other.

Belinda had studied while Mother did her evening shifts. Sitting on stacked pallets, Belinda used the top of the small, buzzing fridge as a desk. It was about the same size as the one she had at school, and equally sturdy, although the school one smelled less damp. Textbooks, protractors and pencils were messy islands at her feet. Each half hour or so, the broken kerosene lamp on the shelf above jiggled shadows and she fetched paraffin. When her attention swam, she turned the radio on, lay on the bed and listened to the World Service, staring at the old struts keeping the walls in place. Moments before sleep pulled, she slapped her cheeks until they were warm and returned to her fridge.

Mother's body sighed against the thin screen door around eleven, and Belinda softened the frown for addressing old enemies – tough questions and equations – and led Mother to their bed, slipped off her shoes and peeled back unnecessary socks. As Belinda put Amma's stub in her pocket and headed to the room that still felt too large for her to sleep in, Belinda remembered taking the weight of her mother's feet on those evenings and plying the flesh around the bunions. Belinda had pressed their unchanging edges for years. Only sometimes, as she kneaded and Mother groaned satisfaction, did Belinda let herself wonder if they grew from walking too much.

14

Belinda wasn't sure if she had slept at all. She stretched. Cool light spread behind the curtain that nearly prettied the room's wallpaper, patterned with branches knotting like Jesus' crown. Nana called it a traditional English style, something along the lines of 'vines' and 'thistles'; Belinda couldn't like it. She rolled over and unfolded the Mary-shaped heap she had moulded the duvet into during the night. Images of the day before returned: she remembered the Yeboahs and the snatched time in their flat: a tiny hour of understanding, familiarity. There, she had been useful to Amma. She had liked that. She had liked that so much. She remembered speaking with Amma in the park and the silenced phone jiggling and jiggling and jiggling as she had talked about Father. The thought tensed her scalp and the veins there became hot, like someone squeezed her head. She tried swallowing and her tongue waved around: a dry, clicking thing not fit for its mouth.

She needed to leave the bed. So, as carefully as she could manage, she did. On her journey downstairs, she stopped for calming tasks. The guest bathroom door needed closing. The large photo of Doctor on the landing had to be straightened. As she descended from the carpeted upper floor with all the bedrooms, down to the floorboarded middle level where the drawing room sat, then past the grand double reception, finally reaching the kitchen in the basement, she noticed her breathing had calmed and her legs had steadied. She tickled the granite worktops she had polished and was pleased. The newness of the chill from both the surfaces and the air was good. She poured herself a glass of water and took it with her as she opened French doors onto the sharp morning. Out there, birds repeated the same string of notes.

She had learnt the names of the most unusual members of the garden. Though she liked the spiky del-phin-i-um, her favourites were the massive hy-dran-geas. They nestled at the back, beyond the pond. Careful to avoid spoiling her hem, Belinda picked her way across the dewy grass in the direction of those flowers, and stood in front of them as they bobbed against the mauve sky. The first trains of the day rattled out of Herne Hill Station. The tumble and clap of rubbish being taken away in trucks was happening nearby; those flowers were too beautiful for it all, and for her. Such precious little lights, shining within dark leaves; hundreds of tiny white wings all fitting together to dazzle. Mary would ask her to pluck one for Cynthia to wear behind her ear. But how would Belinda even know how to break the stalk of so perfect a thing?

Arms raised, she stood in praise of them. She felt herself sway. If she stared long enough, her watering eyes would make the whole world a beautiful blur of whiteness and light. She stared hard.

'What, like a Yoga or something? Early morning yoga? Aren't you a Miss Full-of-Surprises? I didn't know you have these things back home these days. Have you copied from your Aunty? She do it to help with pains in her joints? To be old in Africa is not a small thing, let me tell for free-oh.'

Nana's questions made Belinda's glass slip. The glass bounced, rolled, spilled on the ground. It should have cracked into hundreds of bits for Belinda to bend and collect. Belinda shook.

'Belinda – are you all –'

'Is a shock! You … you.'

'*Hwε wanim!* You not expecting to find me in my own home? Belinda is my funny girl.'

Before she could retrieve the glass, Nana had gone for it, and smiled. 'Aren't you cold? For you "just come", September morning is a no joke. Get this one.' Nana took off her dressing gown and draped it over Belinda's peaked shoulders.

'But, madam, then you will –'

'*Fri hɔ!* Me, I am built of rocks. Put it on.'

The soft fabric smelled of the expensive creams in Nana's cabinets. Belinda concentrated on something moving between blades of grass and heard Nana let out a little, thoughtful puff.

'I know, OK? You feel ashame.'

Belinda's eyes scooped up. Her voice wavered, 'Yes. Yes. That is too real. I am ashame.'

'Why? We can all get … get carry away.'

'Carry away?'

'I think … I think yesterday you became too excited with everything, isn't it? You get sweep up in all of it. I understand. Truly, I'm telling you I understand. Amma is a very … *persuasive*. She used to getting her way. She, she probably take you off to, to, see a white classmate? Or, no, I bet, I bet you visited to one of these galleries she always goes, to stare at these paintings and things. And is so quiet in those, so this explains is why you cannot call to let us know you are safe. Even though you wanted to, because you care about my feelings and how I worry. For you both. I was so relieve when I get home and see you both sleeping in your rooms. Like two black angels.'

Belinda let Nana readjust the gown around her shivering frame.

'I am right, eh? Gallery? Is fine. So I was happy to excuse you at *Ghanafoɔ*. *Adjei!* Those poor Yeboah twins keeping on asking if they should be a search party. But I didn't mind. Belinda? OK?' Belinda felt Nana put a finger beneath her chin and raise it. 'Did you hear? I didn't mind.'

'What will be the punishment? I – I will take all, any.'

'Memory Lane! We are in Form 3 again! You want to bend over? To fetch the cane?!'

'Do you have one? Or I can take branch from a –'

Nana laughed. 'Esther Rantzen has created a Child Line in this country, you don't hear? Even though someone should tell the woman they need one for Mum Abuse also, *me boa*?'

The light played off her velvety pyjamas, off her skin nearly as pale as the older Huxtable daughter from *The Cosby Show*. Belinda watched Nana brush aside silliness and gather herself.

'You are a woman. A good woman, Belinda. Women like us? We don't need for a big person to come and dish out the punishment. We ourselves know our own wrongs and how to fix them. We, we not sitting down: we take the chances to fix when the chances come. *Wa te*?'

'*Aane*?'

'Dazzit. We move forward. That's how to nicen it again.'

'I would like that very much, please.'

'So I have thought about it. How you can redeem it up. But you have to make out to Amma as if is your own plan.'

'Plan. My – plan?'

'Yes. So you start studying in few days. Maybe you tell her you not sure of the route home from this school. You think you will get lost. Or you are frightened to go through Streatham solo. Or whatever good reason you can come up with that's feeling right for Belinda and seems real as your own. Make it as if you need her and so every day she has to take you from this new Abraham College or whatever, and come with you back here. Every day.'

'Abacus. Abacus College. And, madam, it seem –'

'If you can see her, spend more time … Maybe. Just maybe.'

Belinda watched the windows of the Otuos' house flash up in the golden colours breaking through the cloud. Was that a figure moving on the top floor? A dark body definitely turned. Doctor leaving for work? Or, why would Amma be awake and not enjoy-ing one of the last late risings of the summer holiday? Nana focused Belinda again.

'Is this, exactly. This is why she will come to you in time. The gentleness. The little gentle way your eyes are watching. When you look at something or someone, is like your eyes giving them a kindness. And that's what she needs. That will bring out whatever the sadness truly is in her.'

'Gentle? I never think to call myself as this word before.'

'Yes. You much more … how they put it … refine than me. Not too harsh and big and in the face as me.' Nana sighed. 'But can I help it? I am sorry that I cannot. How can I change to become something new now, old like I am, old like Methuselah?' Nana crossed her arms and tutted. 'Perhaps when I get to His gates I will get why I have been given so many curses to bear.'

'Please, madam, don't. A great like you cannot have a badness upon them. I feel is for sure.'

'And I nearly believe you, Belinda. That's this special power you having. You, you are special, OK? Very special. Sometimes I'm thinking you don't even see how much good you can do with this special. If you let yourself. Eh?'

Belinda wanted to believe that, too. As she reached to scratch an earlobe, she was gathered into a hug from all sides. It pulled her up, stood her on tiptoes, tipped her onto Nana's shoulder. Though its soft force seemed to reduce her to Mary's size, she didn't mind. She leant her weight into it and felt Nana lightly roll the water glass over her spine. That was nice too. The skin on Nana's collarbone was soft, difficult to distinguish from the fabric, somehow like the hydrangea's petals. Nana purred. In that embrace, Belinda had time; she understood what Nana meant about herself and change. However quickly she had come up with Mary's Cynthia, it was a struggle for Belinda to think of herself as anything other than she had always been. But the embrace – that closed, opened, and closed again – promised that as Belinda slipped into other ways to find the answer for Amma, when inevitable failure came she would be caught and protected. She had no idea what those other ways might be. But the embrace was sure that eventually she would find the right one.

Belinda wanted to speak. 'I need to work as never before.'

'Of course, Belinda. Of course.'

Belinda lifted her head, looked up. She was certain the curtains up there were shifting.

Amma had been disturbed from sleep, in her room. There was silence, except for familiar voices. She scraped rogue plaits from her forehead and tiptoed along the corridor. Through the lonely sash window on the back wall ahead, she saw Mum and Belinda, down in the garden, surrounded by flowers like doilies. Amma moved closer: Mum's dressing gown flowed around a stooping Belinda. Amma slumped too, as she thought back to yesterday. It had been wrong to do it to Belinda, sitting in the park and watching the poor girl's awkwardness rise. She had been cruel; sometimes it was no more complicated than that.

Amma rested her forehead on the window's glass as Nana softened her stance in a manner rarely seen. Except when Amma had been younger, and especially on their Sundays: out they'd go, Mum and her, necks tied with identical scarves from M&S. First to Bookends on Coldharbour, where the smelly Afghan hound harrumphed in the corner, and Amma was allowed two picture books, Mum buying herself something with embossed lettering, a swooning damsel and man in breeches on the front. Then through the market and Granville Arcade, her tiny hand still in Mum's pocket as Mum teased butchers and fishmongers to get the best deals on cow foot, mutton, red snapper.

Amma's bitter, early-morning mouth tried to remember the slippery feel of cow foot. And while it did, down in the garden,

Mum lunged Belinda into the kind of hug that the Dulwich College boys probably did after sporting success, or even defeat, when only the crush of bodies would do. A large and important part of Amma regretted putting Belinda into a situation where solace from Mum was the best option. An even larger and more powerful part simply felt sad.

The exposed backs of Amma's knees caught the cold. She watched Nana rub Belinda's back.

Getting an A for an essay was pleasingly straightforward. There were rules to be followed, well-selected places in paragraphs where untaught flair was required. Hiding her feelings in order to turn into the kind of daughter Nana Otuo wanted presented a greater challenge. A daughter accepting of a dressing gown draped over shoulders; one who, as Belinda was then, was happy to be led back into the house by Nana's arm. Happy to be led, full stop. Amma pulled on the curtain and the rings on the rail overhead strained. She heard the easing of locks.

Quickly, she padded back to her bedroom, shut the door and pressed her back against it as if someone would soon demand to come in. For thirty seconds she stood, readied. But no one would come for or to her. She straightened up like nothing had happened and stepped around oil pastels. She turned on the lamp at her desk and sat. The trinket box occupied the edge of her line of vision, as did the hand mirror. She caught a glimpse of herself: dry skin, masculine sideburns like an Asian girl's, the gap between front teeth that others would have banished with braces. If she had possessed a better, lovelier face, perhaps all her troubles would have been avoided.

How weak the pre-caffeinated mind could be! How weak! She grabbed at papers and dumped them over her reflection.

It had been ages since the Saturday when she had put away all the important things from the Brunswick Manor Gifted and Talented Residential into the trinket box. On that day, it had rained appropriately and persistently. Amma had waited for weeks and weeks to hear anything, anything at all, but there had been no replies to her texts, voice messages. That Saturday, after closing the box with a definite, final click, she promised herself she wouldn't touch it ever again.

She had had a good run of nearly five months now, so even if it would blight any chance of enjoying these last sunny days before the start of her A2 year, the pressure in her stomach said she needed to do it. She scrabbled at the bottom of her pen pot, fingering tampons and coins and the condom and stamps and sequins, for the key. Her hand trembled as she opened the lock. She pushed the box away.

After a moment, she pulled the lid back further and moved the lamp closer. In the box's first drawer were the smaller items. The 'Programme of Events' for the week at Brunswick – long lectures on Ulysses and Medea and Diego Rivera. The paper crunched as she moved it to inspect a feather from a dead pigeon that Amma and Roisin had picked up. Then two Pearlstein nudes Roisin had given to Amma, with interlocking legs. Postcards that, all through Dad's driving her home on the final day, Amma was certain would fall out, bringing shame and an unconvincing explanation. *Roisin*. The best of the new names learnt that half-term week at Brunswick. Ro. Sheen. That name, like Amma's, impossible to forget among the Edwins and Tillys who'd found their way to that boot camp for the brilliant.

Amma kept sifting through the box's contents. Travelcards: 13 March 2002. Then the mixtape she had played and played, Mum coming in every evening with the same 'joking' instruction that Amma 'turn down the white music. No – come again, the white noise! *Won sere?*' Amma teased the cassette's silky innards, torn when anger stopped her seeing later regret. The first three on the B-side were the songs she had listened to most: 'Girl Afraid', 'Coo Coo', 'Wuthering Heights'. Amma started humming 'Panic', tapping the cassette – until the sun splashed over her too much and she came close to something like contentment.

She gave herself a moment, the cassette limp in her grip now, its ribbon dripping. Though the tape was ruined, the writing remained on the thin white label above the two wheels. 'All for Amma to Take!' She flipped it over. On that side: 'Take the All, Amma!' So typically Roisin: both odd and oddly profound. Thinking about Roisin's savage moving of the nib to write those slapdash capitals brought a smile, a smile Amma guessed was less attractive than the one across her mouth when Roisin had held her face under the sycamores. While everyone else slept soundly in Brunswick's dorms, in darkness Roisin had stared at Amma for what seemed like an hour, before Amma broke the mood with a giggle that soon disappeared, shushed by Roisin plunging her lips at Amma's neck. Amma shot up from the desk, rocking the trinket box, returned to her bed, threw up the duvet, pulled it back and crouched beneath, like she was praying in the dark.

The first time they talked at Brunswick was straight after the horrid icebreakers and watery squash. On arrival, all fifteen of the elite specially selected for seven days of 'prestigious intellectual challenge' were forced to sit in a circle on the newly varnished parquet floor. They were called upon by the 'coordinator' and her dangly earrings to 'share', to bleat out vital statistics, a hope for the stimulating week ahead and something 'quirky' about themselves. After that embarrassment, Amma – '17, SCGS, interested in Toni Morrison and Nella Larsen, can vibrate her irises' – had left to sit on the cold steps and be anti-social. She wasted time there by pursuing a snail's shell with her toes. And then Roisin – '18, Godolphin & Latymer, headed to New Hall, keen on the workshop about jazz, knew lyrics to most winning Eurovision entries' – was standing in front of her. Auburnish hair; a nose ring that irritated the surrounding skin and turned it a floral red; black waffle knit, silver rings, hobnails; an academic witch.

'You like to smoke, I think?' Roisin had said, her tone clipped.

'I do. Sometimes.'

'Let's, then. Let's make this one of those, then. Let's make this a time.'

Roisin had kicked the snail shell away, sat, and produced the necessaries for rollies. Amma had watched Roisin's precise handling of paper and grinding of tobacco with an intensity she assumed came from both her own inexpertise at this and from finding a diversion from the grim, gargoyle-greyness of the place. But when Roisin's tongue darted along the white edge of the paper, Amma was grateful that her skin hid blushes. The perfection of Roisin's motions did it. The pink of the tongue, the pearl of spit at its end. The pallor of Roisin's concentrating face. Amma wanted to touch that face, to check its reality. The waving sensation inside Amma as she kept staring was like lying next to Helena during Sleeping Lions at Prep School. During that pre-home-time ritual, a secret peace came each time Amma inhaled and got more of her oldest friend's almondy odour. Like when their little fingers brushed. But that first encounter with Roisin was much more.

Amma was frightened by the wringing knowledge that she could never tell anyone about her body's response. Because Amma knew the unwieldy truth: no one likes a black girl who likes girls. Friends would wriggle: their liberalism tested by something they couldn't *quite* get on board with. Mum would die. *Ghanafoɔ* would explode in a shower of Jollof.

That first day at Brunswick, on the wet stoop, Amma had been incredibly impressed by herself. First, at her ability to actually animate her mouth to say 'Thank you' for the proffered cigarette and to the slate eyes evaluating her. Secondly, at not stroking the long fingers that proffered; fingers whose peatiness, saltiness, Amma had missed for five whole months, but could almost smell then, filling the air beneath the duvet.

Throwing off the duvet and darkness with it, Amma flipped onto her back, hoisted up her knees and yanked down her knickers. She pressed the heel of her hand hard between her legs at the heat and roughness there. She moved, did the same grinding to the inside of a thigh, then stroked the damp lips, gently, like they were a discovery to her. She rubbed her thumb against her clitoris in tense circles until her breath leapt. She stopped and growled. Her fist thudded into the mattress again and again and again.

15

The next Tuesday, Belinda was opposite Streatham Hill Station. The door she stood at was a thin blue one, pressed between a shop where mobiles became 'unlocked' and one where trainers and flip-flops were sold from wire baskets. Other people stood outside the door too, with the same printed sheet and concerned expression Belinda had – apart from the hunched black man with an itchy, brown hat squashed on his head. Unlike the rest of them, who were confused, his huffing suggested anger that Abacus Educational Centre lacked a proper sign.

At the end of a climb up a flight of dark stairs that reminded her of going to *Ghanafoɔ* a classroom appeared. Everyone scrabbled to find seats and unloaded rucksacks on tiny desks. She looked around: a computer, almost as massive as the ones back home, fat and grumpy on the teacher's table. An empty bookcase gaped. There were green felt panels on walls studded with gold pins and wads of chewing gum. Small flames of Nana's encouragement flickered in Belinda's belly. Minutes passed before a headscarved Somalian woman entered the room and stood at the front with her hands placed together as if in prayer. Her quiet smile undid the scrunching of Belinda's forehead. The woman turned, showed the class the flowery back of her flowery front. She hummed as she pressed her marker across the board's streaked whiteness. The letters of her name were given tall, thin limbs. So neat.

'Mrs Al-Kawthari … easy enough, I think – I think – but somehow its fate is to be mispronounced forever … so … let's try saying it together, shall we? Pronounce it properly and you'll all get As for your first assignment.'

Belinda hoped her laugh was polite enough.

'So, so after three … one, two, three? Three? Reluctance. I see, I see. We've got to start somewhere, haven't we, eh? And so …' the woman jogged on the spot, as though about to launch into a run, her little breasts nudging her shift. '… let's try again. One, two, three …'

'Al-Kawthari.' Belinda rang out loudest. Her armpits felt sticky.

'Super. Really super start. Some Crayolas and coloured paper are whizzing around now for our first little exercise of the course …'

School meant sitting up, so Belinda did: straight and proud like she had been taught and as appropriate for a student of her potential. She had always been in positions 1, 2 and 3 when test results were called out back in Adurubaa. There was no imagining being one of those – Anang, Amoako, Saakye – who reliably turned up at the end of Mrs Mensah's league. Mary would probably have spent her life in the duller ranks of that list too. Although, Belinda admitted – accepting a green, an orange and a blue pen as instructed – not necessarily. Because there were times when Mary was an excellent pupil. Like when it had taken her only a matter of seconds to understand how to fold hospital corners. Or when she had learnt how to remove the candle's dripped wax from the tablecloth without damaging the fabric forever. Or when they had prepared dinner together on Nana's first night in Daban.

In Aunty and Uncle's vast kitchen, using a tea towel, Belinda had gripped half of an avocado and Mary had observed. With her free hand, Belinda tapped the knife against the pear's stone and twisted the blade into the surface. Lifting the knife, sure enough, the pit clung to the serrated edge and left behind a clean space in the fruit. Belinda remembered tossing the pit between her palms.

'So is that simple, OK?' she had said.

'Confusionist! Con-fu-sion-ist! Is exact same like what I did, and it never did come loose for me. Is very frustrating, oh.' Mary threw her arms up.

'But you need to be a little more firm and tight. Else will never work.'

'I was firm and I was tight – I, I want to kill the avocado and Ninja it with my knife.'

'One more, you hear? Then that's last. We cook for four, not four hundred.'

Mary skulked to the fruit bowl, bare feet moving wetly. She stretched her neck and arms like Belinda had seen boxers do before the bell. 'You can't hide from me, Mister Pipstone. The champion will get her winning and tonight is your nightmare day.' Mary put her victim on the chopping board, cut, twisted the halves apart and high-fived herself. 'Hallelujah and hooray – the first of winning.' It took three more attempts, each time Mary pushing away the guidance of Belinda's hands. But when she did it herself, Mary produced a tired handkerchief from her pocket and twirled it like a rejoicing elder at a wedding. Mary bent her knees, humped her back, hobbled, strutted around the granite-topped island. Belinda had howled and suddenly Mary wanted the two of them to go to the garden to celebrate with handstands.

'And don't be a shy or a scared: it doesn't matter because no one is here to see if the skirt falls a bit and then the knickers show. Only me and you.'

Now, Belinda nearly giggled to herself as the man next to her with the hat announced to the group that he was called Robert, and he spoke about what he would do after he had achieved this GCSE in English Literature.

'And you're?'

'Me?'

'Yes. Come on. No one bites.'

'I didn't mention any biting thing.'

'Your name, love?'

'Belinda.'

'Belinda … Belinda …?'

'Otuo.'

'Like the phone?'

'Otuo?'

'0-2-0?'

'Otuo. It means gun, in my language.'

'Crikey.'

'I'm only revealing what it is.'

'That's … fascinating, Belinda, really. Tell us what language that is then.'

'Twi?'

'Ah. From Ghana. I could tell by the cheeks.'

Belinda coughed, scratched her central parting, didn't like the sweetness the pomade left on her fingertips.

'Any other Ghanaians here?'

The girl two ahead in a denim jacket raised her white hand. Belinda splurted out a surprised noise, then scrabbled to push the noise back. 'Sorry, I –'

'Nah, 'scool, listen. It ain't me, course, it's my first-born. His daddy's from Ghana. Said 'e'd take me there one day. See Labadi, get Kente. All that. Thing is, he fucked off back, didn't tell me nothing about where he was. Oh well.'

'That is a very sad tale,' Belinda heard herself say.

'Nah, 'scool. You just gotta get on with livin'. Get me?'

'Black men!' a female voice added from the row behind Belinda, 'and West Africans ones, they are worst, I'm telling! Nigerians, Ghanaians: our men: They behave so up, up, up, and pompous; even if they came here with only two cedis in their pocket and have only add some twenty pounds since their arrival. Every day every day talking themselves up.'

'Seen,' said the white lady.

'Yes,' said the black lady behind.

'Let's not forget names, p–'

'Alice,' said the white lady.

'Sylvia,' said the black one.

'I mean, we're definitely covering some slightly dodgy ground here with our generalisations.'

'But they are not wrong, Miss, are they? And Robel, I am call Robel … I see it all the time. They have no care for women. Women is like things. In my country, women is like goddess. You must look after, protect. You know this, Mrs Al-Kawthari, I bet it, from you own country, right?'

'Hey, this is all about you guys, Robel.'

'Come on, miss, you can't go on like that,' Alice started.

'Like what?'

'All, like, you ain't got a view. It's bait. You blatantly do –'

Mrs Al-Kawthari wandered down an aisle between tables: 'You've been quiet. Yep, you over there?'

Like the rest of class, Belinda shifted her attention to this older woman with smoky, creased eyelids and wispy hair held up by fancy gold shields. She pointed at her chest in disbelief.

'Ask grandchildren if Mahdokt quiet. Laugh at you. Tell you I'm never knowing when to stop.'

'We got wisdom to give,' Alice offered, and Belinda liked that she was trying to make friends.

'Is Mahdokt. My one. Name.'

'Mah-dokt … beautiful … and what does it mean? I bet it means something beau-ti-ful …'

'It is. It means like what I am: daughter of the moon.'

Belinda wondered if Mary might prefer that to Cynthia. It sounded even more wonderful. Belinda and Mary could practise its pronunciation together carefully, repeating it to each other down the line until they got it exactly right. The thought warmed

her all the way through the list of 'Synonyms for the word "Scary"'
that they had to come up with in pairs, and when they started the
difficult first scene of *Macbeth*. Until her phone vibrated. She knew
what the text would remind her to do. No kindness and fun from
the teacher pulling excellent monstrous faces for the witch-char-
acters could soften Belinda's forehead now.

That same afternoon, Amma contemplated the similarities
between her surroundings and the set of the '… Baby One More
Time' video. In English Lit., watching the clock, Amma listened to
each tick, as hollow as every tock, and rapped her pencil against
the desk. Worst luck: none of Britney's backing dancers somer-
saulted between the desks to provide entertaining respite from 'the
horrors of World War One'.

'So, folks, why might Faulks have used this narrative technique
in the extract we're analysing? Can we all remember what we mean
by the term "narrative technique"? Who can remember?'

To emphasise ideas in desperate need of razzmatazz or to lend
important questions greater jeopardy, the little man at the front of
the class stretched his hands out, up, to the side. Mr Stevens –
although 'Titch' was more informative – sat on the edge of his
table, kicking his legs like a child on a swing. Each of the fifteen
girls under his tutelage were destined for As and Russell Group
universities regardless of his efforts. The prospect, the certainty of
success, dispirited Amma. She cast a glance around the class. A
troupe of patient, medieval princesses in forest green; Rapunzels
in a tower. As ever, Helena was doing a much better job at appear-
ing attentive. Her chin was forward, hair arranged over one shoulder just so. Amma pushed lower into the seat and the chair
squeaked. Once the resultant glares drifted away from her and
back to Titch, Dead Nina With The Spots slid Amma a note from
someone. With precision, Amma peeled it open in her lap and a
revealed a scrawled cock. The penis had been drawn with

exuberance, the shaft generously wide and topped with a pointy
Ku Klux Klannish bell-end spraying buoyant droplets. To the left,
an arrow as thick as the shaft, indicating the direction of the dick.
An explanatory caption, in Helena's looping script, 'Titch is a
knob'. Amma winked at Helena, who winked back. The note was a
funny, silly thing to have done. But Amma immediately thought
of Roisin and the rave and then felt terrible. That rave was where,
in a sense, Amma had encountered her first, proper cock. She
wondered if it would be her last. A Garage rave, early March, in an
industrial estate in Battersea, a few weeks after Brunswick. The
final time Amma had seen Roisin before the messages stopped
coming; no more trenchant texted lines that Amma would copy
out and stick on her bedroom walls. They completely stopped, no
matter how much Amma tried for a response. Amma worried the
grey corner of the novel's cover as Titch went on and on.

Roisin had never been to South London, and insisted that they
go to a Big Night she had heard about on some pirate radio station.
They both hated Garage, but Roisin was 'curious'. And she had said
that word so wryly that they had both laughed, and it seemed
enough to stop Amma's itch that Roisin's planned trip was about
wanting an ethnographer's look at how the black half lived; Amma
was to be her helpful native guide. The itch was not new. Even after
Roisin had first fingered her in the toilets at Brunswick, Roisin had
also said something incongruous about how Amma was 'different
from other black people', and Amma had agreed emptily. But it
would have been unfair to press those issues during that conversation when Roisin was bouncing. Amma didn't want to dull the
gleam of future excitements. As Amma agreed to the plan, she did,
however, tell Roisin they'd have to be really careful about kissing
and touching one another and stuff. Roisin laughed again, this
time on her own.

So they went, dressed authentically for the occasion in slinky
Adidas halter-necks and hooped earrings, getting the bus from

Clapham Junction with the Travelcards Amma now stored in the trinket box. After freezing in a queue for an hour, they entered the rave and quickly got the gist. Green lasers gridded the smoky air. On the stage MCs who were very cross with their microphones shouted over blippy beats. They said 'Oh my gosh!' and 'Good God!' which Roisin found particularly amusing. Much of it sounded like speeded-up tongue twisters, like drama warm-ups gone wrong, Roisin had observed. Down on the sticky dancefloor, boys lined the walls of the huge cave. They mimed gunshots at the MCs, whispered into the sides of each other's hoods, slipped packets up their sleeves, picked their teeth with cocktail sticks. All this and always, always monitoring the pool of girls in the middle of the warehouse who simulated many different kinds of sexual positions. Here, female dipping was so low that frayed hot pants could split. The same squatting girls pulled themselves up from those difficult bends with a kind of grace.

Sucking on her Breezer, Amma had wanted to say something about how she loved the intelligence of women's bodies, because it seemed like the kind of thing Roisin might suggest. Amma swallowed the Bacardi harder. While she was gulping, one of the boys decided he had taken a liking to Amma's bottom so he ground at it with all his strength. The pressure against Amma's arse became urgent. First there were hands on her hips. And then there was the cock. Crude and blunt, like it had the conviction to tear through her jeans. She had desperately wanted Roisin to come to her rescue and cut the hooded stranger down to size with an exquisite one-liner.

Sweating, Amma had felt guilty at her revulsion. She was supposed to like this? He a big black man, and she a sexy young sista: this grinding pairing was as the universe should be. She wondered if any chivalrous, protective attempts from Roisin might be correctly understood. The cuss was usually batty boy, but wasn't batty gyal as easy to shout? There was no telling what else a room full of hundreds of black people – black people not like Amma, not like Amma at all – might do, with lesbians in their midst. If that was even what they were. So Amma wriggled away from the erection with a deft dance move. She sidled up to Roisin and chatted like nothing had happened, like she hadn't been ignored, like she didn't mind the strange passivity in Roisin's open face, at odds with the lights flecking it with colour. They'd finally left, the big and sceptical Nigerian bouncer eyeing the two of them when they staggered out, clutching each other. She felt like that man's fixed stare carried such meaning. As if he knew. But he couldn't have known. Could he? That uncomfortable wondering kept Amma silent on the night bus as drunks crooned and Roisin slept on her shoulder, her lips beautifully parted.

Amma looked down at the frozen soldier on the cover of *Birdsong* again. She chewed on the pencil's rubbered end and searched the classroom's long Victorian windows. She wanted space, silence and a fag.

'A fantastically sensitive response from Natalie there about empathy – I can imagine that's precisely the kind of anxiety the prose is working out. Yeah. Can we all applaud Natalie's excellent interpretation there, please?'

Amma clapped and smacked her knees together under the desk. The acrylic skirt rubbed.

'The bit we all love, then, ladies. Your toils will continue elsewhere.'

The girls did pantomime groans at Titch; Amma watched him chuckle and write 'Homework' on the board. Amma picked up her 'Homework' planner. Titch wrote 'Handouts on Language, Form and Structure', and, just like that, three coloured sheets of paper appeared on her desk. He shouted a reminder about UCAS references and they all hummed. The buzzer buzzed and green coats, green bags and green folders became alive, as did Amma's 3310. Even though it wouldn't be from Roisin, hope still pulsed in her throat. A little envelope flashed on the phone's tiny screen. She pressed buttons and the envelope flew open.

'Really, Belinda? *Really?*'

On the other side of the road, by a red Threshers and yellow Pharmacy on Streatham Hill, Belinda watched a van crawl along in a 'sinister' way – the word Mrs Al-Kawthari had most liked when they all gave their answers to the first task. The van reminded her of the bubbles for the old shopping women, but was similar to an ambulance too, and was also like a metal beast with orange lights for horns. Sometimes, it bleeped. The van rested on two huge, swirling brushes, swivelling through a fuzzy, watery smoke. The driver looked a serious man, only moved to pull levers that brought more bleeping and watery smoke.

Amma was too busy ignoring Belinda to ask about it, piling her plaits up and trying to secure them with pencils – which looked dangerous, messy and hard work. Belinda wondered if she might help, but Amma's jaw and the bite around the pencils she held in her mouth suggested otherwise. Belinda took her Travelcard out of its blue holder. She then put it back into the holder. What was the English? Fighting Fire with Fire. She thought of the tie and the lighter and nearly enjoyed her own pun. Belinda put the holder back into her pocket and beamed at Amma. No response. Belinda took the holder out of her pocket again and ran a fingernail down its central fold.

'Oh bloody hell, stop fidgeting or I'll take the thing away from you.'

'Sorry, I.'

'Yeahyeah. *Sorry.*' Amma said 'sorry' like a naughty boy might, then kicked the bus stop's stand. A young woman tutted and checked the sleeping baby in her pram. The white must think the blacks had gone mad.

'What did I do for this one?'

'How can you not remember how to get home? Fuck! Me, you and Mum talked about it like seven times! I can't even stand it. It's so straightforward! This is ridiculous.'

'I ... had a mental blanks.'

'And you couldn't have like, I don't know, figured it out yourself? What if I'd had other stuff to do ... or like, like, somewhere to go, or whatever? Then you'd be fucked, wouldn't you?'

'You are angry because you had appointment I have inconvenienced? I assumed on school days you are quick quick to come back to Spenser Road straight after lesson to begin the home assignments as soon as you can. What was your appointment, I wonder if I can maybe ask?'

'No. I, I didn't have anything on today. But, I could have, which is the point. Really important point.'

'I remembered that the whole number had a "3" in it, in some place, but not sure, completely so. I thought is best thing to ask, and for you to collect. Me: I'm never thinking I'm causing such massive commotion commotion. Imagine if I lose myself in this place. What would I do then, eh? Or you prefer it like that?' Belinda saw Amma's tension slowly come undone.

'But I don't get it: why not just ask my mum?'

'I think you shouldn't pronounce the word as that. Mum. Like is a curse. Be very very grateful for all that you have for a family.'

'I bloody am, I don't need –' Amma pulled the straps of her rucksack. 'I am grateful.'

She yanked the straps again and the paler bits of her hands were turning red and Belinda worried.

'It will break, stop that.'

'I hate being called spoiled. It's the kind of thing she trots out too, like, twist the knife. Mum. All the stuff about her having to walk miles for water and then look at Princess Me.'

'I don't think of you as a princess. Princesses have a politeness and also a charm.'

'Be!'

'And also I never mention "spoiled". That's something you put in there all by yourself. I only ask that you remember what goodness God has given to you.'

'I've got lots – you're absolutely right.'

'Yes. Much more than many others. Much more than me, for one instance. Have you thought on that?'

'Please. Literally, I'm begging you, yeah? I can't deal with that guilt shit and everything else.'

'And what everything else? What else?'

'Look, just because I've got, like, I'm lucky and privileged and all that – and I know it, I know it – it doesn't mean I can't wish what I had was better. I mean – Shit.' Amma placed her left boot on top of her right. 'Where's this fucking 133? Note that, Belinda. 1. 3. 3.'

'Thank you … Captain?'

'That's weird.'

'Yes, I suppose is.'

'I do quite like it though … Captain …'

Amma smiled and sighed very loudly and the young mother was startled. The woman, who wore a big white coat that reminded Belinda of the man made from tyres, bent down to whisper something at the baby, stroke its chin and then pulled out the pram's hood.

'One thing I know for sure is this one. Your mum. She is loving you very much.'

'Give me an example, of how you've seen that love. I'm not even being mean, like challenging you for the sake of it, or whatever. I might have missed something that you can see better than me. So like, any proof you've got would be great. I'm all ears, Be.'

Belinda gently wrapped her fingers around the back of her neck to ease a knot there. The noisy traffic all came together in one dull drone. The child's fussing cry and the beast's beeping were absorbed and lost. The fact that Nana had brought her over from Ghana to London, mostly for Amma's benefit, mostly in the hope of soothing and fixing Amma was, to Belinda, a big, obvious example of the care that Amma was blind to.

Belinda relaxed her grip. Had Mother ever shown love like that? How had Mother shown love? When Mother listened and nodded as Belinda described what she had learnt at school that day, even when Mother, with body angled towards the door and eyes on the clock, seemed so keen to be elsewhere – was that patient waiting a kind of loving? When, once, Belinda had been reluctant to speak but had eventually told Mother that two girls had called her an abomination and spat when she tried to join their game of Pilolo; and Mother had roared in response and clattered pots and promised that she would fry the yam and Belinda should rest for once – did that rage count as love? A man with thin, blue-black hair hobbled past the bus stop, pausing after every few steps to bite at his dripping burger.

'Looks like you've got nothing for me,' Amma muttered. 'Case dismissed?'

Belinda pressed her palms together and observed the seal they made against one another. A tight lock; a stop to all her questions, doubts. A siren started then quickly stopped itself. Belinda cleared her throat.

'Amma, you should just trust me, eh? Trust that your mum loves very, very much.'

'That's a little weak, *non*?'

'Trust? The truth?' Belinda clucked. 'You think the truth is weak? Then maybe there is none of the hope for you if that's what you actually believing.'

'I'm afraid, on that one, my friend, I have to agree with you.' Amma kicked the ground repeatedly.

Belinda exhaled. 'I don't like to see you so, eh? You look so … so painful.'

'Cheers.'

'No, I mean that … that I'm scared you will do yourself a bad damage if you keep all this building and building and you don't go to let it out. You will hurt yourself.'

'I don't know what to do with … with this …' Amma's voice shook.

Belinda hopped on the spot. 'Close your eyes.'

'Be –'

'Why not change your record player of always "no" to me and do what I'm requesting for once in your life, OK?'

Two 155s rolled past.

Belinda liked Amma's silence, liked the fizzing in her veins, liked how fast the girl's eyelids snapped to follow the instruction.

'Breathe slow and forget. Breathe. Slow. Nice, and easy, mmm? Nice, and then, the easy. Eh heh. Nice, then slow.'

'Mmmm, rush-hour exhaust fumes …' Amma jiggled. Belinda had made her smile. 'I must look mental.'

'Ah ah! Say nothing. I am Captain now.'

'Right …'

'Pretend you not even here. In this place. You are not cold and not waiting for this 133.'

'It's like Paul McKenna.'

'And now, behind your closing eyes, you … you form a picture of the best place you have ever been. Like one without all of these angers bubbling in you and all your bad feelings. Somewhere so nice and gentle and with all the best people that you love.'

Belinda noted Amma's straining cheeks, uncomfortable mouth.

'You … you think you can tell me about it? Only if you like, of course. Not meaning to be a nosy parker or anything as that.'

'I –'

'No, keep the eyes shut. That is an important bit.'

'OK.'

'So? You don't want to – No. I understand that. That's fine and I'll do no prying. Not me, sir. No way.'

'It's a garden. There are massive oaks and sycamores and stuff. And it's night-time. So it's completely quiet and still. So beautiful.'

Belinda stepped back as Amma's whole face turned in on itself. The woman in the big coat muttered and rolled her pram away. Though Belinda stung with the urge to apologise to this person troubled by her actions, Belinda could not. To ignore the weeping girl who was now slapping her cheeks both to hurt and wipe tears away: that would be cruel. Belinda took a step forward. She touched Amma's green shoulder. Nothing happened for a moment. Amma continued to shake, continued to try calming herself. Belinda watched that irregular movement, her own touch acting as a steady contrast to it. She tried to remember: in her saddest moments, when she had felt unworthiest and most lost, what kinds of things did Belinda want someone to say to her? Slowly, Belinda's lips unstuck. The voice was hers, only more solid.

'I promise this will pass. I promise, this thing you feel? Is too bad and so when you least expecting it will have gone. Because you not an evil. So what have you done to have to get a terrible pain like this forever? What have you done to deserve it, eh? You only a little girl. Not like a Hitler or devil. It will pass. It has to. Eh? Eh?'

16

So Amma and Belinda travelled together home twice, maybe three times a week. Helena had disappeared, off doing that weird thing where she and Max banged for, like, a month solid, and when it was all over pretended to everyone nothing had happened, so Amma was certainly able to spare the time. On most afternoons, Amma and Belinda took the good old 133. Other times, when Amma's legs were restless, they did the longish journey up Streatham Hill on foot, going past the rickety Somali Internet cafés and pizza places selling heart-stopping saltiness for a quid. On the eighth or so time they walked together, Amma stopped them at the Ritzy Picturehouse for a drink. They moved through the brassy foyer, Amma single-mindedly focused, taking them up the stairs to the third floor and the café there.

'It feel strange to be in a cinema, but not planning to see any film. Unless you want us now to be watching one? A blockbuster? In Ashanti New Town, they had one. Some days it served as a church, but on the rest they turned it into a Cineplex, like this, but less … less posh than here, obviously. I would go by it when I did my errands, and they would let you see what you could see for a few seconds, no charge. They put up a big white sheet like from the washing and showed the films on that. So, shall we see a film today? What kind do you like? An action? A rom comedy?'

As soon as they arrived, Amma sent Belinda to order, Belinda flinching and deferential as the coins were counted into her right palm. Amma dumped her rucksack, waited amid the familiar fairy lights and dog-eared posters – Almódovar, Haneke, Allen. The tall guy at the till flirted with customers, coyly playing with his trendy trilby and cocking his head to indicate roguishness. Amma smiled at Belinda's stiff behaviour in his presence, and then Belinda brought over their Cokes and slices of Red Velvet. Belinda lowered the tray and removed the scrunched receipt which she had held between her teeth. Again, Amma considered the ludicrous possibility of fancying the girl now arranging herself in the seat opposite. Wouldn't it be logical and neat if desire were that transferrable? If she suddenly became curious and wanted to know how black cunt tasted different from white cunt? Amma rubbed the grey grime on her shirt's cuff and cracked her knuckles.

'You have no change from it. I even added a few coins myself. So.' Amma nodded and shoved the receipt into her blazer's pocket. Amma tried to imagine Belinda as a lover: Belinda, sucking Amma's lips – 'Seem costly to me for a little piece of something sweet, but anyway, I thank you for it. A nice treat for a hard day's schooling, eh?' – or what about if Amma put her proud little thumb, gently, gently, up Be's arsehole? Amma watched the bubbles whizzing to the top of her glass and smirked.

'What brings you this joy? Is really lovely to see, Amma.'

In the imagined throes of passion, with Amma trying to be creative, super-sexy and risky, a thumb inserted into Belinda's arse would undoubtedly cause Belinda to shout *Adjei!* and wriggle away, stealing up the bedsheets. *Adjei!* like when Mum couldn't find her car keys. *Adjei!* like when Dad sipped uncooled tea. *Adjei!* like the old aunties in the poundshop on discovering last week's deal on pilchards was no more. Amma did not care that it was only funny to her, and broke into giggles.

Belinda's smooth, wide forehead frowned: first at Amma, next at the cutlery, then at the table. She narrowed her huge eyes, the whites disappearing to almost nothing.

'Coasters. These people need to get coasters. Or else someone needs to incarcerate the staff. Quick-smart.'

Amma's laugh was like a wet klaxon. She spat out crumbs. They landed on the toggles of Belinda's coat closest to her throat.

'That's horrible, Amma! Haven't you manners?'

Amma couldn't help it. She scraped the cake's ornate top with the back of her fork, making a gash in the icing, spooned up some of that bloody sponge too. She smeared what she had collected in oily stripes across the table. She did it again. Then again. Belinda was agog. Amma dropped the fork, pressed the mess and walked her greasy fingers all around. She covered everything with shimmering little holographs.

'Speechless, Amma. I am so very speechless.'

For a moment, Amma thought about making it like children's television, being like Dave Benson Phillips and mashing it in Belinda's face. Amma raised the slice, readying it for launching. Belinda's expression – probably as animated as it would be with that fictional thumb lodged in her backside – was priceless.

'If you even try to do this – throw this at me – I – I will walk from this place right now.'

'If you even try to do this – throw this at me – I – I will walk from this place right now.' Amma was disappointed with her mimicry; although the accent was fab, the pitch was slightly too high. Slightly. She tried again, resting the mangled cake. 'If you even try to do this – I – I will walk from this place right now.'

'Yes,' Belinda's tone was steady and sage now. 'The second was a much better. That is very like how I sound, actually. Maybe you have a real talent. Your mother keeps calling you the comedian, but is only now I'm seeing it for myself.'

Amma saw Belinda compose herself, dropping her slight shoulders within the hefty duffle, loosening the set of her jaw. Amma kept looking at the curious, patient girl opposite her; this funny person who was so resilient in the face of her shit chat and shit behaviour and meanness. Amma felt her own shoulders relax. She smiled and poked at the pink pulp on the table.

'You do it too,' Amma said.

'What?'

'You do it too. What I've just done.' Amma pointed at the mushed remains. 'Do it to yours.'

'And why would I want to waste? Your foolish messing is the most greedy and selfish nonsense. What did you even do it for?'

'Why does it need a reason? Is life reasonable? Is it ever reasonable?'

'Oh my goodness – so is that a good cause for spoiling a perfectly good food? I don't think so.'

'What about doing it just to be silly?'

'I can't afford to be silly.'

'It's like Mercutio –'

'We will study *Romeo and Juliet* next term I think –'

'If love be rough with you, be rough with love.'

'Why are we speaking of love? Who is in love?'

Amma breathed exasperation. 'Change the word love for life and – and like, if life is full of stupidness then you should clown right back at it. Take the piss out of it: it's doing the same to us. Do you get me?'

Amma had never seen such consideration. In Belinda, or in anyone else. But then again she had never seen someone pick up a blob of icing, roll it, then press said blob so willingly onto their own nose, then do the same again. In time there were three creamy dots across Belinda's cheeks.

'Beautiful,' Amma purred, as solemn as a groom to his bride. Belinda fluttered her lashes. They laughed. The lump of dough on Belinda's nose flopped off. She stopped laughing when Amma reached into her blazer for her cigs.

'Please. I told you already I don't like this one.'

Amma's clawed hand froze around the box of Marlboros. Amma pushed the packet away, found a napkin instead.

'I appreciate that one.'

'An eye for an eye.' Amma shrugged, got up. 'Shall we see the view then?'

'While wearing this?' Belinda pointed at her new spots.

'I triple dare you.'

Belinda stood, and Amma waited as she did her best to wipe as much of the mess on the table as she could before the dick in the trilby could notice. They walked over to the balcony, opened the sliding door, and the rush hour rushed at them. They clung to the railing, bathed in the red glow of the cinema's neon sign.

'It gives us a power, doesn't it? To be so high.'

Amma hummed approval. She surveyed Raleigh Hall next door, boarded up, fly-posted and flaking. The austere clock-face opposite, the harsh yellow of the McDonald's 'M', the windows of flats above Speedy Noodles, granting tiny access to others' lives. Down by the KFC, hunched tramps whispered and cackled. Incense sellers lined up their wares on pavements. Girls shared chips and checked each other's weaves. The best one: the preaching woman who performed in a bra and a grass skirt, steam blooming from her mouth as she bellowed into the cold air. She waved her Bible, she shook it skywards, used it to hit her bottom like a paddle, kissed it. Down, down on Windrush Square, mixed-race boys on skateboards zigzagged, flexing their ankles to create art. To the right of them, a fat-titted woman was pulling faces at her compact mirror as she applied lipstick. By the benches, an older man squatted to capture his Rottweiler's shit in a plastic bag. In an attempt to sum it all up, Titch might have quoted MacNeice's phrase about life being 'incorrigibly plural' but Amma thought 'ridiculous' was much more apt. All of it. Ridiculous. Too difficult to catch and understand any of it; herself; anyone.

The little dollops were still there on Belinda's glossy cheeks. Amma peeled one off and flicked it onto her tongue. She chewed at Belinda theatrically, winked suggestively. How great that Belinda only responded with a withering arching of eyebrow. How great that she simply turned back to the view, and breathed in, then out.

While washing her hands later, Belinda again admired the lines between the bathroom tiles that she had worked to keep as white as possible. She turned the tap off while Amma tapped and fidgeted behind her. Belinda quickly patted the flannel and moved aside. Best to do everything very quietly. Doctor was asleep, his snore less forceful than Uncle's. Amma opened the glass cabinet, splitting the reflection, then fiddled around in there until she pulled out a small disk with a tail.

'What's that one for?'

'Observe, *ma petite chérie*.' Amma lengthened the string and pressed it into her mouth, sawed then plucked it out. 'Dental floss. Flossing.'

'I know it. We have sticks for this one. Chewing stick. It is starting out big like one of your fingers and you use that one on the big teeth and the back ones that dogs have. Then you pull off some smaller splinters for yourself, and then you do those for … florssing. Or flossing. Florrrssing.'

'Maybe. Yeah, probably. Ooh, watch! This is my best bit.'

Amma held the string out to show its patches of pink and bits of shrimp from the stew Belinda had cooked for them all.

'Disgusting.'

'Granted.'

Belinda's frown hardened. Amma laughed. It surprised Belinda that she found the slight gap between Amma's two front teeth prettier and prettier as the weeks passed. Amma nudged her.

'Lost in space?'

'What?'

'You're very tired, aren't you?'

Belinda liked Amma's damp hand on her arm.

'Perhaps I am. That's never new.'

'There's such red in your eyes.'

'I hadn't really noticed myself.'

'Aren't you sleeping?'

'I am. I am.'

'Do you miss your own bed? I bet you miss your own bed. Even if it sounds babyish and you're all worldly and shit. I probably would. Like my creature comforts, I do.'

'I sleep very well. Thank you.' Belinda smiled at her slippers.

'Joke?'

'Is nothing. Nothing. This. This is much more restful here than I ever had in Daban. You people do nothing. Basically I am doing the same. Strange then I am become old and exhausted looking. Nice of you to compliment.'

'What a fucking Sensitive Sausage! That'll learn me to be sympathetic.'

Before Belinda could tell her in that sentence the better English was in fact 'teach' and not 'learn', Amma had the light pull and darkness came in a blink.

17

O n the Thursday morning of that week in early October, Belinda pressed the flaps over her jacket's pockets until they were flattened. She smoothed Vaseline on her lips and passed her tongue over her front teeth. With heavy legs she approached the study. She stopped herself because the door was ajar, and in the room Nana was spinning on the office chair. Nana's white hair flew up like strange flames. Watching, Belinda fidgeted on the spot, her tights scratching. She nearly liked the girlish noise Nana let out when the spinning slowed and Nana had to clutch the desk to push off again. And Belinda was curious to see how many goes round Nana might have before becoming dizzy. But more than that, the moment felt too private for her to see. Belinda straightened out her annoying gusset, went for the door's handle and coughed like an important man.

'*Agoo?* Madam, *agoo?*'

She heard Nana's feet clatter.

'Belinda? Be – Be – Belinda, *amee*. Wonderful, do come. Exactly the lady I wanted.' Nana's reply was breathy.

Belinda walked in and stood near the line of paperweights. Her favourite of these funny domed things was the one with a tiny lion trapped within it.

Nana tapped her glasses' case. 'Yes, I wanted to catch you before you jet and disappear for the school day.'

'Please, please, I come with a question. May I ask? I hate to disturb … your important time.'

'You want to know of this party? Hmm? Is that one, not so?'
Nana's words changed Belinda's face. '*Hwε!* She thinks I have been
doing juju to see into the crystal ball as Mystic Meg-oh! Otuo will
laugh to hear.'

'How –'

'Can you believe such a thing: first, my daughter comes to offer
me this – this – *adjei!*' Nana directed Belinda's eyes towards a
framed drawing, the size of a postcard: fat flowers with orange
petals, loud against a blue background, with Amma's signature in
the corner. 'Then she asks me of a party. And she wants permission. And she wants permission to take you also. Belinda, I'm not
exaggerating, my eyes nearly literally fell from my head. She has
never asked in months.' Nana clutched the drawing. 'And, and
when ever given me something as a gift? Maybe you are the one
with juju for such things to happen, eh?'

'I. I have done nothing. I have only been around and there. Like
you asked of me.'

'And we thank you for it. Truly. Now, is not, is not like we should
be getting head of ourselves, not as if everything is completely
smooth but –' Nana lifted the drawing, spoke to the air around it.
'Is a start, you know?'

'Madam, I told her, and I was very strong on this one, if we go
to this Lavender's occasion, we definitely have to come and get
your full blessing to go. And we must return home at a reasonable
hour.'

'I agree. Yes. I have called and checked the parents. They seem
acceptable and fair. One even works for the BBC *Newsnight*.' Nana
placed the drawing back but kept fussing with its position. 'I know
the kids they will try to break the law and get some spirits, but
having faces small like theirs will be the problem, so we are safe for
that. And I will be arranging an Addie Lee to collect you at
midnight precise, so that is fine also.'

'Midnight?'

It was one thing to set fire to a tie. One thing to put a cake on your cheeks. But an endless – midnight?

Nana's bony fingers snapped open her glasses' case. 'We, we even had a joke about how I'm not meant to call it a party. It's a – it's a – gathering, apparently. I find their words so silly sometimes.'

'Yes, madam. I know what you mean.'

'And one other little matter, Belinda.' Nana coughed, closed the case's lid. 'This my house been seeming remarkably cleaner and more neat since you arrive. I can eat *Kontomire* off of the floor if I am minded to do such a thing.' Nana laughed to herself, 'so I don't know how and when you doing it, but I know you doing it – cleaning anything and everything, *me boa?*'

Belinda focused on the frozen lion, on the shape of its poised claw. Her face started heating up.

'You understanding we not expecting this from you? Eh? My, my husband he worries that you thinking we want you to do this cleaning scrubbing on your hands and knees? No way, girl! No, absolute no. We, we want you to leave off from this, eh? Didn't we say only study and Amma, those should be your concerns, eh?' Nana sighed. 'I'm not coming to you to be hard-hearted. Don't think of me as a meanie for saying these things. We thankful for the efforts. Truly. How can we not be – my kitchen surfaces have never sparkled like this before. Like stars and bling bling. Really. Is lovely. But is not necessary. *Wa te?* Because am I an invalid? Can I not maintain my own laundries and sweeping? Am I incapable?'

'Madam –'

'Eh hennn. So you going to agree you will end this one, *wa te? Wa. Te?*'

Despite knowing that it would be impossible for her to keep such a promise, Belinda raised her head and limply nodded. She watched Nana's satisfied smile, watched Nana slap the table four times to show that everything was settled, watched the agitated paperweights vibrating against one another.

Lavender's home was long, bone-coloured walls holding paintings framed in ancient gold. Dripping chandeliers – almost as big as Aunty and Uncle's – swayed. And there was so much talk. Talk that rose and bubbled, loud and everywhere. So being calm was not easy for Belinda. Sometimes the talk broke and long whoops of laughter came instead. Beneath those noises, the moody music thudded, wobbling the floorboards. In the corner of a large space similar to the front room at Spenser, Belinda stood very upright with her back pressed against drawn curtains. She wondered if the vibrations were strong enough to bring up vomit from her stomach. In the room ahead, through heavy smoke, forty boys and girls shuffled on an exotic rug no one had thought to move for the evening. The laziness made her hold her cup of peppermint tea more firmly. She had said no to the 'vod and cran' offered as soon as she and Amma entered through the grand door and asked for peppermint tea because Mrs Al-Kawthari drank that from her sensible safety cup. Belinda was curious about its taste and, also, wanted to try something as different as the many-pocketed, baggy trousers Amma forced her to wear to the party. Belinda stared at the nasty colour in the mug.

She looked up. A white boy with dreadlocks like that Cal-i-ban-man on the way to *Ghanafoɔ* hooked his fingers into the belt loops of a girl's jeans. He pulled her towards him. The girl didn't mind, even though she stumbled because the rug bunched under her. Now the girl was even standing on tiptoes to be tall enough to kiss the boy. They both started attacking with tongues and lips. They had never eaten: they knew true hunger. The boy worked and worked her breasts, checking mangoes for ripeness. The girl's hands roamed over his body too. Everyone else – all the whites in denim, in leather, in the same soldiers' trousers as Belinda's own

– paid no attention, carried on with their smoking and their cans. Belinda sipped again and winced. She checked that Amma was not doing the same nearly-sex-nonsense. If any filthy white boy touched Amma, Belinda would have to smash her cooling mug into the back of his head. Thankfully, Amma was breaking off a conversation with one girl to start talking to another.

Belinda would never allow her first kiss to be so public. It would be like a special ceremony when it finally happened. Quiet and holy and only the two of them. She imagined removing her clothes in front of a man. He didn't have to be the most handsome but he needed to be cleaner than the Rastafarian now stroking the girl's shoulders. After Belinda was naked for her man, then he would follow by removing his clothes. Next, their faces would come together and their different breaths would mix. Nothing else. Until one of them fell asleep. She wondered if Mother had ever had it as gently as that. Belinda doubted it.

As she swirled the tea around, a fat boy with sore red blemishes bumped into her. He whined like a goat knowing slaughter is near and didn't apologise before he went off. None of them had any respect for space. Belinda turned her head. Even those not doing the nearly-sex-nonsense were too close to one another. It was strange and probably unhygienic: how happy they all seemed to stand so near. She hoped that they had all used talc, flossed and gargled with TCP as part of their preparations for the night. Belinda started playing Space Impact on her Nokia. Then stuffed the phone back in one of her pockets. From metres away, Amma beckoned for Belinda to come over, and Belinda felt something open softly inside her chest. The girl next to Amma had those freckles Mary would envy and Belinda was pleased at the opportunity to inspect them closely, but the lights flickered, the music fell silent and many male voices swore. The same male voices soon decided they knew what to do. Belinda sipped the tea again, then fumbled to rest the mug on the windowsill.

The power had been out for the whole evening when she had last seen Mother. The old kerosene lamps did little to brighten their room. Mother was quiet as Belinda checked the covered soup bowls and glasses on the table. The silence helped her concentrate on chasing the tablecloth's wrinkles.

'What you have prepare –' Mother had begun as she tugged a ball of *fufu* from the mound and skimmed it across the soup, then held the dripping portion. One eye squinting, she inspected it, tilted it. Red shivered down the white grainy starch, shivered down Mother's fingernails. Belinda watched the mouth snap open to show its darkness. Mother gulped. 'What you have prepare is good.'

'Thank you, Ma. I. I wondered that maybe we should have eaten roasted corns. Since you like it as your favourite. Since it is our final. So. I only wondered. Here we have what we have. And you like. So.'

'They will appreciate this, this your new Kumasi family … this kindness you have for other people. *Ɛfɛ paaa*.'

'Thank you, Ma.'

'Amen.' Belinda had jumped with surprise as the sockets sizzled again, even though that sound pulsed every seven minutes when the power failed. Mother's expression became pained.

'I feel like … I feel like I done it as best I can. The best I could. Raised you as much as was in me for to do this thing well. What I say isn't a new.' Belinda nodded. 'It has tired me. More than I can tell you. I'm feeling … I'm feeling in this body like I never even slept in these years since they take you out from my inside, eh? Me, I'm always lying on this bed, worrying, worrying, worrying for you, if I do good for you. Is not even possible to count eye bags.'

'Ma, I be rejoicing daily for each of the sacrifice –'

'And when you speak righteous to me, and I come and on my table there is some dinner that you have done, it must be true that I have achieve well at this.'

'Amen.'

'And there has always been food. Name one days when you got hungry?' Belinda smiled at the water glass. 'So now there, there is little left. For me to do.'

'True. I am grown.'

'And so you must create your own way. *Ino be so?*'

'I … I will try.' Belinda heard girls stumble and giggle outside.

'When they fetch you tomorrow for Daban and I'm waving at you goodbye – dazzit.' Mother swiped at the air. 'It finish. Then after that pretend our Adurubaa is wash away in flood of God, or volcano fire, or earthquake come to shake our ground and all does collapse. Force yourself believing that here is no longer here any more. Here have disappear. Me! I rhyme!' Mother covered her mouth shyly. 'You have it, eh? Eh? A person splitting themselves in two for two places will find no doctor's medicine to stitch. Is how the elders have it.'

'Ma, then it is.'

'Close your eyes.'

'Yes, Ma.'

'Tight. Shut. Shut.'

'Yes, Ma.'

'Imagine me, pretend me, you have seen on that flood, and some big wave came to wipe me off. Can you picture? Big blue monster come to down me, and bam! Maybe for some moment you clocking my hand sticking from water. Then in few second my hand is going going under. Now. Is only water.'

'Yes, Ma.'

'You have picture?'

'Yes, Ma.'

'And even if you thinking, oh, I will wait until water have drain to come for collecting what is left, you coming to get your *nyama nyama* books or whatever, you will be find nothing and nobody, because here have disappear.'

The crickets had thrummed like the blood in Belinda's ears.

'Thank you, Ma.'

'Is wickedness, and will go spoil your chances if I'm dragging you back to my own – troubles. I do this all as a goodness for you, *wa te*?'

'Ma. My eyes. May I be able to open?'

'*Ma. My eyes. May I be able to open?*' Belinda repeated the words again to herself, to no one, to the busy figures shifting around in a darkness broken up by the tiny flares of lighters, to Amma ahead whose face didn't understand.

'Why are you still there on your lonesome, bella Be? Come the fuck on,' Amma shouted, the girl with those pretty freckles laughed, and as Belinda approached them the lights came back on, as did the music. A damp cheer, and then everyone returned to their chatter chatter chatter.

'I hate this one,' the girl announced before Belinda could introduce herself. The girl walked away.

'How can she hate me? I haven't –'

'Helena means the song, she's gone to change it.'

'Oh. Oh.'

'I'm sorry you're not having a good time, Be. I suppose –'

'I am having a lovely time, thank you very much. I'm … learning a lot of different things.'

'What?'

'The place is the same as a classroom to me. Or at least, that is how I am taking it.'

'How very cryptic of you, dearest.'

'What is cryp-tic?'

'Like, like mysterious?'

'Sorry sorry then. Being cry-ptic is something I think I should try to never be and avoid at all costs.'

As Amma had rightly predicted, the song changed. Out of the speakers, a man was talking in maybe an Asian language. That was funny: there were no Indians in the room. The only brown people were her and Amma.

'Missy Misdemeanor! I fucking love it. Yes! My little guilty plesh.'

'What? What is it?'

Amma drank three gulps, crushed her can underfoot and ran to the speakers.

'Watch,' Belinda heard Amma demand to someone. The freckled girl clapped and encouraged a growing group of blonde girls to join in. Copying the music word for word, Amma started rapping about new shit and about getting a freak on; pushing herself around, narrowing her eyes, clicking in a way Belinda thought sulky, sometimes turning her attention to the boy behind her who fiddled with buttons on the hi-fi. Amma nodded at him, first suggesting she agreed with the volume and then at other times as though she wanted a fight. Amma pressed her knees together and wiggled, drilling into the floorboards.

Belinda played with the soft tuft at her forehead. She saw the outline of Amma's nipples through her black vest top, but was distracted by Helena's clapping – she missed the beat so often. And now, still rapping, still barking out and tossing aside bossy lines, Amma lunged at the blonde girls with her breasts, challenging them to react. Belinda knew she should whisper 'stop' in Amma's ear and then escort her home and afterwards sweep the front steps. But some larger force stuck Belinda in the middle of the small crowd, correcting the freckled one's beat with her own sharper clap. Amma winked at Belinda.

The blonde girls whispered behind multi-coloured fingernails as Amma shouted the song's repeated list of instructions at the crowd. The girls and many tall boys with limp hair who were previously very bored or tired did as they were told, surging towards the speakers in a wave that dragged Belinda in too and she nearly lost her balance. A stranger's grip helped, shifting her, pushing her onto Amma's shoulder.

'Yes, Be!'

Belinda was straightened up and Amma started bumping her hips into Belinda's. It hurt, but the glittery eyes behind whipping braids said that Amma wanted a response so Belinda pushed her hips out too, feeling wider in that part of her body. Belinda waved her arms at the same time. When Amma nodded and yelled 'Bounce!' Belinda nodded and yelled 'Bounce!' Amma screwed up her nose like she had smelled *Kobe* for the first time and continued rapping. Belinda couldn't do the rapping but could match the expression: the faces of the village when she and Mother knocked to ask for evaporated milk because they had run out; the one she did at Mary for leaving streaks of brown in their toilet bowl. Rotating her waist and rolling her shoulders like she did not care about them, Belinda kept on going and the blonde girls pumped at the air and at her with little fists. Though some tiny part of her was unsure if they were doing that sign to truly support her dancing or make fun of her, once more she let Amma's sweating smile rule. Under Belinda's skin hundreds of bubbles rushed. The strangers who were shaking and pointing at the sky did that because they were following her. To check it, she flexed her head. They did it too. She bent her knees again and again. They did it too. It was good, how willingly they let her be in charge; they knew nothing about her.

A breathless Amma slapped a hard high five into Belinda's palm and led her to a table where Amma stopped, picked up an empty bowl cut with icy diamonds like Uncle's whisky glasses.

'Who's had all the booze?'

The room didn't hear. The space where they had stood seconds ago was refilled by others, drifting, sliding, kissing.

'Everyone's so fucking greedy. I wanted to give you a little cheers. That was a-ma-zing.'

'I don't think we even need it, Amma. Any more drinks. No. I enjoyed my tea.'

'It's not about need. It's just fun, Be.'

'I. I have never done anything like that before – dancing as that. I wasn't even feeling embarrassed.'

'You seemed to take to it very naturally, *ma chérie* – Lav?! Lav?! Is there any Pinot N. still knocking about? Lavender?!'

'I need no more. Nothing else. I only want to enjoy this happiness, not add to it, because if you try to add to it, maybe you, maybe you will fail and then everything will be lost. I don't need all. Let us, let us keep things small, eh? Please? Please, can we?'

Amma went back to the empty bowl. She passed her finger over its rim and sucked the red stickiness.

'I hope that you're right, Be. About lots of it.'

Amma moved closer to Belinda. The few footsteps seemed difficult for her. The whites of Amma's eyes were a pink-yellow – they might have been irritated by the thickening smoke.

'The things you offer to me, advice, whatever. I mean. I mean, usually, if, like, you come against someone and you feel their whole world view is basically completely different from your own, you, like, want them to be wrong? Like, spectacularly wrong. Fall from grace. But, but, I'm taking myself out of the equation. I don't want you to be disappointed by anything. Do you get me? I want, I want so much of the stuff you believe to be as it is. So you aren't hurt? And even though I wish we could, could both be right, I'd rather you won than me because, because I can take it.' Belinda wanted to speak but Amma continued, her voice higher now. 'Because I am taking it right now, and look how I'm shaking it all off. Easy peas. You wouldn't be able to do that if like, it all came tumbling down. I wouldn't want you to.'

'How do you know of my beliefs, Amma? And my, my world view, Amma?'

'Well, it's like what you said before.' With concentration, Amma drew her thumb and forefinger close together, and peered through the space she let remain between the two. 'It's small. Very small.'

'You –'

'It's not insulting. It's not patronising. I swear I'm trying to be nice Be, we're – we're different. Obviously. Fuck. And that's actually OK, it's excellent, in fact. You look at things more neatly than me. And sometimes you don't and that is, also like, amazing and gorgeous too. But my mind is constantly changing: it's, like, never neat, and' – Amma's hands whirled – 'going and going and going. I tried being fixed, and focusing on one thing and being very, very rigid, and it proved to be a very, very bad thing for Amma. So.' Amma played with her vest top's strap.

'Maybe you were. Maybe you were focused on the wrong kind of thing?'

'You're almost certainly entirely correct, Be. Even if it does feel shit passing the buck and blaming someone or something else for how I am instead of being, you know, personally accountable for my own actions. Like a proper person. Grown up and shit.'

Belinda laughed. 'And, and Amma – are you a proper person?'

'Not yet. I'm trying to be. Just because I haven't got all the answers, doesn't mean I'm not. Just because I have an extraordinary tendency to fuck up, doesn't mean I'm not. It's the trying bit that counts, Be. And I like you because you really, really try.'

Belinda smiled her biggest smile as a girl more ill-looking than the ones on *Model Behaviour* handed Amma a bottle.

18

Looking over the banister's handrail to the landing below, Belinda saw Doctor yawn, scratch between his legs and rub his bald patch before slipping into his study. As his door closed, Belinda cradled the phone's receiver to her ear. Mary was breathless.

'So, Belinda, explain me again. Is hard to understand. You telling me there was no adults?'

'No.'

'You had free run of the house?'

Belinda released her foot from its slipper and let it nudge a little pile of paint flakes collected on the skirting board. She would deal with it in the cleaning session later that night. That would be good.

At the end of the line, Mary whistled. 'How are adults to be sure you won't do damage? Even on accident? It could happen. And then, then imagine how angry that will make the Mother and Father. They may even have put pepper in your anus as they did in my village too. Is true-oh.'

'Some of the parents here, they, they trust the children to not mess. And no one did. Not from what we saw before we left. And they have, like, a clever spray to get rid of the smell from' – Belinda grappled with the receiver again, whispering – 'their smoking.'

'Yey! And did you join in with that also?'

'Madam!' If Belinda mentioned the dancing or the kissing, Mary would never stop and the phone card would run out.

There was crackling. Mary coughed. 'You. You promised you will call me immediately after it. Now some three days have pass. I have waited and waited. *Adɛn?*'

'Sorry.'

'Also what did they wear? Any special dress? Did they have things newly sewed?'

'It wasn't, like, really a big deal, or like a party or anything, they called it –'

'Also what food was prepared? Did they give you some to take home in a Tupperware? Have you eaten already?'

Belinda dabbed her big toe into the flakes again and a stubborn, dry hexagon stuck. She tried to flick it off but the toe wasn't clever enough.

'Actually, now listen to me: they let me watch the interview for the next housegirl. Our Aunty and Uncle let me. I liked it. I got into the big reception room, the one they use to show off if the Nigerians come, that's where they did it – you remember the place?'

'Of course.'

'Eh hehhn. I sat on the long sofa, with the tassel cushions and in the middle of Uncle and Aunty like I am their real small child. They had a notepad and even gave me my own like I would need to take something down. I laughed. They didn't seem to mind the laugh. But they didn't join in either. So.'

'So, so have they found?'

'My sister. We spoke to about ten. A lot from the North with big scars and the scarves on the mouths. I, I wasn't expecting that because Aunty thinks they are bad.'

'Then they didn't choose?'

'No. And I was glad. I thought, if you are coming to act as you will be a good cleaning person, then how can you yourself be sweating and in a *pata pata* with oil and stew on it? Many of the girls were like this. *Aba*. Cynthia wasn't very impressed either. But she kept it to herself.'

Mary went quiet again. 'Will you greet Amma for me?'

Was it the irritating flake or the request that brought a sudden flush to Belinda's arms? 'I suppose I can do that, but. Like. She might find it weird. I mean, she doesn't, like, know who you are? And, like, like I don't want to … bring in any more things. You see? I have talked to her about you and stuff, but –' She imagined Mary's lower lip pushed as far as it could go – all pink and wet and those eyes: massive and pleading and familiar. 'I'm being silly.' The hexagon curled off.

'Oh, I understand. Everyone is selfish.'

'It's not like that.'

'OK then.' Mary paused, then burped.

'Mary!'

'Excuse – but don't pretend some don't come from your body sometimes – is not like you are like the purest and built from fairy dust.' Mary burped again.

'Ma–'

'I will give you some words to mention next time I am in your chatting with Amma. I will like you to –'

'I will tell her I have a very clever and very nice and a very special friend back in Africa. A friend who has a very big light inside of her. That is the best phrase for you.'

Belinda waited for the bright response, at this proof that she wasn't selfish at all; was in fact the opposite.

'Will you, really, use all those verys?'

'Yes.'

'And mean each one?'

'Yes. Yes, I think so. I mean, yes –'

'You only think so? Ha! You give nicely and then in two second flat – *kai!* – you take it back! Wicked, *wo ye* wicked *paaa*.'

'Don't play rough and tease.'

'But, Belinda, is my very favourite thing to do.'

AUTUMN

19

The third week of October saw the predictable spreading of a cold that had both Belinda and Amma off sick for two days. Throughout the girls' first morning as invalids, Mum was both panicked and thrilled to bits. Transformed into a veritable Mary Seacole – albeit one with a magenta Hermès drooping from her neck – she listened with concern to the spluttered recounting of symptoms. She rushed between Amma and Belinda's bedrooms, applying too much Vicks to their foreheads and shoving her generous bosom in their faces while plumping pillows. Through her wall, a sweaty Amma heard Belinda's thin apologies for causing trouble and fuss. Amma then heard – at fast-dwindling volume – Mum listing the contents of the fridge before making promises to be back from her shift at the Barnardo's shop as soon as she could. The letter flap thwacked as she slammed the front door.

Amma's idle arm swung across the bed, knocking over the Kleenex, the half-read *Orlando*, and threadbare Langston, who always offered such cuddly support during times of strife. She spat greasy phlegm into a ragged tissue and threw it towards the waste-paper basket. It landed perfectly. Her subsequent irritating run of coughs was not enough to detract from the joy of that victory. Reaching over, tasting chalky Lemsip on her tongue, she grabbed the novel and shoved it into her tracksuit bottoms' fleecy pocket. In her grinning piglet slippers, she padded along the corridor to collect snotty, puffy Belinda.

'Twins?' Amma offered, pointing at their matching, inflamed noses.

Belinda nodded slowly. They descended the stairs, tentative on the sisal runner and holding the banister like elderly women frightened of what lay ahead.

Amma loved a good sickie – especially when Mum wasn't rattling around at home. The sick day was a day of untrammelled luxury! It ignored the boring business of being presentable, and instead made completely reasonable the need for things that brought on delicious, drowsy forgetfulness: sticky linctus, eye-watering hot toddies. Settling into the front room, Amma poured herself into Dad's Lazy Boy and sighed until she started coughing again. She undid the top buttons of her striped pyjama shirt and flapped the collar for more air. Belinda took the sofa opposite, robing herself with its patterned throws.

'I only don't want to fall behind with my studies. Today we have an important question about Banquo and –' Belinda stopped to consider. 'In every lesson if, if you blink then you will miss. And I must pass. I must pass the exams or –' Belinda massaged her neck. 'My attendance record in Adurubaa was always consistently at 100 per cent. I've never had a staining like this.'

'A staining! A. Staining?! Total fucking jokes!' Amma grabbed the remote control. 'A little allusion to her "damned spot", am I right? Titch had us learn it off by heart when we were in, like, Year 10. Fucking terrifying sound, all of us droning it out together. Yikes.'

'I think you're talking of Lady Macbeth? Miss mentioned a bit about it in a passing, but we haven't properly studied it in full, so don't spoil please.'

'You're in for a treat. Seriously. Lady M is a-maz-ing.'

'That's what Miss says too.' Belinda looked even more crest-fallen. 'Miss will be so disappointed in my absence. She may even tell me off when I return. It's. It's not right.'

'I think she'll find some way of coping, Be. Eh? People get ill. Then they get better. The world turns.'

'Maybe.'

Amma hoisted her legs up to her chest and swivelled herself in the direction of the screen.

'The easy wisdoms of Mr Robert Kilroy Silk! Perfection. *Entre nous*, I –'

But Belinda wasn't listening. Instead she had reduced herself; hidden the lower half of her body further within the throws' fuzziness. Like some purposeful bird, she nibbled the tip of her thumb. Kilroy kept talking about forgotten Blitz spirit, so everyone in the audience had to clap. The sudden report of their applause seemed to underline Belinda's stillness. Amma repositioned herself. The chair's springs responded to the movement.

'I can help you catch up if you miss anything really important, you know. We did *Macbeth* for fucking years so I've got tonnes of notes and handouts and stuff. You probably won't need them, but anyway … And of course you'll bloody pass, Be. You're really on it. Working the whole time. It'll be piss.'

'I don't always like to ask for help. But if I need it, is really nice to know that's there. So. Thanks. Thank you.'

Belinda took a tissue from the bulge inside her sleeve, wiped a nostril and tried being more positive. 'So, so now we'll sit here for a whole day? And do what? Waste?'

'We can read a bit later, if we really want to. Have you finished the last book I lent you?'

'Nearly. I find Achebe's writing … well … hard to describe actually. Sometimes he sounds like any person you might hear speaking on the street. Like, I mean to say he … he sounds ordinary. But then, on other pages, it feels … heavier. I don't know.'

'No. Totally. Absolutely.'

The two girls sat in a pleased silence, concentrating on Kilroy again. Kilroy's hands moved a lot as he spoke, as if his gesticulations sought to stir into life the passive, hooded dude being interviewed.

'Why did the guest come on to national television like this? See the corner of his mouth there? As if he has never come across water and handkerchief.'

'That's the least of his worries, Be.'

'And how come this Kilroy interrupts so often and everyone allows? Eh? Listen again, he's even doing it now. Each time someone wants to speak he only jumps on top of them. If anyone in the audience did that in their daily lives, someone will surely tell them about themselves.'

'Quite.'

'And, also, can you explain to me his skin tone? He seems fully white, and his speaking and accent agrees with that view also, but the face is more … more orange than usual. Like … like a cross between an English and a Hausa. But then I doubt that. Doesn't seem likely that is his origin.'

Amma laughed herself into another fiery succession of coughs until she had to go for water, flapping aside Belinda's offered assistance as she went. In the glitzy kitchen Mum had bought herself to celebrate early retirement, Amma squeezed two glasses of orange juice with the suggestively shaped juicer and placed them on a tray. She then loaded the remaining space on the tray with Cool Original Doritos, Maryland Cookies, a knife, Nairn's oatcakes, a block of Duchy Original cheddar, five tangerines, salted cashews and – for fun – some Haribo. As she wobbled forward, Amma looked at the pile of crude, inflated packets with their screaming logos. Nothing had the delicacy of the food Belinda had prepared for them in the weeks since she'd arrived; fried yam without the usual bitterness, still crumbly and soft within; *shitoh* with heat that didn't strip the tongue of feeling, but still managed to be spiky and exciting. And, yeah, maybe it was anachronistic etc. to be praising the lady for her domestic prowess as opposed to some higher quality. But, whatever. Amma edited the excess, eventually only taking up the juice and a jug of water.

In spite of Belinda's initial protest, they proceeded their way through varied televisual offerings, with Belinda especially enjoying *Fifteen to One*, astounded at contestants' powers of recall. *Bargain Hunt* also went down really well – even if Amma did have to go through the concept of heirlooms at length when her throat prickled most. Belinda nodded through Amma's careful example: the story about the lightbulb Dad had given her as a memento of his first job in England, on the production line of an Osram factory where he'd met Belinda's Uncle and Aunty of Daban-fame. At the end of the explanation and through the scratchy coughs it forced out of Amma, Belinda rested her eyes on the corner table's calla lilies wearily. As painful and annoying as it was for Amma to do it, switching to *Dawson's Creek* surprisingly reanimated Belinda; as the show went on, Belinda wriggled in the throws, brushing aside her hot water bottle, brimming with wonder at the interesting words they used. Belinda admired the pretty actors as they hopped on and off yachts, but said that the skinny Joey-girl's beauty was spoiled by her constant shrugging of one shoulder. When Joey and Dawson kissed, Amma noticed that Belinda turned from the screen. Amma wanted to tease her for such childishness, but Belinda's frowning and pulling on her Totes socks stopped the urge. As did Amma's embarrassment at immediately thinking of the *Brookside* kiss.

Amma would have been nine or ten. Mum hadn't been a regular viewer or a fan, but in the run-up to that particular episode – maybe because of all the heated coverage in the papers and on the news – Mum went on about definitely watching it, and about how Amma had to be in bed when it came on. But of course Amma, ever the rebel, evaded bed. After story time, after lights out, she crept back down the stairs with trusty Langston in tow. She hid herself in shadows by the front room's door. She waited, frozen like in Grandma's Footsteps, and peered through when the two delicately featured girls put their lips against each other's with such speed and lightness it seemed like it had never happened. But it had happened. Because as soon as the curly-haired one pulled back, Mum stood up, spoke to the screen in Twi and made outraged noises. Then Mum changed the channel and appealed to Dad for equivalent disapproval. Amma had tiptoed away, confused by Mum's determination to watch something she clearly knew would upset her so much.

In the front room now, as the *Dawson's Creek* credits rolled, Amma smiled to herself while Belinda hummed along to the theme tune with impressive accuracy and collected the empty glasses. She rested them on the side table and picked something from Amma's shoulder with a punishing pinch: blue fluff, which she proudly showed on the end of her finger, like proof of something long-contested. With a curious lack of sympathy at the yelp Amma released, Belinda bent down for the tray again. Chatter emerged from outside, beyond the shuttered windows. And it got louder and livelier: Helena 'doing polite', asking to help carry Mum's shopping and complimenting Mum's scarf and clutch bag. Mum replied in her reedy Parents Evening voice; the one she specifically used for talking to posh white people. Amma rolled her eyes and breathed into her palms to check the depth of her unbrushed teeth's stench.

'Oh. Your friend has come to pay a visit to see about your illness. That's nice. It will be nice for me to greet her also.'

Amma noted the sharpness and formality of Belinda's tone that somehow seemed to rhyme with Mum's high-pitched affectations that now filled the passageway. Helena appeared in the door frame.

'Observe! Weep! Bow! Scrape! I did it in Period 3 at Ellie's. Comments? Thoughts? Hey, bootylicious Be! How goes?'

Helena kept shaking her hair. Helena had dyed her hair pinkish. All Amma could think was that it clashed with the green school blazer terribly.

After hearing the sound of Amma's radio speaking what Belinda now knew was the weather for the sea, that night while the family slept she topped up the lilies' water. She moved the flowers around in the vase so they were less floppy. Then she gathered, quietly crushed and threw away the leaves fallen from the long stems and wiped the vase's damp bottom. She wrestled a Kleenex out of her pocket and blew her nose quietly.

Next, she sat in the utility room among bedlinen from the tumble dryer, watched by a slow, pointy fox in the garden that she tried to shoo away with a shaking fist. The copper pipes snaking the wall opposite talked as she worked. Folding such huge sheets seemed more difficult without a small friend to help. As she moved on to the towels, she wondered again why she had lied earlier. Because her attendance hadn't been completely 100 per cent at school, back home. More like 98.9 per cent.

Once. There was once. Harmattan, so the stormy morning air had been a mess. She'd had pains in her stomach similar to the ones before her monthlies. But these were much more like punching than the familiar wringing. Normally, in class, she could manage the wringing, breathing through each twist as she copied sentence after sentence from the blackboard. The pains that particular morning were deeper, longer, more cutting, and forced her chest to do scary hops to find air. When using the latrine only hot, brown water had come from her behind and she hadn't been able to stop herself from crying. Mother had insisted she stay home and roughly tucked her into their small bed.

With her thumb now restraining a Habitat towel's label from flicking up again, Belinda remembered that day: trying to get comfortable on their unkind mattress, clutching her belly. Mother sat closer to her than she often did, close enough for Belinda to smell the remnants of cigarette smoke stronger and richer than the usual. Belinda remembered the clump, crunch and crash of the water pump outside, occasionally waking her. She remembered the white enamel cup speckled with black marks, filled with something hot, green and bitter that Mother pushed at Belinda's lips. And the coolness of the cloths Mother laid on her cheeks. And Mother putting one of their four cassettes into the Fisher Price player. *Akosombo Nkanea*. Maybe because Mother assumed Belinda had dipped into sleep again, or perhaps because of boredom, Mother had let herself sing along, wiggling to the old tune. She clicked her dry fingers and nodded like she and the singer shared the same wisdom. Belinda had been awake. Wide awake, watching it all. Mother had never seemed so young.

Belinda dealt with the last towel, putting them all in the rectangular wicker basket as Nana did. Lifting the load to the highest shelf, she turned to see the fox still out there; red hanging from its mouth. This time Belinda tapped her fist on the glass, not bothered about the noise. Condensation flaring from her lips, she showed the animal all of her teeth and bit towards it. The fox looked up and fled into the bushes.

20

In the dining room, Amma sat at the head and Belinda at the foot of the long table, with flouncy candelabras, uncapped biros and fat highlighters spread between them. Amma played with her pencil case, picking at the elaborate squiggles and hieroglyphs Tipp-Exed onto its plastic. Then she stopped and flipped down the iBook's tangerine lid. Her sigh became a loud yawn, disturbing Belinda from her serious, squinted reading of *Macbeth*. Amma mouthed 'Sorry, *ma petite*' at Belinda's sternness. How funny to think of that girl, a fortnight before, working her thang to Missy Elliott in synchronised sass. Belinda underlined something very firmly and scribbled on her notepad with an air of industry that implied she would not be receptive to Amma's attempts to talk about their now famous performance. Instead Amma put her feet up on the scarred oak. A pattern of grinning pineapples danced across her socks. She peeled them off and flung them aside.

'Weeeeeeee!' she said, as they flopped to the floorboards.

'Amma!'

'Whatever. Sorry. I'll stop. Sorry. Fuck.'

Belinda sighed. 'To give a bit of encouragement to do more work for some more moments I can heat up the leftover okra thing as a snack for late lunch? Yes? In fifteen minutes? We eat then?'

'Yeah, thanks ... you sick feeder, you.' Amma took another salty *tatale* from the saucer nearby. Belinda frowned and returned to her text.

Even though Amma had been pretty pissed when she'd said that thing about admiring 'trying' at Lavender's, it was still on point. So, in the dining room, with Mum rattling around upstairs, sorting out some campaign at the charity shop or whatever, Amma had spent most of the bleak Sunday afternoon, now dragging itself out, doing her best to mimic Belinda's diligence. As Belinda concentrated opposite, Amma grimaced and grunted at the iBook; her task was no meek adversary, nor could the battle with it run on and on. The bloody UCAS Personal Statement had to be finished that weekend 'or else', Titch had threatened. But each time Amma tore herself away from the delicious and distracting *tatales*, what she wrote sounded sometimes a bit Miss Jean Brodie, sometimes a bit business-speaky – and mostly awful. Amma flipped open the laptop and pressed some buttons to change the screen's brightness.

Maybe the difficulty in writing about 'herself' came from the blandness of the 'herself' to be put on the page. The most interesting thing that had happened to her wasn't appropriate for the box on the form allocated for luring offers from History of Art professors at Leeds, Sussex, Manchester, York … Amma felt a bit sick and scrunched her toes, not only responding to the draught or the flashing memory of Roisin's pubes damp with sweat, but also because it was embarrassing and inaccurate to consider 'that' 'interesting'. Amma let her head loll. The word 'interesting' and its friend 'fascinating' were problematic. Like when jolly-hockey-sticks primary schoolteachers had asked about her 'ancestry' for colourful displays on family trees. If Amma remembered boring details like how a distant relative on Dad's side had been an adviser to some chief or that she could bring in offcuts of Kente for her wall poster, teachers intoned the words 'fascinating' or 'interesting' with irritating reverence. For Amma, being interesting was the ability to recite all of *The Rime of the Ancient Mariner*, speaking … Yoruba and Finnish and Cantonese – singular and cool and amazing stuff like that. The blackness of her face or that she'd eaten out a girl and wanted to do it again didn't confer specialness and certainly wasn't important. Amma took a biro from the middle of the table, snapped off the messier bits of its destroyed end and chewed. Tasting bitterness, realising she had sucked ink, she spat.

'Amma! I can't study at all. So much moving moving as if ants are in your pants. And I find conclusions very difficult to do indeed. So please.'

Amma wiped her mouth and watched, through the window behind Belinda, the grey outside whipping away, getting wetter, the sky as blank as the screen in front of her. The funniest thing about Roisin's red pubes was when Amma brushed her teeth at Brunswick and found one of them, prone on the enamel. Stranded saffron.

The time with Roisin had involved a good deal of careful studying, of getting to know: understanding which particular absurdities amused Roisin most. Hyperbolic impersonations were often the thing, so Roisin loved Amma's screechy versions of Mum. There was also watching how Roisin used cutlery to attack meals, then seeing how her mouth closed as precisely around the forkful as it did round Amma's nipples. And learning Roisin's belief that talking around rather than towards solutions was best. The question of whether Roisin was as preoccupied with the same observation of Amma and her responses was beside the point. Amma recorded the moments until she was full with them. There had been so much noise in her head. Now, there were only gentle sounds like Belinda's reedy humming of old church hymns from the village, so much less startling than Roisin's operatic sneezes, her guttural burps. Now, there was no certainty that what Amma had slavishly learnt about Roisin remained pertinent. If they met tomorrow, on the off-chance, what anecdotes might Amma have to lightly colour to keep Roisin's brittle stare focused? What had it all been for? Amma adjusted the screen's angle, wondered uselessly if it would have hurt less and if the hurt would have disappeared more permanently, if the loss had been of a boy's … love rather than a girl's. She shook her head.

'Amma –'

The dumb cursor kept on going: Blinking. Stuck. Repeating. Blinking. Stuck. Repeating. Amma breathed, tried to remember the point: University. Forward. Forward. She forced herself to type.

'The study of any society's progression – and the costs of such advancement – is most effectively conducted by an assessment of the images and artefacts that society chose – or chooses – to represent itself with.'

Amma pressed the delete key and watched the cursor kill her words.

'You have been greedy-oh! Let me have the last one so I can take the plate away for the dishwasher.' Belinda scored the corner of her text with a thumbnail.

'Oh. Those.' Amma pushed the saucer of *tatales* forward for Belinda to stretch to. 'Sure, yeah. Take. With my blessing.'

'Such a big and sad voice.'

'Sorry.'

'It must be the weather. Or maybe the sickness has yet to pass?'

'Yep. Yep, that's the one.'

21

On the top deck of the 133 on Monday afternoon, Amma's responses to Belinda's questions were short or didn't come at all. Like they had been for most of the weekend. Like everything had slipped backwards. No opportunity to celebrate Amma's completion of the difficult UCAS form, and no thoughts about the day at school; only pauses and shuffling.

On the seat next to Belinda, Amma quietly blew and popped spit-bubbles bigger and nastier than Mary's. Then Amma breathed on the window through wet lips, drew a grid and played noughts and crosses by herself, sometimes stopping to give the world below a passing look. A speeding 250 scarily overtook their bus. Amma laughed, wrote in her spoiled Mickey Mouse notebook and put it back in her rucksack. Belinda started to ask what had been written but the hardness of Amma's shoulders stopped her and she hated that she could do nothing. Belinda's mouth tasted bitter. She wanted to get home and roll *Omotuo*. There would be Doctor's soft praise for the smoothness of her Light Soup – the meal she knew was his very favourite. Then scouring the bath's waxy ring of scum as the rest of the house snored, before the hope of gentle, empty sleep.

Loud ringtones sang from passengers' phones and Belinda looked around, her left eyelid twitching. To the left, with their heads bent in towards one another like lovers, two white boys shared a set of earphones, pecked the air and did the same mean faces. The seats at the back were taken up by five Indian boys slapping each other with their striped ties. Some squealed. Others laughed. The whips got more violent, the screams too. Before Telford Avenue, one rocked forward with pain. His glasses fell off, slid down the centre aisle, past Belinda's sparkly Primark ballet pumps, straight towards the stairs. The bus soon stopped, releasing its trapped wind, and the glasses flew back towards their owner who muttered about what his dad would have done to him if they'd smashed. His friends whooped. Belinda pretended that noise caused the heating of her cheekbones.

Two schoolgirls thumped up the stairs, obviously Jamaican because of their crucifixes and the piercings. Sometimes the difference between Nigerians and them was hard to tell, but these were definitely Jamaicans. Their tights were like fishermen's nets, their shirts unbuttoned so the darker of the two displayed some red bra.

'Nah, man, nah. I don't watch dat! Fucking reeks up here, cha.' The darker girl waved her lollipop. 'Come, Monique, I beg we get on some next bus, it's too nasty up in here.'

'I'll be late for my aunty's, you know say they neva come on time in these ends.'

Something passed between the two girls that Belinda didn't catch.

Monique's apologetic voice changed. 'But. What. Is. Dat? Whatdafuckisdat? Proper like someone's got doo-doo on their shoe! Eugh! You people need to fix up and check your shoe, yeah, coz some nastiness is going on in here. Some people are so nasty.'

Monique, the lighter girl, held her hips and talked to the whole deck. Her hair was fancy, fanned out like a peacock.

'Excuse me, yeah, whichever one of you bumbeclarts has come up in here and made it all rank and dat, bes' remember: public transport. We all gotta use it. Save that dundusness for your own home. Nasty, man, proper nasty to do that. Putting me right off my dinner.' She pointed to her lollipop and cackled.

'I'm sittin'. Come.'

Belinda's spine went up and her chin forward like she was lining up for Morning Assembly again. She coughed. 'Please. Excuse me. Hello. I say, hello, young ladies, please. What smells? I been here and I can't smell anything.'

'Be, don't –' Amma whispered.

'What? I'm confused, they aren't making sense, so I'm asking.'

'Is dat one talking to me?' Monique said. 'I beg dat one ain't talking to me. Coz no one chats to me like dat, yunnerstan?'

'Fuckin' 'ell man, my girl's about to blow! You bes' check yourself.'

'Check what? Me, I'm asking straightforward questions. Seems like you've come up here to be noisy for no reason. Everything was calm before this. Why can't people be calm, eh?'

'What the – who even arsked you, bitch?'

'Who asked, I say, asked you to shout your big mouth like this? No manners as though from the bush. Nonsense.' Belinda hadn't realised that she was on her feet and wagging her finger, or that Amma yanked at her pocket.

'Allow correcting me! Fucking Africa Bambara's telling me and whatnot. You must be mad, Boss.'

'Monique, yeah, cool it. Don't make the driver hol' up like last time.'

'Nah this bitch is stepping to me so she must know what she's about to be fucking stepping to me. Coz she have to know I don't even care about merkin' mans, ya get me?'

Monique's fingers became little guns pointed at Belinda. One of the white boys popped out an earphone and tried, 'Girls, leave it, yeah?'

'And who was chatting to you, you butters freak? Don't watch me! Put your fucking Dido back on and suck your thumb.'

'She's clearly an idiot, Be.' Amma pulled Belinda by her belt loops. 'She's just called you an African Bambatta – or whatever. Which is clearly racist and bloody ludicrous. Sit, I said sit.'

'What's your likkle friend going on about?'

'Sensible things. Not like you, who are naughty. You calling me African what? For what? I am an African, but what? You calling that bad? You foolin' with your own history? Have you only rocks in your skull – too much nonsense.'

'Don't test me! Nah! I wasn't even trying to fight this term.'

'I wouldn't dream to test,' Belinda laughed. 'You will fail, without a single doubt!'

The darker girl inhaled and began thumping her knees. 'Ohmygoshohmygoshohmygosh, that is a liberty! Fresh off the boat and cussing so bad.'

'Shutup.'

'Belinda, shh.'

'You have only behaviour like this? Is it nice? To be being this way? It's afternoon. Only 4 p.m., aren't you ashamed? Your family aren't ashamed?'

'Be, don't bring families into this. That's how it alwa–'

'Shutchamouf. Who said you could talk about my family?'

'Oh God. Dear Lord,' Amma sighed. 'She really is an utter *retard*.'

The lighter one ran forward and before Belinda could shield her she'd grabbed a fistful of Amma's braids at the roots. Two of the Indian boys at the back screamed in a pitch even higher than before.

'Think coz you're talking posh I can't understand?'

'Let go of me. Sorry.'

'You and you girlfriend need to apologise.'

'Are you deaf? Sorrysorrysorry!'

'It's not good enough. My feelings got fucking hurt by dat.'

An Indian boy started ringing the bell over and over.

'It really hurts, Be!'

'She has asked you to remove, and you haven't. *Adɛn*?' Belinda slipped off a ballet pump and held it high.

'And what you gonna do with dat?' Monique pulled Amma again. 'You're lucky I don't cut you and your rasclart girlfriend right here right now.'

Belinda swung her bag at Monique. Monique's releasing of the braids and stumbling back into the stairs seemed to happen all together.

'Be? What the fu– Fucking hell!'

Monique hauled herself up, hanging on to her friend and the green rail Belinda had moved forward to peer over.

'I can even push you down more if want. You think I care? I will kick you out of this place with my bare hands. So gerroff. Now. Gerroff and … bloody hell!'

'You don't even know what you fucking done, you ugly, fucking bitch, I'll kill you.'

'Gerroff from here. How can you frighten me? Eh? Ha! You cannot even speak a word properly.' Belinda whipped the bag through the air again and the girls ducked.

'That one goes to Streatham, I know. You, you lot bes' watch. I ain't joking: one of you is dead before da en of nex week, trus.'

Belinda sank into her seat.

They got off the bus, like normal, by the Town Hall. They stood in the cold breeze. The Ritzy's neon sign opposite stretched in Belinda's vision. On the pavement, balls of someone's old weave circled her feet like dried grasses in the harmattan. Amma took Belinda's wrists and smiled away the frowns of passers-by. The ease with which those strangers walked off and did not care was comforting.

'Let's wait here, yeah? For your shaking to stop? You're fucking mental, Be. And, also, brilliant. What even happened to you back there?'

Belinda liked the kindness of Amma's speaking again, but a tight grip and a few minutes of calm would not be enough. The dizziness, the thing inside was not neat or little. This bad behaviour, badness, sickness, strangeness in the blood, handed down from mother to daughter. Belinda slipped herself from Amma's hold and smoothed the sleeves of her duffle, pulling the sleeves even though they would not go further. It would be sad if she broke the coat's stitches but Belinda wanted the sleeves to cover more.

'Be? Come on.'

The thing in Belinda's racing blood was in charge, came and went and slipped out when and how it liked; it cared about nothing. How funny to think about the nasty Monique-girl's shock. That was the good. Less of a joke was the sound of the satchel against her forehead and the small, baby sounds as the girl got to her feet, struggling against something she had not seen coming.

'Let's start – yeah? OK, so. Breathing.'

Belinda dropped her head. Three sequins had flaked off her ballet pump. 'I remember first wondering of it when I was young. Because of during thunder and lightning. In the rainy season our storms are so much bigger than whatever small ones you have here. They come for whole hours and hours at a time back home. And when the storms begin, with the lightning and the lizards running to hide, everyone would get so excited. The village women would together prepare, going to get off their clothes from the line and then the others getting buckets to catch the water when the rains come proper proper. But whenever my mother ran to help anyone, they slid away. They waved her off. They will pretend, like, as though they have seen nothing, rather than go near or have her touching their coal pot or picking up their child to put them inside, away from the downpouring. I tried thinking they act as this because we are the poorest in Adurubaa. A good explanation and I believed in it for a while but –'

Belinda stamped to see if that would trick the dizziness. No.

'I don't understand.'

'Rahab. Ra-hab. Ra-hab. What will you hear when I use this name since you don't know your own Bible?' A car beeped. Belinda jumped. 'They wouldn't allow us into the Church. We try once. The pastor barred us entering with his big arm and so we never return. Instead we did our own Bible study at home every Sunday. She enjoyed Revelations. My reading was much better than hers. Much better.'

'OK.'

'She worked so late, late, late, late, late, late. Always. Do you have to do waitressing at 1 a.m., 2 a.m., 3 a.m.? Who?'

'Let's get home, Be. I. I – Do we need to grab anything from the shops for dinner before they close?'

'Maybe they did it hidden by trees. Big trees. Or, the back of buildings. Different buildings.'

'Be –'

'I don't know the word for one of the men because I never used it out loud before … maybe a customer. One of her customer. Ac-customed to her. Ac-customed to her. Ha! Like customary marriage. That's funny.' On the Town Hall's pointed roof a pole stood where a flag might have flown. The coming clouds were so grimy. Belinda stamped again.

'Let's start walking.' Amma sounded very grown-up and very in charge. Too late.

'One of her customer came to the room and then that was when there wasn't a doubt. Then I knew. I was in the room. She was at work. Waitress. Maybe she mixed up her times and dates. Maybe because the man was too drunk and the error was his fault. But I was in. Doing my homework nicely and then the door knocked. He stood there, you could see his face. I hid so I could see, but not him me. His face' – Belinda sketched his features in the air, spent a long time drawing the big lips – 'at the door, through the net, grinning and licking all his mouth. And him calling my mother's name. He went away after a bit, swearing a lot because he could not get what he came for. I. I remembered his face and his tie. He had on a tie with this, this pattern of swirls. You will recognise yourself if you come across it. Like teardrop shaped and leaves and swirls with other sorts of patterns.'

'Paisley? I'm not sure.'

'OK. OK that. I never asked why or asked her who he was. She got back home from the chop bar that very night and I never ask her why a stranger had come shouting for her that he was hungry hungry for the sweetness, telling that this time he has dollars and dollars, banging and hitting. I didn't tell her of my fear and of hiding myself under the bed until she came back from the waitressing. I had to pretend everything was as normal, because I am a good girl.'

'Belinda.'

'And only a few days after, I cleaned. Did all the usual. The plates in the pink bucket. I did the underwears and put them away. I scrubbed the calabash we used for bathing. I was fixing the bed nicely when I saw it again in between the sheets. Pattern like swirls. Like swirls and tears and things. She wouldn't even clean his dirty tie from where we slept.'

'Oh.'

'I didn't know what I was even doing. I was frightened and had all these questions like what, what will I become if my mother is … is that way? Selling it? Giving it? Is, is that how I became? How much do they pay? Ha? Eh? I just couldn't understand any of it. I knew nothing, nothing. And who was there to explain? Eh? The, the tie was in my hand as a dead fish and I wanted first to spit on it or urinate but I went for a lighter from her smoking. I watched it burn a bit and then the whole middle went up and I felt better and I blew on it and you could still notice some small piece of the pattern left and I thought yes, I will show her to bring her to shame. So I put the burnt thing on her pillow. I pretended I was asleep and I watched her come in and nothing. In the morning, and the next day, and the next day, she said nothing. Never. Nothing. She has never told me if it is or isn't. She will never tell.'

Belinda thudded her chest.

'He might have –'

'Now you think I am less, isn't it? Even less. Disgusting.' Belinda clapped. 'You do and don't lie about it.'

'What? Of *course* I don't. I feel … sorry that you've had all of this going on. Truly. Shit. If that's, if that's what's going on in your head.'

'What can sorry do? Sorry doesn't eat curses.'

Belinda stopped and her hands were freezing. They crawled over each other, searching for warmth.

'You won't tell Madam? Nana? Please. Your mum. She can't. I mean, please. I mean, please, I beg. Really. I mean she will even refuse to even look on me, or have me in her home. I'm begging you to say nothing, Amma! I, I should not.' Belinda reached out towards Amma. 'Forgive that I spoke this, eh? I cannot fail and get ashamed here because –'

Belinda's wrists were restrained again. 'What would I tell, Be? Exactly what? Hey?' Amma sighed, even looked annoyed. 'Cruelty. The cruelty of the fucking world is proved fucking every single day. The unfairness of life is just, like, unbelievable. Unbelievable.'

Amma kissed her teeth, which nearly made Belinda laugh.

'We're all weeping. The whole fucking time. Inside, outside. Fuck.' Amma shook her head and the braids leapt. 'Shit, Be, even if it is all true, what's what your mum did or does or whatever got to do with you? You're your own person. And anyway, who the fuck am I – or is Mum – to sit in judgement? Who?'

Straight after the quiet dinner where Nana talked about the *Ghanafoɔ* fundraiser for HIVAIDS in a few weeks, and who may or may not be on the guest list, Amma started running Belinda a bath. When ready, Amma offered Belinda the good towels and told her to take as long as she needed. So Belinda did. Long after the water greyed with her dirt and her fingertips wrinkled, she sat with her knees hitched up through bubbles. Sometimes she lay completely still, like Monique's promise about death had come true. Other times, she banged the back of her head on the bath's ledge, stopping when the pain went beyond a sting. She scooped water and threw it on her face as though the action might wake her mind up so that she knew what to do next. She could not believe it. Everything was going to disappear – Abacus, Amma, Nana. All of it. She would be sent back, with nothing to show for the time away apart from the solid and certain knowledge that the world wanted no good for her. Aunty, Uncle, Mary: they would hear of it and be disgusted at how well Belinda had hidden a filthy truth from them. She would be left to withstand dust and slaps alone. After a lifetime of being so careful, Belinda was to be punished for her mouth forgetting itself just once. Just once. That was the cruelty that Amma spoke of. Belinda reached for a flannel, dropped it into the bath then wrung it out. Outside, Radio 4 mumbled on, as did Nana on the landing, phoning someone in Takoradi.

Belinda thought again about that final meal with Mother in Adurubaa; the night Mother had asked her to imagine the village beneath waves. Belinda wondered what Mother's face and body had been doing while Belinda's own eyes had been closed, picturing scenes of destruction. It was possible that, while Belinda concentrated and conjured a flood, Mother had sat in the old folding chair and, deep inside, had struggled with the prospect of giving away her daughter; the only thing in the world that belonged to her. When Mother described her own hand scrabbling out of the waves, maybe she had sensed the threat of a rising tear but fought it: she wanted to show no weakness because that might weaken her daughter, and Mother knew strength was needed to face unknown Daban. Mother knew strength. That evening, as Mother had given out her clear instructions about never turning back, perhaps it had been hard to speak so thunderously when, really, under all of that pretending, Mother's feelings were more unsure and broken. Maybe the following day, after the driver had taken Belinda away, when Mother was doing her sticky nastiness with some evil man, Mother might have stared up at the dead insects on the ceiling and not fully felt the pressure of the heaving body on top of her because the scale of what she had lost and the emptiness of what lay ahead filled every space in her mind.

All of that was possible. It *had* to be possible. Because when Mother focused on something simple and ordinary, like sewing in the thin light of the kerosene lamp, Mother could take on the most beautiful softness; a calm that, for a moment, controlled Belinda's spinning worries. It had to be possible, because of the way Mother stopped the nosebleeds Belinda often had when she was little; with the slightest pinch to the bridge of Belinda's nose and admiration for Belinda's calm courage. And it *had* to be possible, because Mother sometimes muttered in her sleep, quietly calling herself the worst names and using curses to describe herself, and then she'd get up the next day: shrivelled, defeated.

Belinda twisted the flannel more, tossed it aside. She wanted to smack her hands down and to make water splash out of the tub and onto the floor. Instead, she pulled at the bath plug's chain with her toes and listened to the drain's burbling. She started to think about how she could leave the room without seeing herself in one of the large mirrors on the walls.

22

Over the following week, the 'line' Amma decided on was dull but effective. When Belinda avoided eye contact or lingered in her bedroom long after Nana had screeched her name and harsh Twi up the stairs, Amma was quick to suggest to Nana that Belinda might simply be a little homesick. Perfectly normal. Pressing Belinda on what she had said might do more harm than good. Amma had never used the phrase 'more harm than good' in her life. Neither had she ever spent so much time preoccupying Mum with questions about the Yeboah twins and MAC rouge; or making empty chat about Helena's portfolio for Central St Martins, Paul Burrell, Alicia Keys' outfits, the square footage of the newest buy-to-let and the imminent fireworks at Brockwell Park. Each time Amma unknitted Nana's brow, distracting her with some conversational bauble, Amma glowed with success. Then she thought about Belinda. How much bravery Belinda had in her; had shown on that bus.

Over those days, the need for Amma to keep quiet about what she knew – or what she supposedly knew – struck her with a kind of solemn force the like of which she wasn't sure she had ever experienced before. She had purpose. This silence was important. And how good to be tasked with a challenge both meaningful and achievable: Amma was tops at keeping secrets.

On the Wednesday after the stuff with Monique, Amma's evening diversion with Mum involved working through the lists of Dad's relatives in Kumasi who had asked for Discmans, phones,

watches and underwear. The TV blathered on in the background.
To help with easy ordering, Amma's job was to mark up the rele-
vant products in catalogues reserved for such occasions: quite a
boring task, apart from Nana orally annotating each of the names
she wrote down with bits of stupid gossip about how that aunt had
an alcohol problem, and that one was a true gold-digger, and that
uncle was having an affair with a nurse and everyone knew.

After *News at Ten* Nana fell asleep sitting upright on the old
Chesterfield. Her silver lizard brooch glinted on her blouse as it
caught the light when her chest rose with each snore. Her honeyed
cheeks seemed softer; her lips, still slick with deep plum red, were
also different – less poised to twist into wryness, maybe. Deep and
structural whorls grooved her calm hands that rested on her knees
like a yogi. Amma scooped her oversized hoodie around herself,
tugging its long drawstring. As she watched Nana sleep through
the chirped summary of rank wintery weather, she wondered just
how beautiful Belinda's mother must be and why beauty always
got ruined or robbed. Or was it only black people's beautiful things
that ended trampled on like that? And didn't they often do the
trampling themselves?

Amma sipped a mug of the peppermint tea that Belinda loved
so much and which she had also started liking. Nana's snoring
changed: now there was an extra, whimpered breath to it that
worried a stray lock of her grey hair. Weirdly, whenever Amma
imagined coming out to Mum – if she was even allowed to call it
that, if that wasn't grandiose – the dreaded revelation happened
with Mum reading in bed, peering at Amma over her ornate
glasses. All fired up with injustice, in the midst of her imagined
scenario Amma raged and her mother did the same. But as Mum's
whimpers kept on coming and dribble crept down her chin, it
couldn't have been clearer: Mum was getting old. Everyone might
joke about 'black don't crack' or whatever, but Mum was getting
old. Amma wanted to forgive this older version of Mum for

making her daughter lie about herself; about the part of herself
that Monique had maybe detected on the bus and found so utterly
repugnant. Amma played with the teabag's green tag. A line
connected them all – Monique, Mum, Belinda, Belinda's mum, her
– all these black women mired in different kinds of shit.

'Mum.'

Nana snorted herself awake, wiping the dribble. 'Eh?'

'Mum?'

'Eh? What, what time is it? *Ewurade* I need my bed.'

'When you and Dad first, like, met. How did it – How did it
feel? Inside? Like, did you have some sort of sensation in your
body because you knew what it was going to be?'

Nana settled and reshaped her blouse, then rubbed her face like
a fretful toddler.

'More than thirty years ago. Often is hard to even remember.'
She yawned. 'Especially when he is around so little these days.'

'Answer.'

Nana yawned again, kissed her teeth, thought. An advert for
cough syrup flashed pinks and golds on the TV screen. She spoke
very slowly. 'I suppose I only could tell that he was different from
others in our village. Everyone else clinging to their *oburoni wawu*,
but for him always an Oxford shirt and these shiny brogues,
perfect even with all the red dust everywhere. You've heard how
he dressed? It was how he wanted to be. Smart. People laughed at
him for doing so, for being professional even though we were
young. He didn't mind anyone. I liked a man with this behaviour.
I thought, he is strong. He will be strong enough to keep me safe
if anything happens. That was my big thing, I was very frightened
as a young girl.'

'About what?'

'I. I thought bad would come around the corner, could come at
any given time, and I would have no preparation or protection
from it. Probably all poor people are the same.' Nana paused.

'Look at your face. I think maybe I haven't given the correct responses as you wanted.'

'It's not that. I don't think I'll ever get it. I mean, I mean I wonder if, sometimes, in a relationship, there are mysteries that happen between two people that only those two can understand, and others ... well, can't.'

'Really?' Nana sat forward, interest animating her puffed eyes. 'And where from this wisdom, small philosopher?'

'It's from a book we're doing in class. That's not the quote exactly but. Yeah.'

The front door opened and Amma could hear Dad sighing in the corridor and shuffling across the Victorian tiles there that Helena's mother cooed over and commented on whenever she came round.

With effort, Nana stood up to go to him. She touched Amma's head lightly. Her fingertips smelled of familiar cocoa butter. 'When you first did your hair in this style with the purple braids and the dark blue ones and –'

'Yeah, you hated it.'

'No, no, hate is strong. Too strong. I only worried it didn't bring out your very best but' – Mum tilted Amma's head this way, then that – 'is not so terrible after all, is it?'

'Crikey! From you, Mater, I will take that as a resounding endorsement. *Merci beaucoup.*'

'There's the true joke, Comedienne. As if you waiting and need an endorsement from me. As if you need an endorsement from anyone. You do what you like with or without that, eh?'

23

Mary had a cut on her thumb from a tin of corned beef. Mary had seen the Nyantakyis next door take delivery of a trampoline for their garden because their grandson was coming over from the US and would love it. Mary had held Driver's filthy tools while he fixed the Mercedes; Cynthia had been scared of spoiling her smock. Mary was annoyed that Afua was able to do the splits, but she could not. Mary had watched Carpenter kill and cook a whole goat to celebrate the birth of his first son. With her spine resting against the wall, Belinda sat cross-legged on the landing, listening, her nose twitching at Doctor Otuo's sugary aftershave that remained in the air even though he had left for his Saturday stroll hours ago. In her hand, she held a small sheet of paper softened with sweat. On it, to help control her thinking: a list of safe and interesting topics to talk about. Belinda's eye drifted near '– Victoria Line & the Tube in general – Tattoos' when Mary coughed wetly and gulped for air.

'*Adjei!* Nasty!'

'Eh? Mary? Mary?'

'*Me ba, me ba.*' Mary's breath strained and her receiver clapped against something.

Unsure what to do with the silence fizzing down the line, Belinda dropped the paper and rubbed the yellow patches on the sandblasted jeans Nana called trendy. Her palms became painful so it was good that Mary soon came back sounding steadier. Belinda felt confident that the rubbing could stop.

'Thanking you for the patience, sister. Sorry,' Mary giggled. 'I am too too accident prone. Is as the rhyme goes.'

'Rhyme?'

'I swallow a fly. I'm not an old lady but the rest is the same. I swallowed a fly.'

'Oh.'

'I don't care. I'm fine now. And – don't tell – but I had some of their water with the bubbles in it to get the insect down? I don't see why our Madam and Master fuss for that water so. We have to drag crates of it from the A-Life! supermarket shop and they do a "mmmm" noise like is golden or like they are on a advert whenever they drink. Why? It tastes same as a normal water to me. Maybe even a little bitter. Perhaps is only poor children like us who enjoy sweets as much as we do.'

'You shouldn't steal their belongings, Mary.'

'What steal? The sparkling water was the nearest one to hand. And it's an emergency, not so? I could have choked to death but now I am saved, all praise and thanks to their San Pellegrinos. Halle, halle, hallelujah. I bet they will get an extra reward in heaven for it. They should even come to thank me.'

Quick feet moved below. Through the banister's spindles Belinda saw Amma coming up, holding her 3310 like it was too precious, the loose bun on her head wiggling, whistling the 'freak-on' song from the party in a bouncy way. When Amma reached the landing, the whistling stopped. Her dark forehead, spotty at the hairline, squashed itself at the sight of sitting Belinda. Then Amma smiled, saluted and put the Nokia away before walking off to her bedroom. Belinda's shoulders jerked.

'I don't mind,' Mary said.

'What?'

'If you want to do like this? I will even be happy to stay here quiet with you like this, with no words and hear you only breathing. You breathe quite heavy, actually. I bet some people will find it a bit disgusting but I quite like it. Is normal to me.'

'I got distracted by something, that's all. Pardon. I'm here now.'

'Your mind always drifting to some other place.'

'It isn't.' Belinda pulled at the split bits of her thumbnails. 'Is it?'

'Of course. I. I thought you will stop now that you are there. Because, because when you did it here in Daban, when you have these small moments with the face still like the world has stopped, I sometimes thought in my head she is imagining a beautiful place for herself. Daydreaming. I wanted sometimes to ask you what you thinking on but I felt a bit shy to. Even though I know you cannot believe that shyness of me. Seems to me like you still doing it, this daydreaming or whatever. Like, like your London is not even enough.'

Belinda stroked one of the spindles, following its ladylike dips. She thought about her new room. She really liked her marble mantelpiece. It had the same olden days feel about it as the spindles in front of her and the lampposts out on the street. She carefully wiped the mantel's grey swirls with Cif twice a day and, like an altar, put special things on it. At the end closest to her wardrobe a Hello Kitty pencil case sat, bursting with more felt-tips and rubbers than she had seen in her life; next to that her passport. Also, Penguin copies of *Macbeth*, *Romeo and Juliet*, *The Tempest* and *Lord of the Flies* for Abacus. A Lambeth Borough Library Card that Mrs Al-Kawthari had helped her apply for. *Things Fall Apart* and *White Teeth* for fun. To the left of those, the Coca-Cola money box for change from her pocket money. Then a letter about a class trip to the British Museum. And her keys with the peg doll key ring Amma didn't want but that Belinda thought was so beautiful: a little Chinese lady with pink blossom trailing down her thin wooden back.

'No. I will like to stay here for a long time. I think. As long as I can. To get myself a future security. One day I will come home.

Maybe come for you, take you to some different places, show you some new things.'

'Little me? You will return to collect Miss Mary for adventures? I don't believe in it.'

'I would do it. I would, whyever not? And also I would like to do something good and big in the place where we are from. Something important. Charity or a school perhaps. Something to help. I'm not clear on, like, like, what it will be. But I will like to … to try.' Belinda smiled to herself, remembering Amma at Lavender's. She shook her head. 'I suppose that doesn't even make much sense anyway.'

Mary's voice was stern and careful. 'In a fact, I think it is a great and good answer.'

'Oh. Oh. Thank you.' Belinda shifted her weight on the carpet, its rough weave digging at her bottom. For a second Belinda wondered if such dreams were useless; how many days until the inevitable, when Amma let slip and it was over? Her next, tired sigh rippled like one that comes before crying. But then Mary started up about the long lack of a replacement housegirl and did an impression of Aunty and Uncle moaning that none met the standard Belinda set. The crumpled list stayed by Belinda's knee, untouched, as Mary kept on and on and on, speaking as if to please only herself, as if no one would be able to stop her, laughing at her own jokes and answering her own questions. So Belinda went back to humming agreement sometimes, tutting disapproval at others, offering suggestions soon batted off. And as Belinda listened, spoke, listened, she saw that she gripped the banister's spindle like she had held up her shoe at Monique; tight and certain.

24

Amma led them over the zebra crossing by Herne Hill Station.

'I think I will find it very interesting. This fireworks display thing,' Belinda said as they walked. Her voice was as firm and game as it had been when she'd accepted Amma's invitation to the event earlier in the week. Amma had been embarrassingly pleased when Belinda had said yes; it was a sign that Belinda's stifling awkwardness and suspicion of her – the furtive looks were the worst – was finally starting to subside. Now, as they got closer to Brockwell, Amma smiled to herself and then at Belinda.

'Interesting? You're a pyromaniac, you'll be in your element, darling.'

'What's a py-ro-ma-ni-ac? That's new.'

'Don't worry, I'm being silly.'

'Remind me. To reassure, these fire-works, they are entirely safe, right?'

'Of course they are, Be. It's a big Lambeth Council type thingy. St John's on standby and shit. I've come every year since forever and there are never any accidents or anything like that. Usually Helena tags along too but, alas, this eve she's preoccupied with the irresistible Maximilian –'

'Mm. I mean. I mean not to sound ungrateful, but. The whole occasion seem strange to me. Is it normal to take days and days to build a model of a human and then you throw on the flames to watch it burn? Why!'

'I know there's, like, obviously historical reasoning for its happening and, like, this will definitely sound quite silly, but there's something appropriately late-autumnal about it? The bonfire getting rid of the old so the new can eventually come. Or something?' Amma noted Belinda's thoughtful expression.

'Tickets, madam,' was the officious instruction at the park's gates.

'Right, yes, sorry,' Amma handed pink slips to the shivering attendant who, without eye contact, tore them with a perfunctory swipe. Amma laughed at Belinda's insistent 'Thanking you very much' as they entered Brockwell, nudged by the chattering groups surrounding them.

'I don't understand those either,' Belinda said.

'What?'

'Those gloves the rude lady back there she had on. It's a cold night so why would you put things on where the finger coverings have been sliced off? Won't they freeze? Fingerless. Adεn?'

'At least the cold is something you won't have to worry about.'

'What?'

'Three scarves on your neck and, erm, are you wearing a fucking gilet under your duffle coat? How many layers have you actually got on?' Belinda counted six. 'Christ alive, woman. You'll evaporate.'

'This cold is se-r-ious. How you can survive it for some six months? Half of your life is lived in a torture.'

'You sound like Mum. She's forever going on about, like, "the wind's wickedness" – like, hilariously –'

Belinda feigned interest in hot dogs and candy floss, and continued to do so as they trudged forward, avoiding all the kids with sparklers. Mum. The word Mum.

'I promised I wouldn't tell. I meant it. OK?'

'I know.'

'It. It doesn't change anything. Honestly.'

'Not for you, anyway.'

'Definitely not for me.'

Amma's attention landed on a brilliant stall and idea. 'Mulled cider, yeah? Yeah.'

'Is there alcohol in it?'

'Tiny, tiny bit. Really not much at all. And it's a traditional part of the event. So.' Belinda sneered. 'Don't be such a flipping grandmama.'

Amma tugged Belinda over, flashed her excellent and expensive fake ID and carried the two drinks away.

'Thank you,' Belinda said as she accepted a fizzing flagon, enunciating each of those words so Amma could not help but understand their more profound meaning. Amma nodded, slurped.

A sound system screeched. 'Dancing Queen' started up. The crowd cheered and quickened its pace towards the bonfire. Eager for a good spot, Amma and Belinda continued towards spectral light and smoke, mulching fallen leaves underfoot, skirting round empty trees. Through the cup's steam, Amma watched Belinda indulge in increasingly large sips.

'You big fat wino.'

'Is not wine. Is mulled cider.'

'When you're pissed on the kerb somewhere, don't expect me to carry you home.'

'Ay! Will I? Will I become pissed?'

'Shut up, Be! And stop walking so slowly, everyone's pushing ahead.'

The echoing track changed to 'Billie Jean'. Amma had misdirected them, to a part of the throng where forward motion was largely impossible. The ghoulish guy's moppy head, crowned with flames, was just visible, but little else was: the view blocked by a wall of six-year-olds sat atop fathers' shoulders and their Barboured backs. Belinda craned her neck to see more.

'Never mind, Be.'

'No, it's totally fine actually. I can get the smell from here. Is nice. Wood smoke. It reminds me of home, somewhat. Like dinner time in Adurubaa, and everyone is out to prepare their evening meals. And, and I'm more enjoying the music than the fire, actually. I love Michael Jackson. Next to Whitney Houston, is one of the artists we like the most in Ghana, even if we know he is ashamed to be black.'

Amma bristled. The sky exploded.

'My goodness – is … my goodness!'

Now the DJ opted for Prokofiev. There was a glittering spillage. Pompoms of colour – electric reds, electric pinks, electric oranges shredded into the night. Hundreds of points of light sprayed and then soon fizzled away. Next, a series of silver droplets showered everywhere. There were whoops, cheers, shouts.

'That last one is my favourite so far. Like crystals. Ooh, Amma, look. Ooh!' Belinda shouted above the rustle of collective excitement. A scatter of purple hearts appeared above, breaking into blue pixels. 'No, no – I preferred that one. That one is, like, amazing! How can they make it happen?'

Amma saw that, despite Belinda's cumbersome layers, she revelled in a new ease: Catherine wheels excited her into squealing, coerced her into bigger gulpings of cider. Abandon lightened her laughter each time a rocket shot up. In pauses during the display, Belinda even tickled the ears of a child in front and made small talk with her. Amma wondered if that was what being unburdened looked like. Maybe Belinda's confident play, her pretending to steal the little blonde girl's nose said: I'm frightened, yes. But at least there will be change now. At least something different will happen to me. No more festering, festering, festering.

There was that, and, for Amma, the prospect of Roisin in a few days. Roisin's unexpected, long overdue text – a demand that they see each other – had come – naturally – without warning on

Saturday afternoon. A simple suggestion of dates and locations and it brought no promise of more, but the miraculous idea that she had been in Roisin's thinking again was more than something, it was certainly a start and it mattered. More unabashed pops above, whizzes, applause. Amma's heart raced like the crowd's feet stamping for warmth. She tapped Belinda's shoulder. But, instructed by a clashing of cymbals, Belinda's gaze returned to the sky.

It ended with 'We Are the Champions' and a battery of fluorescence. Then silence, crescents of smoke and timely rainclouds. Amma rocked on her heels as the blonde toddler's predictable wailing came with the realisation that all fun had been had. Thinking quickly, Belinda offered up the maze of her cornrows – revealed from under the hood for the girl's inspection – and that magically stopped the tears. The little girl traced the patterns quietly and studiously. Chuckling at Belinda, the girl's mother glowed with gratitude. Belinda chuckled back and waved off the calmed child as she was pushed away in her pram. Amma wanted to know why, why it would be easier if that little one grew up to love a Roisin or an Elizabeth or a Susannah, only because she was white.

'Come on,' Amma said.

'Oh, you talk sharp! You going to start making a scene like that child too?'

'I just quite want to leave now. Show's over, right? Sorry. Didn't mean to, to snap. Or whatever.'

'OK then. We walk.'

'Yeah. Let's.'

Once out of Brockwell, back on the main road, she and Belinda made their way back past the launderette, the toy-town train station, the newsagent; the man by his counter waving at them through the window. Amma did not wave back. Instead, she grabbed and lashed out at the bushes; greens and whites flurried and her heels scuffed the pavement. Amma felt Belinda at the edge of her vision, pulling her coat's toggles. Carousers probably headed for the Prince Regent congaed by, towards Rymer Road, much to Belinda's bewilderment.

'Smoking! Yes. Just the thing!' Amma's cold fingers struggled to do what was needed, but eventually she took a drag and was unsurprised when it didn't help. She pulled harder and harder on the cigarette, tutting.

'See,' Belinda said unhappily.

'What?'

'You're uncomfortable. Can only pretend for a bit and then. Then you feel awkward about it all over again.'

'I am but. Uncomfortable, yeah, but.' A car screeched up from Spenser playing reggae that hushed into the night. 'Not about that. Sorry.'

'A lot of sorry from the tigress today.'

Amma stopped under a lamppost on the corner of their street, making Belinda stand still too. Dots swam in front of her eyes.

'What is the meaning of this one?'

'You're my friend,' Amma was methodical, 'and this is … this is the place where our friendship has taken us; where it's reached.' She tugged at her beanie. 'I. I don't want you to feel unsafe ever again, OK? You've had enough … shit, enough shit to deal with. I know that. I don't want to lie, or hide, or be ambiguous.'

'Is so kind for … for someone to be kind.'

'Yeah. Yeah, I hope. I hope it is.'

'What?'

'And I'm not sure exactly how I want you to react, but, but if you can at least, like, do *kind* once I'm finished, I can manage with that. Definitely. Kind would be cool, cool, cool.'

Amma watched Belinda staring at the illuminated air around the two of them, at the dust drifting through the beam. That brightness reflected off Amma's Doc Martens; Roisin had promised to cover those boots with hundreds of tiny, painted flowers. One for each of the different feelings they had for each other. Amma had not been allowed to call her cheesy, because Roisin's face had soon closed. They started walking again.

'Now is when I tell you that I fell in love.'

'Oh.' Belinda reached up to wipe her nose. 'Oh.'

'No. Present continuous. Still falling. And it's confusing and. And not necessarily always great. But. Yes. Here's where I am.' Amma inhaled and nodded with false authority.

'Well, to start. First, I thank you that you wanted to share with this with me. It must frighten to, to do it. Now that you have – said, I mean – now that you have spoken these to me I suppose I can only advise. I only advise this one. I think a love at our age can be a very dangerous *paaaaa*. Maybe it can give you scars for life, can even send you crazy. Me, I don't know entirely for sure. I'm only guessing, because I've never had a boyfriend myself, or something such as this.'

'Me neither.'

'Neither what?'

'Like, I've kissed a few KCS boys at house parties and that, but. No. No boyfriends.'

'So … so, you mean that this one now who you are … loving, you want to call him a boyfriend, but he won't give his love back and this is why you have a pain? Is this it? I tell you for free, Sister, the man must have rocks inside his head if he can't see your real worth and beauty.'

'It's not a boy, or a man.' Amma unwound and rewound the scarf around her neck. Belinda did the same.

'Is not man or boy?'

'No.'

'Then is a girl?'

Amma nodded.

'A girl?'

'Yes. I'm in love with a fucking girl. How do you like them apples?' She unwound and rewound the scarf again.

'Is, is maybe like *Supi*? We have in Ghana. In the girls boarding schools. You have a special girl friend who you spend time with and you never leave them. Like a best friend. Me, I never took one because as I wasn't going to any of those boarding schools of course. And, yes, you not going to one either, but maybe *Supi* works different here, so, so maybe. Maybe what you're trying to tell is that you are sad you have warred with your *Supi*, eh? And I am, I am sorry for that one if that is the reason. Yes?'

'I don't think I quite understand what a *Supi* is because you're talking a lot but, like, not really saying very much. So. Look, I can tell by your rattling on that you get it and …'

'I get nothing.'

'I – We're more than friends, best friends, whatever.'

'Who? Me and you? Me? *Wa bo dam!*'

'Fucking-narcissist-much? Her name is Roisin and. And I think we want to be together. Possibly. We're meeting in a couple of days. And. We'll sort it out.' Amma watched Belinda's mouth slacken.

'Sort it out? You are a joker. How can you sort that?'

'Be –'

'I'm meant to be pleased that you sharing this with me? Happy? Happy for you and this Raysheen, or whatever?'

'I didn't really think about it in terms of your happiness, Be. Sorry. I. It needed doing. I've wanted to for a while now. I thought that –'

'Seem like you never really thinking at all, Amma, if this is how you want to have your life. As a homosexual lesbian.'

'It's just about her, OK? Me and her and love and –'

Belinda clutched her knees. 'A homosexual lesbian! On top of all the rest!' She laughed a scratchy laugh. 'You have to admit, Amma, is a bit funny. Funny, funny funny. Someone should even have joking tears upon their cheeks. Ha. Ha. What? What? Why you seeming as concern as this? *Won sere?*'

Belinda began walking away and Amma followed.

'Be. Be –'

'You have to walk behind me,' Belinda said, staring ahead.

'Walk behind?'

'Exactly. And many, many paces. I mean many, *many* paces.'

Belinda opened the door to 19 Spenser Road. The hush in the hallway and the lights of the alarm system meant that Nana had gone to sleep. That was good. Belinda nodded and left the door ajar for Amma, who she could hear crying. Belinda undid each of the toggles on her coat and hung it to rest on a hook. Suspended like that, Belinda gave it a little pat to congratulate it for serving her well. Perhaps the crying had lessened, she could not tell, because she was busy unbuttoning the gilet, peeling off the jumpers, making them into a pile at the bottom of the stairs she would take to her room when ready for bed. But before bed: work. Belinda went down the hallway to the small toilet at the end before the stairs to the kitchen. She locked herself in. On her knees, she scrabbled into the corners of that tight space to find the cleaning brush. She was pleased at the muck in its bristles. She got to her feet and turned the hot tap on. With ungloved hands, under the stream of scalding water, she plucked the dirt from those spines until they were as white as she could manage. She watched brown dots disappear into the plug hole. Then she picked up a bottle from another corner and squirted its contents under the toilet's rim. Blue dripped down, into the water, in long, long tears. Bent, Belinda peered into the bowl. She scrubbed at its edges harshly, even when her wrist ached and ached.

25

The muscles around that wrist hurt throughout the long week of complete silence between Belinda and Amma. One of those days, at Abacus, Belinda rotated her wrist joint. On the front row Robert complained loudly about his latest low grade. She twisted more. The sharp twinge forced her to bite down. Belinda flattened her palm on the desk, played with her pencil.

Was Amma in pain? Maybe. No. No: because Belinda would never stop remembering Amma's explanation of it. They were 'in love'. Even if Belinda knew the fire awaiting Amma, Amma saw none of that. Only romance and red roses and soft pinks. She couldn't help imagining it again: the girls, this Roisin, them moaning and moaning on top of each other. Such a frightening and rude noise. There weren't that many reasons to think about down there, apart from during the monthly when it behaved badly. But now Belinda had to wonder more, worry more. What did it feel like for another girl to touch the private place? She mostly thought it foolish to worry that a girl's hand there would sting or leave a stain like a birthmark. Mostly. She wriggled. And how disgusting: disgusting to picture the girls' four breasts as they brushed and rubbed, their mouths pushing into each other for angry licking. Their sex acts would be done more dramatically and more horribly than normal people, because the girls wanted to show off as much as they could, to shout that they were different. To Belinda, the whole thing seemed to be about that: wanting to be different. She scored along her palm's deep, dark lines with the pencil's point. Worse than Mother and any just-paid man. At least there was something natural about that.

Robert thumped his folder. Miss kept ignoring the protest, organising colourful handouts for a new task instead. There were sixteen sheets in each set, and each set was placed into a shallow purple tray. Mrs Al-Kawthari's careful handling of the sheets – all the greens together, all the yellows together and all the blues together – soothed Belinda. She liked the easy rhythm of it. She wanted to get up and join in; helping might help her. But then she would have to explain or come up with an excuse for the big, relieved smile it would cause. So Belinda found herself stuck on her chair as Mrs Al-Kawthari reached into the trays and neatened each pile like a newsreader at the end of the show.

'I am always Macbeth, I do the best voice for Macbeth – you all claim so yourselfs. Until what is fair and right occurs, until my essay is remarked, I am on strike. What you mean to give me a C?' Robert's shouting was bad for Belinda. Like when Amma had told her secret, Belinda wanted to cover her ears. Robert's outburst was bad for his clothes too. The seam on the back of his blazer started to split. First it seemed like a straightforward repair job: five minutes of squinting and care. As Robert continued it lengthened. Some fabric from within showed through. The unzipped seam gave the dark oval a frayed outline, hundreds of tiny teeth. Belinda heard her name, announced in that familiar, instructive tone, so she picked up her pencil again because that was active and good and normal.

She imagined the oval getting blacker. She imagined there was none of the classroom: only the blackness. Blacker than her, blacker than the ink on Western Union slips. Blacker than behind-the-oven dirt. Blacker than the smoke of a burning tie. Different, very different from temporary, powercut dark; that darkness held promises and was a mischievous spirit hiding shoes, pens, watches for a time, giving them back to you at dawn. Belinda imagined this black mightn't pass. There mightn't be anything else. She imagined the darkness spreading, pouring from the tear like the skunk's bad smell in the cartoons Mary found hilarious. And somewhere in the corner of all that black, she imagined a huddled person, a tiny version of herself, as alone and as friendless as Mother had been. Because in Adurubaa, when had a woman knocked on their door to lend Mother a few cedis and wisdom and an ear to make all the difference? And now, what person had a few minutes and the right words for Belinda? The little girl at the end of the phone who lived in playtime? Or the one whose homosexual lesbian problem was far too much for Belinda to deal with? Or that one's mother, the woman who Belinda had let down, the woman who might even send Belinda back home to – In the imagined gloom, the smaller version of Belinda rolled into a ball, head tucked in. She heard whispering.

'Line! Your line?!'

'This ruining the performance! Get your skates on, girl, and read, ya unnerstan?' That was Robert.

'Belinda!' Sylvia pressed.

'Sorry.' Flustered, she searched for the right page, not sure what she'd do when she found it.

The route her feet chose after class was long; through back streets between Streatham and Brixton Hills. She did not want to go home. Calling it that was silly. She bounced her rucksack on her back, screwed hands into fists in linty pockets and turned into Lyham Road now. Its early-evening emptiness was peaceful rather than eerie. Clever cats dipped their backs to get beneath parked cars. Behind hedges, through windows much smaller than the Otuos', TVs lit the faces of watchers. Little, blue-haired old ladies. Quiet mums. Serious dads. She wondered how many of those families had homosexual lesbians in them. She guessed none, explaining why their front rooms seemed calm, still. She wanted to knock on a door, any door and ask if she could stay. They would close it on her. That would be right.

She waited at a crossing, alongside three schoolboys whose hair was shaped into wet peaks. The boys burst into sudden laughter. Her shock set them off cackling even more.

26

Though Amma's over-annotated copy of *No Logo* might have protested, Starbucks on Northcote Road was the place chosen for them to meet: an easy 295 from the florist in Parsons Green where Roisin was working and far enough from Brixton to avoid bumping into Mum, Belinda or anyone else. As Amma queued for coffee, she again found crediting Belinda's nastiness difficult. The image of Belinda's turned back after the fireworks was the most inhumane part of it all; a tense, humped thing seen through hot tears. How could they speak after that?

Fixing on the now, Amma flourished a twenty, requested and paid for her second soya latte. She concentrated on things like cutting the wooden stirrer through froth and opening the sugar packet. And then the difficulties of the present came again: that this meeting had been repeatedly postponed by a series of Roisin's laconic texts. And even on this, the date they had firmlyfirmly-firmly agreed on, a good week and a half after first contact, Roisin was late and Amma had been waiting, like a twat, for twenty-five minutes. What was she expecting to come of their little rendezvous? What could she expect? The mood was not eased by the two Brazilian or Portuguese baristas behind the counter who kept singing that Moloko song, making up the lyrics they couldn't quite remember.

Sinking into a leather sofa, Amma smiled at a nearby woman in a primrose twinset who assessed her too intently. Had all the careful amendments to her school uniform been excessive? Was the

kohl on the eyes artlessly smudged? Were the rips in her tights too
salacious?

'Fidgety knickers. Like a Pina Bausch.' Roisin's voice came from
the corner of the café, accompanied by a snatch of busy, outside
sounds: sighing buses, pleading homeless. Roisin's face was flushed
and her irises still that wet shade of slate. There was a force in those
eyes, or perhaps a new maturity. Amma rested the mug against her
teeth and breathed not only through steam but also through the
sensation that the situation was already far beyond her control.

'I've been watching you from the other side of the road for
about three minutes. Shuffling away and all neurotic with your
precious little hands.'

'Are they little?'

'They're smaller than mine. See.' Amma let Roisin's warm palm
press against her damper one. She was immediately regretful
about the giggled, giddy sound she produced. The larger white
hand withdrew and Amma watched the redhead chew her lips and
deliberate.

'What?'

'I'm not sure, Amma. I'm not.'

'Of what? What?'

'I can't tell what you're feeling, thinking any more.'

'Forgive me, like, if I speak out of turn, but that may be a fucking consequence –'

'So we can't begin more lightly? Like, I was going to start with
how much I'm loving this gap-yearing-working shit. We had this
nightmare lady come into the florist, in furs and making demands
all over the place, and I got her to buy the most expensive, beautiful peonies. Fat, rough-looking things – sort of like bloated drunk
old men, but also totally pretty –'

'Roisin – I was really sad to not, not have you around any more.
For you to just disappear like that. So sad, fucking sad, Roisin.
And, and, like, what could I do?'

'I needed … not distance, that's too trite, let's try … a chance …
to puzzle through it all, without, without –'

'Me?'

'Because that's exactly how it seemed; in my head, a jigsaw. All
these fragmented bits that were obviously interconnected but with
a logic entirely escaping me. So I needed to figure out how to get
them, get them all together. Or something. Oh, fuck this.'

'OK. And, you've done that now, have you? Puzzled through?'

'Like, let me load myself up, and then I'll be back, mm? You're
all right for drinks, yes?'

'Yeah. Thanks.'

'And I can't tempt you to a little pastry deliciousness? Their
friands are often actually quite home-madey and tasty.' Roisin
took off her coat, revealed a green apron stamped with a cheery
sunflower.

'No, but. Come back quickly.' Amma reached for that hand
again and clutched it. Roisin smiled a small smile. The twinset
lady, however, winced.

Roisin turned away, counted coins, pointed at something puffed
and crowned with walnuts. Moments like these struck Amma the
hardest: how to behave with someone who you'd loved, had sex
with, when you were back in the world? That had happened every
night at Brunswick: Roisin's honest pressure against the shyest part
of Amma. Then the shift, when all of Roisin's actions softened –
flick of wrist, circling of thumb, adjustment of tongue. It seemed
so full of planning, but also invented on the spot. Now how could
their discussion be so ordinary? Friands, peonies … the weather,
what was on each other's fucking Christmas lists, useless chit-chat
amongst all the yummy mummies and freelancers. They could do
much more than that.

With a dead grin, one of the baristas wiped the table and
collected empties. Amma lifted her mug. She wanted to remind
the girl walking back towards her how her black body shivered

and sweated and changed each time they had said goodnight that week, before they curled into their separate beds. But she also knew that was redundant now. That nightly separation was to be turned into a longer, more final one. Everything was unjust.

'It's good to see you.' Roisin sat, patted her piled gloves and ursine hat.

'And you. You too.'

'I should give you the explanation you deserve.' Roisin used her own wooden stirrer to slice a layer of cream from her mocha then dropped the mess onto a white serviette to ooze. 'I got quite panicked. You, really panicked me.'

'How? I never meant to. I'd never mean for you to feel anything like that, Roisin.'

'It paralysed me. Like, you wanting to see me all the time?'

'But,' Amma needed to go slowly, 'but weren't we both, like, phew! At least we live in the same city so, like, we could almost keep going, keep … being how we'd been? You were fucking crying when we left Brunswick. Cry-ing, Roisin. And you had that silly line: London is a tiny place and we will make it even smaller.'

'I did, didn't I?'

'Yes, Roisin.'

'I think it's different now, though. Isn't it? You see that too.'

Amma's jaw was heavy. She was supposed to be clever. Yet there she sat, eyeing the grim remnants of an overpriced drink, tripped up by her own longing.

She inhaled as Roisin started up. 'Don't do that.'

'Not doing anything.'

'You're being all sweet, and perfect, and lovely.'

'Thank you.'

'It's a problem, not a compliment.'

'Right.'

Amma wondered how an exit might be conducted with dignity; mightn't come across as melodramatic flouncing. She stroked the mug's iconic logo like it were a talisman. She could only produce childish words, 'This is a horrid, horrid way to be dumped.'

'I don't like to think of myself as dumping, as a dumper. "Dumper" suggests powerful, implies a power. I lack that. I'm … stumbling around and hoping for the best.'

'Best for who?'

'Yes. Best for me. All right, for me. Because I'm young, I'm eighteen. So. So, I had an amazing time at Brunswick with you. That is true. Totally.' Roisin scratched her head too much: a bad soap actor playing mad. 'You're too beautiful. And so special. But really, truly, I think I liked it because it was only this … only meant to be this short and fiery and ephemeral thing. A supernova sort of moment. Blinding.'

'Blinding?'

'Maybe I didn't see straight for a while.' Roisin giggled. 'If you'll excuse the terrible pun.'

'But we planned so much. A trip to go and see those curtains at the Geffrye Museum you said were too gorgeous to believe. And going to your parents' flat in Pigalle. And that pub on the river with the burlesquey men. All of that. Look, I had no clue what it was either, but I was certainly under the impression that we were at the beginning of something. That was so exciting and we couldn't have been closer, Roisin.'

'I can't force myself to mirror your heart. I'm sorry for that.'

'But *you said*.'

'I say a lot. So do you. That's the problem with being pretentious.'

'Not pretend for me. And now I sort of feel stuck. Because I'm really into this?' Amma wished she could be less honest. 'Fuck!'

'Amma, listen. I want to do everything. All of it. Life is full of thrills for us. Surely we only limit our bigger selves by fixating on a silly Sapphic … holiday romance.'

'And you were worried about being trite before?' The air around Amma seemed hot and hostile. The primrose twinset lady did not know where to put her eyes.

'It was an experience. A totally amazing experience.'

'Why did you even bother to get in touch with me? It had been months: why not maintain the silence? Would've been easier, surely?'

'I realised that wasn't fair. I realised that.'

'Wait.' In a frenzy, Amma rummaged in her rucksack. 'This is fucking ridiculous – where is it?'

After wrestling with folders and crumpled papers, she pulled out a bracelet. Jangling from it: a pair of little charms, 'A' and 'R' tiles from the Scrabble game they had played the second day they had known each other, when Roisin had saluted the board and wolf-whistled Amma's match-winning 'Faqir'.

'I did this for you. Doesn't look like it, but it was really fiddly. And I spent ages choosing the right shade for the thread because I wanted to get something that went with your hair and your eyes as well. And a colour I was sure you'd like. So.' Amma dropped it on the table. 'But it's nothing that you need to keep. I just thought I'd show it to you before I threw it away or whatever.'

Amma pressed the empty mug. She let Roisin's precise features crunch through a series of useless emotions, none of which ever made the girl's face ugly.

WINTER

27

'*Adjei!* How these people carry on! They've, they've not even let November properly finish before putting on this holly and this ivy everywhere. Don't you think is too much? Amma? Eh?'

Belinda did her best to show interest in Nana's question about Waitrose's glittery Christmas decorations because Amma was examining her shredded cuffs. Belinda's attempt was insufficient: Nana kissed her teeth.

'In a normal sense I would give you one shopping list with all the items on it and you can both do it together. But since you're still pretending each other are strangers, I can't even bring myself to be bothered.' Nana tore the sheet of paper she held in two. 'So you have that, and you that.' Belinda took, then watched Amma ignore her slip. 'I recognise the lady working Till 23. That is where we will meet. She is a very good Akuapem girl and it will be nice to greet her. Since no one else is talking to me around here. I see you in fifteen minutes.'

Wafting her Kente scarf, Nana looked Belinda up then down. With her stubby French plait pointing as high as it could, Nana pushed away her trolley, a warrior ready for battle. In the weeks since the fireworks, Belinda had become excellent at ignoring that look, declining the possibility it was meant for her and sending away the nausea it brought by pressing her thumbs together. Releasing her thumbs now, she spoke to Amma.

'Shall we go then?'

'Suppose. I'm on bathroom stuff. So.'

'Yes. Yes, I will see you.' Belinda clicked her heels, keen for Amma to move forward first, and to avoid accidental bumping into one another. They must not touch. Something about Belinda's hesitation annoyed Amma, who swore under her breath. Belinda picked up a wire basket and squeezed its thin handle.

Belinda was annoyed that everyone was so cross with her. A trip to the supermarket was usually a treat. Mary thought so too. In Kumasi, they were often sent to A-Life! in Adum when extra provisions were needed if guests came for long weekends. In the *tro tro* on the way to the store, there was only one way Belinda could control Mary's mad anticipation about steering the trolley around the aisles: Belinda had to face Mary head on and declare:

'Let's Freeze-Out – Three. Two. One. And we go … now!'

Starting the game, Belinda would stare at Mary without blinking. Well practised at this, Mary stared back; showing Belinda the kind of determination she called on when carrying bolts of Aunty's *ankara* that, at first, seemed too much for her skinny arms. As the *tro tro* hit pothole after pothole, Belinda would continue even through the prickling at the corners of her eyes, and as the image of the tensed child opposite her wobbled. Eventually Mary had to flap and gasp and shout 'Pax! Pax! Pax!' and the two would do battle again and again until the driver announced that they had reached the shop.

Sweaty A-Life! – with its grey meat and crispy-haired cashiers – was not in the same league as gently lit, fragrant Waitrose Balham. Waitrose Balham was a place of many small wonders. Taking a long route, Belinda dawdled by Fruit and Veg. Curiosity on every shelf. The sound of names: pom-egran-ates, ki-wis, passion-fruits. And elsewhere: cho-ri-zo, hal-lou-mi, San-ce-rre. What of those? What could you do with those? In fact, Sancerre was in her favourite part of the store, the bit with the alcohols. Though it was a clearly sinful section, its green-red glow was

magical. Mary would agree. Remembering her old friend so much
was dizzying. Perhaps she hadn't done the thumb thing properly.
She stopped by the coolness of Dairy. She had saved three soaking
saucepans at home, and they might return in time for *Fame
Academy*, something nice to fix on and look forward to. That
helped. She started up again, swinging her basket like a girl in a
fairytale woodland. She hummed a tune, overemphasising the
notes she strung together. She didn't mind if those around –
red-faced men with enormous eyebrows; a group of little, harassed
women who seemed Chinese, but not quite – were keen to avoid
her. She was busy singing a happy song and marvelling at all the
different types of tea towels.

She liked how politely the smart staff – most about the same age
as her and Amma – spoke to one another. It was not a problem
that most of the workers here were black and most of the customers not, because Belinda was quite envious of anyone with a job at
Waitrose Balham. An amazing honour. She might even stop to ask
one of the chatting shop girls opposite what their discussion was
about. They had good nails, neat teeth, small sparkles pinned to
ears. The two prettier ones wore small crucifixes that Belinda
believed, not like Monique's. She might see if she could join in
with these potential new friends, perhaps she could talk to them
about her latest essay, returned that afternoon – a mark away from
an A*, and on difficult *Lord of the Flies* as well. She hadn't been
able to tell Amma that good news; Amma would have turned the
story into one about herself somehow. Those gossiping girls,
Belinda knew, wouldn't do that. Then the smallest one caught her
watching. The others noticed too. They giggled, patted each other
and returned to touching products with clunky guns. Belinda
searched Canned Veg, embarrassment making it hard to find the
black-eyed peas.

The overhead speaker tried to give its message but the crackles
won. At the far end of the aisle, she noticed other, more serious

members of staff. Their arms were crossed and one man kept tapping his shiny shoe. Their attention focused on a black man dressed like a police officer. This black man was at least three heads taller and spoke into a dark radio. Belinda listened to him shout numbers and mention 'distress' which seemed a strange word for such calm surroundings. But they were becoming less calm. Excited customers streamed down the aisle and then to the left. Belinda followed them. She heard Nana before seeing her.

'Amma Danquah Otuo. Amma. Danquah. Otuo. Stand from there.' In the section with the detergents, Belinda and an audience of perhaps twenty found a black girl in black clothes with scrappy braids sitting amongst and trailing her hands through mess.

'Stand.'

Someone – and it was clear to Belinda and probably everyone else, who – had turned the aisle upside down. Like a crazy Art class. Piles and puddles of white, blue, pink, peach. Lenor, Daz, Bold, Comfort, Persil spoiling the floor. Torn packaging and empty bottles everywhere. Each time Nana yanked Amma, Amma said no. Belinda stepped towards the struggling two. Nana's arms stopped fighting and changed, openly begging. While the watching white women muttered away, the big black man persuaded Amma with a voice that moved towards shouting. Then Amma picked up a nearby bottle of Toilet Duck and skidded it at Belinda. The bottle slid through a splash of green liquid and Belinda stopped it with the side of her ballet pump like the football-playing boys in the village when they paused their game to let her walk across the pitch, whispering as soon as she had passed. Belinda bent to collect it, found the space where it was meant to go and pressed it into place before turning back to the emptiness of Amma's stare. Amma's cool look made Belinda tilt her head as if she were about to softly ask a question. Then Amma got to her feet, brushed off her top, punched the air and flopped onto Nana.

From that slumped position, Amma trembled. Belinda thought it was right to do that. It was a struggle in the body, a fight against a tough demon. That was what happened before the pastor came to strike the forehead with the Bible, knock the beast out and bring stillness. Nana looked at Belinda in complete confusion and petted Amma's back. Belinda wanted to hum her tune again. The crowds dispersed and went back to the safe order of their tiny squares of papers: Milk, Bread, Cheese, Apples, Tea.

'I will pay for all these damages,' Nana splurted. 'You only give me a number. Me and my husband we will pay, don't worry for that one.'

The big black man cleared his throat to show his importance. 'Madam, it's not as simple –'

'What else do you need but cash money –'

He bowed, stepped back and Belinda studied how Nana now held her daughter's head. With thoughtful fingertips, Nana grazed the fluffy beginnings of Amma's sideburns and traced the pretty bulge of the lower lip. Belinda was surprised that Amma let her, as if Amma had waited for this to happen, or needed it. Perhaps if Mother had touched Belinda as tenderly, instead of giving her softest touches away to strangers. Maybe then Belinda might have known how and what to feel as she saw those two sad people doing their best to be close with one another. Belinda heard Nana talk to her daughter in a way she couldn't have learnt in any village.

'Amma, what is this? A mental sickness?'

'I want to go home.'

'Darling. Darling. When I'm coming here to see you, and what you up to – you looked as if … you want to destroy yourself. Please. I thought it was … better. I.'

'I don't know what's happening.'

'It was like … you having out-of-body experience. Smashing this Waitrose. What has it ever done to – Amma!'

Belinda felt air rush. Not worried about slipping or sliding or knocking into already disturbed strangers, Amma ran, kicking her legs up and sending her loose laces wild.

28

The next night, in the small hours, Belinda stopped in front of the kitchen's longest window and the moody moon it showed. She dragged the mop again. It drooled over the tiles as it had for the last twenty minutes. She returned it to the bucket and swiped her forehead with knuckles like a labourer. The dishwasher ticked, a red timer winked a change in minutes, and a tear came from her eye. It might have been best to stop then as it rolled out, but it was the loveliest of feelings as the second tear rose: a rushing, like Mary sprinting for leftover meat bones. She didn't want to think about Mary. She shivered, sniffed the third and fourth ones back. The mop slid in the bucket to an angle it found natural.

She shuffled up the stairs, the usual radio-murmur from Amma's door guiding her. Amma sat cross-legged on her bed with a book. In her pink pyjamas, with hair pouring down a shoulder she had an innocence that calmed Belinda. The gesture Belinda wanted to make to her seemed possible, if it were to a girl as gentle as that.

'You?' Amma tucked the book beneath her pillow.

'We need to start somewhere. To get back on the track. I suggest this.'

'Be.'

'Justcome. Justcome. And now.' Belinda's neck did not show the weakness of turning to check if instruction had been carried out. Amma followed, whispering her confusion as they picked down the flights. 'Shh – I only tell you that I want you to help.' Belinda hissed into darkness near the living room as they crept on. 'Is not big. Is not much.'

'I'll – I'll do what I can.'

'I think I need to not be by myself, OK? Is that clear? That's all.'

'Are you all right, Be?' Amma clicked the kitchen's light switch. Black, white, silver. 'Oooh, it's chilly.'

'Now the central heater won't wake up until six. I want you to wipe the front of the fridge. You need take the alphabet magnets off first, of course. I will take care of the surfaces and some other things.'

'It's, like, way way after midnight and I've got – we've got. What?'

'This helps me. I do it often. And it may you, also.'

'Be, this is like some fucking slave labour shit. It's out-rage-ous. Has Mum got you doing this? Or, or was it Dad? Did Dad make you? Is this you, like, paying your way? Like the level of exploitation is un–'

'I choose to do it. I say I choose. It helps me and may do good for you too.'

Amma sniffed. 'I doubt domestic chores will work, love.'

'Have you tried?' Belinda waited as Amma picked the skin between finger and thumb. 'And, also, I am not your love. I don't ask for you to, like, call me words of that kind, please.'

'So this is how it's going to be now. Fucking fabulous.'

'Take the magnets off. Careful on the floor as I will be attending on it again, so it will become slippy.'

Amma plucked lower case letters. The circling of the sponge on the granite tired Belinda.

'You think cleaning will magic it away, Mum thinks it's therapy that'll do the trick. To deal with my … what did she call it … my rages and madness and strong emotions. Therapy! What marvellous ideas you all have.'

'I'm sorry?' Belinda pressed into the sponge.

'What did she call it this morning … the most ridic phrase …
yeah, "getting a white help". As if.'

'What is that?'

'Professional help, dearest. Medical. Head Doctor. Like, I'm
totally interested in the workings of the mind, all of that, and like,
gushing to paid ears is probably excellent, if you're properly
damaged or whatever … and there was this girl from JAGs and it
helped her to stop cutting herself, but I'm not like that. Oh, and
plus they love shoving tablets down your throat, and like tablets
are a definite no-no. They use those things to control black
women.'

'Maybe I like it better when we are silent.'

'Ha.'

Though there was no real need, Belinda abandoned the sponge
and searched for another cloth. 'You should perhaps also throw
out the rotten courgette in the bottom drawer of the fridge. There
are one or two to get rid of. Sorry for the smell.'

But Belinda had more, made Amma jump. 'Was it nice, yesterday? Did you like what you did and what you caused?'

'That's all rather convenient, isn't it? Palm it off onto me and
then you needn't think about it, or your own shit, any more.
Blissful blissful blissful pretendy.'

'And your meaning is what?'

'My meaning is … my meaning is. Fuck it. Pass me some of that
fucking spray … please.'

For a time, nothing but the squeak of chamois and the hiss of
Cif. Belinda liked the gentle strain stretching and disappearing
along her arms as she worked.

'I only feel you need to watch your behaviour, Amma. I'm a
good friend to suggest it.'

Amma pinned Belinda with a bloodshot stare and pointed with
a shaking finger. 'My behaviour isn't your real worry though, is it?
Your worry is what I'm like, Be. It's, it's *what* I like.'

'However you want to put it is however. Look, listen, with, with this your … sad problem …'

'Christ.'

'You have a great power to leave your own mum the most unhappy person I can imagine. And all for the sake that you want to say your foolish words about girls. Why? If it was my daughter I might even collapse. Would you like that?'

'You're nearly funny.'

'There are no jokes. We can joke no longer. Because of you.'

'Your whole perspective –'

'Keep your voice down.'

'Your whole perspective about this is, like, blame-centric. Unbelievably blame-centric. I haven't actually done anything. I'm trying to figure –'

'I don't need to be arguing. I try to help by telling what is true: whatever this you have done or want to do with a girl is no natural thing. Is not. Is wrong. End of the line. If you have any common sense in the head, you better come to learn how to sit on it and shut it down, not go to make a show of everyone and yourself.' Belinda snapped the cloth and sighed. 'Is part of the adult life, Amma – why cannot anyone else see? You don't always get to be the thing that you want or think you deserve, or whatever. You don't, and you have to live with it and move on.'

Amma stepped forward in her piglet slippers; their softness was the only thing reassuring Belinda that Amma would not hit her. 'I probably loved her. She is an absolute twat and she's gone and I loved her. Love. Do you understand what love is? Stupid fucking question. Stupid. Fucking. Question.'

Belinda straightened her back and walked to the sink to wring the dirty rag in the basin. Grey dribbled into the plug hole.

'Be? Sorry. That was harsh,' Amma puffed. 'Be?'

Belinda thought of the boys in Adurubaa, the ones who messed around on the steeper dirt road. Up high, they played with brittle trucks pieced together from sardine tins and bits of tyre. When an unwise push sent one of those battered trucks too far and too fast, there was no immediate panic. They let the toy whizz down, bouncing all the long way until it reached the dip at the bottom and crashed or rolled into stillness there. Then they scurried to check the damage and remake. They never stopped it in the middle of its run.

29

Four lethargic days at school. Momentary intrigue came in the form of a sticky rumour that Millie Lyons from 13S had been off for so long because she was actually pregnant with Mr Lowell's baby. As inconceivable as the tale might have been, Helena set about informing everyone excitedly. Amma did not assist. Evenings at home were no better. Amma returned to spending hours in her garret, the stacked books on the floor joined by more gritty cafetières and smeared saucers. In that festering cage she listened to a lot of Skunk Anansie, annoying herself with the intensity of her need for a role model.

On the Friday morning, Amma swept out of the front door into an inky winter dawn with an impassive face. The air carried the smell that Nana always said meant rain would come soon, and she braced herself against the icy blasts and the lingering shame at how she had spoken to Belinda in the kitchen the other night. Instead of going towards Railton, Amma turned onto Dulwich Road. She went past the tumbledown Regency villas and the long wooden benches outside the Prince Regent, turned upside down until the evening. She picked up her pace by the unloved lawns fronting the Meath Estate. As Herne Hill approached, she tried to remember the last time she had bunked lessons. The guilt that it would waste Dad's hard-earned, immigrant-thriving-against-the-odds cash usually suppressed her desire to truant. On that particular morning she couldn't be bothered to feel empathy for a man so rarely around.

At the train station, she stepped onto the Thameslink along with harassed commuters. Nudging through the packed carriage, she went into the tiny toilet. In the cramped space, she stripped off her uniform and pulled her charcoal Elastica T-shirt, black denim jacket, black Levis and trainers from her rucksack. She changed and checked her hair in the savaged mirror opposite; let her braids fall wherever. She stuffed everything into the bag and returned to the carriage. In the crush, Amma found herself stuck between the turned back of a thin man and the twisted front of a woman in Lycra, fresh from the gym. The train lumbered through south-east London. Amma craned her neck and saw outside, in the gaps between other uncomfortable passengers, lampposts festooned with dormant Christmas lights, wily pigeons, bloated graffiti; the watermelon brightness of the Elephant and Castle then concrete severity rising around them again. Amma enjoyed the feeling of being effortlessly suspended between the two bodies, as well as the woman's tart sweat and the pressure of the woman's stomach against her side. Amma heard her heart accelerate and pressed her lips together. It had often been like that – with Helena, Roisin, all the termly crushes in between – initially exciting to think that her attraction was so powerful and delicious that it could not leave her body and enter the world either as language or action, because its force was so strong and otherworldly that it might make anything happen. That kind of self-silencing, all electric feeling, made Belinda's advice to keep shtum seem a little bit sexier. The woman's warm breast pressed into her, and Amma's shoulder contracted as the river rolled into view. Wasn't it as dangerous to keep something so strong locked in? It could eat from the inside out. The real fear came again as the train stopped between stations and waited in darkness. Even if Amma managed to find some other person 'like' her, to be with and to touch, she could only imagine it being just the two of them; alone, protecting one another by distancing themselves from the harshness of other people. But hidden away from the real world like that, love would become pretend, something false, turned inside out and not itself. The train started up again, its rocking inconsistent. All the strangers in the carriage became uniform as they swayed together, stumbled together, froze.

She walked out of Blackfriars Station. On the streets, vast glass windows repeated the vast glass windows opposite. Shops' shutters were snapped up. Traffic stagnated. Her phone buzzed with a message from Helena: a demand to know her whereabouts, full of hysterical exclamation marks. Amma's Converse scurried until she reached the Tate and the Turbine Hall. There, she looked up into echoing, gloomy nothing. A yelped instruction surprised her, rising high over the spiked chatter of schoolkids. Amma moved on, avoiding collisions with bleary tourists too fixated on maps. She felt like she was in a film and her solitude needed underscoring, as annoying couples appeared around her, kissing with a sensuality too intense for half past nine in the morning. She waited by the lift for a few minutes, stabbing at the button, but nothing magicked it up. She trudged up the stairs instead.

On Level 4, three chatty American women were standing by the installation. Each of them wore a differently coloured version of the same shawl. They discussed what they saw in whispers, putting on and taking off reading glasses to check it and the impenetrable curatorial notes. Amma waited, turning her phone onto vibrate and feigning interest in the other exhibits. That shuffling eagerness and perhaps her unexpected blackness in that whitest of white spaces, eventually startled the women into awkward apologies. They receded so she could take their place.

There were three other Calders around the building, but this, *Antennae with Red and Blue Dots*, was the one for her. She took five steps back from where it hung, accidentally thudding into businessmen behind her. She returned her concentration to the floating being, its wiry black limbs and elegant pops of colour, the forms dominating its centre. Shields. Or scales. Or shadows. Amma unzipped her rucksack, threw a Cherry Drop into her mouth, sucked and crunched. She hated to pin it down to anything specific, but possibly the clarity, the quietness of the great eagle-wing of a thing above, was what pleased her so much. The sculpture kept on wavering. Amma heard the attendant in the corner fiddling with the aerial of a walkie-talkie. She wondered what Belinda would make of the Calder, and the questions she would ask about it. Even if Belinda's instinctive response was a critical one, that wouldn't stop her trying to get to the bottom of its oddness by asking and asking, testing one possibility and then the next.

Amma gave herself another gluey Cherry Drop, and sat on a bench next to two men in raincoats doing slow and inaccurate sketches. The attendant leapt up and scolded one of the business-men for taking photos. A beaming, perhaps six-year-old girl, in a cute combo of Argyle vest, white shirt, festive bow tie and green corduroys entered the room, pushed in a wheelchair by a turbaned man. Amma watched the two of them assess the Calder dispas-sionately. The sculpture eddied and turned in the breeze. The girl applauded the motion. Again, the attendant twitched, then sat back on his stool. It might have been that or the memory of stand-ing on the balcony at the Ritzy with Belinda, or a deepening, deep-ening boredom with herself that made Amma get her phone out from her pocket. The girl applauded the shifting Calder again as Amma scrolled through her Contacts.

Belinda wanted to start that Friday morning, the morning of her last mock exam, simply. Kippers – for brain power – bread and milky tea – to soothe after more bad sleeping. Since it was an important day, Belinda would use a matching cup and saucer from the 'olden days' set, the ones covered with the dark blue drawings of houses, trees and ships. Her revision flashcards would be spread over the table. Between bites of food she would glance over at those notes and be reassured by the sight of her own big handwriting. After eating, she would double-check the contents of her satchel, particularly the number of ink cartridges. Then make sure her black trousers were ironed well, her collar straight and her new Mary Jane shoes unscuffed. The walk to Abacus would be for last-minute running over memorised quotations and definitions of key literary terms which Mrs Al-Kawthari had drilled and drilled into them.

After Amma had slammed the door without a word, Nana's interruption of Belinda's planned breakfast – Nana's tapping of Belinda's behind with a rolled-up *Daily Mail*, insisting she drive Belinda a clever shortcut, demanding Belinda had better hurry because she wanted to leave in three – set Belinda's fingers racing. Her satchel's buckles felt slippery. The bobbly coating of Sure on her armpits failed. In the Fiat, Belinda fixed on the windscreen and its spots, counting and recounting the six buttons running the length of her fitted white shirt. She started going over the best examples of pathetic fallacy in *Macbeth*, but at Brixton Water Lane had to stop, because Nana was shouting at a cyclist who had appeared from nowhere. Belinda flexed her knuckles.

'Nerves?' Nana's laugh didn't believe itself. Belinda's knuckles kept on. Peaking. Flattening. 'Girl, you going to be amazing today, trust me.' Nana adjusted the mirror, adjusted her lizard brooch, adjusted the mirror.

'Thank you.'

'From one village girl to the next, that's my advice to you. Chill-ax.' The laugh again, this time more like a man's.

Belinda reached forward. 'Shall I play the radio, Nana? You, you sometimes like to listen to that Irish man who is on now. Let me find him.'

'No. I want to talk.' The sentence was flat. Belinda pinned her shoulders back.

'That is fine. Like, like good chatting will help me calm before my big test. You are probably right. Nice idea.'

'Yes. Yes. Yes.'

They turned onto Tulse Hill. The light outside went between yolky and dirty. Belinda wished they could open the windows to get the safe, fresh smell of the dry cleaner's they passed. A tiny Nigerian woman with a huge yellow headdress dragged her checked trolley over the zebra crossing. Belinda felt guilty at wanting to roll her eyes at how slow the elder was, about how much time she was taking to signal thanks to Nana, raising her walking stick. Nana was patient and still, bending her red lips into a gentle smile at the elder. Other drivers honked. The woman jumped and sped up. Amma would have been rude about it all.

The car jerked and swung past the massive Allied Carpets and its zigzagged signs shouting prices on the windows. Driving away from the main road, Nana sniffed and cleared her throat. Belinda moved her damp bottom, her sanitary towel feeling three times its real size. The windscreen wipers began to deal with the arriving rain.

They were finally on Streatham High Road. At least she could watch the stationery shop, the Greggs, the Superdrug, the Lidl, the Boots, the newsagent's, the one with pictures of houses in the window, the one with the dead furniture on the pavement, the one for the Turkish, the one for the Polish, the one for the Somalis; at least they all meant she could jump out soon.

Nana clutched the wheel and her pearl bracelet swung as her lips tried out different shapes. Belinda didn't want Nana to speak but nothing was ever as Belinda wanted. 'Eighteen years. Before she came. Imagine what I had to. What I endure in that time. What people were thinking about me for nearly two decades? Rotten womb. Evil. Twenty years of feeling, of almost feeling like, like my life was only standing on the edge of a circle. And even a light skin as this can't save from so much whispering, whispering,

whispering.' Belinda saw a tear. 'I can't have my girl forced to stand outside like I had to. Eh? My Amma cannot. This way she is. This thing she has, this thing making her do public scenes to, to shame us and – No one will be able to protect her from – In our culture, we –' Nana shook her head and drove them away from roadworks.

'Belinda?' They were pulling over on the corner beside Abacus.

'Do Otuos only know the pronoun "I"? There are several others. You are all stuck on one. Constantly. All this of myself, myself. For one tiny blink of second, have you even had a thought to, like, ask me of my feelings?' Belinda pushed the knuckles of her right hand into the palm of her left. 'You know how is been for me having to deal with all of her nonsense and speaking whatever rubbish comes to her mind and her constantly changing and … whatever! Eh? You even know what I've had to put up with from her, how I keep trying to make it better and is just getting worse? Eh? You even considering for a moment that is all giving me pains and maybe I'm hurting and you could think on me for a second? Eh?'

'*Maame?*'

Belinda opened the glove compartment, took out the Kleenex and threw them at Nana.

'You should blow your nose. You have some mucus on you. Is not nice.'

'What kind of behaviour or voice is this for you to use? Belinda? *Wo yare?*'

Belinda undid her seatbelt. She tossed her satchel across her body. She met and held Nana's gaze. Nana's chest rose and her mouth kept opening and then closing like fresh tilapia in the market. Then Belinda saw that, on Nana's lap where it rested, Nana's phone was brightening, vibrating and doing its ringtone. 'Walking on Sunshine'. The screen said that the caller was Doctor.

30

Later, letting herself into the house, Amma stopped in the doorway to perform an inexpert can-can routine. Rucksack slumped at her side, she kicked out, over and over again. She jiggled her foot, flapping the skirt she had hastily put back on during the train journey home, then kicked more in an effort to get rid of the tenacious leaf stuck to the sole of her shoe. Taking a momentary break from her demanding task, Amma looked up and saw her mother at the end of the hallway.

'Fucking Jesus! Mum!'

'Shh. Not so loud, eh.'

After the shock had cooled, Amma noticed Nana's inertia, the strictness of her posture and neutrality of her expression. No briskly brushed colour on her cheeks. Nothing glimmered over her lips. She was handsome, frightening. Amma felt herself frown.

'Fuck, Mum. My heart fucking literally – Like, literally. Shit.'

'Keep. It. Down.'

'Mum, why are you wearing that?'

Like some prodigious magpie decided to perch on Nana's scalp, an enormous black headwrap topped her, rising in spikes and indulgent curves. Intimidating black rocks caught the light at her ears and throat. Beneath those, Nana's dress was a great, irides-cently black thing; puffing out at the shoulders, sneaking in at the waist, billowing over hips and thighs, sweeping the ankles. The fabric's embossed pattern of wavy black lines spread endlessly. Velvety black court shoes squeezed Nana's feet.

Amma's breathing and her heart fought one another. The ruck-sack began to weigh more but she could not or would not let it go completely. She swung her plaits, pushed her shoulders back and chest forward. Licking the salty, chapped skin on her lower lip, she spoke.

'Why are you wearing that, Mum?'

'Amma. Please. You have to come with me, please. I will tell upstairs, I promise you.'

'Where's Dad?'

'On his way. From work. He'll be here soon. Don't worry on that.'

Amma looked around her, redundantly. 'And Be? What about Be?'

'Safe and sound. She sleeps. She needed to. She will come to us soon, when she is ready enough.' Nana's voice flattened and softened more with every response. Amma didn't like it.

Nana reached her hand out. 'In meantime come with me first, eh? Upstairs. So when she wakes we can both be in customary fashion. It will be right for her to see, I think. To show our respect.' Nana took a step closer. 'I won't do you full in local attire like me, but maybe I can give you a wrapper skirt, like you had for *Ghanafoɔ*? Or something nice for the head. And you can add your own black T-shirt, or whatever. You like my design here, innit? I have some offcuts.'

Nana pointed at herself then extended her hand again. There was an unmistakable urgency in her eyes. The gravity of the costume and the weakness of the pleading had a discernible tug to them. Amma watched her own shaky hands releasing keys, coins and a buzzing phone onto the tiled side table.

'You're being totally creeps. Totally.'

'Maybe I am. But is a big news so you need to receive it slowly and calmly. All in good time.'

Amma nudged the rucksack away, walked down the corridor with measured steps and let Nana hold her close. Pressing against

each other, huddling into one another as though shielding themselves from unforgiving winds, they stayed that way as they
climbed the stairs, going past the photos lining the duck-egg blue
walls: the wedding, Dad's graduation, her own christening and
first day at school. Amma at prize-giving days wearing the ugliest
spectacles known to man. Amma, flaunting a flute. Amma, aged
twelve, immensely spotty, jutting out her hip and doing a peace
sign on Labadi Beach. Accomplishment and abandon glowed out
of each familiar image. On most days she walked by those awful
pictures without thought. Now they pushed her even more firmly
into the crook of Mum's arm until the landing appeared.

After unlacing herself from that grasp, in her parents' room,
Amma sat on the edge of the bed and waited, unable to ask
anything else. Nana complained about her ageing back and unre-
liable hips before hitching up her long dress. She got down on her
knees and unclicked the gaudy clasps of the silver trunk stowed
beneath the bay window. The trunk – the stuff of family folklore
– had held Mum's belongings when she first travelled from her
village to London in the seventies. Amma knew Mum now used it
for storing her most ornate traditional material; expensive fabric
bought either from innumerable trips to Peckham Market or – like
the freaky *akuaba* dolls – from trips 'back home'.

Amma peered into the opened chest as Nana dug deep and
unpacked cloth decorated with all manner of colours and shapes.
One with turquoise and gold pyramids was dismissed. Then more,
these covered with linear trees and parrots. Nana seemed particularly enamoured with a blue one, stamped with angular white
shapes like those mini-windmills kids get from fairs, but it was
thrown aside too. The colours of the cloth Mum pulled out became
much darker. Black. Brown. Black. Purple. Red with black. Black.
Black. Black. Mum stopped churning through the trunk with such
speed. When she found one with a pattern similar to the print on
her own outfit she stopped.

After scrabbling up to full height, she clutched the material then flopped it wildly. 'You see the repeating symbol here on this, eh?'

'Yeah.'

'We call it in our language *Nyame Nti*. N-ya-me N-ti. This is one of the easier Twi phrases, I think. It, it means something like you have to have a trust in God. That we should all put our faith in Him. To see us through all things, even when they so bad, even when they so painful. Yes.'

Amma did not tut, sigh, kiss her teeth.

'Now you go there to sit, please.'

Enjoying the simplicity of following direction, Amma moved and waited at Mum's dressing table.

'Fix your plaits into a bun so is easier for me.'

Nana stood behind her, holding out the fabric like some terrifying flag. Then, in a purposeful swoop, she brought the material around Amma's forehead, beginning a process of subduing and sculpting it into stiff waves and peaks. As she continued, tucking errant corners and disciplining looser parts, she explained to Amma what had happened in Ghana earlier that morning, the news Belinda had had to hear. Nana delivered the facts with evenness and resignation, until the fabric was sufficiently manipulated and eventually resembled the crown she herself sported. Amma nodded through it all, being sanguine, being sage, even though it made no sense whatsoever. At the end of the explanation, Mum patted her flourishing masterpiece. Amma slid the chair back. She got up and left the room, not really caring if Mum shouted or tried to stop her.

Amma knocked on Belinda's door, her fist beginning with fast bangs but soon losing its certainty. With no response, she turned the knob, its metal cold against her palm. In the stark, ostentatiously tidy room, Amma had expected to find her friend as a small and shivering thing, pulling itself apart, shrieking itself into hoarseness. Instead, Belinda was standing directly beneath the bulb, light gilding her thoughtful profile. With her beautiful head angled up, it seemed to Amma like Belinda was searching for something in the cornicing.

'Hi. I came to see if ... I wanted to see how you were and if you needed. Anything.'

Belinda turned, the rotation slow and deliberate, before pulling the scrappy hoodie hanging over her shoulders, drawing the stretched arms across her body. Then she seemed to notice Amma's headwrap. And Amma watched Belinda fight to smile: jerking her pinched mouth, working her cheeks. Belinda worked hard, harder until she showed all of her teeth and then eventually froze like that. The sight of such struggling, with all of its stupid, fierce dignity, made Amma's hot tears run and run and run.

31

Ghana – December

The taxi smelled of *Akpeteshie* and bubble-gum. Belinda shifted beneath the car's low, bashed ceiling. The spongy seats squeaked. Then the engine burped. Belinda flinched and the driver found it funny. Of course everyone would laugh at her: in the small mirror ahead she was a stiff brown puppet, done up in shiny black. A silly, frilly black collar at the neck. Black studs at the ears. Two black hairclips keeping picky braids in place. In the months over in London, had her face changed? That's how Aunty and Uncle might begin. *Aba!* So different! We can't even recognise you! Who is this one?!

The driver tapped his chewing stick on the dashboard. Taillights twinkled. In between the lanes of traffic, hawkers shouted in three languages; children and women in *oburoni wawu* balanced cellophaned bundles of Swan's matches, Imperial Leather, Wilkinson's razors on their heads. A boy in a large hessian sack with slits for arms and legs marched in front of ten men. In their dirty blue overalls, they chatted cheerily, carrying a huge log past honking *tro tros*. A scratching girl followed them. Umbrellas sprouted from every part of her: golf umbrellas, polka-dotted umbrellas, some black, some covered with bug-eyed Disney princesses, some with Chelsea FC logos, some longer than the girl's body itself.

Accra. Acc-ra. Before, simply hearing the city's pretty name used to do so much to Belinda's stomach. Aunty and Uncle returned to Daban from weekends away in the capital – she there on pleasure, he on business, they always said – with their receipts and tickets. If Mary wasn't distracted – by turning rice jars into musical instruments or straw brushes into a rowing husband and wife – she and Belinda arranged the different stubs of crinkled paper into categories, passing their fingers over the names of Accra's exotic districts and weird dialling codes. Belinda gulped three times but her throat still throbbed. The taxi made its way towards McCarthy Hills and its flashy malls catching the last of the fiery sunset. Flyovers looped and sleek guard dogs leapt. A strange kind of planet.

Mary had always been tiny, weighed little. So when the truck hit her, when she had run into the road and a truck hit her, she had floated high, trying to see the clouds better. In the sky, Mary had become an angel. God would cherish her. That is what Belinda heard Doctor explain as she held Nana's mobile close to her ear that Friday morning in the Fiat. But Doctor had not been there to see the accident for himself. And the sharp dreams Belinda had had every night for the two weeks since the news meant Doctor's nice words were difficult to believe. Belinda was sensible. Mary had come down, bounced off the bonnet and opened on the tarmac. Mary. Mary had been broken into tiny pieces. The tiny pieces could not be a whole. Mary was dead.

Mrs Al-Kawthari had been best with it and with her. The first time she returned to Abacus, a few days after finding out, Belinda had spent the whole lesson not focusing on Robert's interesting comments about the Coca-Cola adverts they were annotating. Mahdokt whispered to ask Belinda if she was 'all right' each time Mrs Al-Kawthari turned to write 'persuasive', 'bold' or 'colour' on the board. Are you all right? Are you all right? All because of the bags beneath and glassiness of her eyes. Are you all right? Are you all right? So desperate for a simple yes and light 'thank you for asking'. At some point, Belinda had become aware of the class leaving and of Mahdokt directing Mrs Al-Kawthari to her desk. To begin, Miss hadn't asked anything, only stared with a troubled expression and Belinda wondered how it cleverly managed to match her own insides. Then Miss had reached out for Belinda's wrists and held them through Belinda's slow explanation. The simple, steady tightness helped the words to feel more real. Miss had nodded, said sorry, sorry, sorry. Everyone was so sorry.

Now a motorcycle tore alongside the taxi. Its shirtless rider grinned as he rose up and moved his weight all the way forward, pushing out his elbows like a bird spreading its wings. He pressed the handlebars and then more roars and smoke came until fumes blackened everything. Belinda listened to the driver swear and complain until the darkness started to lift and the motorcyclist whizzed off, weaving between cars. Soon he became only a quiet rumble, a sound beneath the trembling within her. Belinda clenched.

She hated the trembling. It came whenever it liked, in little fits. Sometimes for minutes, often for longer. Even though her body was obviously weird and often wrong, it had never done anything quite like this before. The trembles had arrived about three days after she had first heard. When they started, and Nana and Amma had fussed and wrapped Belinda in all of the special Heals' throws and bought Peppermint Tea and spoke softly, the trembles still went on until the end of *Buffy*. They were like a shiver from the inside trying to get out. Or a dizziness with complete control of her. A bit like what happened when she thought she caught the scent of Mother's talc on the breeze; similar to when she hadn't eaten for a while or if she got out of the bath too quickly and needed to sit on the tub's edge for a minute, until her heart calmed. Belinda made her right hand into a fist and rolled it into her cupped left as the driver took the next turn.

When Belinda felt the quivering grow, as she did when the taxi swerved again so the little pot of coins on the dashboard spilled pesewas, she prayed. Behind pursed lips, she begged for the thing that in the past had helped her to burn ties, to dance freak-ons, to stand up to crazy Jamaicans on the 133. She twisted the fist in her palm. Because that thing – blessing or luck – had clearly forgotten her. She had no idea where it had come from in the first place, where it had gone to, how to get it back. She had no idea about anything. Traffic lights sent their loud green across her knees.

'Shall I play some of our local songs so you can remember our heritage and culture? Eh? Eh?' the driver offered. Belinda did not respond.

Bats carved overhead as she waited in the hotel courtyard, standing under a yellow moon and opposite five evenly spaced teak doors, each one lit with a single bulb and crowned with a striped awning. She remembered how fast night swept in here; how thickly dark nights could be. Pale stars pulsed. Something growled and wind passed through the orange trees' leaves, making a sound like light rain. Wood smoke from a nearby coal pot drifted around.

Eight hours to rest, then up early for the coach to Kumasi. A week until the funeral. A bitterness sharpened at the back of Belinda's mouth.

The porter arrived, bowing his square head. His name was Ade. Ade wore a very smart, white *batakari* and a sad face. When Ade bent towards her luggage, Belinda bent too.

'Stop that – it's OK – please. Is too much for Madam, at this time, and in the way that you are … and you must be bringing gift gifts gifts, from the UK for your poor relatives here – I come correct?'

'But –'

'Exact, then is too much, please.'

'I can manage, seriously, is fine – but thank you.' She scooped up handles, threw a strap over her shoulder. 'I can manage.' Weighed down, her walking across the gravel was lopsided.

'I pass through … here? Ade? Or here? How do you not, like, get lost all the time?!'

Over her soft panting she heard his sigh as he directed her through the foyer. Following a narrow corridor lined with more teak doors, her shoulders started to sting. Ade kept time with her and stopped himself from helping even when the holdall knocked against her side and something pointy in the bag jabbed her. Walking, still walking, she gasped and struggled and grunted.

Ade flashed a card, a box on the wall beeped and revealed a massive family room at least twice the size of Amma's. In it, everything was different shades of cream: the frothy carpet, the silky curtains flirting with the louvres, the trumpeting flowers in the vase. All for her? The Otuos had been too generous.

Ade did his best smile and spoke in the direction of the Samsonites. 'You strong like a female ox. Really. I think you must be one.' Belinda plucked off her earrings. Ade's gaze scanned the bed and the suitcases again and then Belinda remembered herself: where she was, what she was here, now. She presented him with a £10 note. He pretended surprise, took the tip and quickly left.

Belinda eased the zip at her back until the two panels of waxcloth peeled themselves away. Freed, she fell backwards onto the bed and bounced. Remembering again the noise she made in the Fiat after Doctor had had to say his news three times, she seized the bedsheets. It had been a big, pure shout. Loud enough to make her ears and hearing feel funny for a while. Nana had immediately copied her yell; her eyes wide, her mouth a perfect 'o', her tears fat and fast. And the two of them went on like that for a time, as if taking it in turns: one yelling and then the other, until Nana grasped Belinda's shoulders and Belinda wished the pressure would go on so she could sink, sink, sink. Minutes later, as Nana reversed the car, Belinda counted the days since she had last spoken to Mary. By the time they drove past the messy Hootenanny's pub, she had worked out that it had been five weeks.

Five whole weeks. Belinda sensed she would always think about the silence of those five whole weeks; might spend a lifetime trying to find forgiveness for it.

Belinda pulled the sheets again, breathed then let them go. She gathered up the black dress around her. Its embrace crunched.

32

'*A*goo? Madam, *me se agoo?*'

Belinda yawned and kissed her teeth, long and slow like Mother might have. She needed a second or two to work it out: the heat, the bedclothes smelling like no fabric conditioner she ever used, the murmured *Ga* on the other side of the louvres. Understanding and remembering more, Belinda loosened her nightscarf and looked up. She was disappointed by the blankness above. Outside, the *Ga* got angrier and water slapped against asphalt. Ade's knocking continued.

'*Me se agoo?* Is a morning call, from your London? You wouldn't like to take it?'

'*Amee. Me pa wo kyew.*' Belinda drew the covers around herself and Ade passed a cordless phone on a silver tray through the opened door. She reached over wearily.

'Be?'

'Amma.'

'Yeah. Hi. I. Wanted to check you'd arrived safely. Did you? You did. Obviously. Because I'm talking to you now. So.'

'Yes.'

'That's excellent.'

'OK.' The silence crackled. Belinda kicked up the sheets, then exposed and wriggled her toes.

'Is this, like, too early? I wanted to get in there quickly.'

'Get in where?'

'I don't know.'

'OK.'

'Good flight?'

'Was so so.'

'Manage to, manage to start that book I lent you? The Mansfield? They're brilliant little things, you know. And easy to whizz through. Not that you can't read longer things.'

'OK.'

'Just promise me you'll give them a go. Soon. Yeah?'

'Soon. Yeah. Soon.' Belinda passed her tongue over fuzzy teeth and slippery gums. Would continuing to repeat Amma's words pass for conversation? Belinda could just about do that. Sensing she wouldn't be offered such a gift, she sighed and nestled into the pillow behind her back.

'I'm … getting on with things. Over here in rainy Blighty. I got my final uni offer yesterday?'

'I suppose it's congratulations then. So congratulation.'

'I'm going for St Andrews. Probably.'

'The Scotland one, isn't it?'

'Yep. One of the northernmost unis in the fucking country. Somewhere far, far away where I can –'

'Can what?'

Belinda heard Amma doing something to the receiver – perhaps moving it awkwardly.

'And how about you?' Amma used a different tone now, 'Is being back … weird?'

'Is fine.'

'Not finding our groove today, are we? Our … flow.'

'No. No flow.'

Amma tutted. 'Be, look. This has all thrown me. If I'm honest. Sorry. I still can't. I seriously can't imagine your … grief?'

'Grief? Is that what you call it?'

Amma clucked. 'Look, shit probably seems so dark now because it is, but, I promise, the world turns.'

'Does it?'

'I think so. I'm certain, in fact.'

'OK then.'

Another long pause opened up and widened between them. Then Amma coughed. 'I'm, erm, seeing Kweku Yeboah tonight. For a drink? We've been texting? Quite a lot, actually. He's got wittier via SMS. And apparently he's on course for a First at Imperial. So.'

'Who?'

'Fair enough, I suppose that's a fair question: he was one of the dudes at *Ghanafoɔ*. With the jheri curl, remember? We're going to the Prince Regent.' Belinda could not think of a time when Amma had ever been this shy. 'Mum is pissing herself with excitement.'

'I thought.' Belinda's forehead hurt. 'Kweku as in a man Kweku? What of all this because you won't' – now she handled her receiver roughly – 'you don't choose boys? Then now why is one taking you for a candlelight dinner?'

'Aren't you relieved? Pleased? I mean, Be, what the fuck?'

'So this girls thing. Is coming like something you can turn it on and off like a switch? Now you want to turn it off? But this is not how you spoke of it before. You said –'

Amma sniffed. 'I have nobody. I'm just like, this fucking half-of-a-person skulking about with absolutely no one, no hint that it might, at some point, get a tiny bit better. I'm just me. I'm only me.'

Belinda scratched her chest and dry white lines appeared. She wanted to offer something soothing because Amma's voice stretched painfully.

'Amma –'

Belinda flicked the nightscarf against her forearm, a glossy black wave, rising and falling. She let it go, then watched it skid and ripple over her skin, dropping to the marble floor in a small heap. She frowned. The two of them – Amma, Mary – in their own, very different ways, in their different times and places, had made Belinda think and laugh so hard. And she knew helping Amma now with quick gentleness might be an easy show of thanks for that. She waited for the trembling to start.

'Fuck, Be. Sorry.'

'What for now?'

'I wanted it to be about you. I've fucked it, *como siempre*.'

'Is it Italian? I don't speak any Italian.'

'Tell me how you're doing.' Amma quietened. 'Please.'

'Amma.'

'Please. It's mental, Be. The whole thing. A child? A little child. It's not fair.'

'Maybe I was horrible,' Belinda said, as brooms grazed the courtyard, running *challewattes* smacked, more water splashed. 'All those months together – and nothing. I can't even remember if I ever knew her birthdate. I should have done it better. Been better to her.'

'For fuck's sake. Be nice to yourself, Belinda. For once in your life.'

Belinda pulled the sheets over her feet, pressed her ankles into each other.

'What you're going through, what God or Fate or chance or whatever has decided to put you through, is completely fucking horrendous. And what good comes of you, like, adding to the shittiness by beating yourself up and looking to make things even worse? Take the pressure off. Be? Fuck, I bet you're not even listening. Hello?'

'No, no I am. Is just. What you're telling me to do. I don't know where to start.'

'Yes. Leopard. Spots. *Plus ça change*. Et cetera.'

'What?'

'Nothing. I'm being a prat. I'm sure it's difficult to break old habits, Be. I get that.'

'And you?' Belinda swallowed. 'Will you take your own advice? Be nice to yourself also and really think about what is … what is going to be nice for you … in the long run. If you get what I mean. Because maybe a candlelight dinner with some boy is even going to mix you up even more. It might make you less on your own for one evening perhaps. But maybe it isn't something you truly want. Maybe is something you don't even need to do. Because maybe your own way is the best way. For you.' Belinda tried to breathe as her heart pumped. 'You just have to give your own self a time and space. I think. *Wa te?*'

Belinda could hear Amma humming as she tested and decided against different responses in her head.

'Shall we both promise give it a try? This whole being kinder shebang? See how we get on? Hey? We can but fucking try.'

'Yes, Amma. Is true,' Belinda said, heart still thudding away. 'We can only fucking try.'

33

Shooting Star Express Number One Coach pulled into Koforidua. Noisy air conditioning quietened after a wheeze. As though in Nana's car, Belinda reached for her seatbelt but found nothing to unclick. Far away at the front of the bus, the conductor fired out sentences and pointed with a forceful biro. He told passengers they had only fifteen minutes to refresh themselves at this rest stop. Then the vehicle would set off again to complete the final stage of the journey to Kumasi. He promised to leave behind anyone who decided to be too slow. He clapped twice to end his speech and the well-fed aunties, fragile elders, loud been-tos and important Chinese piled off, stepping on the backs of each other's sandals.

Resting her forehead on the stiff curtain framing the window, Belinda watched the conductor, who was now on the tarmac, press his little machine to keep track of numbers. So many rules. So much to check. She nodded to slip her fake Ray Bans down from her forehead to her face. Once space became available, she too stepped into the soupy heat. Out there, smells of sewage sat in the air, smells ruder than when the bin men came with the huge truck to collect the rubbish on Spenser Road. Some of the Chinese coughed, eyes nearly watering, and covered their mouths before stumbling to the small stalls and loos. Under a brown sky, Belinda loitered among the other parked coaches and waiting *tro tros*, their cracked windscreens painted with slogans written in a familiar, shouty font: '*Yesu Mo*', '*His eyes watch us all … including you!*', '*Beware the silver-tongued man*'.

Mary loved those weighty mottos, especially if they had spelling mistakes. In fact she had loved everything about *tro tros*. On *tro tro* rides, especially those that took the busy route from Daban to Adum, Mary saw life and all of its surprises, so different from the silence and routine of Aunty and Uncle's house. On *tro tros*, passengers pressed into cramped space with their rusted machetes, crates of Gulder, dried grasscutters, baskets of pink shallots; toddlers groaned wildly from their mothers' backs. Drivers used fists and fingers to angrily gesture at pedestrians not paying attention as they crossed Lake Road. While Belinda usually did her best to make sure that their shopping bags did not get in anyone's way or focused on holding the loop of frayed rope above her head for safety, Mary could not help but get involved in the minivan's noise and mess.

Belinda remembered that, on one of those journeys last year, she and Mary had been sitting on fold-down seats next to a smartly dressed City-woman. The City-woman had a very straight back. Belinda had peered at the young woman's newspaper and its centrefold showed farmers standing near piles of coconuts and a government notice about not urinating in public places. Beneath those: the mysterious daily Anansi sketch that Belinda and Mary often found Uncle thinking about while he had his morning cigarette. Belinda watched the City-woman grimace at that day's difficult puzzle. In the first rectangle, Anansi stared at the sun with wide eyes. In the second, the spiderman was halfway through eating a chicken drumstick – its huge bone pointing out of Anansi's thick lips. The third box was entirely black. The final one showed the question mark with the red dot that ended each and every strip.

The City-woman thrashed the pages and Belinda had been shocked by the anger with which she spoke. 'If I had my chance to, I will find this Anansi cartoon-drawer and tell him a piece of my mind for challenging my brain so like this each day. Every blessed time I try but I never can get at the answer of this cartoonist, or even close to his sense, even if I try my very hardest. Nothing at all. A wicked man *paaa*.'

'I. I don't think is supposed to be like is in a schoolroom,' Belinda had heard Mary say.

'What you mean?'

'Forgive. Forgive me coming in your personal and private chat, but. Well, why you carry on like every little thing it has to have answer? Maybe is fine fine to sometimes only have the questions, and leave there? There is so very much I do not know or understand. But is not causing me a rage and a heartbreaking. If someone just tell you answer, or, or even you are clever enough to work out the answer for yourself and get it, then bam: is finished. You have your answer and no more guessing and thinking. What is the use if all is finished and completed and there is nothing else left to do?'

The City-woman nodded, smiled and said to herself: 'Out of the mouths of babes and sucklings.'

Because she couldn't and didn't want to think about that any more, Belinda repeatedly struck the coach park's cracked earth with her heel, squashing termites that covered an old flyer for Milo with each movement of her foot. She stopped. The action was making her too sweaty: the temperature in Koforidua was even higher than in Accra. She longed for a smack of thunder louder than baking trays tumbling from Nana's carousel cupboard. She needed a shocking flash of rain. Eventually, she found herself walking forward, away from the vehicles, their spluttering engines and their black smoke.

Big white letters wobbling on the roof of the building ahead told her the rest stop was called Best Salvation. In front of shops selling gizzard kebabs, oily patties and sarsaparilla, three thin boys played a game of catching marbles in painted calabashes. The youngest boy was distracted, kept picking at the diamanté design on his T-shirt, bright spots sketching the skylines of cities faraway. Near them, two women in faded aprons sat on a bench. The battered silver dishes at their feet displayed swollen tomatoes and dripping guavas, the fruit on the top of each pile cut in half to show juicy insides. The limpness of the women's dark arms and bowed heads, the carelessness of their legs, the not-minding if flies trekked the bones on their shoulders felt completely right to Belinda. Not embarrassed that they had noticed her staring, Belinda went past the women to the fishy WCs, ignoring their boasts about how they could steal her fine-fine sunglasses and fine-fine Nike shoes from right under her nose if they wanted. When they joked and called her '*Akwada bone*' for showing neither respect nor manners, she didn't turn back to tell them she was no child; had not felt like anyone's child for so long.

In the shadowy cubicle, exhausted again by the journey done and the idea of how much more lay ahead, Belinda pulled her knickers down and sat heavily on the seat. She leant forward to trace the crosses and flames scratched into the wooden door. Old copper pipes whispered. A tank somewhere gradually filled up. A girl hummed senselessly as she washed her hands in the sink. Belinda pushed but nothing came out of her. Because she was so bored of sighing, deep in her chest she held on to the rush of breath aiming for her lips.

Belinda wondered what Mary would have asked for as a Christmas gift this year. Would Mary have made the request shyly or without fear? Would Belinda have trawled the narrow aisles at Morley's with Nana, searching for something shiny Mary could carry about with her and show off when she wanted? And would Uncle and Aunty have bought Mary a special gift too; a reward for working alone since summer and being grown-up? A pinkish bike Mary would be allowed to ride round the edge of the garden after finishing the laundry, the dishes, the silverware? When she first pulled it out of the box would Mary have screamed until her throat hurt? And would Mary have screamed even more knowing how much Aunty and Uncle sometimes enjoyed her being 'too much'? Later, would Mary have feasted on salty scraps of goat from Uncle's plate? Would her serious mouth have chewed and chewed tough flesh, not wanting to swallow and waste precious meat, chewing and chewing until any flavour had disappeared?

Might Aunty and Uncle have sent Mary to school properly? Would Mary have been better at Mathematics than she had expected? Might she perhaps find herself placed as No. 1 in a few algebra tests, and then recite all of her correct answers down the line to Belinda? And would Belinda have nodded at the meaningless combinations of letters and numbers? One day, when her reading and writing got better, might Mary have told Belinda about how she had also read *Lord of the Flies* like they had at Abacus? Might Belinda and Mary have shouted about Piggy and shouted about Jack?

And one day, when her age and the time were correct, might a man have seen Mary at church or by the seamstress' shop and taken her as his own? And, as the years went on, might Mary have been magical enough to make him stay? Clever and magical enough to distract the force, the *thing* that eventually seemed to sweep everyone away; made them disappear or turned them to nothing? In the cubicle, Belinda rolled the heel of her hand against the bulge of her forehead. She kicked up the puddle of water seeping across the floor tiles. She tightened her body and pushed down. A steady and strong stream ran from her.

It was a mean trick the world kept playing: making her feel like certainty or calm had finally arrived. Letting her think that because she finally worked out the wool settings on the washing machine, understood Doctor's weird respect for the ginger woman Cilla Black and now knew how to get from Tulse Hill to the Whitgift Centre, she could relax; that she had worked enough to make sense of it and could stop.

She wiped. She stood. She flushed. She washed her hands and walked out, passing the crumpled women who were complaining about how Nkrumah was the country's last honourable leader and they wouldn't see his like again. She wanted to ask them how they managed to cope with how unfair everything seemed to be, to use Amma's phrase. But the women would have found her ridiculous and laughed at her with all of their teeth, so loud the noise might have made Belinda lightheaded and set off the trembling. So Belinda asked nothing as she bent down for four guavas she did not want to eat, leaving her change as she went.

Back in her seat, Belinda shuffled closer to the window to allow the quiet Chinese businessman next to her some room. He checked his even, tidy fingernails. He rested his briefcase on his knees and took out his laptop and a little padded ring that reminded Belinda of the balloon animals on a particularly good episode of the *Blue Peter* programme. The engine began and the green fruits in Belinda's lap rocked. The man slid a disk into the computer then put the ring around his neck and headphones into his ears. Switching between English and Twi, the conductor did another bossy performance at the front. Smiling, the Chinese man pressed the mousepad and wriggled as the film started. He adjusted his neck ring and concentrated, paying Belinda no attention at all. Belinda found the sight of him strangely calming.

34

The final stop in Central Kumasi was at Kejetia. When they arrived, the conductor saluted. Passengers were shooed out into a square minutes away from the zoo where Belinda and Mary had settled for a crocodile rather than an ostrich, and had later made a scene almost as bad as Amma's foolishness in Waitrose.

Here, everything blared and honked and irritated. Crowds gathered, shouted for no reason then moved on. Belinda slid her tongue over the roof of her mouth. In exchange for her rusted coins, an Albino boy collected her things and got her yet another taxi. A sweatily overdressed driver appeared, popped up his car's boot and tried to impress her with his smart hat. He said it was called a fedora. He asked if she knew of the Godfather of Soul. She didn't. Lifting the hem of her wrapper, Belinda pretended to be a classy lady, letting the driver open and close the door delicately, as if a slam might break her.

In the back seat, she soon gave in to the driver's insistence that she stroke the fedora's proud purple feather. She passed the hat, and a twitching smile, back to him. It seemed to do good because soon he stopped his chat and did his job properly. He went from Kejetia to Fanti New Town, then through Adieba and Atonsu. Every time he found a road ahead was too potholed, he stopped to think up a different route, petting the flopping pink flower in his lapel as he frowned and came up with a new plan.

When they finally reached it, Belinda saw that the track through poorer, Old Daban, was exactly the same as when she'd left. Along it, people from houses smaller and less fancy than Uncle and Aunty's busied themselves. By the Sunlight Soap billboard, women with long breasts carried armfuls of laundry to scrub in the stream. The Methodist Believers' Church was still as rickety, only now it was decorated with huge paper flowers for Christmas. Further along, the wrinkled moneylender drove his cane into the ground with fierce twists; toothless elders hacked sugar cane into pieces and a fat girl cooked turkey tails by a ribbon of sewage. As the taxi passed by, its wheels sprayed them all with red dust.

They drove up the avenue of palm trees marking the start of the foreigners' villas: the enormous, four-storey for the old professor and his wife, both of whom had skin even fairer than Nana's; the modest one for the Frempongs from Atlanta, with their three watchmen playing draughts on the porch; then the Nyantakyis with their enormous courtyard, in which their visiting grandson played on the trampoline that Mary had mentioned with the hottest envy.

In loose pyjamas, the eight- perhaps nine-year-old seemed to be having the best time of his life. The car threatened to pick up speed but Belinda wanted to stay and study his actions. His lightness. The way he seemed to fill up the sky each time he flew through it. He tried and failed to backflip, landing flat on his stomach, laughing, then whizzing up to do it again. His body delighted him. He spread-eagled his arms and did star jumps. He hugged his knees close to his chest, turning into a firm ball, striking and rising from the mat. He soared, his face full of both real fear and real joy. Up, up, up he went, driving himself with his own power, pushing so far from everything. The little boy stopped to wave at Belinda. Pressing against the window, she did the same back.

The driver eventually dropped Belinda off at Aunty and Uncle's perimeter wall, whistling to himself as he sped away. Carpenter's stall and its stack of tables and traditional stools remained in its usual spot, yards from the gate. And there, through the railings, the mango trees in the front garden she had sat beneath to sort through Aunty and Uncle's boxes shipped over from the UK. And the corner of the garden that, each evening, was turned bluish by the pool's lights. Ahead, up, the red slate roof, so impressive compared to Adurubaa's corrugated iron. On the veranda, two rocking chairs swaying to different beats.

Belinda pressed the buzzer. The gates unwound with a whine and Belinda clutched her middle and tilted, bowing at the house. She fell to the ground, limbs and crinkling black cotton covering themselves in dirt. Every time she breathed – because she had to keep breathing – pain hit and her legs became less willing to cooperate. Someone's quickening feet were getting nearer. Her throat throbbed.

'*Adεn?* Eh?'

'*Adεn?*' Aunty and Uncle's questions came out between little coughs and claps to her cheeks.

'*Me se! Me se adεn?!*' A much thinner Aunty came down low to Belinda and spoke hoarsely. The weight of Belinda's skull increased. Tasting grass, she tried to smooth her breath. Aunty's hard rubbing helped. Aunty held Belinda's shoulders and Belinda wondered if Aunty had wanted to do the same to Mary, but could not because the small girl's arm did not meet the small girl's shoulder did not meet the small girl's chest. Belinda screamed and crawled into Aunty's lap, getting tighter as fabric folded round her.

Belinda thought of Mary's mother. Wherever and whatever that woman might be. Somehow Belinda hoped Mary's mother had felt it deep, deep inside her body when Mary's spirit was taken. On that day, Mary's mother might have been fetching water or prodding avocados before buying. And then suddenly, in the middle of that ordinary task, Mary's mother would have found herself thrown back by a pain she had never experienced before but understood immediately. Onlookers maybe stopped to put their supporting hands on the woman's back, like Aunty did to Belinda now. What was the point of anyone's helping hands? The mother might eventually have been put upright, but the woman wouldn't walk in the exactly same, normal way ever again.

After she had wiped herself down and steadied herself like they told her to, after the heat of embarrassment sank and stilled around her ankles, Belinda sat in the massive reception room with the two of them. Like when the trembling came, she tried to do very little. Sometimes, the ceiling's pine tongue and groove was calming, with its straight lines following one another. She squeezed the green coconut given to her, put its straw between her lips and sipped at the cool saltiness. She studied her surroundings. Again, everything, everywhere, was like nothing had happened and this was a perfectly acceptable world. Same tasselled rug underneath her. Same chandelier above, icy as ever. Same old side tables with tiny claws for feet, today holding three plates of Aunty's greasy Jollof. Belinda wondered how quietly her voice would come out if she pushed the straw aside to speak.

'Is shock. You have a bad shock and who can blame for that one?' Uncle said, from the armchair beside her.

Aunty nodded from the other sofa and smiled. Her black head-tie wagged stupidly. 'Shock. Yes.'

Belinda became interested in the two large vases either side of the telly, covered with those blue, Chinese-style drawings also on Nana's special crockery. Mary had loved cleaning those vases. While they had polished, Belinda let Mary wear the nicer pink rubber gloves. Belinda took the yellow pair while Mary buffed the show-off vases with slow-motion care, sometimes pretending to drop them, catching with seconds to spare. If Mary had been less cautious and clever, if one of those two vases had cracked and split into pieces – so what? Really, so what?

Uncle stretched his legs, letting out little, tired puffs, and then put his feet on the chunky ottoman. He grinned with satisfaction as though finally achieving the rest he deserved.

'Darling?' he asked.

'Yes, my darling?'

'Why don't, eh, why don't we see what is on the television? Check, dear.'

Aunty's flitting between channels brought so much colour and colour and colour and screaming and applause and singing and silence and beeping Belinda worried she might be sick. She bit the straw. A saxophone did a familiar tune through the speakers.

'Oh, we all love this one very much, don't we? Is so nice.'

'Yes, dazzit. Leave it here, dear.'

'Oh yes. Yes, this is a good one. Belinda, you know it well, eh?'

The *Cosby Show* titles were starting; the opening where the background was a child's drawing on a wall, a painting of a city, something like that. Dr Huxtable was first on, in an orange suit and pulling silly expressions to give his old-dog face youth. Next, the wife Clair appeared – too attractive for the Cosby man, Belinda and Mary always agreed – swinging her bouncy relaxed hair. The kids followed, one by one, different kinds of brown and all friends. They played around too, doing ridiculous walks across the stage, wearing clownish clothes several sizes too big for them. As the tune continued, Aunty and Uncle clapped along, Uncle even sometimes imitated the saxophone when it hit the highest notes. Aunty seemed to like that a lot. When the programme started, with all the patterned jumpers and padded shoulders and the laughs from the audience, Belinda found it hard to concentrate. She guessed Clair was putting up with something bad Cliff had done because that was usual. Aunty was transfixed, folding a leg beneath her bottom and leaning forward so her black *pata pata* rode up. Every few minutes, Aunty repeated Clair Huxtable's quick replies to the doctor's silly behaviour like she could not believe the woman's intelligence.

Though it might be hard, Belinda did want to forgive Uncle and Aunty for not offering some special, elders' wisdom capable of fixing everything. Forgiveness would be the kind thing to do. Perhaps kind to herself too, just like Amma had said. Forgiveness would recognise that, once, Aunty and Uncle had been so very good to her. The first and perhaps greatest gift they had given was complicated work. At the beginning of her time with them, the newness of the jobs – starching shirts, hanging dresses in an order according to their shade and colour, defrosting the chest freezer – and the need to teach them to a restless pupil, demanded all of her attention. The images of men's clumsy hands claiming Mother's thighs and breasts had no opportunity to appear in her mind. For that gift, she would always be grateful. Belinda flattened the straw between her teeth. She pulled at it slowly, bent it in half, then back on itself.

Now Theo and Vanessa Huxtable were planning something stupid that would surely fail but would only result in short, easy punishments. They sat on a park bench, their heads craned in towards one another and the green of the park's grass blazed up from the screen and painted Uncle's concentrating forehead. How was forgiveness actually done? She had never seen it happen before: someone doing wrong, someone else seeing around or through their hurt, everyone eventually moving forward together like a Tampax advert: with big smiles, all walking in time towards something brighter and better. She liked the idea of trying to be better. But how was it actually done? Belinda turned to the side table and picked up the plate of Jollof, ignoring the cutlery bundled in the blue napkins they used when guests came for dinner. She rested the plate on her lap and scooped a great handful of the rice into her mouth. Out of the corner of her eye, she sensed Aunty and Uncle half-smiling their approval. As if food could stop the hollow feeling inside, Belinda pushed more and more into herself, swallowing messily, like Amma standing at the fridge and eating salad straight from the bag. Belinda knew orange oil must be smearing her lips and teeth. She slurped more coconut water and then returned to the rice, enjoying the little bits of chicken, corned beef and prawn. It was like she hadn't eaten for months. She kept on going, moving so fast. Now Aunty's half-smile became more concerned. Belinda continued, shovelling, gulping until only traces of palm oil were left. She lifted the plate and licked in long stripes.

Pretending that she had not been staring, Aunty squealed at Theo's sudden dancing, then cackled from the back of her throat. Belinda poked her bloating stomach while two black beetles on the side table fought for a grain of dropped rice. They kept getting close to the edge and nearly toppling over, but before a full fall they managed to quickly drag themselves back up to flick their legs at one another. In the process of all this, they often lost the grain and so stumbled endlessly, trying to find out where it had been left.

Later they moved to the veranda where huge moths threw themselves against the wall lights, mosquito coils sent up scribbles of smoke and the generator moaned away. Uncle made a big fuss of dragging out an extra rocking chair from his study so Belinda could join them and 'be comfortable'. Once settled, Uncle began to browse through a book with a picture of a furious horse on its front cover. Every few minutes Uncle sat up, pointed at a page and shared a fact – about the size of the Zulus' assegai or the diet of Lord Chelmsford's men.

Aunty mostly ignored these outbursts of information. She was busy taking the jokers out of a worn deck of cards, organising everything for Belinda and her to play Spar, a game the limping Mrs Aberese had introduced to the local womenfolk a few weeks ago. Carefully, Aunty went through the rules, her powdery fingers sensibly lining up several cards in several rows on a stool. The fingers' movements were slow. Belinda liked that. Belinda nodded as if she understood each instruction.

Dealing out the remaining cards equally between the two of them, Aunty quietly told Belinda about the first place she and Uncle rented when they arrived in London; a damp room above a newsagent's on the Loughborough Road, not far from Spenser Road. It was a place where any peace she and Uncle managed to find was soon interrupted by the scratch of a rat's claws on floorboards or the Irish couple next-door's arguments. Aunty said all of this shaking her head. It made Uncle peer over the top of his little reading glasses and mutter '*Ampa, ampa, ampa* – we have come so far you will not believe' to the calla lilies in the garden. He poured the three of them more *Akpeteshie*. When Belinda refused the top-up, Uncle pouted, so she took what was offered. To drink it, you had to wince first and then soften your face and throat to let its bitterness slide down and away.

The sharp palm wine smudged the world. As did Aunty's singsong storytelling of that past in distant Camberwell – first jobs, first evening class at Borough Poly. Aunty went on, discarding a few jacks, a king of spades, sketching out their wedding day in 1971. Much of this Belinda already knew, so her attention wavered like the breeze slipping by with its faint smell of someone's burning rubbish.

Adjusting the positions of the diamonds and clubs she clutched, Belinda wondered how much Mary's passing made these two old people think about the closeness of their own deaths. She assumed they could not avoid that thought; it must be with them often.

If Uncle stopped turning down a page's corner and Aunty stopped reshuffling the deck to tell Belinda how scared they were of disappearing, Belinda would probably ignore their tearful mouths and instead, after sipping *Akepeteshie*, fix her loose headscarf. Then she'd tidy up the monkey nut shells on the balustrade in front of them or go inside to find matches to relight the sputtering coil. She would do nothing, just like when Amma had opened up and spoken about herself, because more than nothing would be too much to cope with, alongside everything else. As Uncle frowned at the stool, Belinda's tiredness became a hand moving up from her neck, crawling across her scalp and resting its mean weight on her forehead. It was not only tiredness after the travelling and the drink: she was tired of herself.

Belinda swung forward on her rocking chair and reached out to add the queen of diamonds and the seven of hearts to one of the rows. Quickly Aunty beamed and whooped louder than when Mary managed a one-handed catch. Aunty raised her palm, preparing to strike the rows viciously.

'*Me yere! Gyae!* The girl has done a beginner's error. Won't you do a rematch? Is a first go, *me sroe*?' Uncle pouted again, added more to their glasses. Aunty's smile fell into a tight line.

'No. Is OK. Is totally OK.' Belinda snatched at Aunty's winning hand, started laying down cards for a new round. 'Like, fair is fair is fair. I can learn from this one. I will do differently next time. You watch and see.'

35

Well-wishers came over during the next three days. Hundreds of them tramped to the reception room, rubbed with pomade and wearing their best purple, charcoal or red robes. The husbands usually started by talking about sympathy and fate. They discussed the lack of good driving in Kumasi. Help of all kinds was promised by the wives. Gathering God's lambs and Belinda writing and giving a eulogy were mentioned. Then the visitors tried to find a way to be normal, asking Belinda about the snow, and white people. The children also asked about London and then pleaded with her to use more of a Queen's English voice. Belinda shook her head; the children's begging faces were so much duller and more stupid than Mary's. Belinda offered malt and minerals, only to be refused. She excused herself and returned with felt-tips for the kids, Marks and Spencers' belts for the husband, leather purses for the wife: Nana had stocked her up well. Aunty thanked the air for its generosity and everyone was happy with the gifts. They all held clammy hands to pray and Belinda 'hallelujah-ed' in the ragged way her mother had taught her when they prayed together in their tiny room, just the two of them because Pastor would not let them into the church.

Belinda spent much of those visits from mourners picturing Mother in that reception room, paying her respects: Mother recalling lines from First Corinthians because it was the only part of the Bible she knew to recite. Or Mother nicely complimenting the plans for the funeral and the guest list and all the rest, even though the scale of the thing confused and angered her. Mother brushing dust from her good black dress, her desperate fingers itchy for one of the cigarettes in the black clutch given to her by a customer.

36

On the fourth day, fed up with the prospect of doing the same performance again, when the Otengs and the Afriyies arrived at nine in the morning, Belinda did not leave her room to greet them. Uncle knocked and knocked on her door. Called her name. Shouted. Through it all, Belinda sat up in bed and held herself very still.

'*Me yare*,' Belinda snapped, eventually.

'*Wo yare?*' Uncle asked.

'*Aane.*'

'Oh dear, dear, dear, dear. *Aba!* Then please allow us to –'

'I only need to rest. Like, a break? That's all. Good morning to you. Good morning and good day.'

Belinda heard Aunty. Uncle coughed. Another, louder conversation with many different voices bubbled up from somewhere. Finally, silence; they had given up. Later on, there might be some cost or consequence for Belinda. But, for now, she had won herself some space. It was enough. She turned towards the window and the band of light there in which specks of dust floated. She did not care that she had allowed that floating dirt to gather. She did not care she had not reached for a mop, broom or sponge in weeks. Belinda raised her hands in the air and, as she moved, the capped sleeves of her nightdress shuffled down to her shoulders. Warmth slid over her skin. After melting out of that pose, she punched her pillows until they were plumper; beating so much that two freed feathers dived down to the floor.

Belinda rummaged in her suitcases, clawing away layers of sensible underwear Nana had packed until she pulled out grammar questions and Amma's *Collected Works of Katherine Mansfield*. In the conversation they had had on the doorstep before Belinda headed to Heathrow, Amma had handed over the book roughly, saying that the stories were 'strange and unshakeable'. Belinda would do the reading before the boring chore of task-sheets and homework: yet again going over how to use apostrophes and then the differences between there, their and they're. Later, she would attempt to start on the eulogy; one thing at a time.

Sat with her back against the headboard, she held the book carefully, smiling at how far and wide Amma's interests were: the girl who enjoyed things by the gloomy author on the back cover here also loved decorating her own tights, Missy Elliot's noise, the TV show where people had to cook disgusting, ungenerous meals very quickly, and Audre Lorde with her funny, flattened afro.

Belinda met the stare of the pale author in the photo and flipped to the contents page. There, right up against the spine and folded tightly, a tiny piece of yellow paper nestled. As though doing something forbidden Belinda checked around her before opening the wedge. The handwritten paragraph revealed on the creased sheet had neither a date nor an underlined title:

He manages like somebody carrying a box
that is too heavy, first with his arms
underneath. When their strength gives out,
he moves the hands forward, hooking them
on the corners, pulling the weight against
his chest. He moves his thumbs slightly
when the fingers begin to tire, and it makes
different muscles take over. Afterward,
he carries it on his shoulder, until the blood
drains out of the arm that is stretched up

to steady the box and the arm goes numb. But now
the man can hold underneath again, so that
he can go on without ever putting the box down.

Below it was the name 'Jack Gilbert'. Near that, in Amma's big capitals spreading up over several lines, the word 'COURAGE'. Belinda traced the shape of Amma's precise letters on the page.

Mrs Al-Kawthari had taught them all about symbolism. Belinda understood that the man fought and kept going, no matter how tough his challenge became. In giving her this poem, Belinda understood that Amma wanted her to make her mind and body a wall. Sometimes. Belinda might have to be clever and change the way she strengthened herself; try out different methods, techniques. Yes. The message was appropriate, beautiful, true. Even more than that, Amma's giving it clearly showed how much Amma cared.

But Belinda also found symbols very difficult. They could mean many things at the same time and could make you feel different emotions and ideas all at once. The image of a wrestling man with his parcel did show bravery. But it also looked ridiculous. His terrible twisting and frowning was foolish, like a frustrated, idiot stray dog in Adum chasing his own tail. Belinda was not ungrateful for Amma's writing, not ungrateful at all: the idea of being COURAGEous appealed. It was different from anything else the world offered her now; sorrow, silence. The problem came from the clash between the final word pressed into the bottom of the page and the image of the sad, fighting clown Belinda couldn't escape from. Partly, the man and his on-and-on struggle with the box seemed like something silly from *ChuckleVision*. He might trip over at any minute and a whole audience would not be able to contain themselves. Because all of his nonsense effort like he might burst a blood vessel – and for what? With the big toe of her left foot, she idly chased the feathers loosened from the pillows, moving them this way and then that across the tiles. The fluffy little things looked so helpless. She kicked them into a dark corner and lifted her head. There had to be more courageous things to do than just fighting and gritting teeth. There had to be.

37

Aunty announced that there was last-minute funeral shopping to be done, so – before any excuses could be made – on Wednesday afternoon, Belinda was bustled into the Mercedes and sacks and bags were pressed into her lap. She tried to hide behind her fake Ray Bans.

Aunty's driving was clunky. She did strange things like heading straight towards the busiest roads at Atamanso and going the wrong way around the roundabout at Yaw Ampofo Avenue. She blamed the stubbornness of the gear stick and steering wheel for her slow progress. Aunty chatted away – about how many of the staff had all left the house in the days immediately following Mary's death: the nightwatchman first and then several others soon after; about how she wanted to experiment with what she grew in the garden, about how her catarrh seemed worse lately. As they passed the Golden Bean Hotel, the wooden elephants either side of its gates hailing the sun with their trunks, Belinda wondered if the flaps on Aunty's neck and the lines round Aunty's lips were as mean as Mother's were these days. How much older did Mother look now? Perhaps too old for her crumbling rouges to do any good. But maybe some men liked touching, kissing, pressing the skin of someone broken by time and who clearly needed looking after. Belinda wanted the *Akpeteshie* from the first night. It would smear and soften her thoughts.

They found themselves at the end of a long, slow tailback near the GOIL station in Ahodwo. Aunty turned to face Belinda head on.

'Belinda. This I have to say. So please let me. Is not easy. We – me, your Uncle – we both thought it very nice, very nice indeed, the whole way you cared for Mary. Like even as if you were kin. Your behaviour was a great honour and credit to you.' Aunty clutched her knees. 'I probably should wait for Kofi, for your Uncle to give the news but. Seem proper, now. It will only be correct to reward you. For all you did for her.'

'Reward?' Belinda slipped off the sunglasses, squeezed their arms as far as the screws allowed until they creaked, then stopped and squeezed them again. 'I don't deserve or need or. Like, I don't want anything. Seriously. Thank you.'

Aunty inhaled and exhaled through her nose several times, before then pounding the air. 'So we haven't signed off on all the details. There are different possibilities. Your Uncle maybe perhaps wants to include you in our wills. Or we will get you some A levels. Or in time we set you up with a small shop or small business. In London or Kumasi. Something along the lines of these. We not sure which. So much in our minds, *ino be so*? We will find the best one in God's time for you. And it will help to bring you happiness and a hope. It will be a great blessing. Because we have to find a positive in tragedy? *Wa te?*'

Belinda pulled at the frayed lip of the sack on her knees. Using two tensed fingernails, she extracted a long, thin piece of its hessian and rested the thread on her palm.

'No. Aunty. No. I don't think I want any of that. Please.'

'But, Belinda –'

'These thing you speak of? Like, they are nice for someone else. Me? I am not so sure.'

Just like Nana's had in the Fiat, now Aunty's mouth worked furiously. 'So, Belinda, what? You want what? What should we do for you now, eh? Now children behaving and doing and acting as they want and wish?' Spit sprayed from her. 'Running where they know they should not run. Who know what world we living in

now. An upside-down one. *Me se* an upside-down one, *paaa*.'
Aunty thumped her horn, pointlessly and madly, over and over
again. Even though Aunty had never been angrier towards her,
Belinda didn't mind or care. Belinda rolled up the window, then
rolled it down.

When they eventually arrived at Central Market, Belinda
remained slack and flat. If any of the harassed customers at the
huddled stalls had glanced up from weighing garden eggs to look
at her, her expression would have frightened them. Her stillness
came partly from concentration. Stepping round the homeless
lying face down with cups at their heads for coins, she tried to bat
away thoughts of the coming days. She walked behind Aunty,
often stopping to dodge tired donkeys carrying huge bundles of
piping.

The day's heat pushed hard, bullying and prickling. Aunty's
black linen blouse sweatily glued itself to her shoulders and arms
and she continuously wiped at herself, blotching her foundation.
As if the conversation in the car hadn't happened at all, Aunty
listed the jobs still to be done, her hands flying everywhere as she
spoke about the drivers, the undertakers, the performers, the
caterers, the pastor needed final checking. The eulogies, the liba-
tions, the prayers all were yet to be confirmed. Recently received
donations had to be accounted for. Recently presented invoices
had to be paid. So much! Good-ness, good-ness gracious! Aunty
stopped to inspect pawpaws sold by a tall man in a big pink
dashiki.

They carried on, making their way through the market's
constant naming of its goods, the trilling of bicycle bells, armies of
cows blocking paths; past posters against skin bleaching and
HIVAIDS, the Devil, Malaria. In the section with the snails and
crabs the smell was too much, stronger than the hand Belinda
clamped over her nose and mouth. The shouting and selling
became faster.

'For the tables? To cover the tables nicely? Yes?'

Now Aunty stomped towards the cooler, shadowier textiles area of the market. There, glass cases of metallic satins shone and flashed. They walked in, the ground here wetter underfoot. Women beckoned Aunty and Belinda from the stoops of shops, wafting fabrics in their direction. They hissed to get attention. Some urgently chirped 'Hello, hello, hello' just like Belinda used to do on the phone, trying to draw back Mary's cracking, fading voice.

Aunty stayed closer to Belinda, nudging and steering Belinda away from an abandoned pile of tyres ahead and then away from a row of lean-tos – each one on stilts rising out of black muck – towards a large wooden shack, held together by beams green with damp. The owner sat within it on a bench counting the stacks of material around her. Her hair was wild, arching in every direction. Dragging up her drooped vest to hide the long gap between her breasts, the owner invited Belinda and Aunty in. She pushed aside the oily bowl at her feet and wiped her lips. Courtesy stopped her from offering a dirty hand – instead she gave them both her wrist to shake. Aunty cleared her throat.

'I come to this shop on a recommendation, madam. And we come to do a great business with you, I hope. We make preparation for a funeral and need some of your goods.'

'Amen. And so sorry sorry sorry. And I promise you won't find a better goods anywhere than here in this place. Welcome welcome welcome.' The woman clapped happily. Flies flew from her. Belinda focused on material hanging in a drape from the ceiling; its designs of huge green limes falling through a tangle of red spirals.

'Me I am Mrs Asare. And this my … niece, Belinda, has recently returned from London, UK.'

'Eh! *Abrokyriefoɔ! Akwaaba.* You are welcome. Let me hear your good London English and I will have to give you *kama kama* price today. Very welcome welcome! Oh, fine! And me they call Gifty.'

There was something likeable about the owner, who now thrust her thumb at her chest. She was full of alertness, sayings about lazy husbands and the smallness of Aunty's waist. With all her energy and ease she could not have been more different from the sour checkout girls at Woolworths. Belinda's gaze soon moved past the owner's busy mouth and elbows to rest on the fine tribal scars beneath the woman's eyes. On both cheeks: three thin vertical stripes and two smaller, fatter horizontal ones. As a child, whenever Belinda saw them, marks like those had sent her wriggling. She had found the patterns very pretty but also very disgusting too.

In the shop, staring at those scars, she imagined it happening: the cry of the infant Gifty when the elder's blade slit, the applause as the baby's squeal stretched, the flesh being opened up. The elders marked children at a very young age so the pain would not be remembered. Even though it made sense, it was also terrible that a child was introduced to suffering – was given the same box the man from Amma's poem shuffled from shoulder, to hip, to knee – only weeks after arriving in the world. And perhaps that bleeding child screamed long after the ceremony had finished.

'You watch on as in wonder?' Gifty smiled at Belinda with yellow teeth. 'You don't know this one? *Kai! Abrokyriefoɔ!*'

'No. I know it well,' Belinda replied, coolly. 'I suppose I, like, forgot about it? That's all.'

'Come. You all curious as cat. I won't bite you.'

Aunty started to speak. She stopped and searched her clutch for something. While Aunty then turned to tug a corner of a black cloth sprinkled with stars, Gifty offered up the scratches to Belinda. Belinda's fingers found the woman's scarring unfriendly to the touch, almost like it might graze. Belinda pulled back and yanked on the pockets of her boyish cargo shorts, fiddled with their buttons.

'Miss Gifty. May I please ask? Please. It doesn't anger you? That they hurt you, when they cut like this – and all for nothing?'

'Nothing?'

'They tried to make my mother do it on me in Adurubaa. My home village. She would not allow it. Her words were that is like animals, old-fashioned. She thought we all see who we are anyway and so we don't, like, need marks to remind. I think she was right. It must hurt very much as well. For the small child in that horrible time. For the woman who has to watch on at the side and do nothing at all. Isn't it nasty and bad?'

Gifty's pencilled eyebrows slid up. She handed a purple heap to Aunty, not breaking eye contact with Belinda once. 'See all we three of us in this small place? We Ghanaian women, *wa te*? We know how to take a pain, a real pain. All kinds of pains. We queens for it. We not winning all things, but that is our good skill. And we proud on it. And your mother should be proud on it too. Mark it on the wall, is true. You think Yaa Asentawaa is remember here for all time because she turn her back on tough things? Because she didn't want to see through some real hurts? *Kai!* She was made of rock and stone like us.'

Although the back of Belinda's tongue tasted bitter like she might be sick, and although it mightn't do anything good, she wanted to speak and ask questions.

'Maybe. But, like, really, aren't we actually made of flesh and skin underneath it all? Aren't we made of much, much softer things that break too easily? Isn't all this always talking of rock, rock, rock a fantasy?'

Belinda sensed Aunty's movements: Aunty frowning at one style, checking another then frowning at that. Aunty moved too quickly and was making herself sweat more.

'Madam, the child means means what?'

Belinda let her chin fall. The world down there against the splitting yellow lino was a mess of empty water bags like snakes' skin and three sets of feet: Belinda's in scuffed Nikes with once-white ticks grubby after days back at Daban; Aunty's in ceremonial sandals crowned with yellow pompoms and the woman's, all wrinkled and exposed. Belinda wanted to look up and describe Amma and Mother and Mary as well as she could. And say she had been there when Amma had run out of a supermarket in tears, alone. And was there when Mother quickly changed from sadness to fury each time sat at their small table, counting and not believing how few cedis were in her purse. Belinda wanted to talk about how she had also been there when Mary cried for her own mother and family, and seen Mary struggle to control the noise. And Belinda wanted to say that nothing worthwhile had come from any of it. She raised her head.

'I mean something along the lines of, like. I, I suppose I'm trying to simplify, so –'

'Belinda, honestly!' Aunty shouted. 'Ho-nest-ly. You have to stop! I beg. We focus on the task here. Please.'

Silent, Belinda let her arms dangle. Passing her lower lip over the upper one, she felt just how rough and dry they both were. She found her tin of Vaseline, applied some and returned to standing still.

Aunty shifted her head-tie to bring up its big drooped wings. She pressed her handkerchief to her forehead and then pointed at stacks of black high above her. 'That one. There. Right there. For the chief mourners' tables. Fifty yards. I'm sure Mrs Gifty will only charge us for forty. Sister, fetch for me, eh? *Me sroe.*'

Belinda stepped aside so the owner could grab a long rod with something like a claw on its end. Gifty moved back over to Aunty and stood on the tips of her toes, straining her arm as the pole reached to the distant shelf. It took a few tries, and when the hook eventually eased the fabric down and fell for her to catch, Gifty cheered like a child. She battered the cloth with slaps to remove its thin coating of dust. Aunty started asking for more samples, crossing her arms and uncrossing her arms, tapped things into her cell phone while Gifty ran around. Belinda looked away.

Through the doorway she could see the entrance to a shack opposite. Standing there, a woman leant against a pole. A tasselled blue thing was knotted around the woman's head and trailed down her neck snakily. The woman pulled out three small green oranges tied into the top of her wrapper skirt, tore into them with her thumbs one at a time, then threw pieces into her mouth casually. She split the fruit into more bits and handed some to the seller in the neighbouring stall and to other, passing traders. While Aunty filled her sack with yards and yards of purple, black and brown, through that narrow slit of the door, Belinda saw children swarming to snatch more segments of orange, until the woman found she had nothing left to give away. When the children continued to pester, the woman took off her *challewatte* and waved it at the thieving crowd, laughing as they scattered.

38

Making her way down the long corridor the next afternoon to see Uncle in his study as she had been instructed, Belinda sympathised with and felt as frightened as the naughty ones at her old school, called to the Principal's office to face the anger of his famous, wicked cane.

Aunty had been quiet and brief when she had given the order to visit Uncle, her eyes fixed on the tiled floor, shutting the door almost as quickly as she had opened it. Getting closer to the study, passing the utility room, then the first guest bathroom, Belinda dabbed at the slippery dampness gathering above her hair-down-there, scraped back loose tufts from around her face and rolled up the sleeves of her shirt. She saw Koromoa, the incredibly slim, quiet pool boy, wandering to the furthest end of the pool, squatting and turning the stiff wheel there, turning and turning to slowly unfold a white skin across blue. Behind him, sprinklers waved glittering arcs across the lawns, the water striped with shadow and falling gracefully. Their steady hissing and Koromoa's steady rhythm helped her breathing and the clamminess of her hands when she reached Uncle's door. She rapped her knuckles against the *nkyinkyim* symbols carved into the wood.

'Come, come, come, come. Sit, sit, sit.'

In his black *batakari* with the clever silver embroidery at the neck, Uncle stood holding the edge of the desk. His shoulders seemed as high and bunched as Belinda's. Belinda sat wincing a little at the pink sunlight washing over Uncle's dark, ringed fingers and over the room's oak, brass and leather. Uncle pulled out cigarettes and a lighter then played with a Lucky Strike. He couldn't get the lighter going so Belinda took it from him, flicked its wheel and returned it.

'Do again. You'll see it work.' A flame appeared and she smiled.

'Something you learn in London?'

'No.'

'That's a relief. Is a bad habit, this.'

'Yes. It is.'

'For old-timer like me, is fine. But for a young lady like you, you shouldn't smoke at all, I don't think.'

'Yes. I mean, no.' Belinda pressed down on her chair's armrest, pushed her arm forward until the elbow cracked. Uncle licked his lips and drummed his fingers, clearly finding it difficult to look at her for long. He coughed, then concentrated on his cigarette more. Her ability to discomfort him nearly made her feel powerful. She watched soft blue smoke curling away from him, drifting up and around the room.

Belinda and Mary used to find the study particularly difficult to clean because of the amount packed into the space. Unlike the order of Aunty's largely empty 'relaxation room', Uncle's study was overloaded and crazy, almost as busy as Amma's bedroom. In Uncle's study, several different Turkish rugs covered the floor. They were angled in odd ways and sometimes layered on top of one another bumpily. The clashing patterns could almost make you feel queasy if you looked too hard; Mary had always insisted they did – an excuse for not having to dust them. Occasional tables with gold lions' paws instead of castors were strewn with sticky coasters. The tall cabinets lining the walls displayed some things that seemed worth showing off – carriage clocks saying different times, pigs dressed as humans with slots in their heads for coins, little bronze statues, photographs of Uncle smiling next to bald, suited men who now reminded Belinda of Richard

Whiteley – and then lots of other things whose value was not clear – shelves of unopened letters, and empty record sleeves, papers with curled edges, birthday and retirement cards with washed-out balloons on them. In the corners of the study, slippers and sandals climbed on top of one another, umbrella stands overflowed. In the centre of everything, an enormous globe sat fatly. It opened at the middle, revealing hidden bottles. Each one had to be individually taken out, wiped down, put back in the exact same place. A few had always been very unloved and untouched: Belinda remembered a curvy one called Courvoisier. Others were much more used, marked everywhere with Uncle's oily, wide thumbprints: Ballantine's, Johnnie Walker, Chivas Regal. She knew so much about the small and stupid details of these people's lives. Far too much. In her seat she lifted her bottom up and down, wriggled slightly. She shielded her eyes as the sunlight hit her face more forcefully.

'You well, Belinda? Keeping well, eh?'

Belinda nodded.

'OK. Good. That's good news.'

'Yes. Praise God.'

'And you willing to hear a foolish old man for some few minutes of your day?'

Belinda nodded.

'Eh heh. Dazzit. You a good girl really.' Uncle sucked in another drag then rubbed his right eyebrow. He swept something away from his nose and took a deep, serious breath. 'So some time, early nineties or something like this, I paid for your Aunt and Nana and some few girlfriends to get a luxury weekend. Like a thank you for not minding or moaning about my hours at work. For everything, really. Spa. In a countryside. Green. Horses. Very expensive. Chinese giving massages. Jacuzzi and Champagne. Manicure.' Uncle batted his eyelashes.

'Nice to reward and treat. Good to rest,' Belinda said.

'So I myself kept the kids for two whole days. Antoinette was eight and Stephen ... then Stephen will have been five or so. Ask your Aunty how bad I am with ages and she will continue going for three hours. Anyway, I cared for the kids. We did all you are meant to. Park and swings and ice cream and la la la. Then we were walking by this South Bank. Did you visit it when you were in London?'

'No.'

'A shame. Is nice.' Uncle tapped the cigarette, salting the *I Love Aburi!* ashtray. He inhaled again, waved the Lucky Strike around like a wand, smoking much more dramatically than Amma ever did. 'Anyway, we walked there. Pointing at boats and doing I-spy and whatnot. A man came to take our picture, called it professional, told me some ridiculous London prices, spoke of how beautiful the little ones were and the usual nonsense to get you parting with cash. I agreed because the kids' noise can be so on and on and on and Ariston. I like an easy life. So the kids they started fixing their hair all proper and Stephen is shining the shoes and he had on this silly bow tie thing he loved and he was getting it perfect. They carried on about how much they wanted to give Mummy the picture when she came and how nice it would be for Mummy and la la la.'

'Very lovely and sweet. Children.'

'Before the man could take the snaps,' Uncle shook his head, crushed the cigarette, 'I remember it so clear like it was happening before me right now; before the man could snap, Antoinette was practising her best smile. And she did it for ages, Belinda, I'm telling you five minutes or more, she wouldn't stop grinning until she thought she had it correct and the good photographer stood patient. All of a sudden she vomit everywhere, all on her dress, everywhere. *Aba!* And she cried' – Uncle put both hands on his cheeks – 'that is "ruined, everything is ruined" and I had to clean her up but she still really went for it. Bawling *paaa.*'

'Oh. Children.'

'But my Stephen is creasing himself. Almost wetting himself and coughing and choking with the laughter. And so Antoinette runs and punches him square on top of his black head. Bam. *Kai!* The photographer must have thought we are only recently from the wild.'

'Oh dear.'

'The next is important, *wa te*?'

She nodded.

'*Hwɛ*, Antoinette hit Stephen and he wept. Hey! How he wept, like he was even given a brain damage. And at first Antoinette's mouth was hanging down in a shock. And then she looked more and screamed – high pitch – because she realised her crime. You know it?'

Belinda saw the joy in Uncle's face: his delight at his story and the way he had told it; his pleasure at having an audience. His eyes, nostrils and mouth were all wide. Now she had to do her bit. She shook her head, made her own eyes wide and expectant too, leant forward a little in the chair in the hope that her cooperation would make things finish sooner.

'My Antoinette she cried because she came to see the worst thing is to hurt another only because you yourself hurt. It doesn't help. It does no good. It only brings on extra, extra hurt.' Uncle reached for a carafe and filled two tumblers with filtered water; he passed one over to Belinda and she gulped greedily. Water ran down her chin and she had to wipe with the back of her hand. Uncle held his glass up, let the liquid slosh at the sides. 'You see, in this … difficult time, we should all support each other. Instead of scaring or hurting one another more with strange actions, weirdness? Eh? I had mentioned several times now that grief, is grief that works in mysterious ways, causing you to be a bit … different. But your Aunty she won't believe me. She worries on how you will speak when it comes to you doing this eulogy. She wants me to take this honour off you. She worries you will bring a disgrace and a shame – as if we can take that now, as well as everything we have on our plates.' Uncle took several long gulps and sighed. 'She fears you greatly. And, more than that one, she fears *for* you. You know you can stop her feeling that. You. Is in your power. If you only hold yourself together. Eh? *Wa te?* Is for you to do.'

For such a long time and in so many places – in the village, in Daban, as she left for London, while she was there, and now, now more than ever – Belinda had been required to listen closely. It had been exhausting: all of her efforts to hear and properly understand the words of others and what lay behind their words. Belinda twisted her top and noticed Uncle's finger pointing at her and the veins pumping at his temples. She wondered what sort of person she might be if she stopped just soaking up the instructions and opinions of Uncle, Aunty, Amma, Mother, Nana, Mary – every-fucking-one. She wondered what sort of woman she might be if she were able to listen to herself a little bit more, and to *really* act on what she heard herself say.

'*Me se, wa te?*'

She made a short promise to do better, be better, to give a great, nice, short speech at the funeral because Mary would expect her to say some words. She flashed Uncle a smile and, so her voice wouldn't quiver, slowly asked his opinions about the prospects for Saturday's weather, if the funeral might pass without a downpour. She saw his mood lighten. He shared his thoughts about the telling colour of clouds, the ominous behaviour of the cockerel. He went for another cigarette, stopped then rotated the ashtray clockwise while moaning about the state of the local roads, worrying about guests' journeys to the funeral venue. He reminded her of her appointment at the hairdresser's on Friday to make sure she looked nice for Saturday and she thanked him for the reminder. When the conversation dried, Uncle stood and rearranged his *batakari*.

'There is also another reason to have you in my study today, Belinda.'

'And that is what, my Uncle?'

'I hope is not a mistake. I don't believe so. Because I feel you will want to see this. Is nobody's right to keep any from you. And is to help you end and move on. Even you can keep them forever if you choose to. Or even you can throw them out on the rubbish for incinerating. If is what you want. I will leave for you to decide. Because I respect you as an adult to make such decisions. So.'

Uncle opened a drawer in his desk. He lifted up something rectangular, a tray or board, covered with a silky black sheet. He slid it over to Belinda and it rasped across the wood as it came towards her. She reached to remove the material but Uncle stopped her, softly telling her to take her time, to take it away, gesturing for her to leave. So she carried the tray out of the study, back down the corridor she walked through half an hour before, the small windows now showing the neighbours' two thin cats fighting in the garden, throwing half of a hen's carcass up into the air between their arched bodies.

In her guest room, at her dresser, Belinda rested the tray. She lifted the cloth, feeling oddly like a magician. First she saw Connect 4 counters – jolly red and yellow circles scattered everywhere like cheerful pocks. The box of Connect 4 had been in Mary and Belinda's annexe when they had arrived, along with some buckets and old sleeping mats. Its presence in their room was never explained. Belinda had sometimes thought perhaps the labourers who had built the house had been fans of the game and accidentally left it behind. Or maybe it was a gift from Aunty and Uncle that they had forgotten to present to the girls in their usual, grand way.

Belinda tossed two discs between her palms, their small clatter so familiar. She and Mary had mostly played it in the rainy season. If they were busy outdoors or on the veranda, as soon as the wind changed, they would leap up from their stooped sweeping, race in with laundry from the line and wait for white scratches of lightning. In that stolen moment when outside work would have to wait, on the small, wobbly table in their room, they set up the game, standing the blue grid between them: a holey wall. Without words, as the rains pounded, they started, Mary's expression becoming more intense as they continued. Mary wasn't always interested in winning. Her aim, Belinda recalled, swatting flies off her knees, was often to make as many diagonals on the grid as she could, whether it brought victory closer or not. Mary liked that kind of row best, she always said, because they were shooting off somewhere. She preferred them because diagonals were a bit wrong, a bit naughty.

Belinda screwed the counters in her palms and let the weak beginnings of a tremble pass through her. She put the counters down and looked through the rest of the tray's contents. Mary's crumpled tabard. The porcupines' quills they picked up from near Gardener's beloved mango trees. The ragged head-tie Mary had brought with her from her village, a tattered thing decorated with *adinkra* symbols. Also some pesewas, some disintegrating cedi notes, some groundnut shells, some rusted bottle-tops, some beads. Then photographs.

In the blurriest ones, it seemed green, white, yellow and sometimes streaks of brown had been thrown together into a washing machine and then spat out. Belinda put those to one side. In the better ones, although Belinda hid just out of shot, Mary was clearly visible; Mary wearing a shirt far too big for her, pulling the silliest face, or doing a double thumbs-up, her body all skinny legs and arms and elbows. In some Mary held on to the proud zoo steward, who aimed her stick at the viewer like a rifle. In others, Mary was mid-sentence, her mouth doing all sorts of strange shapes. In others still, Mary stood in front of caged parrots and toucans, raising her arms to imitate their wings. Each image was a little record of Mary's fearlessness, of Mary's unwillingness to be restrained even though so much of the world had told her to still and quiet herself. Mary did not listen to all of that. She cartwheeled away from those limitations, made a joke of them because they stood in the way of her experiencing things and getting more. Mary had always wanted more. Just like Amma. Belinda shuffled the photographs.

What was hardest to understand was how Amma – with all her words, shouting, action, colour; all that life – why someone with that inside would truly want to make themselves less by having a stupid candlelit dinner with a boy she could never like. What faces would Amma have to do, sitting opposite him, eating her food slowly, while he did stories she would never enjoy? What idiotic faces?

Two girls in a sex-romance was unnatural and Belinda could not and would not yet contemplate what a life like that might mean for Amma. But the idea that her friend in London might leave the Kweku boy an apologetic voice message, turning him down, warmed Belinda's stomach and relaxed the muscles in her cheeks. Amma should do and be as she wished. She should never be small. Sitting at the dresser, Belinda knew that before the funeral she would say something like that in an SMS to Amma. The phrases would come out wrong and Belinda would be frustrated as she typed and deleted and typed and deleted, but she would try her best, and eventually press the little envelope button and Amma would understand and do her prettiest smile: the big, toothy, honest one that did not happen enough.

Neatly collecting together photos of a frozen Mary hogging the frame, Belinda imagined Mary and Amma meeting, a tiny girl and a taller one, the tiny one asking questions and the taller one answering in riddles, the taller swishing purple plaits the other one pulled to check closely. The taller girl wouldn't like the attention, would try to disappear. But the tiny one – too quick and too quick-witted – would follow, matching step with step, now demanding that the taller give her a piggyback, chasing and surrounding annoyingly. The taller one – too lazy, too cool for that sort of play – might try to distract, try to disappear again, while also laughing at the power of the tiny girl's persistence. The image of them whizzing around one another in fast, stumbling, giggling circles made Belinda laugh too. Belinda laughed and laughed and laughed.

39

The swinging sign was painted with an orange woman's head. Her expression was proud despite wonky eyebrows and a stubbed nose. Her hair, flecked by the artist with little bits of white to make it look healthy and glistening, was plaited into the shape of a huge black crown. Beneath her, in big blue letters, it read His Way Is The Way and The Only Way Ladies Salon. Belinda and everyone in Old Daban called it Pokuaa's Place. The tiny hairdresser's perched over La Parisian Chop Bar at the top of a steep flight of wooden stairs – like the kind you might find leading up into a tree house, Mary had said, each time she visited. Mounting those stairs on Friday morning, the day before the funeral, Belinda felt sickened: by the mix of sweet shampoo smells from above and frying from the restaurant below, by fear she had left it too late to write a good eulogy, by having to do a eulogy at all. Climbing further, she extended her legs beyond the penultimate step that had been replaced by cardboard scrawled with the message 'YOU WILL DROP'.

At the top, she took a moment to catch her breath. Although early in the day, Old Daban, the scratchy town out there and below her, was very much awake. Down on the ground, in a horrible group, a few vultures hobbled then took flight. To the left of the dry patch the birds left, four girls dressed in white played *Ampe*, having fun before staring at sums for hours. They kicked with such speed and their feet slammed, sending lizards everywhere. Enjoying their performance but suggesting they move elsewhere, an old Hausa woman prepared *kenkey*, spooning dough into corn-husks. A dusty midget pushed a wheelbarrow past them and did a weird, jutting gesture with his elbow so everyone shouted '*Fri hɔ!*' which the little man seemed to like. Far, far in the distance were the swaying palms behind which Aunty and Uncle's developed area of the town hid. A burst of light and some delicate, golden clouds decorated the furthest parts of the sky beneath which those wealthier houses sat, like even nature and God preferred New Daban to Old.

Belinda turned, entered the shop. A window's loosened mosquito netting waved at her. As always, the broken hood dryer, green and tall, dominated the room. Torn pictures of Janet Jackson, Mariah Carey and Whitney Houston were tacked onto the walls. Belinda and Mary had spent hours facing those bossy singers while their braids were undone or redone.

'*Agoo?*' Belinda asked.

In a flash, Agnes and Akosua swooped. The two young apprentices who worked for Pokuaa and had done Belinda's hair every fortnight when she lived with Uncle and Aunty said sorry sorry sorry sorry-oh for the loss. Akosua bobbed around, her hot-combed curls flapping about; Agnes pushed her lower lip in and out. They both told Belinda that Mary was a pure innocent living in Heaven now, and they should make a joyful noise unto the Lord. They hurried through it all to get on with praising Belinda for the many blessings heaped on her. They moaned about their uniforms, old aprons so bad in comparison to Belinda's London clothes and Nikes.

Perhaps to stop it all, perhaps because there was little else to do, Belinda replied in a voice she thought was the same as theirs; high, fast and shrill. It startled the girls into accusing frowns. Belinda worried Uncle might hear about her strangeness and subject her to another of his sermons, but then Pokuaa stumbled in from the even smaller bedroom out back, brushing aside a brown net.

Pokuaa was as fat and queenly as when Belinda had left, and brought into the room the strong menthol whiff of Robb. She sprouted a red comb and rolling curlers poked from the pocket on her massive right breast.

'Agnes, Akosua. *Gyae.*'

The girls moved and Pokuaa came forward to hold Belinda's cheeks in rough palms. 'How is it, eh? I won't call you a little one any more because you have been in the world now and you have come fully grown-up. Eighteen soon, *me boa*?'

'*Aane.*'

'A woman now.'

'Yes. I suppose so. I am a woman,' Belinda replied flatly.

'Well, you are welcome-oh. Is good to have you home. Even if a sadness called you here.'

'*Me da ase.*'

Pokuaa grabbed Belinda's hair, crunching the strands between her fingertips. '*Ewurade!* Sister, is come very dry. I think you want us to fix this for tomorrow? Expensive for your Pokuaa to right this one.' She screwed up her mouth. 'You don't have no good oils in *Abrokyrie*? Eh? Is coming rough like you are even from deserts like in Bole.'

'*Ampa, ampa,*' Agnes agreed.

'*Me pa wo kyew*, please I'd only like a simple cornrow. Nothing, you know. Fancy. Or anything.'

Pokuaa tilted Belinda's chin one way and then the other. 'Yes. Your master he gives you all these cedis cedis to do whatever style and you only ever want a normal thing. This one been your way since I'm knowing you. *Me boa?*'

'Does it even matter? Eh? If I'll be covered up with some, like, headgear or headwrap. Who'll even care what's underneath? And why do we even have to do it, anyhow? Making myself pretty and doing beautifications. A child is dead. Is not a fashion parade.' Belinda exhaled and blinked several times while Pokuaa whistled a long note through her teeth and the apprentices muttered hotly. She swallowed her thick spit, blinked again.

'Sorry.'

'Yes. You have to speak more better than this, more nice. Is not correct.'

'No. Sorry.'

As though Belinda did not know the way, Pokuaa led her to the chair and sink near the Dark and Lovely poster. Its pink *Special Offer!* expired in July 1995, but that didn't stop the woman in the picture from chuckling over her slim, oiled shoulder. Once seated, Pokuaa flopped a cape around Belinda.

'Now, *me sroe*, promise not to –'

'– jump as grasshopper when we do our work! We don't like a jumping, jumping grasshopper!' they all shouted Pokuaa's old catchphrase in unison, the apprentices nodding approval towards Belinda's joining in. They patted her to show congratulations for remembering the words perfectly. Belinda smiled at how easy it was, in this situation, to be redeemed.

The apprentices stood to attention like the gloved men who directed traffic at Kejetia and quickly pulled at Belinda's head, jerking her neck as they unravelled her old braids. The teeth of the comb often went too close to her scalp and scraped. She enjoyed the slight pressure and the yanking. The apprentices' focus entertained her too, with their fingers picking madly as they stared at Belinda's skull like they were trying to see into or through it, while Pokuaa yawned a lot and rested all her weight on one hip, like Amma when Nana lectured. Once the tangles were pulled and teased into an afro, once the toughest knots had been cut out, Pokuaa and her girls sectioned off and flattened portions of Belinda's hair, then plaited from the front, their knuckles skimming her forehead. They passed the strands over and under one another, steadily moving to the nape. Outside, down in Old Daban, someone cheered and turned up their radio when *Yaa*

Amponsah came on. The person sang along badly and loudly. The apprentices were unimpressed. Sometimes, Agnes paused to clap moths to death, or Akosua took a break to run down to La Parisian for scraps of meat, mango, and watermelon from the cook who wanted to romance her.

Eventually, Pokuaa left the girls to do it without her. She wandered round the room instead, swigging from a bottle of Sprite.

'See how correct and good my two have become. They have skills.' Pokuaa punched her chest to deal with a troublesome, bubbly burp. 'To start with, they hated learning how we do our things, how it has to take time to get the craft proper-proper.'

'Agnes hate more than me, if you remember right,' Akosua added.

'They both hated learning because I wouldn't let them go quick quick like they wanted, from one style to the next to the next. First they wanted to learn relaxing, next second is extensions, now is kinky twists. Ah-ah! I keep telling them *aba*, you have to go slow and go over things well before you can move on. You have to go back before you can go forward. Else you won't truly have learn anything solid and for sure.'

Pokuaa's words brought silence. They seemed to change the temperature of the air around Belinda. Pokuaa had been talking normally, but the wisdom of what she had said was undeniable. The tension in Belinda's jaw disappeared and her shoulders sank. She let her head drop back heavily and comfortably into Akosua and Agnes' hands and they received her weight in silence and carried on, made nothing of the sigh and hum she released.

'Pokuaa, you are right,' Belinda replied, carefully. 'I truly agree with you. You put it well. Much, you know, much better than I could.'

In the background of the mirror's reflection, Pokuaa lifted herself from the seat, her smile and dimples deepening. She yawned once more and stretched to the ceiling, then humped over, picking up bits of old weaves, kirby grips and tissues, collecting them in a fist. She shuffled around, her big body close to the buckled floor, the loose skin on her arms flapping as she reached for more. When satisfied she had done what she needed to, Pokuaa stood and nodded before shaking the gritty rubbish into the bin. She dropped herself back into the seat and splayed her legs out so Belinda could see the frilled knickers hidden up inside her skirt. She fell asleep, the empty Sprite bottle rolling at her foot, her deep snore making the apprentices snigger. Belinda wanted to go to pass Pokuaa a cushion for her lolling head, cover her with a cloth, give her the dignity she deserved.

As the afternoon slid on, Belinda became bored, then annoyed, then upset by the reflection in front of her. It was one of the reasons she hated visiting the hairdressers: the punishment of having to stare at yourself for ages. The puffiness around the nose; the plump cheeks; the speckling rashes and ripe spots on the forehead: the lack of anything fine or delicate. While Agnes and Akosua rubbed pomade between her cornrows and began a conversation about what jobs they would really like to do, Belinda remembered how her face appeared in the driver's mirror in the first taxi from Accra Airport to the hotel; how she had wondered if Aunty and Uncle might find something new or mature in her cheek, nose, brow. What they would never have noticed but what became plain to Belinda then, was how the resemblance to her mother was fading.

Even as Mother spoke harshest – teaching Belinda how to sew on buttons, telling Belinda not to cry about being banned from Adurubaa Baptist Centre, giving Belinda sentences to spit at any boy who might stand too close – Mother's huge eyes implied something else, seemed to glow if you caught them at exactly the right second. Those eyes often distracted Belinda, which annoyed Mother because she would have to repeat herself again and again to drag Belinda's attention back to where she needed it to be. Belinda had always imagined that flicker was some last glimmer of Mother's youth, still there glowing away, holding on. Belinda had searched her own black irises and told herself Mother's light was in there, too. Not exactly the same, but nearly. And the moment when it could be detected was frightening and exciting and only for her. Now, while Agnes fetched more pomade because the pot was empty, Belinda squinted and frowned, struggling to make out the light or find anything there at all.

'I have an itch. Sorry, a big, bad itch. *Ewurade. Adjei!*' Belinda suddenly rose, her cape waving outwards. Akosua kissed her teeth at the interruption. Belinda turned from them to sort out the emerging tears before making a clumsy pretence of scratching her back.

40

Later that evening in the guest room, in the silent stillness between dinner and what she expected would be another night of broken sleep, Belinda had to let it happen. There was no doing otherwise. Lying on her bed, reading Amma's poem again, Belinda's nose and mouth squeezed in on each other. The poem dropped from her grip. Her neck shook, breath stuttered and the spotlights in the ceiling seemed to wink. At first, single drops slipped down her cheeks. They reached her chin then waited there, hanging before plopping onto her top. She tugged her black T-shirt until it pulled at her neck. Curling up, with knees creeping close to her head, the tears came faster, strings of mucus dripped from her nostrils and she spread wetness across her face. She forced herself against the sheets. With Egyptian cotton rustling in her ears, it was unclear if the tears were for Mother, Mary, or for Jack Gilbert's words – or about how unprepared she felt for the morning ahead.

Moving to the dresser took effort. Once there, she laid Amma's paragraph on the dresser next to the tray, her notepad, biro and cell phone. She knew she had to do it now: write the eulogy, something straightforward about the girl who had been her friend and her sister. She wanted to write it as Mrs Al-Kawthari told them an essay should be composed, with a perfect thread running from beginning to middle to end; arguing the same case throughout but using a variety of different examples and quotations. It sounded so sensible when Mrs Al-Kawthari put it like that, pointing to a diagram of equally spaced and identically sized rectangles and connecting arrows drawn on the whiteboard to show what she meant. But rather than starting, Belinda fiddled, nearly unpicking some of her fresh cornrows, before caking together the stray crumbs of soil around the spider plant. Eventually, she smoothed down a new page on the pad and clicked the pen's end, the nib daggering in and out. She found herself drawing a picture like one of Mary's, making two circles, one bigger than the other, then large triangles beneath these. The triangles grew thin legs and twiggy arms. Those bodies needed eyes, noses and smiles too, so Belinda put those on, then tore out pages and pages, screwing them up, tossing them. She didn't move for a time. Soon, her beeping Nokia flashed up the sign meaning a reply was coming through. The name under the tiny, spinning envelope was Amma, with a response to Belinda's last text. Seeing her name and thinking of Amma was a helpful little nudge.

Belinda tried to write a description of the first time she and Mary had met: the date and the place; the length of the journey from when Mary was picked up in Baniekrom to when they both arrived in Daban. Mary's appearance: the manly *oburoni wawu* she wore – a checked shirt and black church trousers. On the page, Belinda put down bits of the conversation they'd had: little things Mary had revealed about her interests – singing, stories, eating – and her dislikes – being made to go to bed early, being made to wait. At the end of a snaky arrow that wriggled to the edge of the paper, Belinda made a note to later include compliments because she guessed that was the kind of thing you were supposed to do too. Belinda stopped and rattled the pen's lid. She picked up Connect 4 counters and photographs and put them down. She looked at the sentences she had managed in the last few minutes.

For Belinda to say something true tomorrow, the kind of words Mary would *really* like, she would have to take special parts of her time with Mary – the safety of hearing the same whistling snore beside you each night, the calm which came from knowing the specific way to perfectly teach, entertain, care for another person – and let them out into the world for others to have. It was so hard to hand those things over. To strangers, to anyone.

She stood and paced between the bed and windows, crossing and uncrossing her arms, opening the louvres then flipping them shut. She took out her frustration on the scrunched paper, kicking until eventually all the white balls formed a rough pile near the rattan, with the odd one rolling loosely in the corner. Belinda looked at the mess she had made. She thought again about how, after she had left, Mary had had to tidy that vast house by herself. Each and every day. With no one to set exciting challenges and no one to laugh when Mary raided Aunty's wardrobe and she tried to recreate Aunty's grandest headdresses. Mary had had no one at all, but she had persisted on. Something like a tremble started spreading across Belinda's ribs. But it soon stopped.

Belinda returned to the dresser. She picked up the pen to start again. She wanted to see what she was capable of.

41

The room's grainy darkness was swept aside when the door clicked open early the next morning. Belinda, who had been half-awake, heard that click and rolled over to see someone standing in the light, their shy feet playing with slippers. For a slow, blurred moment she thought it was Mother: there and quietly waiting. The person carried a sharply ironed black kuntunkuni dress. It was patterned all over with red and brown shapes like arrowheads. Its puffed sleeves had little bows tied into them. The neckline was the shape of a love heart and just below it the gold lizard brooch Nana had given to Belinda twinkled. Aunty, at the doorway, offered the dress to Belinda, and Belinda sat up to press the lamp's switch.

'Good morning.'

'Yes. Good morning. I hope you are well. You have perhaps forty-five minutes for showering and so on. If you want to take some drink or even just a little water there is a flask in the dining room for you. And *Koko* in the pot too. Not as nice as the one you used to make for us, I'm sure, but I prepared it in case.' Aunty sucked in her lower lip. 'I leave this one here, eh? This is your morning attires. It will make you look so fine and pretty. I've put the others already in the Mercedes boot, for afternoon and then the evening parts, so you not to worry for that. I know you have enough other little jobs to be getting on with. So, here.'

Aunty came in, with her smell of coffee, toothpaste and camphor, with her gentle, little walk. The rubbish in the corner didn't seem to trouble her, or at least, she didn't comment on it. She draped the outfit on the rattan chair, patting it down gently then patting the air closest to it. Perhaps because sleep dulled the edges of her senses or because of the murkiness of the dawn, Belinda felt like the old woman was disappearing before her, like smoke being troubled by wind, so that soon the faltering figure yards from her would be rubbed out, leaving nothing in the room but the potpourri, the heavy furniture, the morning chill, the glow around the alarm clock. And even that, in its own time, might fade too. And that was fine, right, even, because none of it mattered any more. None of it. As Aunty headed towards the door, Belinda remembered what Macbeth says when he hears about his Lady's death: how life is only a walking shadow. She had liked the line very much. Mrs Al-Kawthari had put it up on the OHP and asked for volunteers to talk about it. Robert had said it was about God and the riches awaiting us in Heaven. Belinda had not been afraid to only say she found the sentence complicated, beautiful and true.

Sitting forward now, Belinda watched Aunty stop at the end of her bed suddenly.

'A child should never mourn for a child. I say a child should not. Is not the order of things. Is not correct? No. No. No.' Aunty's head shook, the long tail of her nightscarf whipping back and forth. She pushed until Belinda heard the bed's frame creak. 'Sorry, eh. Sorry. You don't need this at all. Look at me: getting all my emotions. I'm emotional.'

The clarity of the voice woke Belinda more fully. Listening to the sound was like testing a new bruise. It made Belinda's stomach light and floaty. Belinda wanted to shove the dress at the woman, force her back out into the passageway, turn the lock and hide. But she didn't do that. She had to practise being a bit braver. So she pulled herself across the mattress and rearranged her nightie politely. At the footboard, she reached out and took Aunty's hand.

Belinda held the small, darker knuckles and the pappy, soft fingers. She looked up at Aunty's confusion.

'I will be OK. It will be OK. It just has to be.' Belinda gently brushed down Aunty's arms, the silk of the dressing gown cooler than expected. It was rare for them to stand so close. Belinda had almost forgotten how much taller than Aunty she was and how much broader her own shoulders were. And because it was exactly the kind of thing a child would not do, she pushed those shoulders back, lifted her head, pointed her nose and clapped Aunty's sides twice.

'So let's get ourselves going, eh?' Belinda made busy gestures, scooped up the dress and a towel. 'Because the sooner we start, means the sooner we finish. *Me boa?*'

In the car, on the short trip to the Dabanhene's huge compound, the three of them barely spoke. Not about the order of service, nor the well-wishers on their way to the water pump who waved from the roadside, nor the clang of the bottles in the boot which came each time the wheels struggled over a small boulder. In the back seat Belinda's body followed the movements of Uncle's driving, swinging one way then another, her eyes fixed on the orangey stripes in Aunty's wig. Near the start of Old Daban, a woman with a lopsided weave and a dirty, fluorescent jacket appeared out of the dawn darkness. Over crackling Highlife music, with no concern for any late sleepers, the woman shouted something quick and stuttered through a megaphone, directing them like they were not local.

The building came into view, a pale pink, missing much of its plaster and with leggy watermarks stretching down from the tin roof. Stunted, papery plantains grew around the perimeter in clumps. Though wide and important enough to have perhaps nine bedrooms spread across its one, sprawling storey, the front was unswept so singed grass and bottle-tops did as they liked across the paving. The edges of the windows and the arch they drove through were covered by giant bites – like a monster had feasted. As if it needed making plain, as if she were suddenly concerned, Aunty rotated a bracelet on her wrist and called it a great honour to have a lying-in-state hosted here at the Dabanhene's house; a great kindness and gift for Daban's highest chief to extend since Mary was not really from these parts, since Mary lacked her own proper people to do such things. Uncle argued through the window about parking, Aunty took her bracelet off and replaced it with a new one from a small purse and Belinda reached into her bra for the eulogy tightly packed in there. She smoothed it on her lap and concentrated on the bullet points on the page. She let the words fill her until the engine stopped. Outside, a scrappy gang of children fought about who would open the doors to let her, Aunty and Uncle out of the Mercedes. The kids shouted and spat. One boy wrapped his arm round another's neck and squeezed until a man in a purple *joromi* pulled the two apart and walked off. Seconds after he had left, the fight started again. Belinda did not wait, did not try to stop them herself. She slid off her seat and into the day. Out there, opening the boot and unloading Schnapps, Gulder and Supermalt, the clouds felt swollen and hung too close to the top of her head.

42

By six thirty, the Dabanhene's courtyard rang with conversation. The rows and rows of chairs Belinda had helped arrange were full of restless mourners. Shifting black, red and purple were everywhere. Eventually Uncle stood up and started his traditional libation by waving a stick at the crowd. His robe kept falling, bowing out from his shoulder, so Aunty rushed forward with her knees bent to put it back where it needed to go. Tapping her cheekbones, Belinda listened and watched as Uncle accepted a small glass. He poured the first little splash of liquid to the ground, shakily asked heavenly hosts and the ancestors to gather and drink. He asked those who had gone before to protect the little one on her journey, and told the crowd it was their obligation to honour the dead and all that has passed before the moment they existed in. He said in this way they were forever connected, living and dead, present and past, and to break the bonds was a foolish sin. After each demand, the audience hummed agreement and Belinda hummed too: she remembered Pokuaa and Pokuaa's truth. But then Belinda felt squashed as the crowd hummed, getting louder and louder as Uncle roared. He called for more Schnapps. Belinda rode forward in her seat a little, wondering if his rage was because he too was helpless, ignorant – like all the rest of them. He gave more, messier slops to the greedy spirits until the whole glass emptied again. The audience hummed for the last time and returned to their talking, satisfied, entertained, while Aunty went to Uncle, stroked his bald head, Uncle rubbed a licked thumb across Aunty's eyebrows, she touched his cheek in gratitude. They seemed so separate from the swirling colours, people, patterns, sounds. Aunty whispered into Uncle's ear. They nodded at one another and Aunty made herself the right size to slot under his yam-like arm.

Watching those two, Belinda felt little desire to blame them. Despite the noise of all the chatter and one woman demanding mashed banana for her furious baby, Belinda felt a kind of settling; an understanding that, really, Uncle and Aunty needed only each other, had no need for her. Not like Mary, whose needs had been so obvious from the moment Belinda caught sight of the girl's ashy skinny limbs. Not like Mother, who Belinda pictured entering their old room in Adurubaa, the exhausted woman calling out for Belinda to help her unzip the back of her uniform. Belinda shivered.

Through the clear aisle between the banks of guests, two wiry men marched to the left, heading for the room where Mary had been laid out. A matching pair with exposed, fuzzy nipples, they wore black bands on their foreheads and wrists; bands marked with cowries and battered copper crescents. They pressed blunt ceremonial knives into their palms and brought no blood. Mourners waved programmes at them and Belinda quivered again as those printed, miniaturised Marys swung in the dimness.

Next came a horn player, hard at work, his eyes streaming. He paused to take in more air. The mourners shouted appreciation. He returned to his serious task. Behind him, more men came, all flicking horsehair flyswatters to clear the way for women: the blank Queen Mother with bowed, cropped head; her sisters and their children, whispering amongst themselves and pointing out dignitaries. Drummers entered, striking the instruments slung on their hips with a tumbling rhythm. Their walking was slower than its accompanying music and the contrast annoyed Belinda. The crushed corner of the eulogy dug deeper into her nipple as she watched them all climb up a small flight of steps, approaching that door where Aunty and Uncle waited solemnly.

'I can't,' Belinda whispered to herself. 'I can't, can't. Can't.'

The horn blowers and drummers stopped. From somewhere, a lone, high voice began singing praises. To help it, the musicians came together, more harmoniously now, to play a tune heavier than the last. Belinda tried to hold herself still.

'He comes. Look!' someone shouted.

Underneath a large, fringed parasol that worked up and down, tossing its tassels, the Dabanhene was big and smug and jewelled. The crowd rose and followed him as he padded through.

'*AGOO!*' the Dabanhene shouted as he reached the steps. Magically, the door opened and Belinda heard Aunty groan. Belinda's ankles tingled as the mourners tutted sympathy and shuffled forward. Belinda leant on the pink balustrade. The queue kept on. Clasping, she folded herself to vomit. Retching produced nothing.

With her wig loose, Aunty emerged to congratulatory pats as she passed through the dark jostle. A glow filled the space she had left in the doorway behind her. As she came closer, Belinda slumped into her. And many propped Belinda up. Arms encased her.

She found herself drifting, being easily led. She was turned in a stiff semi-circle until she stood side on to the bed. Belinda sucked in her tears. Someone like Mary lay there. You could only see the top half of her because peach and cream satin covered the legs. Her hands had been folded onto her chest. The forearms were scrubbed and well oiled. The fingernails had been cut and perhaps someone had used a toothpick to remove the grime usually there. Lace and ruffles exploded at her neck.

Aunty reached out to the child until Uncle forced her to withdraw. The face. Blusher tried to pretty the cheeks. A grown-up's lipstick wet the mouth so it seemed as though it had eaten recently.

White pearls sat on her earlobes. Light gathered on her forehead in a great, smooth pool, broken by the only sign of what had brought them to this: one new scar. Diagonally opposite Belinda, a woman beat her chest and screamed like the scream fought out of her windpipe. Then a great wave hit and pushed Belinda. Tottering around the bed, noises came from the very bottom of her. It had waited and it had her entirely, though she pleaded for it to stop. It rocked Belinda at the hips as she continued round the bed. Her middle disappeared. She tore her headdress off. She spat and phlegm came with it and more screaming but she couldn't scream loud enough. More mourners piled in, groaning at Mary, speaking in tongues, men crossing themselves, men battling invisible spirits set on getting the resting one. Some passed Belinda as she stumbled round each corner. An oily-eyed elder, breath whiskied, told her she had done well but not to overdo it. She nearly tripped over her skirt with all the jostling, until she faced the bed head on. Mary, fast asleep, while Belinda herself had been up for at least half an hour, reading or cleaning the mildew between the shower's tiles. Mary, fast asleep, even though the cockerel had announced himself beneath their window. Mary, dreaming, even though a black ring roared around her.

43

After being fetched by screeching, witchy women, after being handed mints, and after she had been pushed up onto the back of the small stage, Belinda found herself in the company of another version of Mary: a huge photo of the girl, surrounded by plastic roses. The picture had been a bad choice. The image's overexposed glare robbed Mary's skin of its brown and replaced it with something harsher, bluer. Belinda reached out, grabbing for the microphone's stand but pulled its cords and wires accidentally. The huge speakers screamed in protest. The whole congregation moaned. Belinda stepped back, her feet tapping the pallets beneath her. She did her best to remind herself what Mrs Mensah had taught her in Declamation – projection and the diaphragm and eye contact – but that schooling seemed so long ago. She had learnt so much more since then.

The long wait to get started was the fault of the local pastor down there: the gum-chewing man meeting mourners, doing grand hugs and slaps to backs. Working along the rows in his silver-buckled crocodile boots, he small-talked with Aunty, Uncle and the others at the front for ages and did the handshake ending with a click. The rest of the crowd twitched more than Belinda. Women angrily patted itchy weaves. A few men with pockmarked arms sucked Fan Ices, careful that the drips missed their big watches.

She touched the head-tie Aunty had made her put back on. She picked out the damp eulogy and scratchy biro from her bra and re-read the words, resting the sheet on her left palm to cross out one or two of the longer sentences. She kept scribbling and scribbling but the poor ink wouldn't do its job. She stopped when the pastor saluted to those in seats further away. He licked the drooped ends of his moustache before sitting himself down and gesturing towards the stage. Uncle folded something in his lap and Aunty did the smile where you could just make out the glint of her gold tooth.

Stepping forward, sticking to the tarpaulin and having to pause to unstick herself, Belinda glanced at the audience and at the expectation of their set eyes. She tried to meet their gaze, choosing to focus on one grandmother in particular who tore at the corner of a water bag and sucked it seriously. Under the hot pressure of their eyes, Belinda understood Amma and Mother more because the audience's stare was so very loud and so ready to judge. It was the kind of stare that must have terrified Amma in her dreams and Mother in reality; one whose demands Belinda herself had anticipated and acted on for years.

But it was also a funny look. A strange look. Yes, it pushed and demanded as though in charge and it knew best. But Belinda was not convinced it saw very much at all. Whatever she was about to offer them on the stage, it would only be a small part of her. So much else was there, but that challenging, bullying look – the fair-skinned man peering over round spectacles, the lady next to him craning to see – it only wanted simplicity, something it could easily call 'good' or 'bad'; it wasn't interested in important or difficult detail, it wasn't interested in offering support or encouragement. Belinda checked her paper one last time, rubbing its edges already roughed and greyed with her sweaty dirt. The prompts and points there now seemed like someone else had written them. She cleared her throat for a long time.

'*Nananom, abusuafoɔ.* I wondered if I might come today and only hold on to the microphone so you would have just heard me breathing my breath for a while.' Someone tried a laugh and another joined in. 'And I would have been happy with that one for two reasons. First, because it would be truthful and correct: any words I have are useless in the face of this Almighty's power.'

'Amen!' Aunty shouted.

'And second because the breathing will show I am still alive. To hear all my breath loud on the speakers like a great wind. But a silent wind. None of my poor chatting and useless ideas, made-up things I'm speaking of only for the sake of it. The silence would have been good. We can sit in silence and properly see our stories and memories of Mary and polish them up. Or, even those here today who have no thoughts of her, no stories or anything, maybe even the silence will have given them a chance to consider their own type of Mary – because we all have those smaller or weaker than ourselves who need to be protected and saved, who we should protect and save.'

'Amen.'

'Protecting them and saving them.' Belinda pressed her forehead and paused. Uncle shot up, picked up his falling robes, passed them over his forearm. Uncle sat back down. 'I was going on about silence. Yes. I like it most because it gives you a gift. A minute when there is no work and you can see the many pieces of the world not fighting at each other, and when all is not moving is a special thing. So in my plan, when I prepared this first I said I will only stand here and not move or speak, but I thought more about it and I felt the opposite, because isn't silence quite difficult and bad as well? If it's silent, then you get to hear how much you have lost. You hear that you are surrounded by nothing, and if you are one who seem to keep losing then you really don't want to hear that. Is too painful, to only be reminded of what you don't have and how much you want to have.' The tremble came up from Belinda's thighs. She turned the paper back into a tight square, running her nail along its edges. 'Mary was my friend. My sister and my friend. Thank you for your time. We wish she rests in peace. Amenandhallelujahhallelujah.' Belinda shuffled backwards, off the little 'x' marked on the floor in sticky tape, not looking where she was going. She nearly knocked over the portrait. No one clapped. She was pleased.

Leaping up to the stage in three long strides, the pastor waved his handkerchief and the audience copied with their own. It was like she had never spoken, like the last minute or two had never happened. As they waved, everything shimmered with white for a moment and Belinda watched the pastor's pleasure at the sight he had created. He owned it all. Then the pastor fell to his knees and struck the platform with his fists. In a shaking scream, similar to Uncle's during the libation, she heard the pastor shout they had to cleanse themselves with and seek wisdom through prayer. He pounded and pounded, and told them the Devil – the ever-watchful Devil – was coming for them and they needed to be armed against wickedness. He told them to search their souls and cast out the sin there. Wickedness lay in the hearts of all men but wickedness could be killed, killed, killed. He yelled about the need for them to pray daily and to open themselves to the Lord's mercy with all their hearts. Mary would have loved his performance, given him an eleven out of ten. He shrieked, he spoke in Jesus' blessed name. He was clear that His was the only way to achieve the glories awaiting in Heaven, then stopped to mop his sweat. The mourners whooped, jumped from their seats, hopped on the spot and flapped their handkerchiefs again.

At her corner near the back of the stage, Belinda untied the childish bows on her sleeves and twisted them round her index and forefingers. She waited for someone to show her where she should sit now she had finished. Everyone seemed too busy rejoicing at the directions given by the pastor to notice her. She didn't mind. She scraped her sandal against the tarpaulin. The pastor rose to begin explaining exactly how to avoid abomination.

Rubbing the tarpaulin again until it squeaked this time, she tried
not to disapprove of the audience for taking so much delight in
being instructed. Instructions made things smaller, more comfortable. She knew the need, the longing for comfort, had seen it in
many different forms. Hitting the wrong note, the pastor began
singing the hymn about being joyful and filled with the light of
day.

Like the pastor, the Dabanhene knew about drama. When he came
to the end of his short speech about great oaks, Dabanhene paused
and nodded for no clear reason. He extended and lowered his
right arm, jiggling his gold bangles and their shower of tiny beads.
Once the arm was flat and parallel with the stage, he swept it to the
right, towards the entrance of his home.

Squeezed in next to stocky female twins, pinching at the sides
of her nose and the oil gathered there, Belinda didn't realise that it
was going to happen right then. The twins did, and were first to get
to their feet as the horns whined their ancient, rough noise. Men
shuffled out of the Dabanhene's gates. They propped up a little box
on their shoulders. It was stupid to be surprised by it, but the size
of the coffin made Belinda tug at one of the twins' tops. She could
only relax her grasp when she felt everyone else bossily moving on
around her.

Belinda got up and hobbled through the seats like the rest, the
whole crowd following the pallbearers, Dabanhene and the elders
down to the town's graveyard. As they went, people fanned themselves as usual and kissed their teeth and clapped their hands.
Some checked their cell phones and fingernails, some muttered
'Adɛn?' and 'Aba!', others sweetly sang lines of the hymns from
earlier in the day. Men worried about dragging their robes in dirt.
Mothers worried children weren't close by, but were soon reassured. Taxis honked, the drums kept on, confused goats were
frightened away. When they reached a hillier section of the road,

keen girls all dressed in white with black swished round their necks pushed ahead. They told Belinda 'Sorry sorry sorry' as they passed her. Belinda caught sight of Aunty and Uncle ahead. They nodded and she nodded too. While the congregation trudged on, Belinda pressed the pimples on her hairline and watched her footing. In the graveyard, strangers' headstones pointed up at angry angles. The crowd thinned down to single file to weave between the crosses and monuments.

The coffin was like a neat slice of wedding cake. Looping curls of silver and pink, fussy like best handwriting, wound around the box. It waited by the gashed earth that the men would rest it in. The mourners admired, clucking. Belinda made herself look at it. Her phone vibrated in her handbag but she let it rumble on. She brought her ankles together, fixed her head-tie and straightened her dress so that it was less bunched around her breasts. She passed her hand over her puffy face and then saw that eyeliner had rubbed onto her palm in streaks.

Belinda's inspection of her messy hands was interrupted by the shouting of the young pallbearers on the opposite side of the grave. They stripped off and swirled the cloths that had been draped over their torsos moments before, then called for hammers. Three little boys, perhaps six or seven years old, flitted back with tools heavier than their tiny limbs. The children hurried off with handfuls of sweet *chin chins*, nearly falling into the hole not meant for them and only laughing light squeals at how narrowly they had avoided an accident. Belinda wondered if she had ever laughed like that when she was their age.

The men started to thud away the casket's handles, eager for the shiniest decorations, the ones that would fetch the highest prices in the market. She knew it was what always happened at funerals, and that the bashing and breaking was no worse than anything else she had seen in the last few hours – but as the men's blows against the handles kept on coming, the sound became a hard hiccupping against Belinda's skull. Her chin jutted forward like it was being pulled and her whole body tightened. Belinda tapped the heel of her court shoe into the red earth, matching her galloping blood. Soon, wrenched free of its metal, the coffin's surfaces were all marked with deep black gouges.

Someone tried to move Belinda with a shove. She remained where she stood. The pallbearers strutted and touched their muscles. Some yelped for the crowd to cheer. There were whines from older mourners about sharing, relatives and fairness.

'Sister!' an excitable man said, pushing a brassy knob towards Belinda. She let it fall from his grasp and roll at her feet. It was not enough.

Back in the seats again, Belinda's face drooped like the flesh might slip from her cheeks and pool on the ground. Her gaze wandered to the leaves of banana trees, wings of green fixed to the earth but trying to fly. Once, she popped open her purse and removed her cell to scroll through Amma's gentle expressions of concern. Occasionally, she gave her collarbones a delicate, checking touch. She often redid her head-tie, making her temples ache more, and so she had to loosen the knot, start again.

Mourners often turned round to Belinda to ask what was wrong. Belinda shrugged. After one particular woman asked Belinda that same question for the fifth time, Belinda focused on the stranger's alarmed eyebrows. Belinda considered telling the woman that she was actually thinking about Mary's annoying fake laugh. That laugh was such a pain. Whether they were separating out the silks and delicates or snapping okra tails, Mary would do it whenever, wherever. A flat sound Mary made until Belinda was frustrated into shaking her, thrilling Mary with the pleasure of having forced a reaction. Belinda would only let her go if the girl's jaw and lips straightened properly. When Mary did her very best to be like any ordinary, nice little girl and pushed aside what she wanted to be like for the sake of them both so that chores could be done efficiently: wasn't that when Belinda had thought her best? Funny, so funny to think of what Mary had sacrificed. The woman became bored of waiting for Belinda to respond and so instead called out to one of the passing serving girls for more beef *Chichinga*.

Belinda bit down hard as she tried to convince herself sacrifice was Mary's way of showing love, was Mother's way of showing it, was Belinda's too. She bit harder because she could not and did not believe it. Why should love be about sacrifice and giving something up, about not doing? Why should it be about standing back to watch as waters washed everything away? Why wouldn't you at least try to withstand the flood, throw out a rope across the swelling waves for a desperate hand to seize? Belinda's heart punched and she found herself beating at her thighs. In Jack Gilbert's poem, however stupid the stumbling, struggling man might seem, at least he was doing, doing, doing.

Her heart punched even more as eight drummers near the stage shouted out and started their own stamping repetitions. Hunched over their instruments, the men winked, yelled insults at each other between beats and dared each other to strike faster, louder. Sweat poured down their creased faces as their hands whipped. Peering over a crinkled grandfather who moaned, Belinda sat up, stretching to see. She wondered what the drummers imagined chasing as they played like that. The crowd was delighted. The drummers knew their chase was an impressive one, acknowledging the mourners' awe at the speed of their hooked sticks with cheeky grins. The singer wouldn't be outdone; she turned herself into a dancer now. She did hundreds of quick shuffles towards where the drummers were stationed. There, her feet hopped and scurried on the spot. She clapped at her enemies. The cowbells liked what she did and spoke up and in time with her pattern. Then the *seperewa* player woke and added strings too sweet to be drawn into the messy fight. Belinda sat up even taller. The singer clapped again and the drummers responded. A barrage of thuds came. They pursed their lips and clawed. The rhythm wiggled. It slowed and sometimes stopped without warning then picked up a thread of sounds from earlier. Knowing backing singers cheered and waved Kente scarves, and from the crowd, the singer's strength and her entire body's working suddenly had Belinda standing and cheering too – 'Go on, girl!' – as the singer's movements mirrored the men, pulse for pulse and hit for hit. When the tallest drummer stepped forward from the chorus and amazed all with a tricky sequence, the dancer snatched bits of air like she was stealing his notes. He went harder and the singer went with him, spinning her head, her colours spiralling: gold on the arms, red on the mouth, oranges on the terrifying chest. Round, round and Belinda was getting nauseous. Round and round and round and the singer's neck let her go even faster. And suddenly the dancer was stopping. And suddenly the dancer was walking into the crowd, and approaching Belinda.

'We will do you next.'

'Me?' Belinda could not meet the certain gaze directed at her. 'Seriously, thank you, but it's not –'

'We'll not have no, eh? How will you not come to celebrate life? Eh? Young woman as you? *Bra*.' The woman took Belinda's lack of response as victory. 'Good girl, and come with many, don't let it be solely me and you here with everyone only watching on. It will shame the dead girl. Bring aaaalllll.' The singer tramped off.

The cowbells did a slow introduction before Belinda had managed to gather Aunty and Uncle, and drag them through to the front of the crowd, each one of them doing stretches to warm up for the show. The music came back, so loud and keen to shake Mary. Belinda listened to the singer follow the form by whining into the microphone to start. Knowing their part, the singer's backing troupe hummed agreement. The singer's voice came back

– richer and more hoarse this time, the kind of voice that Belinda recognised so well: a rough cry, begging for fairness; a broken howl, hungry for pain to stop; a scream that stilled the elder's blade before it split an infant's flesh; a rasped plea to be understood. A cracked, cracked wailing for someone to end solitude. Belinda let the voice have her.

> *Belinda Asare! Belinda Otuo! Belinda of London and our*
> *   Daban, yes.*
> *Mmmmm*
> *Belinda Asare! Belinda Otuo! Belinda of London and our*
> *   Daban, yes.*
> *Mmmmm*
> *They have not forgot, how could they forget? They sent for*
> *   her, she comes to see.*
> *Mmmmm*
> *She cannot sit there, who could sit there to have tears alone?*
> *Who will hear?*
> *Who will hear?*
> *Is anyone to listen for her?*
> *We will hear!*
> *Her heart is paining, listen for her.*
> *We will hear!*
> *We will hear!*
> *Let her come!*

More drums entered and Belinda's band of supporters began to dance towards the centre.

> *Let her come!*

Uncle received the praise of all the old men. Aunty did too.

Let her come!

The cowbells struck sharply. Two elders hobbled up to put notes on Belinda's forehead, only for them to whirl away.

Let her come!

Belinda grimaced. The audience didn't like that. She angled and flattened her feet repeatedly and smacked down her heels. She swaggered, she rolled her shoulders with threat, like the boys on Atlantic Road. She walked, marking out a circle for herself and, once marked out, she beat her breast. With her only sense of Uncle and Aunty being that they drifted nearby but had given her the space she needed, wanted, she turned her palms upwards, seeking the sky's forgiveness, as was the traditional way, as had always been the way. She bent and, following the rising of bells and the beating, approached the Dabanhene, her head low. Bowed, her sight stuck itself to the rich cloth across his lap; darkness shot through with thin threads of light. From under his parasol, he touched her head, but the weight rested on her crown felt too light, like his noble hand might even go on to tickle her. So, with a heart fluttering now instead of punching, and with a rush of wind about her, Belinda jumped high and skipped back, the whole audience whistling at her skill, raining pesewas on her. Her calves stiffened but she spun and spun as the singer had, her gut and head raging, catching the coins and grabbing the notes. The whole scene, blurred and spilled and came together, again and again; came together with the sound of Pokuaa's words, and stealing the show at Lavender's party and Mary's beaming, beaming face. She stopped, only to leap high again and kick with straightest legs, growling in some new language. Movement filled her thighs and knees. Everything tingled or twinged. Her fingers itched. Planted on the red earth, Belinda bent, her hips going right, left, right; her bottom: right, left, right; the lower half of her finding itself. Her fingers, her hands circled and shaped the air with someone else's cleverness, and as she watched them, she thought that she had created something beautiful. The drums stopped. She did a 'listening' mime: the *seperewa* piped up again. The singer bit on her fist.

> *She is strong!*
> *Belinda is strong, the daughter of Asare cannot fail, she come*
>   *to this like warrior.*
> *She has not forgot!*
> *I say to you, if you could not see, you cannot make this one*
>   *lose it!*
> *She has not forgot!*
> *Why would she forget? It lives in the blood, it's only London*
>   *where they take her.*
> *Is not far?*
> *Is not other side, is not other side – oh, where is her sister?*
> *God's hands!*
> *In God's hands!*

The singer paused for ice water, the instruments rumbled, lonely without their leader. The sound system crackled and a tinny hymn blared out at double speed.

'I think,' Belinda puffed, to the air, to no one, 'I think I've done my bit for now.'

'More than!' Aunty replied.

Finding their way through the crowds, they were greeted by admiring strangers who grabbed out for different parts of Belinda. It took them some time to get back to their seats. Once there, Belinda saw that a toddler in a dirty smock had been plonked on the chair next to hers. As Belinda sat, the toddler stuck out her legs. Belinda noticed a puddle beneath the child and dampness crawling down to her hem. The toddler's dumb smile upturned itself and the child stared at her dimpled knees. The child opened her mouth to cry, but the noise disappeared under the grizzling sound system, scratching hymns, women collecting donations, anger at too-small portions of red snapper, gossip about who had been given discounts by the seamstress and who hadn't, a stranger still weeping, tired grandfather coughing, village boys with their backwards caps still rapping. The infinite drums.

'I've. I've left something,' Belinda said to Aunty.

'Oh, let me –'

'Don't worry.' Belinda rose. 'I'll soon come. Please.'

Belinda struggled up a steep road, moving away from the Dabanhene's. Loose stones and potholes troubled her. A few times Belinda lost her balance, fell over and had to scrabble in the dust. She spat on and brushed off her grazes. Panting, she removed her head-tie, used it to wipe herself then threw it away. She continued, her painful sides contracting and expanding as the breath demanded. Belinda took her time now, the ground getting even harsher the further she went, the going increasingly difficult. Her traditional sandals were useless – appropriate and correct and golden, yes – but terrible for anything more than being pretty.

Proud, once she reached the top, she looked down over what had been conquered. The funeral continued below, now a tiny black whirl against the sunset. She turned and passed through the part of New Daban where the land had been cut into mad pieces, construction sites shooting up between the dry grasses as they liked. Each plot she walked by had a makeshift sign announcing who would eventually move in when the dollars, euros and pounds came from London, from Atlanta, from Rome, and had done what they were saved to do. Sarpong. Agyeman. Adu. Each site was so wide, with thin white cord tied between poles to divide out endless rooms and rooms and rooms.

The size, emptiness and possibility of it all almost made her cry but she stomped on with bent knees, and received the respect of the woman on the steps of her kiosk, the shelves stocked with hundreds of identical orange bottles of bleach. The pointed woman stopped attacking her toenails to ask how the day had passed. Belinda, half-answering, walked behind the woman, through windowless cement shacks huddled together, past the daughters squatting at coal pots, fanning embers, lifting lids and nodding into spicy steam. She dragged herself around the other small families crouched inside shell-like homes, slurping *garri*, blackening slices of plantain. A balding dog showed a liking for her, but soon noticed a spewing bag of rubbish and pushed its nose into a nest of newspaper there. Insects were musical and bullfrogs belched. She hopped over the lazy dribble of green sewage to where the tarmacked road began, rubbing away new dust and dirt from her clothes.

Waiting, she clawed at her top to gather the notes and sticky pesewas bunched up in her bra. Counting more than enough, Belinda bundled cash into her fist. A *tro tro* passed; a shirtless boy called for passengers from its open door, the bones of his ribcage becoming more visible with each intake of breath and shout. A fleet of oil tankers boomed by and she listened to its rude roar. Its black fumes faded into grey. Finally she flagged down a taxi.

'You know Adurubaa? Adurubaa, eh?' Belinda spoke slowly to the driver through his window and showed him her full palms and all the rewards there. She didn't mind the keloid on his chin; long, sore and shiny like he had been in a bad fight recently. He smiled to reveal three missing teeth. He pushed his tongue through the gap and found that hilarious.

'Adurubaa is the one in Brong Ahafo, isn't it? I know it very well well. I have a very best way to get there. Is good-oh. Don't worry. Please sit and enjoy this journey. *Me pa wo kyew, bra.* Welcome.'

She slipped herself onto the back seat, pulled the door closed with all her strength. After letting her shoulders fall, she did not listen to him discuss his connection to her village, or ask him about what he was eating from the plastic container on the dashboard, or tell him to lower the volume of the reggae on the radio. Instead she shook off her sandals. She placed her hand beside the right ankle and lifted it up onto her lap. Her foot, so used to shoelessness, was still tough and hard and yellow. White lines spidered its drier, powdery patches. She cracked her fingers and used her thumbs to work the tenderest flesh; right there, in the middle of the flaking heel.

Acknowledgements

First of all, huge thanks are due to the educators. Thank you Linda Callow, Sara Pettigrew and Samantha Mackenzie for making English lessons electric, unmissable moments in my school day. Your unwavering confidence in my abilities as a reader and a writer has been transformative in ways it is impossible for me to fully explain here.

Thank you to Bernard O'Donoghue for his wisdom, to Kathryn Holland for making me think harder than I wanted to, to Andrew Blades for clear-sighted guidance, to Sally Bayley for her openness.

I am also indebted to Susanna Jones, Andrew Motion, Ben Markovitz and Jo Shapcott for their instructive insights when I undertook the MA in Creative Writing at Royal Holloway. Equally, I'm grateful for the energy with which my fantastic course-mates – Andrew W. Campbell, Jacqui Hazell, Ben Martin, Colin Tucker and Marshall Veniar – engaged with Belinda's developing story.

Thanks so much to my early readers: Michael Amherst, Rachel De Wachter, Brenda Fitzgerald, Anna Kelly and Andrea Varney. Your beady eyes, encouragement and sensitive suggestions made such a difference. Thanks to Erin Michie for her incisive comments on the manuscript.

Those at Writers' Centre Norwich, especially Lora Stimson and the team behind the Inspires programme, played an enormous role in helping this novel find its way into the world. Thank you for taking a chance on me! And to the extraordinary Daniel Hahn:

the biggest of hugs. None of this would have been possible without you.

Special thanks to Juliet Pickering at Blake Friedmann who is the most supportive, most perceptive and coolest agent that I could have hoped for. Thanks to Helen Garnons-Williams at 4th Estate for instantly understanding and being so enthusiastic about what I was 'trying to do' with this novel. Thanks to Iain Hunt, Jordan Mulligan, Olivia Marsden and Michelle Kane for all of your wonderful help too.

Next: family. Mum, Olivia, Jenny: thank you for hilarity, steadfastness, love. And extra gratitude to Mum for sorting out my dodgy Twi!

Thanks to my in-laws Jane and Julian for so many things, but particularly for setting me up with a little writing spot in the 'lavanderia'! And to Derek and Liz for their limitless generosity and interest in my writing.

And finally, thank you Patrick, for being my fiercest critic, my loudest cheerleader, my kindest listener. Thank you for giving me the space to write but always being right there, just when I need you. You are a wonder.